Twisted Sister

The nun approached, dropped her black carry-on bag, and bumped into me. "Oh, sorry, Sister. I'm not usually . . . ouch!"

I looked down at my arm and saw the syringe. A syringe that the nun held, had stuck me with, and then tucked into the sleeve of her robe.

A haze started to cloud the room. My mind was . . . fuzzy. *Fuzzy Wuzzy was a bear. Stop that, Pączki!* I laughed. The fuzzy nun pushed me into the bathroom. "Ouch!" I bumped my head on the wall. "Daddy calls me *Pączki*." I giggled, stumbled. "It's a Polish prune-filled donut."

I rubbed my arm. Make that three arms. I saw three arms attached to me on one side, four on the other. "You pinched me. That hurt. Nuns shouldn't . . . pinch . . . What did you give me? I hope to hell that syringe was sterile!"

Without a word, he pulled off his veil.

He?

Books by Lori Avocato

ONE DEAD UNDER THE CUCKOO'S NEST
THE STIFF AND THE DEAD
A DOSE OF MURDER

Forthcoming

DEEP SEA DEAD

LORI AVOCATO

One Dead Under The Cuckoo's Nest

A PAULINE SOKOL MYSTERY

AVON BOOKS
An Imprint of HarperCollinsPublishers

This is a work of fiction. Names, characters, places, and incidents are products of the author's imagination or are used fictitiously and are not to be construed as real. Any resemblance to actual events, locales, organizations, or persons, living or dead, is entirely coincidental.

AVON BOOKS
An Imprint of HarperCollins*Publishers*
10 East 53rd Street
New York, New York 10022-5299

Copyright © 2005 by Lori Avocato
Excerpt from *Deep Sea Dead* copyright © 2006 by Lori Avocato
ISBN-13: 978-0-06-073167-0
ISBN-10: 0-06-073167-2
www.avonmystery.com

First Avon Books paperback printing: October 2005

Avon Trademark Reg. U.S. Pat. Off. and in Other Countries, Marca Registrada, Hecho en U.S.A.
HarperCollins® is a registered trademark of HarperCollins Publishers Inc.

Printed in the U.S.A.

10 9 8 7 6 5 4 3

This book is dedicated to all the men, women, and children whose lives are touched by any form of mental health difficulties.

Acknowledgments

Thanks to Sal, Mario, and Greg for all their encouragement. To agent Jay Poynor. You are great! Thanks to my editor, Erin Brown, who always comes up with wonderful suggestions to make my work even better. And last but certainly not least, thanks to all the readers who enjoy and support The Pauline Sokol Mystery Series.

One
Dead
Under The
Cuckoo's
Nest

One

"This won't hurt."

I looked at my well-meaning best friend and roommate, Miles Scarpello, and then snorted immediately after he spoke the foolish words.

My second best friend and roommate (Miles's significant other), Goldie Perlman, joined in. "Really, Suga, it won't hurt. Blow." He waved his hand in the air like a magic wand but only managed to snag his lovely ecru silk scarf with a long, coral-painted nail. Goldie looked lovely in ecru. Matched his skin tone and made his golden-haired wig look more real.

Then again, Goldie looked beautiful in any color.

And always real.

My father added, "Come on, *Pączki*, I want a piece of cake."

Everyone in the room leaned near, as if a budding thirty-five-year-old didn't have the wind to blow out thirty-five stupid birthday candles. I groaned at Daddy's pet name for me. He had used the endearing Polish term (for a big, fat, round, often prune-filled Polish donut, pronounced more like "paunchki") since my birth, when I weighed in at a svelte ten pounds, five ounces. Okay, maybe *svelte* wasn't exactly the correct term, but I remember seeing myself in the reflection of the metal bars of my bassinet and thinking I looked svelte and the nurse probably had her finger on the scale when she had weighed me.

My mother, Stella Sokol, blew out a breath and said, "Really, Pauline Sokol. You are making a mountain out of a molehill. Turning thirty-five is not the end of the world."

I looked out the window of my mother's house. It wasn't hard to do from my seat, since she pulled back the "winter" drapes to let the sun shine through the sheer white ones each spring season. Yep. The world hadn't ended and was still out there in full force.

And I was officially thirty-five years old.

And single.

And childless.

And in a profession I knew very little to nothing about— but wouldn't trade for the world. Sure, I had thirteen years experience as a registered nurse, but being a "slightly experienced" medical-insurance-fraud investigator was just fine with me right now.

It was this stupid birthday thing that bugged me.

I looked around my parents' house, which, by the way, was straight out of a *Leave It to Beaver* television show— with color added—and thought some days I might go insane.

Not that insanity ran in my family, but then again, there was that aunt back in Pennsylvania who used to wear five dresses at once when she traveled to Hope Valley, Connecticut, to come see us. Aunt Flo had insisted her dresses wouldn't get wrinkled in her suitcase if she wore them all in the car. Once, when she'd had surgery on her knee, she put three fitted sheets on her bed so that post-op, she could peel one off each week, and she wouldn't have to do a lot of laundry.

I thought that was very clever.

I turned back to look at my family and wondered if Aunt Flo had been the only one with "those" genes. Daddy was already licking cake frosting off his finger before my mother even had a chance to pick up the knife. He reached out again. She swatted his hand away.

Uncle Walt, my favorite uncle, who had lived with us since I was born, slept soundly—in his seat at the dining-room table—with telltale frosting on his lower lip, too.

Miles and Goldie giggled like little kids while pouring each other champagne into the crystal goblets my mother had had since the fifties. Wasn't love grand?

The room was full of nieces, nephews, siblings and their *spouses*. I tried not to look.

Next to me at the table was Nick Caruso, a fellow investigator. Okay, I was stretching it. Nick was truly an investigator. Me, I was still a "newbie," as my seamy boss, Fabio Scarpello (Miles's uncle, since Miles had been adopted into the Scarpello family) would call me.

But hey, I'd finished two investigative cases, and didn't get killed once.

As for Nick, he had become a bit more than a peer. We'd recently started dating. Dating. A term I'd almost forgotten. It hadn't taken me long to get back into the swing of it, pretty much like riding a bicycle.

But, and I have to be honest here, Nick didn't "do it" for me completely. Some might find him nice-looking, dressed impeccably in camel hair, suede or expensive linen anything, but I never got detonation—only a few shimmers. Nick was a doll, though, and treated me as such.

Then still, sitting across the table, and at the invitation of my mother, was . . . Jagger.

Oops. There went my heartbeat in a pitter-patter rhythm, and I hadn't even looked at him that closely.

Jagger'd worked on my two cases with me, although, to this day, no one, including *moi*, knew who the hell he worked for. FBI. Insurance company. PI. No one knew, and Jagger didn't share . . . anything. But he was darn driven.

Our eyes locked. Make that his locked mine as usual, and he gave a slight smile. I'd never done very well with that body language stuff, and trying to read Jagger was like fingering Braille. Not a clue. For all I knew, the smile could've come from some thought he'd just had—and not one about me.

He looked toward the cake, whose frosting was now nearly covered in wax. For a second I thought about those wildfires that burn across millions of acres out west.

"Blow, Sherlock," he said.

Sherlock. Damn. He used that pet name on me and each time my pretty damn high IQ took a nosedive to zero. And that "blow" part didn't exactly have me thinking birthday cake.

Nick touched my arm. "Go ahead, Pauline."

I yanked my eyes from Jagger to smile at Nick. Then I turned toward the cake, and puffed out my cheeks.

Eeeeeep! Eeeeeep!

Daddy jumped up. "Fire! Fire in the house!"

Mother shouted, "Calm down, Michael. There's no fire. It's only because there are thirty-five candles on Pauline's cake, and *that huge number* set off the fire alarm."

Amid Goldie and Miles's snickers, Nick patting my arm in sympathy, Uncle Walt snoring and Jagger just, well, looking—I tried to shrink down to the size of the stupid burning birthday candles which, by the way, were already half gone.

I blew and missed five.

Mother shook her head.

Daddy snagged another finger-full of frosting, then spit it out into his napkin. "Damn wax."

And Jagger motioned for me to come with him.

After I'd politely excused myself and given Nick a peck on the cheek, I walked into the hallway. Empty. Then I looked in the kitchen, which also had not changed since the Nixon era. Still aquamarine Formica, with pine cabinets and no dishwasher per my mother. Also no Jagger.

I leaned against the wall.

Maybe I'd imagined he wanted me to follow him. Maybe he only had a crick in his neck. Maybe he had to use the "little boys' room," and I'd die of embarrassment waiting for him in the hallway.

I spun around.

A hand grabbed me and yanked me through the kitchen and out the backdoor.

"What the—"

A finger covered my lips. A Jagger finger.

I had to literally bite my tongue so that it wouldn't snake out and *lick* him.

"Keep it down, Sherlock."

I looked around. This was my parents' house. The neighbors had all lived around here a thousand years and didn't pay much attention to anything except Lotto and *Wheel of Fortune*. No one would care what I said to Jagger.

So I pushed his finger away. A bit reluctantly, sure. "Why are you so secretive?"

He looked at me. "I need your help."

If the March 24 air was a bit warmer than seasonal today, you couldn't tell by me. I'd frozen on the spot when I heard those fateful words come out of Jagger's sexy, full lips. Whenever he asked for my "help," it meant donning my horrific scrubs. Scrubs I'd vowed (twice now) never to wear again. Because if he was asking for help—my help—that meant I'd have to go undercover again—as a registered nurse. And I still had scorch marks from burning out of that career.

"No!" flew out of my mouth.

Once again Jagger touched my lips. He leaned closer. I inhaled him. Male. That was Jagger's scent. I could become a gazillionaire if I could bottle Jagger's male scent.

"This will be a short case, Sherlock. I only need you to escort someone to the Cortona Institute of Life, outside of Hartford. You know, that psychiatric hospital near the river. Catholic place. Run by nuns." He released his hold a bit. "One, two hours tops."

"Why we?" I meant to say *me*, but with his hand over my lips couldn't make myself clear. Besides, my hormones were wreaking havoc with my intelligence. I'm not sure if the left side of my brain or the right was in control right then, but there sure was a body war going on—and I knew either way I'd lose.

He moved his hand. "A nurse has to escort this woman there. I'm telling you, Sherlock. Two hours tops. Trust me."

"I . . . I don't know if—"

Jagger opened his black jacket (oh, yes, Jagger usually wore delicious black) and pulled out an envelope. "Almost forgot. Here." With that he turned and walked down the steps. Over his shoulder he called, "Oh, yeah. Happy B-day."

My heart flipped like an Olympian off the high dive with only a tenth of a point to go to win the gold.

I looked at the envelope. Jagger had given me a birthday present. I touched it gently as if it were made of precious eggshells. With my mind still on the envelope, I heard his words.

Trust me.

Those fateful words must have been spoken to many a victim throughout the ages.

"Pauline, come in here. You have guests," my mother called through the window she'd opened and then quickly shut, before I could answer her.

I rolled my eyes. Guests. All I had was family and my two best friends in the world. I started up the steps and then remembered . . . I had Nick!

Oh . . . my . . . God.

I'd forgotten Nick. And Nick liked me. Nick had actually asked me out, and I think, at least one time, he'd said that he liked me. I stuck Jagger's envelope inside my blouse. I didn't have pockets long enough in my jeans and figured it may be a present that shouldn't be bent, folded or mutilated.

I had to stop thinking about Jagger.

Once inside, my mother said, "Did Mr. Jagger leave?"

Damn. Even *she* couldn't stop thinking of him.

I sat back down next to Nick and leaned closer. He turned and kissed my lips. Yikes. It felt better than an envelope next to your breast.

From the corner of my eye I noticed my mother's eyebrows rise, and then she motioned for my father to look. Daddy licked frosting from his fingertips and nodded at me.

Great. At the age of thirty-five, I got approval from my parents for a kiss. What would they do if they knew Nick and I were sleeping together? That was a rhetorical question, by the way, since we actually hadn't progressed to that stage in our relationship yet.

But I was open-minded.

"Pauline, I asked you if Mr. Jagger left," Mother repeated.

I nodded. "Yes, Mother, *Mr.* Jagger left. He said to say

thank you." Okay, he said no such thing, but my mother liked him so much I thought I'd make him sound polite.

My nephew Wally, my sister Mary's kid (Mary was going to be a nun at one time, but had chosen married life with kids thrown in to boot instead—after the good sisters had put her through college. Yikes.), shouted, "Open your presents, Auntie Pauline!"

I looked at Mary, dressed very much like the modern nuns. She always dressed in plain skirts and plain blouses, and I swear she sometimes wore a veil when home alone. I truly think she missed her calling. "Okay. Will you kids help me?"

A million nieces and nephews descended on my stack of loot. Well, at my age, the stack wasn't too big. Mostly envelopes and two fancy birthday bags, which I knew had come from Goldie and Miles. I touched the envelope inside my blouse. I probably should stick it in the pile, but decided it might have something in it that I didn't want the kids to see—or Nick.

Nick likes me. Nick likes me. Nick likes me!

Lately that had become my mantra to wash away "Jagger" thoughts and keep our relationship strictly business. Speaking of business, I groaned inside at the thought.

Scrubs.

Nursing.

Damn.

Wally held up a gift certificate to the local Stop and Save. Had to be from my parents. My mother thought I didn't eat enough and probably never cooked. Okay, I ate lots of takeout and was a confessed lover of hospital food. I figured no one could call me desperate until I started liking airline food.

Next was a check from Uncle Walt, my savior. He'd loaned me money on more than one occasion, which helped me get my new career started. Wally said there was four zeros on it, which meant Uncle Walt had either given me a hundred dollars or ten thousand, and Wally wasn't counting the cents.

I looked at the brightly colored birthday bags and turned to Goldie and Miles before even opening them. "Thanks, you guys. You didn't have to."

Miles reached over and took a bag. "Okay, I'll return it."

I grabbed it back. "No way in hell."

Mother clucked her tongue. "Pauline Sokol. There are children in the room."

"Sorry, Mother," I said when I could have argued that "hell" in itself was not a bad word. Maybe if I had kids I'd feel differently.

I pulled the ribbon off the first bag and reached inside. Something soft and silky touched my fingers. I grabbed it and pulled it out. "Oh, my God!"

"Pauline!"

"Okay, I'll give you that one, Mother. Sorry. But, this is so . . . sexy!"

"Pauline!"

I looked at my mother's wild eyes and decided against giving her a lecture that sex was a normal (and damn fun) human experience and my nieces and nephews probably knew more about it than she did, but instead I said, "Sorry. Sorry. Sorry."

I held up the bright green camisole top from Miles. Then, I noticed Nick's eyes light up. That'a guy Miles. He sure knew how to buy a present.

"Hurry up, Suga. I can't wait!"

"Okay, Gold. Calm down." I took his bag and shook it. "Hmm, let's see. A car?"

He and Miles laughed.

"No? All right." I squeezed the bag. "A new condo!"

Goldie grabbed the bag. "You'll be thirty-six by the time you open it."

My hand flew to my chest. I really thought I was having chest pains at that thought. In the meantime, Goldie had pulled out his present from the bag.

"Here, Suga!"

I looked at the lovely beaded necklace—and my face caught on fire. I couldn't look at Nick because the necklace was an exact replica of one that I'd borrowed from Goldie one time—and in the throes of passion with Nick, the beads exploded—and Nick and I didn't.

I leaned over and kissed Miles and Goldie. "You guys are the best."

Nick reached into the pocket of his chocolate suede jacket. He pulled out a little box. "Open mine next."

Jewelry. Damn.

I really wasn't the jewelry type.

It kinda hurt that Nick didn't know that. Despite the kids' fussing, I took it to open it myself. Slowly I pulled the red ribbon and started to lift the top off of the box.

Nick leaned over. "Happy Birthday, Pauline."

Some days I wished Nick had some kind of pet name for me. Not a donut though.

I kissed his cheek and pulled the top of the box off. A key chain. Not any key chain but one with a black remote box that I figured locked and unlocked my Volvo's doors. It also had a panic button on the top. Maybe Nick thought I'd need that in my line of duty. (Guess he knew me well enough not to buy me a gun, since I could hurt myself or someone else, having a history of shooting an elevator—twice.) I smiled at him. "This is a perfect gift, Nick. Really perfect." And it was. It was Nick's and my relationship.

The *envelope* poked into my skin.

As soon as everyone left, I kissed Nick appropriately,

and he also appropriately said he'd call me—and I knew he would.

Then, unable to wait to open the envelope until I got back to the condo, I ran into the bathroom. I was worse than a kid on Christmas morning.

I slipped the envelope out of my blouse and stared at it. Then I told myself I was so interested because it came from the mysterious Jagger. That was it. He wasn't the giving-birthday-presents type. No, Jagger was so different, in a wonderful, mysterious, sexy sort of way that I couldn't imagine what he had slipped into this white envelope.

My fingers shook. Pausing, I reached for Mother's can of Renuzit air freshener, sprayed, inhaled and felt a bit of comfort. Her overuse of the pine scent (throughout my entire life) had led me to an addiction. It'd become a nostalgic salve for my soul. Inhaling, I held the envelope to the light to see what I could.

Nothing.

I felt stupid and swore I'd never let anyone know how foolish I was, shaking, inhaling and gingerly tearing at the seam to open it. The silence of the room filled with the *drip drip* of the sink faucet and the singing of the paper tearing.

Then, I pulled the envelope open.

Papers. It was filled with papers.

I looked up and saw the reflection in the mirror of some writing on the back of the envelope. So, I turned it over before I took out the papers.

Monday morning. Nine sharp. Front of your office. Dress in blue scrubs. Don't bring a purse.

Jagger's handwriting.
Jagger's instructions about the case.

His stupid case.

He had to ruin my birthday present by writing directions on the back. I seethed for a few seconds then let inquisitiveness take over.

I yanked at the papers.

Holding them up in front of me, I read the first few words.

And cursed.

Big time!

Two

I leaned against the blue sink in my parents' bathroom and let out a string of more curse words—some I don't think have ever been used in any X-rated videos yet. Then I sprayed my mother's Renuzit again and inhaled. I didn't actually inhale the spray as it dotted the air, more like breathed in a bit of the scent. Usually that familiar fragrance calmed me.

Not now though.

The papers dangled in front of my eyes. But it wasn't Jagger's handwriting on these papers.

It was slimy Fabio's.

Case #3. Psychiatric fraud. Fabio was going on a trip to the Mohegan Sun casino, so he'd written info on picking up the file at eight Monday morning. I hoped he lost his brown polyester shirt and brown polyester pants on the slot machines. Then I thought it really wasn't fair to wish bad luck on Fabio.

He was giving me my third case. Another chance to earn some much-needed money.

I looked down at the envelope and sighed. Jagger'd made it seem as if this was a birthday present. Or, had my thirty-five-year-old mind had a moment of insanity and foolish hopefulness, and I only *wished* it were?

I had to reign in my Jagger-thoughts.

Pauline Sokol, medical insurance fraud investigator, was about to solve another case—and hopefully this time I wouldn't almost get killed.

It'd happened before—twice.

"You're going to be late, Suga!"

As Goldie called out to me a few more times, I looked at myself in the mirror. My undies were pink today to match the bra. Not that I thought anyone would be seeing them unless I, God forbid, got into an accident, but I stood there in my room partially undressed because I didn't want to don my *scrubs*.

They lay on the bed looking so very blue and innocent.

Wearing them meant going back to a career I'd burned out on after a long thirteen years. Oh, it had been fulfilling and what I was cut out for at the time, but nursing was a tough job. Emotions got involved. Skills had to be tweaked constantly. And the hours were murder. I'd be another gazillionaire if I had a penny for every time I'd had to do shift work while my friends partied. Weekends. Nights. Holidays.

I'd had it.

The scrubs glared at me.

I cursed Jagger with one of those X-rated curses I couldn't believe I even knew. My mother would be in the confessional on my behalf if she heard my language or at the very least she'd have the priest over to "exorcise" me.

"Suga!"

I grabbed the top of the scrubs. "Be right there, Gold." Goldie was a fellow investigator at my firm, so he'd offered to give me a ride to work today since my Volvo was in for a much-needed tune up. I didn't exactly have a lot of liquid assets, so until I got paid, the car just might be held hostage by Tony the mechanic. Tony was an old friend and ex-patient and gave me good deals, but even good deals needed cash for payment, and I hated owing friends.

The bottom of the scrubs glared at me. "Stop it!" I shouted. "Just 'cause Jagger needs help, doesn't mean I have to like wearing you." Admittedly I was glad to have been "instructed" to wear the drab blue since it seemed to be a "mourning" color.

Anxious to see the file about my case, I ignored my outfit in the mirror, grabbed my purse and headed down the stairs.

Goldie sat in the white beanbag chair holding Spanky, a shih tzu-poodle mix weighing in at five pounds and eight ounces, although lately the little pooch tipped the scales closer to eight and had to be put on a diet. Miles and I were co-owners of the dog. Since Goldie had recently moved in, we allowed him to adopt a third of little Spanky. At this rate, we'd get more pet for our money with a school of goldfish.

But we all made wonderful doggie stepparents.

I slumped down on the white sofa.

Goldie looked at me. "You look gorgeous, even though I know that outfit is killing you."

"I feel as if I have on a second skin. One that I'd shed months ago and did not want back. More like snakeskin."

Last night I'd told him about Jagger needing my help, since Jagger hadn't said to keep my mouth shut. Besides, I could trust Goldie and Miles with my life. Whenever I mentioned Jagger though, Goldie always gave me some kind of lecture. This time it was "Jagger's like chocolate. He'll make you feel on top of the world—then mess your hips up at the end. But you can trust him with your life."

And trust him I did.

If I sat down and analyzed why, I'd probably be shocked to realize that I shouldn't, in fact, trust him. But I did, and that made my learning this job a hell of a lot easier—and safer.

On the way to the office, Goldie and I stopped to get coffee at Dunkin Donuts. That was Jagger's and my "hangout." Whenever we had business to discuss, we headed there. He always ordered for me without asking since, I admit, I am not one for change. Hazelnut decaf, light and sweet. French cruller. That was me.

Jagger was black coffee sans donut.

Most mornings at the office, Goldie would fix me his New Orleans favorite of chicory coffee with hot milk and plenty of sugar. But since I had to be there so early, he needed the caffeine on the way.

"Any idea what Fabio has for you today, Suga?" Goldie pulled his banana yellow sixties Camaro into a space outside our office building.

"Nope." I got out and yanked my Steelers jacket tighter. Although the March weather had turned milder, I still needed a jacket, and my favorite football team came in parkas, windbreakers and sweatshirts.

Could a girl be any happier?

Inside the building I gave a nod to the receptionist. "Hey, Adele, how's it going?" I walked into her cubbyhole of an office. She'd been with Fabio for years, but he'd never given her a bigger space. Schmuck that he was.

"Morning, *chéri*. Adele is wonderful today." She leaned back in her chair and gave me a wink, a smile and a wave of her white-gloved hand.

Adele was an ex-con from Canada who'd gotten her hands burned in the joint and always spoke of herself in the third person. When I first learned this, I was appalled, intrigued, and sometimes weirded out about that third-person thing, not to mention the ex-con part.

I'd never known anyone who'd gotten more than a parking ticket. As a matter of fact, when the hospital was building a new parking garage and we had to be shuttle-bussed into work, I myself had gotten fifty-one parking tickets because I stubbornly insisted on parking closer to the hospital in a stupid space that had a meter. I'd run out as often as I could to shove coins in, but often got caught up in patient care and forgot.

But Miles knew a cop . . . *Poof*. There went my tickets.

I took a sip of my coffee. "You certainly seem in a good mood, Adele."

"He's out of town. Two weeks. Two glorious weeks." She motioned with her head toward Fabio's office. Black tendrils bounced with her movement and her black, very low-cut dress allowed the cleavage to jiggle.

I think Adele shopped at Frederick's of Hollywood.

I smiled to myself and thought it a shame that someone like Adele had to go to prison when she had stolen only to get enough money to help her dying mother. A modern-day, kick-ass female Robin Hood. Damn shame.

Then it hit me.

"Fabio is gone already?"

"Two weeks, *chéri*!" She swung around, and the wire from her headset caught on my arm. Coffee spewed from the cup onto the floor. Not that it mattered on the already stained royal blue rug. It looked like some kind of modern art.

"Damn! Are you all right, Adele?" I grabbed a tissue from a box, covered with a crocheted cat, on her desk.

"I'm fine." She puffed up her black hair. She liked to change the color several times a year. I liked her in red, myself.

Adele was always managing to get hung up on some wire when I was around. But she always made me laugh and had welcomed me to the job so graciously and warmly that I considered her a second mother.

Stella Sokol would not like that.

I couldn't even imagine what she'd say or do about it, although penance, prayers and pine-scented Renuzit surely would have something to do with it.

"I hope Fabio left my file for me. I thought he'd still be here to give it to me and fill me in on the details." I sat on the edge of her desk, careful to stay clear of any Adele wires.

She pointed to a manila envelope beneath the cat tissues. "He was in such a hurry to go, he left it here. He said luck would stay with him at the casinos after he mumbled something about getting lucky last night."

We looked at each other and let out a collective "Eeeeeeyew!"

Goldie came around the corner. "What the hell? What'd I miss? Tell me, girlfriends. Tell me!"

We laughed and filled him in.

Goldie added a few "yucks" and a screech, and then said maybe Fabio had won the daily lottery and not . . . what we were thinking.

"That's more than I like to think about Fabio at this time of the day—or any time for that matter." I looked at the cat clock above Adele. One paw was on eight. One on the ten. "Shit. I have to go." I'd almost forgotten about meeting Jagger.

I only hoped his little "chaperone" deal was finished by noon. I looked at my envelope.

Because I had my third case to begin.

* * *

After my goodbyes to Adele and Goldie, I hurried outside. When I saw the black Suburban pull into the lot, my heart did a stupid happy dance.

Too much caffeine in my decaf coffee. Had to be it.

Jagger pulled up next to the curb and looked at me.

"What?" I shifted from foot to foot. "I wore the damned scrubs like you said."

"No purse. I said don't bring a purse for this job."

Shit. I'd forgotten. I really had to pay more attention to the details. Especially Jagger details. "I'll go give it to Goldie—"

"Get in."

He looked anxious to leave, so I hurried around the other side of the car and got in. Nick always opened the door for me. Jagger, well, was Jagger.

"Take out your essentials and leave the purse under the seat," he said as we spun out of the parking lot.

I gave him a dirty look, figuring his eyes were on the road, but he stopped at the light and looked at me. "Essentials. No crap like makeup, perfume, or money. You won't need money."

"Fine." I'd learned a long time ago not to argue with Jagger. Okay, what I really learned was *when* I argued with him, I lost. I opened my bag, took out a comb, lipstick, tissue and tried to nonchalantly take out a Tampax—just in case.

When he jammed on the brake, the Tampax flew out of my hand, harpooning itself in the lambskin collar of Jagger's aviator jacket.

He pulled to a stop sign, turned and shook his head.

I reached over and grabbed the Tampax without a word. Somehow that made me feel empowered. If I'd broken down into hysterical sobs, as I wanted to do, or died of embarrassment, which was my second choice, Jagger wouldn't respect me. One more shake of his head and we were off.

Another thing I'd learned about Jagger was when he shook his head at me once, he was perturbed. Two shakes, well, no one would want Jagger shaking his head at them twice. *Exasperated* was the word that came to mind for two shakes.

We turned onto Interstate 91 headed north.

"You said this was only going to take a few hours. Where are we going?"

"Airport."

"Airport!" flew out of my mouth so fast a hiccup followed. I ignored it like the harpooned Tampax. "I'm not flying anywhere." Not being a frequent flyer, I needed a few doses of my Xanax before stepping down the long jetway to confinement, and I didn't bring any. Sadly, Pauline Sokol was not a world traveler.

"No, you are not." He turned off the airport exit and before I knew it, we'd pulled up to the curb beneath the "arrivals" sign.

"You can't park here," I said after reading all the warning signs. "You know how tight security has gotten since 9/11."

This time he merely looked at me. No head shaking.

Made my day.

"That state cop is coming over. You better drive around the airport a few times."

The cop came near, leaned over, looked at me. "No stopping—"

Jagger bent forward.

The cop looked at him, tipped his hat to me and said, "Have a nice day, ma'am."

When I was with Jagger, the same physical things often happened. Heart arrhythmia. My high IQ tanked. And jaw problems. The "problem" was that my jaw would drop down to my chest when he'd say or do something oh-so-very Jaggerlike.

"What the hell? Why didn't you have to—" No need to finish. It was foolish to ask Jagger anything. He was as closemouthed as a clam dug out of the Rhode Island beaches. I should have known and not wasted my words.

"There." Jagger motioned with his head toward the far door. "There she is. Mary Louise Huntington. Go get her."

I looked up to see a young woman with blonde hair about my length coming out of the door. I stepped out of the car and squinted. "Holy shit. She looks like me!"

"Atta girl, Sherlock."

Pleased that I'd figured something out but having no clue as to what, I started walking toward the woman, who was now followed by a nun. Another state cop came out of the far door near the baggage claim amid a crowd of people. A flight must have recently landed.

When I got closer to the woman, I said, "I'm here to escort you." To a mental institution, but I didn't say that out loud. "I'm with him." I turned around and pointed.

That jaw thing happened again.

No black Suburban.

No Jagger.

No idea what the hell I was doing.

I only hoped the woman, who looked even more like me close up, wouldn't freak out and give me a hard time.

"I need to pee," she said and turned around. The nun was nowhere in sight now.

"Oh, wait," I shouted as I followed her inside. She hurried toward the ladies' room near the baggage claim carousels. "I'm supposed to stay with you."

I bumped into an elderly woman, coming out of the ladies' room.

"Watch it, bitch!" she shouted.

Appalled that a granny would speak that way, I offered an "excuse me" and went inside. Mary Louise must have gone into a stall. I leaned against the sink and waited. "Er . . . you all right?"

Silence.

Jagger surely would be back from driving around the airport by now. He would do more than shake his head if I messed this up.

"Look, Mary Louise, is it? I need to know that you are all—"

The door opened.

My jaw dropped to my nipples this time.

Mary Louise Huntington stood in front of me as if I were looking in a mirror.

"I . . . did you notice how much we—"

She took off her jacket. Beneath she wore drab blue scrubs.

Just like mine.

What the hell?

Before I could say a word, she hurried out the door again. I followed close behind. "Oh, no, lady. You are not getting me into trouble with Jagger."

The nun approached, dropped her black carry-on bag and bumped into me. "Oh, sorry, Sister. I'm not usually . . . ouch!"

I looked down at my arm and saw a syringe.

A haze started to cloud the room. Or maybe it was . . . my . . . mind. My mind was . . . fuzzy. Fuzzy Wuzzy was a bear. Stop that, *Pączki*. I laughed. The fuzzy nun pushed me into the bathroom. "Ouch." I bumped my head on the wall. "Daddy calls me *Pączki*." I giggled, stumbled. "It's a Polish prune-filled donut." Jagger.

Where the hell was Jagger?

I rubbed at my arm. Make that three arms. I saw three arms attached to me on one side, four on the other. "You pinched me. That hurt. Nuns shouldn't . . . pinch . . . what did you give me? I hope to hell that syringe was sterile!"

Without a word, she pulled off her veil.

He?

He pulled off his veil, and he wasn't at all like Goldie. It didn't seem as if he usually dressed like a nun. I pushed at his chest and made it to the doorway of the restroom. Thank goodness there was no door that I had to open. My three arms felt as if they were made of rubber. Whatever was in that shot had kicked in, and I felt like crap.

My mouth went dry.

My skin prickled.

My heart raced until the room spun, turned dark and started to wink out.

In the distance, on the other side of the glass doors, watching—stood *Jagger*.

Three

Talk about cottonmouth.

My eyelids refused to open and my mouth felt as if the dentist had left reams of cotton between my gums and my cheeks. Cool air swirled around me and I heard the hum of an air conditioner.

And there was a familiar, medicinal smell in the air.

My forehead wrinkled as I tried so damn hard to open my eyes. Maybe I'd overslept, and Goldie had left for work without me. Why did Miles have the A/C on in March? Was it really March? What the hell was that smell?

Just because I'd turned thirty-five didn't mean I should be losing my memory. Airport. I thought about the airport. What was that all about? I sucked in a breath and decided I wanted to sleep for about a year.

But I had a case to start.

That's right. I had a case to start. Open, eyes. Open, says me.

My eyelids moved in slow motion, until I could see through a haze. Stark white. Miles's condo was done in designer white. White beanbag chair. White leather sofa and love seat.

I lifted my head. White walls. No window. Twin bed

with some kind of iron footboard. Not Miles's condo by a long shot. More like a hospital. Yeah. A hospital bed.

Had I been in an accident?

Frightened, I tried to push up to a sitting position. Hm, nothing hurt more than a few sore muscles and my arm. If I'd been in an accident, I'd expect more pain. I went to grab the iron bedrail.

My hands were shackled to it!

The "scream heard round the world" came out of my mouth with such force, I thought I'd damaged something important in my throat.

Silence.

My head flopped back down. I shut my eyes to try to think. Airport. Me. Woman. Man. Nun. Male nun. Jagger. *Jagger.*

Jagger watching through the glass doors—and doing nothing to help me!

Without attempting to get up, I screamed, "Jagger!" My screaming kept up until the door opened. "Jagger?" I asked hoarsely.

But it wasn't Jagger who came in. Nope. It was the nun. He came closer and looked at me with clearly forced sympathy. "You are going to hurt yourself, my child."

"I'm not your child, buddy. And why the ridiculous outfit? What the hell is going on?" I yanked at my hands. "And I demand you let me out of this barbaric get up! Where am I anyway?"

Silence and more staring.

"Come on, buddy. Black does nothing for you anyway against that pale skin. Why the hell are you pretending to be a nun?"

The "nun" came closer. "I am a sister of Saint Margaret of Cortona. I am Sister Dolores, Mother Superior."

"Yeah, right, buddy." I clucked my tongue. "Oh, I get

it. Dolores from the Latin *dolor* meaning 'painful.' Good one, buddy. But even though you apparently are a real pain in my—"

The "nun's" eyes darkened.

"Do not be so ornery, my child."

Suddenly I felt as if the wrath of God was going to sweep me into hell. I looked through the blur at the "nun's" face. Oops. Looked real. Looked sincere. Looked female. "Oh, dear. Sorry, Sister. I mean . . . in the airport that man dressed like a nun gave me some kind of shot. Some kind of intramuscular mickey. Please let me up from here. I'm confused and pissed . . . er . . . angry."

She, and I mean *she* this time, patted my arm. With a deep sigh she said, "I do not know what you are talking about, my child. There is no man. This is not an airport."

"I *know* this isn't an airport. And I know what I am talking about. Bradley International! It's in Windsor Locks, outside of Hartford. You have to know about it."

"Of course I know there is an airport there. That's about a forty-five-minute drive from here. But what does it have to do with you?"

"I was drugged and kidnapped from there!"

It seemed like hours before the nun came back in. Well, it was close to an hour, I was guessing, since my watch had been pilfered along with my scrubs. She'd turned and scurried out when I'd told her I was being held here against my will. Why she hadn't come back with the key to unlock these shackles and send me home was beyond me.

Sister Pain in the Butt was looking at one juicy lawsuit. I'm sure Miles knew some good lawyers.

Miles. Goldie. Mother. Dad. Uncle Walt. My four siblings. Ex-nun, Mary, my oldest sister. I lay looking at the ceiling, wondering about my family. Daddy would be worried. Mother would be beside herself, and Uncle Walt, the consummate Rip Van Winkle, would lose sleep over my disappearance. Without a window I couldn't even tell if it was night or day. How long had I been here?

Tears welled in the corners of my eyes. Not that I was scared, okay, maybe a little, but I was going to let anger take front and center. That emotion might get me farther than being scared could.

I lifted my head up enough to see my hands and feet. Shackles were designed to keep patients from harming themselves or others. And, damn it, they were pretty escape-proof. I yanked at my hand. Even Houdini would have a time with these. Sister Pain, or someone else maybe, had tightened it so that I couldn't wiggle my hand through.

Why would she be holding me here? In a hospital?

Jesus, Mary and Joseph. This was no ordinary hospital. This had to be the Cortona Institute of Life, and Mary Louise Huntington should be lying here manacled to the bed—not me. She was the nutcase. Me, I was as sane as . . . well, I was sane.

Talk about having a bad day.

I actually chuckled at the irony. "Sister? Hellooooo! Sister Dolores!" I lifted my head. "Hey. Someone!"

Silence.

Damn it. I had done my psychiatric nursing training in a similar mental institution—not my favorite subject, by the way. And I knew from experience that no one was going to believe a patient. I had to convince Sister Dolores, or whoever came into the room, that I was not Mary Louise.

Suddenly the door opened.

A petite nun, dressed in the same black-and-white habit as Sister Pain came bustling in. She gave new meaning to the word *perky*.

When she got close to the bed, I thought of strangling her to escape, but knew that wouldn't bode well with trying to convince anyone I was not mentally disturbed. "Hello, Sister. My name is Pauline. Pauline Sokol."

She made the sign of the cross, then shook her head. My Catholic upbringing said shaking one's head like that was not part of the ritual.

"I am Sister Christina Elizabeth Zawacki." She chattered on about something (I think I heard the words corn, sunshine, and pea soup) and placed her hand against my temple.

I flinched and pulled away, and then realized she was trying to take my temporal pulse. I cooperated by moving closer to her and waiting.

"Good girl."

I smiled at her. "Sister Christina Elizabeth, there's been a mistake. I'm not Mary Louise. My name is Pauline Sokol."

She stared at me a few seconds.

I bet she wished she had a nickel for every patient who pulled that line on her. But mine wasn't a line! I decided Sister Wacky was just that. She might be my ticket out of here. "You see, Sister." I motioned for her to come closer. "May I call you Sister Liz?"

She chuckled.

"Fine. Look, Sister Liz, a man shot me in the arm with something at the airport."

She lifted the sheet to uncover my arm. "There are no bullet holes in your arm, Mary Louise."

Sister Wacky it was. "I know that. You see I mean that he shot me with a syringe. Some kind of medication that knocked me out. I'm a nurse. I was supposed to chaperone Mary Louise Huntington from the airport to here.

And she looked an awful lot like me. What a coincidence, huh?"

She pulled at her earlobe as if that helped her to think. "I guess."

"The guy I work with can explain it all." And he'd better soon, or I would strangle *him*.

"Oh, my dear. It all does sound bad."

Hooked. I had Sister Wacky hooked like a New England scrod. "So, if you let me up, I'll be on my way. I have to get back to work."

"Where do you work?"

She hadn't budged to get the key, but I smiled and said, "Scarpello and Tonelli insurance company. I'm an—" Oops. That almost slipped out. I was consoled, though, by thinking I'd caught myself in time, but if you couldn't trust a nun, who could you trust?

Sister Wacky leaned near and rubbed her hand across my forehead, much like my mother used to do when I was sick as a kid. Very compassionate. "Poor child."

"What?"

"I thought you said you were a nurse, child?"

Why did these nuns insist on calling me a child? Wait, maybe that was better than reminding me I'd turned thirty-five a few days ago. I really hoped it was only a few days ago. I decided I liked being called "child."

"Oh, no. I *am* a nurse. You see. That sounds bad. I mean it sounds as if I really am mixed up or lying." I chuckled. "But I'm actually a very honest person. Sometimes to a fault. Who tells their elementary school principal that they didn't do their homework 'cause they were watching *The Brady Bunch*? I had a wicked crush on Greg."

She wiped harder.

Damn. I relaxed and blew out a breath. "Are you the charge nurse?"

"Oh, no." Now she chuckled, and I figured whoever ran this place didn't think Sister Wacky was charge-nurse material. "Sister Barbara Immaculatta is the charge-nurse on Ward 200. She doesn't use her family's last name. Sister Dolores is the Mother Superior."

"Already met her. Could I please talk to Sister Barbara without the last name?"

She did the earlobe pulling thing again. It was getting annoying. Of course, I couldn't fault the dear nun. When you're shackled to a bed, *everything* is annoying. I grabbed her habit. "Please, Sister. Please let me talk to whomever is in charge."

My grip tightened.

Fear built up in her sparkly eyes. "Oh, dear." She tried to move away.

Suddenly I felt like a mental patient as my teeth clenched. "I'm not crazy! Let me talk to her! Now!"

Sister Wacky pulled away so fast, the sound of tearing fabric filled the little room. As she scurried out and slammed the door, I thought how sad it was that my life was going to end in this closet of a room with me as a mistaken-identity victim.

Never to be married.

Never to give birth.

Never to sleep with . . .

I opened my mouth and once again screamed, "Jagger!"

He'd come. I knew he would. Jagger would come in some stupid disguise. Most likely a doctor. Yeah, I had it all figured out.

I yelled again, "Jagger!"

No one came. So, I laid back and decided to give into the crappy feeling I still had of being drugged. Normally

I'd keep screaming to get out, but knowing the inner workings of a psychiatric hospital, I knew I'd lose brownie points for that kind of behavior.

Maybe I could fall asleep and wake up at home.

Yeah. I yawned. *This was all a bad dream.*

Sunlight touched my eyes.

I slowly started to open them, then stopped. "Please, Saint Theresa, please find it in your heart to let it have all been a bad dream. Let me be home." Saint Theresa was my favorite saint and never let me down.

But as my mother always said, some prayers go unanswered for good reason. By the smell in here, I knew I wasn't home. I opened my eyes. "Okay, Saint T, there better be a good, noble reason for my being here." I could see a light coming through the window in the door.

A ray of hope.

I was going to kill Jagger.

As soon as I allowed myself a momentary curse, the door opened. A different nun came in. Actually stomped in with purpose. She was much taller than Sister Wacky and very slender. Model material if I ever saw one. The unflattering black robes hid what had to be a dynamite figure. Made me wonder why a woman who looked like her would turn to the nunnery. Then I admonished myself for thinking so selfishly and thought that she must have had a calling. And she had chosen to devote her life to God. Had to admire someone like that.

She came closer and stared at me with gorgeous deep green eyes. I wondered if she was Irish. A tendril of reddish hair peeked from beneath her veil. At least that blew the old adage that nuns were bald.

"I'm Pauline Sokol. It's very nice to meet you, Sister."

She leaned closer. "The chart says you have blue eyes, Mary Louise. Do you wear gray contacts?"

"I . . . no. Wait!"

She pulled back with the reflexes of someone who'd worked with the mentally ill for some time.

"That proves it. I have gray eyes. Me. Pauline Sokol. So, please let me out of here. If you get my clothes, I'll call a friend for a ride."

Then strangle him for getting me into this.

I paused for a few moments. Had Jagger really known that I'd get shackled to a bed in here? Had he really stood there watching me get shot in the arm like that? And had he really not come to get me out yet?

He would come and get me, I knew it.

I lay silent for a few seconds. Then, it dawned on me. "Son of a bitch. Why, you son of a bitch!"

The nun pulled back. "Excuse me, child?"

I clucked my tongue. "Sorry. I wasn't talking to you."

She looked around the naked room. "Oh . . . I see."

"No! No, you don't see. And I don't see anyone in here either. I'm not seeing things!"

"Do you see me, child?"

I clucked my tongue. "Yes, of course."

Things were taking a downward spiral.

Because right then, I realized that Jagger had told me to wear my royal blue scrubs—the same color Mary Louise Huntington had on.

He *knew*.

She stepped closer and patted my shackled hand. "I'm Sister Barbara Immaculatta. But you can call me Sister Barbara."

Barbie Doll. I decided she looked like a nun-covered Barbie doll from some career collection. Maybe she entered the nunnery after her breakup with Ken. "Thanks," I murmured, still taken aback about the scrubs. I felt my eyes tear up. Maybe because I was stuck here so helplessly. And maybe because this had to be the pinnacle of betrayal on Jagger's part.

I thought he liked me—as a friend.

Sister Barbie Doll rubbed my hand. "If you promise you will not try anything foolish, like running into the wall, I'll let you go wash up and have breakfast."

Run into the wall? Nothing like giving a whacko a stupid idea. Then again, I was sane. She must have gotten some good vibes from me to trust me like that. "I promise, and thanks. It would be wonderful to take a shower and get dressed."

She raised one eyebrow.

"Okay, shower and stick on a hospital gown."

Soon I was showering under the watchful eyes of Sister Wacky who looked more upset than I felt. I guess Sister BD really didn't trust me to run into a wall or drown myself. Then again, it had to be a policy around here.

How in the world would I ever get out of this place?

Sister Wacky handed me a pile of clothing after I'd covered myself in a towel. My hair dripped onto my shoulders, and I figured they'd never trust a mental patient with a blow dryer or curling iron. Great. Not only was I going to be miserable, but I was also going to look like crap and have a bad hair day.

There had to be laws against holding someone against their will.

Yeah! That was it. I looked at Sister Wacky. "There are laws against this, you know. You could be a codefendant in a lawsuit for holding me captive."

She smiled. "We have the necessary paperwork for having you involuntarily committed, child. It's called a ten-day paper. We can keep you that long before we decide what needs to be done for you. But we will help you get back your life."

I got teary-eyed at that thought and grabbed the clothing. While I shoved on the hospital johnny coat with blue cotton pants, I said, "I want to go home." The damn top only had a few ties in the back to hold it together. You know, the kinds of backless gowns that patients in hospitals wore. Who ever came up with these "fashionable" outfits? I know they were used so patients couldn't pretend to be a visitor and try to escape. Not in this attire.

Sister rubbed my arm. "Your doctor is due here any minute, child. Why don't you relax until then? Have your breakfast with the other patients."

As I followed her to the communal dining room, I got a load of the unit. Not too drab-looking out here in the patient lounge, with colorful red, blue, and yellow printed wallpaper. Some nice landscape paintings like the ones sold at starving artists' shows hung on the walls above vinyl couches and seats sans pillows (obviously so patients wouldn't smother each other).

I figured since this was a private institution, it was kept up pretty nicely. The patients had to have damn good insurance or their own money to come here. I knew private places like this were not cheap.

When we got to the doorway, Sister Wacky stepped to the side—and I got a load of the patient population here.

Yikes!

And I thought the bunch in *One Flew Over the Cuckoo's Nest* were weirdos. Jack Nicholson would seem normal compared to this group. I looked at the staff standing around the room, half expecting to see Nurse Ratched.

No Nurse Ratched here. Only a hippie-type girl, with stringy, long brown hair and tight jeans, waiting by the door. A very young-looking nun who had on a different type of habit stood nearby. Wait. I recognized her as a novice, in her black skirt and white blouse. Most likely a nursing-student nun, here for training. Hmm, maybe she could be my ticket out of here.

Sister Wacky gave me a little nudge. "Hurry in, child, or there won't be any food left."

"No shit, Madonna," a rough-looking teenager said from her seat near us. "Get the whacko some runny freaking eggs and burnt bacon." She pushed her dish so hard, it slid off the other end of the table.

The hippie hurried over while the room burst out in an uproar. "Nice one, Ruby! Now it's off to solitary for you." She grabbed Ruby with such force, it sure as hell shocked me. Ruby, however, cursed and yanked her shoulder free.

"Get your freaking hands off of me, Jennifer, before my old man sues you for molesting me."

A beautiful blonde girl, who'd been on the other side of Ruby's dish, brushed her lap off with a napkin. "You'd need witnesses for that, Ruby, and none of us here saw a thing. Did we?" She eyed the crowd.

Several who'd been screeching about the mess calmed down and nodded, as if the girl had some kind of control over them. Hmm. Interesting.

Ruby spit at her. "I'm really scared, Jackie Dee. Ohhh-hhh. You've got all these crazies on your side. Big shit."

"Let's go, Ruby. And stop causing trouble amongst the patients," said Jennifer—who must have been a psychiatric assistant—as she pushed her toward the door.

Sister Wacky made the sign of the cross and looked at me. "The courts cause so much trouble for us with these wealthy drug-addicted children." Another sign of the cross. "It's either here or jail, and since their parents can afford the high cost, they always come here."

I nodded and decided Sister Wacky must have gotten some good chemistry from me to slip and discuss another patient. Patient? Now I was thinking of myself as a patient.

Jagger was a dead man.

The scrambled eggs weren't nearly as runny as Ruby had said they were. Nope. They stuck to the inside of my mouth as if my saliva had dried up. Of course, maybe I'd lost my appetite after finding myself held captive here. That'd sure do it.

I took a drink of the milk they'd given me to wash down what I could while scanning the room for a means of escape. When I looked at Jackie Dee, I gasped.

An older lady sitting near me leaned over, "Jackie Dee pulls out her own hair."

I wanted to say, "no kidding" when I'd noticed she had a gigantic, monklike bald spot on the back of her head, but merely nodded.

"Eats it too," the lady added.

My milk sputtered out onto my dish of eggs. No great loss. The novice nun looked at me with a frown.

"Oh, boy. You've pissed off Novitiate Lalli," the woman said, moving away from me. "I'm Myra Jackson, by the way. Depression. Two attempts at suicide. Call me Miss Myra. Lalli is spelled L—a—l—l—i."

"I'm—" Damn. Who was I supposed to be? "Pauline. Mistaken identity."

Miss Myra gave me a "yeah, sure" look.

Novitiate Lalli stood above me. "We don't spit out our food here. If a patient can't behave, as in the case of Ruby Montgomery, they are taken out of the dining room. Is that clear?"

Tight ass was pretty clear, but I smiled and nodded. "Yes, ma'am."

"I'm Sister Appolonaria LaPierre. Novitiate Lalli for short."

"Pauline Sokol." I held out my hand. She raised her eyebrow.

"Nice to meet you, Mary Louise Huntington."

I clucked my tongue.

There went her eyebrow again.

"Yeah. Nice." I wiped up my mess with the napkin from my lap. Now I really had no appetite. I tried to sit quietly when one of the nurses announced it was time to count the "sharps." I remembered from my days as a student nurse that the psychiatric patients couldn't leave the dining room until all the knives, forks, and anything sharp were accounted for. Risky group with a sharp in their possession.

A quiet-looking woman across the table stared at me. For a second I was glad the sharps had been turned in. But I noticed a faint smile and a pleading look in her eyes. She shifted in her seat and mouthed, "I don't belong here either."

Yikes!

I turned toward Miss Myra and whispered, "Who is that woman in the green blouse?"

Miss Myra turned to me as if I'd disturbed her. Maybe I had. Maybe she was in some psychedelic daydream. "Margaret Seabright." She laughed. "Claims she doesn't belong here. But if you ask me . . . What?" She turned in the other direction. "What?"

No one was there.

"Cut the shit," she continued, and then turned back to me. "Margaret's as nutty as a chocolate-chip cookie."

Suddenly Miss Myra was not a font of knowledge that

I could rely upon, and I think *her* chocolate-chip cookies were full of pecans.

Margaret, however, did look pretty sane to me.

"Come along, child, your doctor is here."

I swung around to see the welcome face of Sister Wacky. I wanted to throw my arms around her in a big bear hug, but thought better. Physical contact had to be frowned upon in here. Instead I stood up and walked with her toward the door.

Then it hit me. My doctor! Had to be Jagger. Good. I was in a ripe mood to confront him.

Margaret looked at me and mouthed, "Please."

"Don't start bothering the new patient, Margaret," Sister said as we passed the table.

I turned and smiled at her, hoping she'd get my "we'll talk later" look.

"Which way?"

Sister took my arm. "The examining room is down the hall. Either it or the doctor's office is used for patient-doctor visits."

Several of the patients milled around the main sitting area, some talking to themselves, some arguing with themselves, some so wrapped up in their own worlds they sat like statues. I said a silent prayer to Saint Theresa to help these poor souls—and not to forget my poor soul in the process. When we got to the door, I turned to Sister Wacky. "What day is today?" Sure, it sounded like something a mental patient might ask, but I had to know how long I'd been away from my family.

"Tuesday, child." With that she opened the door and ushered me in.

I let out a sigh. As long as it was the Tuesday that followed the Monday I'd gotten my new assignment, I had only been gone overnight.

The stark room held a mint green examining table in the middle, with glass-front cabinets—all locked, I was certain—along the walls. A doctor in a white coat sat with his back to us, reading a chart. My chart, I guessed.

Oh, God. I had a chart in a mental institution.

Sister pulled the roll of paper on the table so I'd have a new sheet to sit on. She patted the table. I sat.

"Our regular doctor, Dr. Pinkerton, is out for a few days. We have another doctor who will cover for Dr. Pinkerton. He'll start with your intake exam. Dr. Richard Plummer." She looked at the man reading the chart. "Doctor?"

He swung around on his chair. "Sister, I seem to have left my stethoscope at the nurses' station. Would you be a doll and get it for me?"

Her cheeks turned redder than this "visiting doctor's" hair. But as a redhead, he wasn't bad-looking. His mustache was a much deeper, more auburn shade. Damn. I had no business ogling the guy who got me in here. I had to smile at the nun's reaction to being called a doll.

The nun hesitated. "I'd be glad to, sir. Shall I send in another chaperone until I come back?"

"Just leave the door open."

Great. Privacy is what we needed.

The sister walked out.

The hum of the ward filled the air.

The new doctor leaned forward.

And I fell off the examining table as I reached out . . . to *strangle* him—D E A D.

Four

I grabbed the "doctor" by his lab coat's lapels and tugged. "What the hell! What on earth! What *were* you thinking? Why'd you do that to me, Jagger?" Okay, admittedly I did more than "tug."

He, in return, kicked the door shut with his foot and yanked at my hands until my grip was broken. "Calm down before they really lock you up!"

My eyes grew large. "Lock me up? Really lock me up as opposed to . . . what? . . . the fake shackles I've had on my . . . Let me go. I won't touch you."

For a second he paused, then released. "Are you all right, Sherlock?"

I slammed my fist into his chest. Ouch! Damn, the guy was solid as a stinking rock. Then I kept swinging like some pint-size boxer—careful not to touch his face. Only thing was, he again grabbed my arms and this time held on.

"I thought I could trust you, Sherlock."

His voice came out in a sexy tone. Shit. I had to mentally order my hormones to cease and desist before my mind lost all control. Why'd he have to call me Sherlock? Damn it all. Damn him. That could be my undoing. "Let me go."

"Not a chance."

"What are you going to do with me? Keep me hostage here until . . . until what? What the hell am I doing here?" Those last few words came out a lot louder than I'd intended.

The door swung open.

In rushed Sister Wacky, who was looking pretty good to me right then. I *really* wanted to hug her. I knew I could trust a nun. Behind her came running a million-pound fullback. He grabbed me so fast, my hands slid from Jagger's before he could even let go. Damn the king of disguise.

"Ouch!" I shouted.

Jagger yelled, "Stop that! Let her go." He looked from the fullback to me. "She'll behave. Won't you?"

I bit my lip. Literally. Ouch again.

"Yes. Let me go, and I'll be fine. I'll be a good girl."

The orderly looked from Jagger to Sister Wacky, who nodded. With a *thump*, I landed on my feet like a cat from a ten-foot-high tree. I looked Jagger in the eyes. "Thanks. For nothing."

Sister Wacky came closer. "My child, Mary Louise. If you cooperate, things will go much easier for you."

I wasn't sure if she meant that I'd get out of here faster or that while I was marooned here, the stay would be more pleasant. "Please—" I swung around to Jagger. "Please, Dr. *Dick*, discharge me from here." I turned toward the nun. "And my name is *Pauline*." Damn. The words came out on a shaky note. I felt heat burning in my chest and my eyes started to tear. I did *not* want to cry.

The sister made the sign of the cross.

The fullback orderly walked out the door, chuckling.

And I stared at Jagger.

He didn't take his gaze off of me this time. "I know this isn't easy on you." He looked at Sister Wacky. "Let's humor her and call her Pauline." He put his arm around the nun and guided her to the door. "I need a few more minutes alone with this patient."

With her full cheeks bright red, obviously from his contact, she nodded. "Are you sure you'll be all right? I can have Spike chaperone if need be."

Spike? The name fit the big lug like a size-million glove.

Jagger smiled at Sister Wacky.

Ah, that smile, I thought, until I remembered he was the reason why I was here.

What I couldn't figure out was . . . what the hell for?

It seemed as if hours had passed since the nun and orderly had left me alone with Jagger. I'd plopped myself on the examining table and shut my lips. Had to. If I started to talk, or answer his numerous questions, I feared I'd melt into a puddle of tears.

With a burning sensation in my throat, I watched the second hand climb ever so slowly around the clock behind him. A plain, stark, black-and-white office-type clock. Made me think of Adele's cat clock, which made me miss her and everyone else.

"Look, Pauline. It kills me to see you here, but there's a damn good reason for it."

My interest peeked. Shit. I pulled my gaze from the second hand before it hit twelve. Midnight. The witching hour. I wished I was home in my own bed, snuggled with Spanky.

I tried to ignore my curiosity, but Jagger had used my real name. When he did that, instead of calling me Sherlock, he was dead serious. I couldn't ignore that. "What is it?"

He looked at me. "What's what?"

I let out a long sigh. "The reason, Jagger. What the hell is the reason I am locked up here against my will?"

This time he started to shake his head, but stopped and said, "You won't be here long if you cooperate."

Typical Jagger. Even when I was being held hostage in a whacko hospital, he wouldn't tell me why. I folded my hands across my chest. That's when I realized I didn't have on my bra (The nuns took it so I wouldn't hang myself with it, and right then I just might have done that if I'd had my 34B handy. Guns I didn't know from caliber, but bras I knew cup by cup.) Suddenly I felt naked.

And, believe me, you don't want to feel naked around Jagger, especially when you are so pissed at him you still want to strangle him. I tightened my arms, as if that might keep him from noticing, but all it did was pull his focus to my chest.

I think Jagger blushed.

But with the red wig, I wasn't sure if it was a true blush or a reflection of the Ronald McDonald color. I wanted it to be a real flush—however, that didn't seem like a Jagger thing.

Stop it! I had to get back to the matter at hand and not let his being here distract my furor. "What is really going on, Jagger?" Okay, it did come out a bit shaky with tears but, damn it, I felt like crying. Maybe that would get him talking. Appeal to his senses, his humanity.

"Oooooooh!" I opened the dam and let the tears begin. With a few added sniffles and sobs, I started to wipe at my eyes. I might not be good at lying, but I was totally good at acting.

Jagger looked a bit shaken. Then, since the guy must have been made of steel like his chest, he said, "Don't waste them on me, Sherlock. You're here and when you do your job, you'll get out."

Dumbfounded, I sucked in a breath and the last sniffle. "Creep."

He nodded, in what I termed was agreement. "It won't take long if you help me."

I grabbed the end of the exam table—and tightened. Ouch. I eased up a bit and said, "Help you, as in escort Mary Louise Huntington? For only a few hours? Oh, wait, you forgot to tell me the best part. That I was going to get kidnapped. Is that the kind of help you mean?"

"It isn't easy to get someone into this place. That guy dressed as a nun is the one you need to find out more about. Have you seen him since being here?"

My heart started to race a bit. I could see the guy's evil face poking out of his habit. Then I rubbed my arm as if I could feel where the needle went in. "No. Why? What the hell was that all about?"

"I'll fill you in later."

"I want answers now, Jagger!"

"Look, Pauline—"

Gulp. Guess he wasn't going to meet my demand.

"—The less you know the better. I need you to stay here a few days and keep an eye out for that guy."

"I have a case of my own to do, you know."

He merely looked at me. Of course Jagger knew about my case. He seemed to know everything, but really wasn't good at sharing. In my anger I pictured him as a selfish kid not sharing his toys.

"I know about your case. Fabio gave you that one so you could . . . it's a small case, Pauline. Won't take you long."

Now my heart sank. There was a connection, a reason why Fabio had given me the psychiatric case—so I could get stuck in here for Jagger.

Sister Wacky shoved the door open. "Everything all right, Dr. Plummer?" She gave me a sympathetic look. I really liked the woman now.

"Fine. I have a bit more to discuss with my patient—"

"Oh, dear." She touched her short-nailed finger to her lip. "Oh, my."

"Is there a problem, Sister?"

"Why yes. Mary . . . Pauline is due for her first treatment. Dr. Pinkerton wrote the order before he left."

Treatment—in a mental hospital!

Now my heart really raced.

It wasn't *my* treatment she was talking about but Mary Louise's. How was Jagger going to get me out of this one?

"And what treatment is that, Sister?" he asked.

"ECT." She looked at me.

ECT? My mind searched my old mental nursing files. What the hell did that stand for and why the hell did they have to use so many abbreviations in medicine?

Sister touched my arm. "Electroconvulsive therapy, my child."

I swung around to Jagger, who at least had the good sense to look stunned, as I murmured, "*Electric shock treatment*."

Before Sister could explain, I screamed, "Jagger! Jaaaaagger!"

Dr. Dick gave the nun another *Playgirl*-centerfold smile.

"What is a Jagger?" the nun asked me.

Dr. *Dick* interrupted with, "That's just a term Pauline told me she uses instead of cursing. She uses 'Jagger' instead of those nasty four-letter words."

I turned toward him. "Jagger *you*, buddy."

* * *

After my "foulmouth" incident, I watched Sister Liz, as I fondly called her now, leave. I used to have an internal feeling that I was always safe around Jagger—until now. Now I turned my feelings of safety to Sister Liz.

She had to be my ticket out of here.

Jagger leaned closer to me.

"Don't touch me, or I'll deck you again." Not that I could, but the words gave me some kind of power.

"Look, Pauline, this is a job. How we got here doesn't matter. You said you'd help me, and—"

"Not that I want to harp on it again, but getting here as a *patient* was not in the plan. Where the hell is the real Mary Louise?"

Jagger glared at me.

For a few seconds I only stared back. It was so easy to mindlessly stare at Jagger. I used to enjoy it. But now, being deceived like this kinda took away the fun. Damn it!

Then he touched my arm, and I didn't pull back. Not that I didn't want to, but suddenly his touch was comforting. Jagger may have gotten me into this, but in my heart I knew he wouldn't let me get hurt. After all, he could have let me get killed several times before on other cases and never had.

"Look, Sherlock, we need to find out more about the guy from the airport. Be on the lookout for him. His name is Vito Doran. Works as an orderly."

"What if I see him?" Okay, with Jagger's hand still on my arm, my temper had defused—for now. Hey, Jagger's touch could work miracles . . . and he knew it.

And I knew I couldn't fight it.

"If you see him, tell me."

"Oh, sure, Dr. Dick. I'll phone you pronto. How the hell am I going to get in touch with you? They don't exactly give me phone privileges around here. They don't even give me my clothes."

Jagger shook his head—once. And then he grinned.

I mentally slapped myself in the head. Of course, Jagger would always be around or at least popping up when least expected.

I chose to look at that as a bright side to my incarceration.

He let my arm go and turned toward the door.

"Okay. I'll watch out for Vito." Before Jagger stepped out, I said, "Oh, hey. Where's the real Mary Louise?"

He paused and said, "Missing."

"Miss . . . *missing*!"

Jagger stopped, turned and shook his head.

"Sorry. I didn't mean that to come out so loudly. But, I mean, *missing*?"

"Yes, Sherlock, she disappeared at the airport."

Now I shook my head, this time in disgust. "Great. I'm trapped here. The male 'nun' is on the loose, and your client is missing. Some case we got here." He didn't move, so I said, "Speaking of cases, what about mine? Number three? How am I going to do it while here helping you?"

"It'll get done."

That was it. Short and sweet. It'll get done. And, it probably would, because I'd make damn sure that Jagger paid me back by helping me out. I needed money real soon.

"You're going to pay me for this, too." I said it with as much bravado as I could muster, knowing I couldn't force Jagger into doing anything he didn't want to.

He merely looked at me.

For a second I thought I saw disappointment in his eyes as if I was accusing him of trying to cheat me. Then, I realized Jagger had every intention of paying me, and really didn't stick me here for any other reason but his case.

What a guy.

I groaned. From behind Jagger I could see Sister Liz approaching. Yikes! She was coming to get *me*. "Jagger, do something."

He looked at me. "About?"

Through clenched teeth I said, "The treatment. My treatment. The brain-zapping thing. *My* brain."

While he looked at me the nun came closer.

"Are you finished, Doctor?"

He nodded.

"Fine. We need to get you upstairs, Pauline, before you are late. No one wants to be late for *that* technician."

I looked toward Jagger. Make that looked toward where he'd been because now it was an empty hallway. Gone. He was gone like some magical creature.

And me on my way to get my brain zapped.

Sister Liz took my arm to guide me upstairs. We never had to leave the patient unit. There was a locked stairway that she opened and, I assumed, if I ran down instead of up, the doors would all be locked too.

No means of escape.

"Um, Sister Liz—" I paused on the stairway and looked at her. "Can I call you Sister Liz?"

A ruddy hue spread up her cheeks. "Oh. My. I guess that will be all right."

Great. One step closer to becoming friends with my ticket out of here. "Wonderful. I really don't feel too well. My head is killing me. Sinuses. You know."

She nodded and guided me to the door, which she unlocked. Stepping aside so I could walk in, she said, "Oh yes, child. Sinus problems are horrible. I suffer in the spring, so I barely go outside."

I may never see the outside again.

"Yes. But since my head hurts, perhaps my treatment could be postponed."

Sister stopped. "My, no. We have to keep our schedule around here. Sister Barbara is quite adamant about that. No. You cannot postpone anything. Besides, my child, your head will feel better after . . . you know."

You know. You know. You know!

Yeah, I'm guessing a gazillion volts of electricity could make a headache go away if your head didn't zoom off your neck in the process. Sure I knew this treatment wasn't that much electricity, but I preferred *no* electricity to my brain.

I looked around the room. Stark. A treatment table with that paper roll thingie tucked beneath. A few cabinets. And a horrendous looking gizmo of a machine near the bed sprouting wires and leads and electrodes. On a nearby table were a tongue depressor and some gel.

I could bite my tongue during this treatment.

I did not want my tongue bitten by anyone, even me.

Well, I'd learned to save myself in my past cases, and now was no exception. So, I took in a deep breath and shoved Sister Liz with all my hundred and fifteen pounds. This was one time I wished I was a plus-size kinda gal.

"Oh!" From the corner of my eye, I noted that the sister had landed on the treatment table. But that was all I saw since I ran so fast to the door. Shit! It was locked. I hurried back to her and stared to grab her habit. There had to be a set of keys hanging from her rope belt. "I'm so sorry to have to do this!"

"Stop, child!"

I felt something and grabbed with all my strength. A hundred pearl-looking balls scattered to the floor. Sister's rosary beads. Oops. Not only did I face a brain zapping, but surely I was now on the wrong side of the higher-ups, who'd probably punish me for trashing a blessed set of rosary beads. I quickly said a silent prayer/apology to Saint Theresa so she'd pass it up to them for me.

While preoccupied, I felt something on my shoulders. I spun and came around face to face with Spike—and he didn't look any too pleased with me.

Within seconds, I was strapped to the treatment table with Spike standing guard at my feet. Sister Liz stood in the background, fingering her broken beads. Every muscle hurt, especially my arm where I'd received that shot at the airport.

I looked at her. "I'm sorry. I'll buy you a new set. It's just that . . . Please. Listen to me. I am *not* Mary Louise. And I'm a Catholic! I am *Pauline Sokol*, a nurse—"

The door swung open. In walked what looked like a Swedish masseuse, dressed in a white pantsuit. Gigantic. Arms like boiled hams and a head of straight brown hair. I had no idea if it was male or female.

Sister Liz nodded. "She's going to behave now, Gretchen. Aren't you, Pauline?"

I looked from one to the other to Spike. I should lie here quietly, I thought. After all, the procedure couldn't be too dangerous, or they wouldn't be doing it on the mentally ill. Then again, I was sane, and what the heck would happen to my normal brain cells once they fried? That, I hadn't learned in nursing school.

Then again, maybe I too didn't have any normal brain cells. After all, I'd taken this job.

I felt a glob of gel on my skin and Gretchen sticking the electrodes to my head.

I could lose my memory. Never know my family again. Never know Goldie or Miles. Never know . . . Spanky.

I sucked in a breath as Gretchen continued to connect

the machine's electrodes to my head. Then, I started to shake my head so vigorously, the leads pulled off. Amid Gretchen cursing in some European language, Spike's warnings, and Sister Liz's prayers, I fought with all my might to get out of this treatment.

Boom!

I screamed, thinking my head had exploded off my neck in time to see Dr. Dick hurry through the door. "Sorry I'm late."

"Late!" I screamed. "How about stopping this insanity!"

Within seconds, Gretchen had me reconnected, the machine made a soft whirring sound, and I shut my eyes, ready to convulse.

Nothing.

I felt something poke my arm and peeked out of one eye to turn and see Jagger glaring at me, with a look of "you'll have to do better than that" and noticed the electric chord in his hand.

"What the hell is wrong with this?" Gretchen said.

"Must be some kind of electrical delay," Jagger said.

Before anyone else could speak, I lifted my chest in a dramatic convulsion and even went so far as to arch my back. Suddenly I was Meryl Streep performing as if my life depended on it.

And apparently it did.

Five

Exhausted, I lay on the twin bed in my room after Sister Liz tucked me in following my "treatment." She'd hovered about like a helicopter, every once in a while poking at the blanket. I wanted to see Jagger to "thank" him, but he'd disappeared before anyone caught on.

Thank him. That was perfect.

For crying out loud, he'd gotten me kidnapped and admitted to a psychiatric facility against my will, and I wanted to thank him for pulling the plug before my brain fried. What was wrong with *that* scenario?

This time *I* shook my head. I had to get out of there . . . soon.

I did try to convince myself that in this job I might have to do things that I wouldn't normally do, but being locked up was not one of them.

My eyes started to close. Obviously stress and the threat of losing brain cells had taken a toll on me. I decided to give in to a short nap. After all, plenty of foreign countries had siestas every day. One couldn't hurt me. Then I'd be in better shape to plan my exit from the Cortona Institute of Life.

"Stop! No!"

My eyes flew wide open. The voice shouting in the hallway was female. Sounded a bit like Margaret Seabright. Then I heard Miss Myra shouting too. I had to see what was going on and if I could help. So, I un-tucked myself and jumped up. Thank goodness the higher-ups hadn't deemed it necessary to have me on "constant" watch. I wasn't sure if they even did that kind of thing anymore, but back in my psychiatric training days, a staff member had to watch "at risk" patients constantly. That meant in bed, in the john, in the dayroom. The patients even had to sleep with their hands outside their covers, since most were either suicidal or homicidal.

Well, at least those in charge gave me some credit for sanity.

I grabbed my hospital robe and ran to the door. When I swung it open, I saw a scuffle in the dayroom. Miss Myra was pulling at someone. Jackie Dee sat twirling her hair. I imagined she envisioned a real feast soon. A huge person pushed Margaret up to the wall. At first I thought it was Sister Dolores in her whites, but when I got a load of the arms, I knew the wrists were way too big for a female.

That had always been dear Goldie's one flaw. And I do mean one.

I ran to the side wall—and froze.

It was him. The man who had given me the intramuscular mickey at the airport. Vito Doran! I ran forward and grabbed at his arm. "Leave her alone!"

With one turn of his head, he gave me a look that sent me flying. Well, his left arm was what actually sent me to the floor, but the look would have done it.

"Ouch!"

Ruby grabbed my hand and yanked me up. "If you know what's good for you, stay out of it."

I would hope at my age I would know what was good for me, but Ruby's tone gave me pause. Did she mean she'd do something to me . . . or . . . that *he* would?

Before I was able to ask her, Margaret was led out of the dayroom toward a locked door.

"Shit," Ruby mumbled.

"Shit?" I repeated.

She turned to me as if I didn't know what the four-letter word meant. Maybe she, too, had heard that my version of cursing was "Jagger."

"Why do you say that?" I asked.

"Cold wet packs," she mumbled and I figured Ruby had been swaddled in them before.

Now it was Margaret's turn.

I would have loved to go help her, but knew I couldn't if I ever wanted to get out of here. A chill raced up my spine at the thought of the cold wet packs. That I remembered from the old days too. When a patient got "out of control," their clothes were stripped off, wet sheets were wrapped around them like a cocoon of comfort to calm them down.

Once I had to sit in a tiny closet of a room with a patient swaddled in the sheets, who kept seeing bugs on the walls. I had to take her temporal pulse over and over until, thank goodness, my shift ended . . . because I was starting to see those bugs too, and was ready to call my mother to borrow her flyswatter.

My heart ached for Margaret. I looked at Ruby. "What'd she do?"

Ruby gave me a vacant stare. "Grabbed his cell phone—"

"—And was going to call someone to help her get out of here. She said she doesn't belong here," I added.

"She doesn't." With that Ruby headed off toward the

TV, plopped herself in front and stared at a commercial for low-carb snacks.

I leaned against the wall and knew I had to find Jagger . . . fast. Maybe I could succeed at getting one of the staff's cell phones.

The instincts that had served me so well during my nursing career said Margaret Seabright was right. She didn't belong here . . . and who else didn't?

I looked around the dayroom to make sure some staff was within listening distance. Of course, in a psych hospital you didn't have to look too far to find any staff. The patients were never, or at least should never be, left alone. I shut my eyes and told myself I was Meryl Streep again. With that thought, I opened my eyes and started to wail.

"Ooooooh! Ooooooh! I need to seeeeeee . . . Dr. Carpenter." I looked at Spike heading toward me.

Ruby turned around from the TV long enough to whisper, "Plummer."

I paused my wailing to let that sink in. Oops. Wrong building trade. "Doctor. My Dr. Plummer. I need to see him!"

By now Spike was within breathing distance, but hadn't grabbed me yet. Sister Barbara was fast behind. Suddenly I worried that she might have some kind of "calming" shot in her hand, so I eased up on the Meryl bit and wiped at my eyes.

"Oh, Sister Barbara, could you please call Dr. Plummer for me? I'd really appreciate seeing him right now."

She stopped within a few feet, her forehead wrinkled in what I could assume was suspicion. Maybe my transformation was too quick. Maybe I was too good an actress. Or, maybe the nun bought my act and thought I was really whacko. Either way she didn't stick any needle into my arm or any other body part.

Phew.

"What is wrong?" she asked.

Damn. Now what? I couldn't say I needed to fill my partner in on our fraud case. So, I said, "It's . . . personal. You know, Sister, no offense, but it's between my doc and myself. I really feel the need to talk to him."

From behind her I could see Ruby smirk. Hmm. Maybe I could use her. We seemed to have made some kind of connection and at least I knew Ruby didn't eat her hair, talk to herself or throw herself at walls. Not that I took a drug problem lightly, but Sister Liz insinuated that Ruby was "normal" and here instead of in jail. Besides, the kid appeared perceptive and clever, as lots of drug addicts are. She probably was a rich kid hooked on coke and who knew what else. At least she wasn't wiped out all the time.

Geez, now I was relying on a rich, bratty, teenage druggie.

I gave her a quick wink and turned toward Sister Barbie. "Please."

"You know, you're lucky he left orders to call him if you asked us to. That's pretty unusual. Most doctors don't do that unless it's an emergency. I'll put in a call to him." With that she turned toward Spike. "Stay with her until her doctor arrives."

Yikes. "I'm just going to watch TV," I mumbled, quickly took a seat next to Ruby and glued my gaze to the set. That way Spike wouldn't have any reason to manhandle me.

Every once in a while I'd sneak a peek at him. Yep, within manhandling distance. Even though I didn't watch daytime TV, I was suddenly very interested in why women cheat on other women who are their ex-lovers' relatives and never moved out of their homes, along with only wearing bright red and sharing a common bathroom, courtesy of Mr. Springer.

What was this world coming to?

"Pauline?"

I swung around to see Sister Liz. How cute. She'd used my real name. Our bond tightened. "Yes, Sister?"

"Your doctor is here to see you."

Maybe I sprung up a little too fast, but my action had Sister Liz pull back, clutching her new rosary beads. Spike was fast on the nun's black, sensible heels and he looked anxious to subdue me.

I felt bad about the rosary, but stood ready to go. "Where to, Sister?"

She motioned for me to come with her. Spike joined in. Guess once you made a bad name for yourself on this unit, it followed you until discharge.

Please, God, I prayed that there was a discharge—soon.

Sister opened the door to an office and moved to the side.

"Thanks," I whispered as I looked to see Jagger, still with his carrot-top 'do on and looking delicious, sitting at an oak desk. The guy fit into any situation. I wondered if he'd ever taken acting lessons, and who the hell did his makeup?

He gave Sister Liz his usual smile. For a second I wondered, too, if her sisterly insides reacted like mine always had when he looked at me. *Of course they do*, I thought. Nuns were human.

"I'll be fine with her, Sister. If I need anything, I'll holler."

And Spike will attack me. Once the gang left, I looked at Jagger. "Vito Doran ruffed up Margaret Seabright today."

He stared at me.

"Margaret is the patient who said she doesn't belong here."

"I know."

"You do?" I hated sounding so fascinated by what he said and reminded myself I was still pissed at Dr. *Dick*.

"You know. You know? What the hell does that mean?" I flopped onto a straight-backed chair and let my legs dangle over the side—not out of reach of Jagger's legs, though.

He pulled sideways.

"What's the matter? Don't trust me?" I asked.

"As a matter of fact, no. Now, what about Vito?" He eased farther to the side.

I curled my lips. "She tried to grab his cell phone to call someone, I guess." Damn. That sounded stupid. "I mean—"

"I know what you mean. Did he say anything to you?"

"Me? No. He merely flung me across the room."

Jagger's no-nonsense look appeared to crack. Maybe he felt a bit worried about me. "I'm assuming you're all right."

My legs kicked out farther. I admittedly wanted to make contact. "All right? How can I be all right in *here*?" My left toe brushed his leg.

"Look, Sherlock—"

"Don't 'Sherlock' me." *Please don't, because it melts me to the very core, and I lose all rational thought.* I held my legs close to the table now and leaned forward. "Jagger. Jagger, please. I have to get out of here. I mean . . ." I sniffled and this time it was for real. Damn it. I really didn't want to do this, but he was too much a reminder of the outside world. "Isn't there a way I can come back undercover to help?" What a waste of words. I already knew the answer to that one. How could I, after everyone had seen me as a patient? I knew in my heart that patients wouldn't confide in a staff member. But to one of their own, they might.

He took a deep breath. "Vito Doran is working with someone on the inside here. We have to find out who."

"Working at doing what?"

He looked at me for several seconds. I could almost hear the cogs in his brain turning. "They get people to fly out here to the country, thinking they are coming to some resort. People who need some R & R, like with relationship problems or alcohol or just too much stress. Here they're promised luxury in a wealthy New England setting. A resort."

I looked down at my hospital johnny coat and fuzzy slippers. "Yeah, this is the Ritz, this is."

"Once they get the person's insurance approved with some fake diagnosis, they keep them here until the insurance runs out, they've collected, and I'm sure, pocketed the profits."

My hand flew to my face. "Wow."

Actually, that was quite the ingenious plan, if not the illegal one. I thought for a second and asked, "Don't the people who get released report it to the police?"

Jagger merely stared for a few seconds.

"Oh, right. That's why we are here."

"It's not easy to prove they didn't belong here, and there haven't been many reports . . . yet. Once you've been in a mental hospital, sometimes your credibility to report things like this falters."

Once I'd let it sink in that, again, I'd learned there are really bad people in this world, I said, "Then what? I mean . . . do they hurt the people?"

"So far, no."

"So far?" My eyes filled with tears. I looked past Jagger to the bar-covered window. From there I could see that the Cortona Institute of Life sat miles from the main road on secluded grounds. It resembled a college campus, and Jagger said it used to be a mansion, a private residence, for some wealthy psychiatrist who left the nuns the money to open the hospital.

What a coincidence.

I looked back at Jagger. "If by 'so far' you mean they haven't killed anyone yet but you think they will, then I insist you get me out of here. Now." A stupid sniffle followed. I pulled myself straight until my back hurt and added, "No, I *demand* you get me out of here."

Sister Barbara came to the door. "Everything all right in here, Dr. Plummer?"

I gave her a smile and wiped my forearm across my eyes. Good. She'd think I'd had some epiphany of sorts. I'm sure weeping patients were a daily occurrence around here.

Jagger walked to the door.

I got ready to scream that we weren't finished yet. I was still here, for crying out loud!

Slowly he turned to look at me, but said to Sister, "Make arrangements to give Miss . . . Sokol a weekend pass. I know it's soon, but she needs it. Her . . . mother will be picking her up at three. She lives nearby."

My hands flew to my face. My mother! He was having my mother come to this hole to see me in this condition!

What really ticked me off was that he had already planned to let me out temporarily and wasn't meeting my demand. Damn.

I wanted to yank him back by his lapels and tell him, "No way," but I was getting out. Consoled by the fact that

Mother would probably say a million novenas and eventually be fine, I remained silent.

Sister Barbara eyed me with a look of what I'd call suspicion and said, "Yes, Doctor. She'll be ready for her mother."

"Pauline! My Pauline!"

After I got decked out in my civilian clothes, the stupid scrubs, that is, Sister Liz led me to the waiting area, where I froze on the spot upon seeing my "mother."

"Suga? Don't look so frightened. Momma is gonna take you home for a bit."

I don't know who looked more shocked, Sister Liz or me. Okay, she had it over me, but seeing Goldie dressed in a Chanel winter white suit, fire engine red spike heels and matching purse, smelling of Chanel No. 5, I couldn't move.

This was my mother?

Truthfully I felt a bit relieved that it really wasn't Stella Sokol standing there. I had to hand it to Jagger. He had protected my mother from, I'm sure, a fainting spell like the one she'd had when Mary had said she was engaged, the day she'd moved out of the convent. I wouldn't even think about Mary's soon-to-follow pregnancy news—*very* soon after the marriage.

Damn it. I felt as if I somehow owed Jagger now.

Wasn't that just beautiful?

He got me locked up, and I owed him for being considerate to my mother. Oh, well, at least I was getting to go see her and everyone else.

Goldie wrapped me in a bear hug that crushed my chest to his. Felt wonderful. I kissed his cheek and whispered, "Get me the hell out of here, *Mother*."

He signed the appropriate papers and assured Sister Liz that he'd have me back on Sunday at three.

Not if I had a breath in my body.

On the way out, Dr. Dick gave me a nod. Oh, boy. He wasn't going to let me off that easily. I smiled and told myself to play along. But, come hell or high water, I was *not* coming back.

Sister unlocked the door to the tunnel that ran throughout the buildings. Imagine being so sick that you couldn't be trusted to walk outside. I said a silent prayer for all the inhabitants of this place and tightened my hold on Goldie's arm.

He patted me gently but remained silent as we made it to what had to be the last door. I could see the outside through the bars on the windows, and as we stopped in the foyer, my heart skipped like a kid's on the last day of school.

Then, Goldie shrieked.

My heart stopped.

And Sister looked as if she'd seen a ghost.

Vito Doran, most likely a real ghost now, lay sprawled out in the alcove near the window—a brown metal broom handle protruding from his chest.

My first instinct was to run over and do CPR or at least check for a pulse, but I'd seen enough corpses to know Vito was not among the living. It was way too late for nursing care, and this couldn't have been any accident.

Our suspect had been killed.

Six

"Pauline," my real mother called through the bathroom door. "Are you using up my Renuzit *again*?"

As I sat on the edge of the tub, I inhaled once more. The pine scent wrapped its familiar comfort around me.

Dorothy was right. There was no place like home.

I sprayed again, thinking of Vito's body, and didn't even remember the trip here.

"Pauline Sokol, stop wasting that air freshener, unless you have a whopper of a case of the runs," Mother ordered.

"I'll buy more."

"You know I have a supply in the closet . . ."

A supply? Last time I had looked, Mother had fifteen cans. All pine scented. All with red discount labels on them. She really cleaned out the local pharmacy when they had a special. I only prayed that the good folks at the Betty Mills Company, makers of Renuzit, wouldn't ever discontinue this scent.

After a quick inhale, like some whacked-out drug addict, I stood and went to the door with the can still in my hand. When I opened the door, Mother grabbed the can.

"Where did you go these last few days that has you acting so crazy?"

I paused, my eyes widened. "You have no idea how accurate you are, Mother."

She shook her head—only her head shaking wasn't like Jagger's. Mother's was a typical mother-type shaking that said, Stop acting like a child and tell the truth.

Before she could continue to reprimand me—since I really wasn't in the mood—I grabbed her by the shoulders and hugged.

With her mouth squished against my shoulder, she reached a hand out and pressed it against my forehead as she said, "You feeling feverish?"

I kissed her cheek and let go. "I'm just glad to see you."

"You saw me a few days ago. You really are acting . . . Where's Mr. Jagger?"

"Why?" I started to walk down the hallway toward the kitchen.

"Why? You have to ask?" She put the Renuzit on top of the refrigerator, as if I couldn't reach it.

I sat on the stool next to the breakfast counter and rested my elbows on the aquamarine Formica. Then I plopped my chin in my palms. "Yes, I have to ask."

Mother opened the refrigerator and started to pull out food items. I'd forgotten it was nearly suppertime. Tears welled in my eyes at the thought. Supper at my parents' house. What a comfort. What a wonderful feeling. What the hell was I thinking?

My recent hospitalization, or incarceration, as I liked to think of it, had affected me more than I'd thought.

Behind the refrigerator door, Mother said, "Well, since you took off without a word, your nice Mr. Jagger called me to tell me you were okay. He said not to worry." She set a bag of potatoes on the counter. "You should go back to your nursing."

Friday night. Mother's potato pancakes. Talk about a nostalgic moment. I ignored the comment about my past career.

"Don't make Jagger sound like some kind of hero." I leaned farther into my palms almost wishing I could get sucked into my hands and disappear.

Mother shoved the first washed potato, skin and all, into the blender. "Shame on you, Pauline Sokol, for talking badly about Mr. Jagger."

Uncle Walt came in with his hat in his hands. He hurried over to me and gave me a hug.

I inhaled Old Spice cologne and smiled.

"Glad to see you back." He turned to my mother. "Michael is parking the car in the garage."

She nodded at him as if she wanted to say, where else?

"Glad to be back," I mumbled. He had no idea how glad I was.

Like some kind of octopus, Mother worked in a frenzy. She kept blending potatoes, onions and flour while she poured me a glass of milk, and I think set the table at the same time. "Here. Drink. Maybe your calcium is low."

Could be, since I didn't have my calcium and magnesium while incarcerated. I wasn't in the mood for milk—more like a Coors—but I also wasn't in the mood to argue either. I sipped on the damn milk as my father walked in followed by Goldie and Miles.

I jumped out of my seat and ran to hug all three of them.

"Pauline, you *are* acting very oddly," Mother said as she added salt and pepper to her mix. "Very oddly indeed. I wouldn't be surprised about that calcium. Miles, you're a nurse. Does low calcium make you act cuckoo?"

Miles chuckled. "Not sure, ma'am, but my best guess

is no." He walked toward her. "You didn't put enough salt in."

Mother slapped his hand away as he lifted the Morton's saltshaker. "Her and that job," she mumbled.

Daddy hugged me back. "We missed you, *Pączki.*"

I was never so glad to be called a fat prune donut in my life.

Then I looked behind Goldie.

And hurried off to get some more Renuzit.

Once inside the bathroom, I sat holding a new can pilfered from Mother's private stock without spraying it. Not wanting to damage my lungs by inhaling too much of the nostalgic scent, I figured just holding it would help. What the hell was Jagger doing here? Hadn't he caused me enough grief, for crying out loud? Here I'd planned a restful weekend with plenty of time to ponder a million reasons why I was not going back to the Cortona Institute of Life no matter what. Then he shows up.

"Open up, Sherlock."

Taken aback, I rubbed my finger on the cold metal can. "I'm—" Damn. I didn't want him to think I was peeing or something like that. Funny how you never want a gorgeous guy to think you go to the bathroom. As if *they* never did. "I'll be out in a few minutes."

"I'll wait."

"That's rude." I sat down on the wicker laundry basket.

"Open up. I've brought you clothes to change into."

I looked down at my outfit. The stupid scrubs had welded themselves to my body. I'd forgotten I was wearing the fool things. "I don't need to change now. Go away. I'll talk to you later."

It did almost seem rude that Jagger would stand outside

the bathroom like that, but then again, I had no doubt that he *knew* I wasn't doing anything embarrassing in here—and he *was* Jagger.

I reached over and opened the door. "Give me them."

He looked past me for a second, then handed me a brown Stop and Save bag.

"Where did you get my clothes?"

"Never mind. Change."

"Not until you tell—"

"We can't work on your case with you dressed like that. Miles gave them to me. Change. I'll be in the kitchen with your mother."

"No! Wait!" Damn. He sauntered down the hallway, knowing full well that I would not dillydally when I knew he was spending time with Mother. What the hell would they talk about? I ripped off my scrubs and slid on my jeans. When I contemplated my mother telling Jagger some horribly embarrassing story about me, I stopped mid-thought and inhaled.

Jagger's scent.

He'd touched my clothes . . . and they'd never be the same again, or ever be washed.

After I was dressed, I hurried out, only to find everyone sitting in the dining room, eating Mother's potato pancakes, and chatting up a storm. I heard snippets of: Pauline did *that*? Pauline ate *what*? Pauline dated *whom*? And, Pauline should be *ashamed* of herself. (That last one from my mother.)

With my face burning hotter than the fried potato pancakes, I held my head up and yanked my chair away from the table. They all turned toward me, silencing the room until I felt as if I might scream to fill in the void.

"Please pass the sour cream, Goldie," I said with as

steady a voice as I could manage—which was about as steady as a drunken sailor at sea during a storm.

Goldie gave me a consoling smile and handed me the container. I spooned a glob on my dish and, after serving myself some pancakes and applesauce, ate in silence.

Jagger wiped his lips with one of my mother's linen napkins. "That was wonderful, Mrs. Sokol. I've never had potato pancakes before."

Mother looked rightly horrified along with sympathetic. I never could figure out how she could manage so many emotions at once. She'd make a wonderful mime.

Me, I hated mimes and clowns.

We all helped to clean up while Mother served coffee and *pączki*, which I passed on. Goldie and Miles agreed to play a game of Scrabble with my folks. Uncle Walt feigned being too tired and decided to watch TV and, I'm sure, take a snooze. Jagger took me by the arm.

"I'm sorry to have to rush off, but I want to show Pauline something."

Mother grinned.

Shoot.

Father kept his gaze glued to the Scrabble board, but I think he winked.

And Goldie and Miles looked at us . . . and smiled.

Jagger eased me toward the door. "Get your jacket."

I was ready to protest, but then remembered my job. I had a case to work on, and tonight *I* was going to use Jagger.

Not that it surprised me, but I did notice Jagger knew exactly where to go for my fraud case. The psychiatric practice of one Dr. Pia De Jong. From my reading the file, it seemed as if old Doc De Jong had a slew of teen patients. Way more than the ordinary practices, and each patient had very good mental health coverage. Hmm. All were supposedly being treated for depression—and the number of patients had increased dramatically in recent months.

Soon we were on the outskirts of Hope Valley, pulling into the driveway of a lovely white Victorian house. The sign hanging by the drive said FAMILY PSYCHIATRY. It listed Dr. Pia De Jong and another name that had been scratched out. Interesting. She worked alone. Was that so no one would catch her committing fraud?

I knew, with Jagger's help that we'd eventually find out.

Obviously that's why Fabio had assigned me to this case. He must have known that I'd need Jagger's help, since Goldie and Nick, both assigned to their own cases, wouldn't be available. I wondered if Fabio also knew that Jagger was working a big case at the Cortona Institute of Life.

It'd shock the heck out of me if Jagger had confided in Fabio—but it wouldn't if Jagger had convinced Fabio to give me a connecting case.

There were lights on downstairs, two cars in the parking lot and a red Mercedes in the doctor's space. That was one thing about mental health professionals: They could name their own hours. Many worked evenings to see more patients. If she had so many teenage patients, she probably saw them after school was out.

Jagger pulled into an empty space by the front door. As soon as he shut off the motor, a young man of about sixteen came shuffling out, followed by a stressed-out-looking woman. Obviously his mother. I felt sorry for both of them, knowing it was not easy growing up in this day and age. Being a teenager had to be a bummer. I'd seen it with my brother's son, and figured out that God made teenagers to lessen the pain when kids moved out of their parents' house. Actually, he probably had it in mind that parents would *want* their kids to move out by the time they got through the teenage years.

This poor kid, who probably wanted to be anonymous, wore black leather everything with a metal something hanging from every place where a hole could be punched.

Anonymous? I don't think so.

Without looking at me, Jagger said, "Come on."

"Come on? Where?" But before I could get an answer to my question, he was already up the front porch stairs.

I hesitated, knowing—just knowing—that Jagger was going to get me into some kind of mess, once again.

The waiting room had no receptionist and two doors. I figured one was for patients to come into and one to go out of so that they couldn't see each other—this because the doors were set off by a long hallway. The décor bordered on French provincial invaded by modern.

I plopped down into a black brocade high-back chair and set my feet on a leather-and-chrome footstool. If this doctor did her own decorating, she might need some mental health counseling herself.

An air cleaner, very common in psychiatrists' offices since so many patients smoked before going there, hummed in the background. Jagger had seated himself in a matching chair and was looking at *Time*. I wondered if he was reading about politics, religion or celebrities. Couldn't be the last. Jagger would not be impressed with anyone's celebrity. I assumed he was a political reader.

Suddenly a door clicked in the hallway, which we could no longer see from there, and another one shut. I looked at Jagger, who didn't move.

"What the hell are we going to say or do here?"

"I'm going to try to help you, Ms. Knight."

I spun sideways to see a woman standing a few feet away. Yowza. Not just any woman. Her features were smoothly covered in flawless skin the color of a not-yet ripe peach, highlighting cheekbones worthy of nobility. Her eyes, which I noted were focused on Jagger, were a brilliant oceanic blue. I decided they were contacts, as I looked around to see whom she was talking to.

We were the only ones there.

"Your brother, Colin, has told me a lot about you, Alice. I am Dr. Pia De Jong. Please come in." She held out a perfectly manicured hand, like that of someone who modeled real diamond jewelry and had been insured by Lloyd's of London.

I looked around again. None of my brothers were here. What the heck was she—

Jagger took me by the arm. "Go ahead, Alice. The doctor is going to try to help you."

"I will help," the movie star/doctor said.

Suddenly I was being whisked off to the Cortona Institute again. Not physically, mind you, but all in all, it felt the same. Confusing. I was losing control and had to gain it back again. It was all a job. A weird job.

I pulled away in protest, but not before I dug my nails into "Colin's" arm.

"Ouch! Stop that, Alice." He said my "name" with his teeth clenched, and he gave me a Jagger look.

That yanked my confusion back to normal. To my case. That's what we were doing here. Against my better judgment, I had to trust Jagger where insurance fraud was concerned.

He knew his stuff. I'd give him that.

And I had plans to use him, learn from him and suck his brain, to become the best investigator that I could be.

Then I'd work alone.

I sighed and walked past the doctor, refusing to inhale. She had to smell wonderful. I knew it just as I guessed she wore Armani, walked in Prada and carried Gucci.

This doc made pretty damn good money.

But was it all legal?

I eyed the couch, done in pale yellows, whites and rose, as I headed into her room. The room offered a feeling of comfort, much like four walls of sunshine. I decided I'd better not lie down on the couch with Jagger in the room. Nope. I needed to stay upright and keep a clear head. I'd been so confused lately being around all the mentally ill, who knew what I'd say.

Suddenly, it dawned on me.

How would I know *what* to say?

What in the hell had Jagger/Colin made up? What had he said about me? What was this doctor going to do to "help" me when she couldn't take her eyes off my "brother"?

I sat on a floral high-back chair and leaned forward just enough so that I partially blocked her view of him.

She got up, sat on the edge of her desk.

"Do you have your insurance card, Alice?"

My heart stopped. My eyes widened, and my hands froze.

Shit.

Jagger lifted out his wallet and took out a little white card. All I could see was Alice Knight and Blue Shield.

Damn, he was good.

Even had a fake insurance card. I only hoped he wasn't committing any fraud.

Then I reminded myself who I was working with.

The doctor took the card, made a copy on her machine and handed me a clipboard. "Please fill out both sides, Alice. Then we'll talk."

I took it and the pen she had tucked in the metal holder

and looked at the questions. Damn. I had to make up a lot of information. Had Jagger already told her some of this? I looked at him, but his attention was on the good ol' doc.

Make that on a certain part of her anatomy.

She kept crossing and uncrossing her legs. Legs to die for. Legs any Rockette in her right mind would envy. Sure, I was proud of my Maciejko legs that I'd inherited from my mother and grandmother, but truthfully, they weren't De Jong's.

I cleared my throat in order to get Jagger's attention. Nothing.

So, I leaned over and jabbed him with the doctor's pen.

"Ouch!" He finally turned and glared at me. "What is it, Alice?"

I had to hand it to the guy. He always stayed in character. I, however, had a hard time remembering what character I was supposed to be. Since leaving nursing, I'd gone from, well, a nurse to a seventy-something to a nutcase, to, well, apparently another nutcase. Pauline Sokol was getting fuzzier and fuzzier in my mind.

"I need help with this, *Colin*." I put a lot of emphasis on his name, hoping that he'd get the hint.

Then again, this was Jagger I was talking to.

He gave the doctor a warm smile. "I'm sure you want to speak to Alice alone." Before he could stand, my hand was on his jeans, just below the knee, not some place good, yanking him back into his seat. But he managed to brush me off and stood. "Calm down, Alice. The doctor is only going to talk to you." He turned toward Dr. De Jong. "I'll be filling the paperwork out for her in the waiting room." He looked at me. "In the waiting room, Alice." He reached into his pocket and took out his glasses.

His words had come out in a comforting tone, as if "Alice" would freak out once her brother left the room. Was I supposed to? I sat still for a few seconds, watched him take the clipboard from my hands, nod at the doc, and go toward the door.

I opened my mouth, and then shut it just as fast.

Jagger left.

The doctor turned to me and said, "Well, Alice, it's just you and me. You can feel free to discuss your problem."

My problem? What the hell was my problem? I wanted to scream Jagger's name, but figured the doc would call 911 and have me locked up. *That* problem I would deal with later.

I smiled at her and then realized . . . Jagger had put on his *glasses*!

Seven

Jagger had put on his glasses.

Jagger didn't *wear* glasses.

I finally realized that they were the ones he'd used on a case before. There was a tiny camera in the frame. He had gone out of the room, knowing full well there was no receptionist, planning to "investigate" the files of one Dr. Pia De Jong with the fabulous legs.

I hoped he wasn't thinking of her legs.

Then I hoped he got the goods on her, so my case could end soon and I'd get paid. Money issues had been pushed into the back of my mind since being incarcerated. But then again, there was my share of the rent to pay, food to buy, and a car payment due soon—for a Lexus I didn't even own but had cosigned the loan on, for a "good" friend.

"Alice? Alice, I am speaking to you."

I looked up to see an annoyed look on the doc's face. Yet she still looked damn fetching.

"Sorry. My mind wanders. I . . . I don't know where to start. Maybe if you tell me what my brother said before bringing me here, I can start from there." Yes! That was a

great idea. I was getting better and better at these investi-
gation/undercover/fake patient things.

Then I thought of Vito Doran's dead body.

I shivered.

"Are you okay?" She leaned back in her chair, not really looking as if she cared if I was all right or not. I actually think she looked at the clock.

"Hmm? Oh, yeah." *I'm fine except for worrying that
Margaret or I might be killed soon.* And it never left my
thoughts that the real Mary Louise was missing too.

"Colin said you were not sleeping well . . ."

I know she was talking, but suddenly I had a vision of
Jagger standing next to my bed, me with Spanky curled
up under my arm, and me wearing my slinkiest, thinnest
nightie and his scent overpowering the room.

How the hell could anyone sleep with him there?

"Alice, have you ever been diagnosed with ADD?"

I looked at her. ADD? What the hell? "No. Why?"

"You seem very preoccupied, even distracted, or is it a
reluctance to talk about your depression?"

Depression? I was one of the most carefree, happy
people I knew other than Miles and Goldie who had it
over everyone where happy was concerned. Depressed
indeed. "I don't have ADD, and I am *not* depressed." I put
her straight.

Her look said she didn't buy it.

What the hell had Jagger told her?

"Are you going to tell me what my brother said or
not?" It came out much angrier than it needed to, but
seemed to get the point out.

"He said you've suffered a loss of appetite lately—"

*You've never eaten the food at the Cortona Institute,
lady.*

"—Have difficulty with relationships—"

Okay, so one of my boyfriends tried to kill me, and my infatuation with Jagger borders on psychotic sometimes, but who wouldn't have difficulty with that?

"And," she continued as she used one of her lovely fingers to push aside a strand of hair that had fallen on her forehead, "you have threatened to run away."

From a mental institution that I don't belong in!

Jagger was a pip. At least he related true life to his lies. Guess that made them seem more real. I could easily explain all of this to her if I leaked my cover. It was tempting, because I knew a psychiatrist had to keep info confidential, but then again, this broad seemed as if she wouldn't believe a word I'd say. She believed Jagger though.

And my being here, telling her lie after lie, would give him time to get some pictures of her files.

So, I began my elaborate story. I told her that my brother was the cause of it all. Ha. Ha. She never once looked as if she bought it. Before I knew it, she was shoving three boxes of pills at me.

"One in the morning, and one at night."

Knock. Knock.

Jagger stuck his head in the door as I took the medication samples from her.

"Colin, I don't want any medication," I said.

He looked at the doctor and then at me. "You need to do what Dr. De Jong says, Alice." He turned away from me. "Shall we make another appointment?"

"Most definitely," she said and gave him a sexy smile.

"Most definitely," I mumbled, cursed under my breath, and stuffed the pills she'd given me into the couch below the cushions.

I looked up to see both of them staring at me and realized my cursing was getting way too ripe and grabbed the damn pills from under the cushions.

Once outside, I turned to Jagger. Not only turned to him, but slammed my fist into his arm. "What the hell were you thinking? First you lock me up in a hospital, and now I'm also going for outpatient treatment. If I'm not crazy for working with you, I will be soon."

"Pipe down until we get into the car."

That was it. Ever the consummate investigator. Damn, but he was right. Since we couldn't see the waiting room on our way out, we didn't know if there were other patients there. The doctor could be coming out behind us any minute. Jagger would have seen if there were more patients when he'd left her office. I remained silent until we got into his SUV.

Then I punched him again.

This time he grabbed my arm. "Stop it, Sherlock. You know of a better way to get into her office to investigate?"

"I . . . well . . . I could have gotten a job as a nurse—"

"You see any nurses, receptionists or other staff around?"

"Damn it. You didn't have to say I was depressed. Why couldn't *you* have been the patient?"

He looked at me, stuck his key in the ignition and turned it. When he looked back, he started to drive out of the parking lot.

"Okay. Okay. Big deal. You have more experience in this field than I do." I folded my arms across my chest before I clocked him again, causing us to drive off the road. "So, what did you find?"

"Every teen she sees is treated for depression. Not an easy diagnosis to prove or disprove."

"Obviously."

He shook his head . . . once.

"But if I could get a look at the files, I may be able to determine more with my background," I said.

He nodded.

Before I could ask any more questions, he'd pulled into our Dunkin Donuts. I liked to call it "ours" even though it really wasn't, and I'm quite positive Jagger wouldn't look at it as ours. At the drive-thru window, he ordered our usual. When he handed me my extra light, extra sweet hazelnut decaf and French cruller, I said, "I have no appetite."

He curled his lip. "I had to come up with something."

I took the coffee and donut and only wished I didn't have an appetite. The truth was, after the days in the mental hospital, I felt as if I could eat nonstop. If I kept that up though, I'd really be depressed.

I took a bite of donut, chewed and swallowed. It dawned on me that I'd missed our donuts and coffee together. "So, she treats lots of teenagers. That doesn't sound like fraud to me."

"No, it doesn't. But when you look at the numbers and the fact that everyone who comes to see her gets prescribed medication, put on her billing system, and is seen for an abnormally long time, it needs to be looked into. Plus the increase of teen patients has been recent."

"That's easy for you to say. How the hell can we prove these kids aren't depressed? I mean, nowadays, almost all teenagers have something to be depressed about. Have you ever seen one who wasn't?"

Jagger merely looked at me. Of course he probably didn't know any teenagers. It was dumb to even ask him. He took a long, slow sip of his coffee. That wasn't unusual, since he drank it black and often had to wait for it to cool. But this time, I could tell he was thinking. Think-

ing of my case and how, more than likely, *he* could get
something out of helping me.

Jagger firmly believed in that old adage of one hand
washes the other. Hand washing I could take, but if he
got into the old maxim of you scratch my back, I'll
scratch yours, I'd be more confused than ever—and in
Nirvana.

"I'm working on it. We'll get you in to read the files
soon." With that, he set his coffee into the console holder,
started up the car and drove off.

I grabbed my coffee so I wouldn't be wearing it and
kept trying to take sips as he slowed or stopped at a light.
Soon, we had turned into the parking lot of Miles's
condo.

I got a bit teary-eyed at the sight of my home and how
I wouldn't be staying.

I sniffled it back before Jagger caught on and got annoyed with me. When he stopped, I grabbed my stuff,
opened the door and got out. "Thanks."

Before I knew it, he was leaning over and the power
window was gliding down. I tried to get to the sidewalk
before he could say anything, but I dropped the rest of my
cruller, which I'd saved for Spanky. When I bent down to
get it, I heard, "Be ready Sunday at one."

I swung around so fast, I lost my footing and landed on
my back like some kind of bug who'd been sprayed with
Raid. Thank goodness the grass cushioned my fall.

From a distance I heard, "You all right, Sherlock?"

Shit. I lifted my head just enough to say, "Yes, I am,
and I am *not* going back. Ever."

"Margaret's life is in danger. And Mary Louise is
missing."

For a fleeting second, I was ready to say, *Then call the*

police, but I knew, just knew, that we had uncovered something at the Cortona Institute of Life, and until our work was done, others could be in danger too.

Damn my Catholic-school-induced conscience.

I held Spanky close to my chest and ignored the doorbell. When the brass clock Miles had bought in Switzerland chimed only once, the term "death knell" came to mind. Again the doorbell rang.

I shut my eyes and thought of the nice day I'd had yesterday. Nick had taken me out for lunch. We'd agreed that we really weren't dating any longer, but would remain friends. We both needed some space and time. I actually needed to get this case finished to be able to live like a normal person.

Usually "needing more space and time" would be a lame excuse a guy would use to break up, but I used it anyway. I figured Nick would be one less person worrying about where I was or one less person I'd have to lie to about where I was going. At least I had about twelve hours of worry-free time. My folks bought my lie about going to spend time in Vermont with my friend Jeannine. I'd never shared with them how I'd cosigned her loan, and how she'd taken off in her new Lexus, sticking me with the payments. Miles and Goldie knew all about where I'd be and I knew, true to their promises, they'd stop by and visit my parents—like two busybody old-maid aunties. How I loved those two. All my bases were covered.

The bell rang again.

"Come on Pauline, or you'll be late getting back."

"Go away, Jagger. And don't even think about reminding me about Margaret and Mary Louise." I looked at the little overnight bag that I'd packed and remembered how I tried to think of any excuse not to go back.

But I couldn't.

Still, I'd give Jagger a hard time so he wouldn't take me for granted. I kissed Spanky on the head. "I'll be right back, sweetie." I always told him this, thinking dogs had no concept of time. Even when I went away for a week or more I'd told him I'd be right back. I only wished it was true this time.

I stood, set him down on the couch and lifted up my little bag. I knew one of the nuns would search it, so I only brought a few magazines and tapes to listen to. Anything to take my mind off of where I'd be. I also brought a small notebook and several pencils to write notes about my case.

I'd never admit this to anyone, especially Jagger, but I was a bit excited about this case. Even though it wasn't mine (Jagger always did pay me something though), I felt an overwhelming desire to stop whoever was committing the fraud.

All I had to do was picture Margaret mouthing to me that she didn't belong in the Institute.

I opened the door. My heart momentarily stopped, and this time it wasn't because I was looking at Jagger.

Facing incarceration again had caused the anomaly.

Jagger pulled into one of the reserved spaces marked for physicians.

I shook my head, grabbed my bag and got out.

"You can't just go walking in alone. Wait up," he said from behind.

Goldie's yellow Camaro sat in a restricted parking space for visitors and I noticed Jagger nod to him. Obviously my family had to bring me back, since they took me out. Goldie stepped out and walked as if in slow motion. Guess he really didn't want me going back in either.

Not that I was in a hurry to get inside, but I was still pissed at Jagger, mostly on principle, that I was the one being readmitted. I stopped for a second and looked up.

It was quiet except for a distant foghorn from a boat that chugged up the Connecticut River. The windows to the main building were empty, but on the western side, I could see someone pressed up against the glass, mouth wide open, hands flailing and eyes glaring in horror.

Yet I couldn't hear a sound.

The place was obviously designed so that passersby couldn't hear the ranting of the mentally ill. The thought gave me no comfort at all. Winter ivy climbed the walls of the giant redbrick buildings. A steeple of white stood on the end building as if it had been a chapel at one time—or maybe it still was. I could use one. My first thought had been that the Institute looked like a typical New England college.

I stopped and turned toward Jagger.

"I'll be one step behind you," he said.

I knew that was his way of trying to calm my fears. My feet felt like lead weights as I nodded and moved up the stairs clutching Goldie's arm between mine.

"All right, Mary Louise, you can keep your notepad, but not that pencil. It's too sharp. I can get you a crayon though," said Sister Liz in the readmitting room.

Bummer. Good thing I'd thought to hide a tiny pencil in my sock. It was only a few inches in length and no wider than a coffee stirrer. I'd gotten it out of Uncle Walt's old golf bag. He used it to write on his scorecard, but it had been a few years since he'd played.

Goldie sniffled and moaned a few times about his "daughter." Then, I kissed him and whispered that I'd be fine and to keep an eye on my family. Having come from a broken home, I could see the pride in his eyes at being given this chore. He kissed me and nodded to Sister Liz as she unlocked the door to let him out.

Glad they didn't do a strip search, I smiled and said, "That's fine, Sister Liz. A crayon would be fine. Could you please go back to calling me Pauline? So I'll remember to answer you. I don't want to seem rude."

She hesitated, then probably remembered my "doctor" had said to humor me. "Of course, Pauline. I'll get you something to draw with. Any particular color?"

"Black." Oops. That choice had to be telling in some psychotic way, but truthfully I'd said it since it resembled a pencil.

"Black. Okay. Black it is." She turned toward the door when it opened with a swoosh.

In waltzed Sister Barbie, carrying a tray of colorful pills. "Everything all right here, Sister? If so, you are needed out on the unit."

Great. If they started to medicate me, I could lose all logic and not be able to do my job. I always wondered how anyone could function day to day, especially at a job, when they did illegal drugs. Give me a clear head any time.

Sister Liz gave me a sympathetic look and walked out.

Damn. Did she know something? I tried to look calm, even pathetic, so Barbie wouldn't force drugs on me. She held the tray and said, "So, how was your visit?"

As if I'd tell her that Jagger and I investigated Dr. De Jong. Instead I practiced my lying and said, "Fine. It was fine."

She gave me a "yeah, right" kind of look. Amazed me how modern nuns were nowadays. Well, excluding Sister Liz. She was adorable and very much like the "old" nuns although she really wasn't that old.

When I went to Saint Stanislaus Grammar School, no

nun ever gave me a "yeah, right" look or was as pretty as
Barbie. Nope. They all looked like, well, proper nuns.
Once they gave up having to wear habits in public, the
nunnery went downhill. It was like letting kids wear jeans
to school. In my opinion, that was the beginning of the
many behavioral problems in schools.

I had problems of my own, I noted, when Barbie took
out a little white cup with a green pill in it. "Your doctor
prescribed this for you, Mary Louise." She held it out toward me.

It was then that I not only decided I would kill Jagger,
but also *how*.

"I . . . Can't you please call me Pauline?"

She rolled her eyes. Damn! These nuns were way too
modern for me.

"Fine. Pauline, take your medication."

"My doctor said I didn't need any."

"Doctor Plummer may have said that, but Doctor Bran-
don Pinkerton, the head of the Institute, my dear, has a
standing order that new patients be medicated. It is for
your own good, child." She wiggled the cup toward me. "I
will inform Doctor Plummer of the policy we have here."

Instead of trying to argue, and I do mean trying, since I
had very little faith I could win against Barbie, I took the
cup, opened my mouth and stuck the pill under my
tongue. While she watched me like the proverbial hawk, I
took a cup of water from my bedside table and drank.

The pill floated from beneath my tongue!

"Swallow, Pauline, before you choke yourself." She remained glued to the spot. "Don't make me have to get my
flashlight to check your mouth. This has been a long day.
Just swallow, dear. Please."

My tongue fished around my mouth, but to try and get
the damn pill back into its hiding place proved useless.

Then Sister Barbie patted me on the back! I swallowed and felt the damn pill sliding down my throat. Shit. I consoled myself with the thought that the pill might be Prozac, which wouldn't take effect too quickly or knock me out. The drug peaked at six to eight hours.

No problem.

In my foggy haze, the furniture in my room started to wiggle. I sat bolt upright in my bed to see it clearly move across the room. When I flopped back down, I decided the pill wasn't Prozac at all.

I called it the Green Demon, and didn't even remember getting into bed.

My eyes fought to shut, but I tried to force myself awake to think. It was no use. The lids closed like a curtain on the final act of a play. Deciding to give in to the feeling, I lay still. Then my door opened.

A shadow of a figure stood by the doorway. At first I thought it might be Jagger, but it wasn't his size. My mouth went dry and my heart started to pound so loudly in my drug-induced state that I worried that whoever it was would hear it. Like some paranormal evil spirit, it moved across—no, glided across—the room. Couldn't be Sister Liz either. Way too tall for her.

As a matter of fact, from this angle, it almost touched the ceiling light above my bed. Of course, I couldn't be too accurate with drugs in my system and lying down.

Not certain if what I saw was fact or drug fiction, I remained still—and the evil spirit rummaged through my drawers!

Paralyzed with fear, I now couldn't move if I had wanted to.

Why would someone sneak into my room? Why wouldn't they think I'd wake up? And why me?

Someone here must suspect me. But of what? I'd been so careful.

I thought of missing Mary Louise, dead Vito Doran, and poor Margaret. Great. Just the kinds of thoughts I needed right about then.

The figure dug into my bag and even looked inside each of my shoes. Damn, that would have been a good place to hide something. But then again, I hadn't thought of it and this spirit person had.

A tickle started in the back of my throat. Had to be from fear, or the dry air of this place, but I tried not to give in to a cough. I certainly didn't want to startle him, her or it. What I wanted was to open my eyes a bit more than a slit to see if I could tell better who it was. But other than the fact that it wore black—and this place was crummy with black-clad nuns—I had no clue.

Suddenly, it turned and came closer.

Gulp.

The figure remained hovering near for what seemed like hours. I tried to identify a scent, but nothing. The tickle became worse. I swallowed as nonchalantly as I could.

The figure remained, its face a blur, and then it just turned and walked out.

I coughed my brains out when the door shut, and then tried to get up. My body remained stuck to the bed as if it were ten times my actual weight. I hoped I hadn't been given some paralyzing drug. The room remained a foggy blur . . . until tiny butterflies flew toward the window. Green ones with yellow wings followed by toads hopped across my bed. Then a large cockatoo flew in from the window. I tried to reach out, to shoo them all away, but nothing.

Instead I shut my eyes and let them make a racket. Someone would hear and come get them out of here.

"Pauline, Pauline, wake up, my dear. I need to check your vital signs, child."

My eyes fluttered. Sister Liz, a hazy Sister Liz, stood in front of me. I opened my eyes wider to see the room. My hands shook but not as much as my voice. "Are . . . they . . . gone?" I grabbed the covers tighter even though my hands still trembled.

"They?"

"The . . . birds . . . the butterflies," I mumbled. "That damn toad kept me awake."

I felt a hand on my arm and turned toward her. "Sometimes it takes a while to get used to the medication."

Get used to! Some psychedelic pill had me hallucinating the rain forest in my tiny, stark room, and I had no damn intention of getting used to it or taking a pill again.

I inhaled and wanted to ask her what the hell I had been forced to swallow, but it probably was some usual "cocktail" they gave all the newly admitted patients. Maybe Jagger had prevented them from giving me one the other day, but he might have a harder time going up against the head of this place.

I shut my eyes a second to think and ask myself what the hell I was going to do next.

The only question that came to mind was, Had someone really come into my room or *not*?

Eight

Once Sister Liz had left my room, I made my way to the nurses' station on wobbly legs. "I want to see my doctor immediately," I said to Novitiate Lalli, who was behind the glass window typing on a keyboard.

She kept typing until she appeared to be done.

I wanted to bang on the window, but thought better than to do that. "Sister?"

Finally she looked up. "Doctor's name?"

"Plummer. Dr. Plummer." Thank goodness I remembered this time.

She reached for the list of phone numbers then looked up at me. "You know, your psychiatrist is not at your every beck and call, Pauline. He has other patients too."

Yeah, right. Not *my* psychiatrist.

She leaned closer and eyed me up and down. "You don't look so great, so I'll call him this time. But don't be surprised if he reprimands you. Go sit in the dayroom."

I think she smirked at me.

I bit back that he had left orders to call him whenever I wanted. No sense in making enemies around here. I didn't know who I could trust or who I should watch out for.

On my way to the dayroom, I said a silent prayer that

she'd learn more compassion if she was serious about this nun thing. Before I knew it, Spike came bounding down the hallway. Oh, boy. I grabbed a pillow, sat and became a statue.

He came so close to me I could smell that he'd recently had a cigarette. "Your doc is here. Get up."

I sprung up like a Jack in the box so he wouldn't man-handle me. I had visions of poor Margaret, whom I hadn't seen today yet, being shoved around by Spike. Of course, the stupid Green Demon had me knocked out for so many hours that Margaret could be asleep along with all the other patients. Without windows in the room, I couldn't tell if it was day or night.

"Lead the way," I said to Spike with a bit of humor that went way over his basketball-sized head.

Once down the hallway, I paused. Through a window in a door I could see someone, one of the patients who looked a bit like Jackie Dee, wrapped in white sheets, ly-ing still on a twin bed with rails, and some nun I didn't recognize was sitting at the side.

While I was zonked out, Jackie must have had some kind of incident that landed her in cold wet packs. My heart broke as I walked past the room, unable to do any-thing to help. I had to constantly remind myself that this was a hospital, and although some of us really didn't be-long here, most actually did.

Spike opened the door to the doctor's office. I held my breath for a second. Jagger sat on the end of the examin-ing table. He looked as if he'd walked in off the street. Al-though in full character makeup, he hadn't bothered to put on a white coat.

Damn. The medication must still be in my system.

"Here she is, Doc," Spike said and promptly headed off after Jagger nodded at him.

He looked at me and said, "Close the door."

I did and turned around to him, thinking he'd move and let me take the table. But no, he remained, so I sat in the rolling doctor's chair. I wheeled closer to him.

"What's wrong?"

"I . . . Barbie gave me a green pill—"

"Goddammit."

"On that we agree."

He merely gave me a Jagger look and said, "I'm not even going to ask who Barbie is."

Good, I thought to myself. He didn't need to notice that the head nurse/nun looked like a real doll (especially since I'd heard my niece say Barbie and Ken were splitsville). Damn. I was becoming jealous of a doll or a nun—take your pick. Either way, it was pathetic. "Look, I know you didn't want me medicated, least I hope you didn't."

He merely looked at me.

"Okay. Okay. So you didn't, but when I'm in the position of a patient, I don't have much room to argue."

"Why the hell didn't you stick it under your tongue until she left, and then spit it out?"

I slapped my hand to my forehead. "Gee, why didn't I think of that?" I rolled farther back.

He leaned forward. "You all right? You don't look all right."

"I'm flattered. But what I wanted to tell you about was my drug-induced trip." I proceeded to tell him about the rain forest and finished with, "So I really can't be certain someone was in my room." Nor am I sure there are toads—or are they frogs?—in the rain forest.

"Did you . . . When your mind cleared, did you check your drawers to see if anything was disturbed?" He tapped his foot on the edge of the exam table's step.

Why hadn't I thought to do that? I watched his foot a

second longer then looked up. "Of course. You know, Jagger, I'm not allowed many personal belongings around here. So it didn't take much to scan what I had to see if it was touched." I ran my hand across my nose to make sure it hadn't grown. I was getting damn good, and much quicker on the uptake, with this lying stuff.

Jagger stood and walked toward me. He hooked his foot on the wheel of my chair and spun me toward him.

"Hey! Watch out!"

"You need to work on credible lying, Sherlock. Go back and check. It's late tonight, so I'll see you on rounds tomorrow." Then, while I was paralyzed in stunned silence, he touched my cheek and said, "Watch your back." His finger ran slowly down my skin.

At least I convinced myself that it had . . . in a very sensual sort of way.

Now I really wouldn't be able to sleep tonight.

I mumbled inside my head all the way back to my room. Dr. Dick had called Spike to escort me and gave him a reminder to keep his hands off me unless absolutely necessary. I figured my idea of absolutely necessary and Spike's version weren't even on the same wavelength. Nevertheless, I made it back to my room unscathed, and as soon as he left, I hurried to my drawers.

"Shit," I muttered when I opened them to find my undies scattered about.

I always folded my undies.

Someone actually *had* been there. Because even on drugs, no way could I be this messy.

Sleep didn't come easily, once I'd confirmed the suspicion that someone had invaded my space. Why me though? Who would suspect me of not being a real patient? Was that really what someone supposed? Or was it a coincidence? Or had a real patient done it due to their mental health issues, and was I—or at least my undies—an innocent bystander? Whatever the reason, someone had violated my undergarments, and that didn't sit right with me.

But who?

I'd pondered that thought over and over during the night, which had led to my not being able to sleep. I came up with a suspect list though. I wrote it on the paper I'd brought there, and rewrote it over and over. It was a short list, unfortunately. Novitiate Lalli was on the top of it—mainly out of principle and the fact that I plain didn't like her. The figure could have been her size, I rationalized. And, maybe she was in on the fraud. That way she might know I really wasn't Mary Louise Huntington.

I had cut the nuns some mental slack. After all, they were chosen for a life to serve God, so they wouldn't come snooping in someone's drawers. Novitiate Lalli hadn't taken her final vows, so that made her a suspect along with, unfortunately, Ruby. Maybe Ruby was being buddy-buddy with me to get some info. Maybe she was involved in the fraud. Anything was possible. Hell, maybe she was a plant, like me, but for the opposition.

Despite my eyes trying to close, I had thought about the figure being male. Vito was out of the picture now, but maybe Spike had been in on it. I wasn't sure if the figure could have been his size or not, since I had been lying on the bed, not to mention the Green Demon in my system.

Things looked different from that lying-down angle. That I knew, from having slept with a few guys who, prone in bed, looked damn decent, but when they got up and gravity was involved, their sizes changed—and I'd realize I was *not* that desperate.

So Spike, who, come to think of it was always around,

could have been the culprit. The question of why me had stuck in my mind until sleep finally took over.

Now I had to get up and see what I could find. I consoled myself with the reminder that the faster I helped Jagger crack this case, the faster I would be out of there. So I got up and headed out to the dayroom.

Several patients rested on the pillowless red vinyl couch, watching the TV. Two men stood near the doorway, waiting for their pills, I assumed. Ruby and another young woman sat on the yellow vinyl chairs, Ruby's with a crack up the back. On the wall above was a starving artist's Picasso-style painting in oranges and reds. Didn't seem a good idea to have such a confusing, modern painting in this place. We all needed reality, not more bewilderment. We were all supposed to remain there to take our medication, and then we'd be sent off to eat.

Suddenly I craved Mother's potato pancakes.

My eyes started to tear up, so I immediately cut that thought short. Of course, as a patient here, I could probably get away with being "weepy," but I wasn't that good an actor. I'd probably blubber out that I was a PI.

When I walked toward the couch to find a seat, I felt someone come up behind me, causing my breath to hitch and a chill to race up my spine, as if I were pantless and my johnny coat was slit all the way up my back.

"How was your visit?"

I swung around to see Ruby standing there.

She just moved up a notch in suspicion if only for the fact that she managed to creep up on me like that. Either I was getting way too paranoid or she was a suspicious, sneaky teen.

"How did you know I was out on a visit?" I sat on the couch.

She flopped down next to me. "I know."

"You know *how*?"

She shook her head—kinda like Jagger. "Look, I find things out in here. That's all you need to know. What the hell else am I going to do to pass the time?"

What'd all that mean? Was she trying to tell me something? Like she had some inside information? I wanted to ask her if she knew what had happened to Vito, but didn't think it professional to ask a hospitalized drug addict for case information.

Then I thought of Jagger, who'd more than likely do *anything* for a case.

"Is Margaret around today?"

Ruby clucked her tongue at me. "Where the hell else would she go?"

"I . . . I don't know." Annoyed at her tongue clucking, I couldn't think too straight. Kids nowadays had no respect for adults. When I got out of here, I planned to have a nice, long talk with all my nieces and nephews over the age of reason. "What I meant was, did you see Vito bothering her anymore?"

Ruby jumped up.

She knows something, I thought, but then looked to see Sister Barbara heading down the hallway with her medication tray. Now I didn't know if Ruby was freaked because I'd mentioned the late Vito, or if she'd sprang up so fast to get her much-needed medication.

Damn.

I watched as Barbie doled out various colored pills. Most of the patients gobbled them down like tiny life rafts. How sad. Then I wondered how many stuck them under their tongues until I saw Novitiate Lalli making everyone open their mouths, stick out their tongues so she could aim her flashlight into their mouths as if she were on some big dig looking for a treasure.

I knew that was for their own good, so no one could stockpile medication and end it all by taking them in one death-inducing swallow. But it still bothered me that she looked as if she *enjoyed* her job way too much.

The novitiate moved further up my suspect list.

Her motive had to be money, and being a new nun seemed way too convenient. She might be planted here pretending to be a nun. I'd bet she was originally a nursing assistant. Now I was determined to find out.

But I had no clue how to go about it.

Sister Barbie turned toward me. Shit. I was *not* going to take any more of her pills. Without a thought, I mumbled about having to use the powder room and rushed off. If she wanted to medicate me, she'd have to find me. I ran down the hall to my room, ready to open my bathroom door—but it was already open.

Along with neat underwear, I have always kept the bathroom door closed. It was ingrained in me as a kid, and my brothers were probably the only males in Hope Valley that put the toilet seat back down.

Slowly I peeked around the corner. The stark white toilet sat undisturbed, seat down, and the tub empty. There weren't any shower curtains or rods in patients' bathrooms. Couldn't trust us. We all had to use the communal shower.

Yeah, this really was the Ritz.

I tiptoed in farther.

Bang!

"Shit!" I shouted, thinking I'd been shot. Then I looked down to see no red liquid oozing from any holes in me, nor was there any pain. I hurriedly spun around. The door to my room had slammed shut. That was the noise.

The question was, Who slammed it? And where had they been hiding?

And would I soon be following Vito to that big hospital in the sky?

Nine

After realizing someone had, again, been in my room, I actually did have to pee. Nerves. The door to the bathroom was fixed so that patients couldn't lock themselves in, so I shut it and kept my ears wide open. But what the heck would I do if I heard something? I had no idea.

I needed to learn to defend myself, and made a mental note to ask Goldie how.

That conclusion hit me as I finished up and washed my hands. Jagger had always been around and made me feel safe. It occurred to me that when I had asked Novitiate Lalli to call him, he was there in no time. I wondered if Jagger stayed somewhere in the Institution, but I knew he'd never tell me. I scanned the room with the thought that Jagger might be watching. Then I told myself he was not some pervert, and that I was acting as crazy as the staff might think I was.

I did not want anyone to think I was crazy.

My behavior, not mentally ill behavior, was all I had going for me to get me out of there. That, and finishing the job for Jagger. Thank goodness Fabio was away, or I'd have lost my job by now. Unless he worked with Jagger. I shook my head. No way.

Then again, Jagger's cases always did coincide with mine. One more mysterious Jagger tidbit.

As if I didn't have enough on my plate, now it seemed that someone was spying on me. I didn't need more bad news along with finding out who killed Vito, and why patients were being held here against their will. Damn.

Chills chased up my spine at the thought. I'd been followed before on another case—by a *murderer*. No great surprise, but it gave me pause.

What the heck had I done to get on someone's bad side at the Institute?

Then again, someone committing fraud for big bucks probably didn't have a good side. Still, I had to find out not only who it was, but why. Why target me?

I finished up and headed out to the dayroom. The place was bustling with activity, and Sister Barbie Doll was gone. Good. No pills for me. Across the room on the yellow vinyl chair with the crack in the back sat Margaret, staring into space.

I smiled at some of the other patients and staff, and nonchalantly, I hoped, worked my way over to her. Ruby wasn't around. Good, since I wasn't sure if she was friend or foe or just a very confused, drug-addicted teen. "Hi," I said and sat down next to Margaret.

She turned but didn't really smile. A blank look covered her face, and I worried that she'd been heavily drugged or had an electric shock treatment. Damn. A wave of nausea floated inside my stomach at the thought. If it hadn't been for Jagger, I . . .

I made a mental note to remind him to be around for my next "treatment."

I felt horrible for Margaret. She sat so still. I looked in the direction she was staring. Spike sat in a chair next to the nurses' station, reading a magazine.

Our jailor.

I leaned toward Margaret. "I know how you feel about him. He's a bit much. Isn't he?"

She didn't turn, but kept staring. "I . . . don't belong here."

My heartbeat fluttered. I leaned closer but tried not to let Spike think I was chatting with Margaret. In order to do so, I had to call on my nonexistent acting skills. I started to twirl my hair over and over and hum the song "When the Saints Go Marching In." I think Saint Theresa must have mentally nudged me that time and put that appropriate tune in my noggin. Amid choruses, I tried to communicate with Margaret. " 'When the saints go' . . . I don't think you belong here . . . 'marching in.' "

Margaret leaned forward slightly, a hint of a smile on her face.

Great. She got my poor attempt at acting. We won't get into my singing ability, but I will say that in second grade, Miss Burdacki, the music teacher, told me to mouth the words while the other kids sang.

"Let's turn sideways . . . 'go marching in' . . . so he can't see our lips." I finished humming instead of using words.

Margaret turned toward the television.

There was my buddy Jerry on the screen. His large men in black were pulling apart two females. All I heard among the bleep-outs were "sister," "baby's father," "whore" and "hamburger." I didn't know you could say "whore" on television and didn't even want to think about what the "hamburger" part was about.

I peeked over to see Spike. Still reading. He seemed

engrossed in it, so I turned to the television but said to Margaret, "I'm in this place against my will too. How did you get here?"

For several seconds she hesitated. I noticed her fingers folded on her lap with the two thumbs twirling around each other.

I twirled my hair in unison in case old Spike looked up.

"I have a drinking problem. Or . . . at least my husband said I did." She sucked in so much air, I thought my body would be pulled toward her. As she blew it out in a gust, she added, "I drank martinis at lunch with my garden club. But Stephen said I needed to get some help. More like a rest from the stresses of my life. Stephen's friend was a travel agent and said he'd heard about this place . . . and here I am."

I blinked. Didn't help to digest the words any better. "I thought you said you didn't come here on your own?" I was getting darn good at talking with my lips firm.

"I was told I was coming to a resort."

"To get rest and relaxation."

"Massages, facials and eat healthy," she whispered.

And here she'd ended up at this Ritz.

"So, what happened that you couldn't call Stephen and go home?"

Despite our jailor sitting a few feet away, Margaret turned to me. "I don't belong here," she reiterated, then went into statue mode.

"I . . . wait, Margaret!" I looked at Spike, who had set down his newspaper and stood.

Damn.

I'd have to reconnect with Margaret some other time. I really didn't want her to suffer from something because of what I did. Before I knew it, Sister Liz had bustled out of the nursing station toward us.

"How are you today, child?" she asked, looking at me.

"I . . . okay." Why'd I say that? I needed to see Jagger.

"Okay. Okay. Okay," I started to sing. Margaret looked at me. I think there was a hint of a grin on her lips, but Sister Liz merely frowned. For some reason, I think she liked me.

"Oh, dear," she muttered.

"Okay. Okay. I need to see my doctor. Okay?" This last part I sang so loudly, Spike was over in a flash, holding my arms behind my back as if I were ready to attack Sister Liz's rosary beads again.

I tried to pull free. Wasted effort. Before Sister could stop Spike, Dr. Plummer zoomed around the corner.

"Let her go!"

I wanted to wrap my arms around Jagger's neck and whisper a "thanks" in his ear. Okay, I wanted to wrap my arms around him for the hell of it, but did neither.

Spike looked at Jagger and then let me go. "She needs the wet packs," he mumbled and walked toward the nurses' station.

My eyes widened at that thought. Staff stripping me to my undies and wrapping me in wet sheets. That was one experience I did not want to have. The thought alone was claustrophobic. Calming. Yeah, right.

Darling Sister Liz said, "I think she's settled down now, Doctor. Do you want to speak to her?"

"I'll take her to the office," Jagger said, taking me by the arm.

Now that touch felt . . . good. Safe.

Once in the office, he sat on the chair and motioned for me to sit on the couch. Why the hell didn't we go into the exam room? I obeyed and flopped down.

"Margaret was talking to me."

"And?"

I hesitated, thinking I really didn't have much to report, but what I thought and what Jagger thought could be very different. So I shared with him what she'd said, finishing with, "Then Spike attacked."

I think Jagger winced.

"Find out more."

"It's not easy with old Spike watching."

Jagger brushed a strand of red hair from his forehead. I was getting real used to seeing him as Dr. Plummer. But, then again, Jagger as a janitor made me hot on a past case.

"We need to get a move on things here. If Margaret is being heavily medicated, we might not get much out of her." He stood. "Also, I wrote an order not to medicate you, but if that damned efficient nun insists, you have to protect yourself. I don't have to remind you that this is a private place and they can do what they want in some instances."

He was protecting me. My heart warmed. Then I realized Jagger would always look after the innocent. "Great, but she's got that novice nun, who, by the way, is first on my list of suspects—"

"Why?"

Yikes. I knew it would not be a good idea to tell him it was because I plain didn't like her, so I said, "She's . . . nosy."

He shook his head . . . once.

Phew.

Then he said, "She's a nun and a nurse in a mental hospital. I'd think being observant would be a good trait."

I curled my lips at him, knowing damn well it would be. "I don't think she's a real nurse, and anyway I've never seen her giving out the meds. She's always given the job of checking everyone's mouths with a flashlight when pills are given out."

"Open up."

I stared at him.

"I said open up."

After a few hesitant seconds, I opened my mouth and Jagger proceeded to show me how to hide a capsule under my tongue, flip it up and out when she looked under and then back again to spit it out later. Somewhere along the line there was a sneeze involved, an occasional cough or some other variety of distractions. Damn. He was ingenious and good at just about everything.

The process was tricky, so he'd taken out a Tic Tac from his pocket and we practiced for several minutes. I wondered what the nuns would say if they saw my "doctor" teaching me this trick. I kept harboring that question because Jagger was getting closer. Touching my cheek. Breathing his faintly coffee-scented breath at me . . . and making me feel as if I'd been drugged again.

The pheromones jumped from Jagger to me like some mystical, magical crickets. Similar to tiny Jiminy himself. Only these had the power to make a fairly intelligent woman lose her mind.

During the entire process, I swallowed seven Tic Tacs—whole.

Finally I pulled my coherent thoughts forward and said, "I've got it." I popped a Tic Tac into my mouth, shut it, and eased back so as not to be too noticeable when it was the real thing and the nuns were watching.

Damn it but he grinned.

And, as usual, my face burned, letting me know I was redder than the emergency call bell light. Oh well, I told myself, at least red goes with this stupid white hospital johnny coat.

"Talk to Margaret," he said as he stood. "And, by the way, Ruby Montgomery's doctor is Dr. De Jong."

I sat stunned. "Really?"

He looked at me, walked to the door. "Use her for your case," he said and opened it.

I forced myself up as if I were twice my weight, walked to the door and turned. All I could think to say was, "There's a difference between 'observant' and 'nosy.'"

I had my work cut out for me, I thought, as I walked into the dining room for lunch, took my tray and got my food. Rubbery chicken. Yuck.

The room held three long dining-room tables parallel to each other with uncomfortable straight chairs for us to sit on. Guess the Institute didn't want the patients taking their time eating while the staff had to stand around and watch. Food was served cafeteria style so we each had to get in line and grab a brown plastic tray at the end of the room near the door.

Although the wallpaper was a bright white with green flowers, this room was my least favorite one—not that I really liked *any* rooms in this place. But too many of the patients looked sicker—sadder—while trying to eat. This place didn't give the atmosphere of any restaurant I've ever been in.

Ruby was across the room, and Margaret sat near the window with the dark green drapes that matched the wallpaper. Who should I pick to interrogate first?

And what would I ask Ruby?

I wimped out and went with the "easier" job. "Hi, Margaret," I said, sitting down next to her. "Chicken doesn't look too good today."

"Never does," she said, spiking a cherry tomato with her fork and nibbling at it.

I chuckled, then leaned near. "Look, I know you don't belong here, but I need to know more."

She held the tomato out in front of her lips. I looked to see Novitiate Lalli standing watch. Smart Margaret. She hid her lips very nicely. "Need to know?"

"I . . . well . . . I'm here against my will too. I have friends on the outside that maybe could help."

Margaret turned and looked at me. Her hazel eyes watered. "I have a nine-year-old son."

I felt my forehead wrinkle, but didn't say, "So what?" Instead, I picked up a forkful of the rubber chicken and held it near my mouth. "You must miss him terribly."

She nodded. "I brought my tennis racket and golf clubs." With that, she shoved the tomato into her mouth.

I almost grabbed her hand and yanked the tomato back so she could explain that tidbit of info. What the hell? Had Margaret turned into a "real" patient? Maybe she was shy of a full deck. Damn.

"Golf clubs?"

"They said it was a resort when my husband signed me up," she told me again.

I wondered if her husband had something up his sleeve. Maybe he knew that she'd be kept here like this and wanted to get rid of Margaret for a while. Then my Christian side said not to judge him, and that he had innocently sent Margaret here for R & R.

I was going with that theory.

I set my forkful of chicken down and took my roll into my hand. Despite it feeling like a month-old sponge, I ripped tiny pieces off and ate them. Occasionally, I smiled, laughed, looked at Novitiate Lalli and nodded to throw off any suspicions. "Tell me more," I mumbled.

"When I got to the airport, I expected a limousine. Instead, a nun—a huge nun—"

"Vito?"

"Hmm? Oh, she never said her name, but she was odd-looking. Very hairy. Maybe Italian."

I nodded. "Okay, he . . . she . . . what happened next?"

Margaret took a sip of her milk, swallowed and continued, "The nun wasn't very nice. I wasn't used to being treated that way."

"Where are you from, Margaret?" Why that mattered, I had no idea.

"New Orleans. My husband is a lawyer. We live on Saint Charles Avenue."

Impressive. I'd seen tours of houses on Saint Charles Avenue on the travel channel. Margaret must come from money. Now it made sense. Garden club. Martinis. Saint Charles. And, of course, a lawyer and golf. That's why I had asked. Yes! My investigative instincts were sharpening.

Someone was pretty desperate (or dumb) to mess with a lawyer's wife. Hope he did criminal law.

Margaret's accent had first made me think she was from New York, but there was a softness, a Southern gentleness, which I now picked up on.

"Anyway," she said, biting into a chocolate-chip cookie (store-bought), "that nun took me to get my luggage. After we went outside the doors, I expected a limousine, but she shoved me into a white van. I didn't want to be rude or seem uppity, so I didn't say anything. Also, I knew I was coming to a Catholic-run resort, so it made sense that a nun would pick me up.

When we got here, she—the nun—and I think Spike took my luggage, purse, cell phone and airline ticket. Before I knew it, I was medicated and all my personal items were gone. Even my hand-embroidered linen handkerchief that my grandmother had given me."

I smiled at that. How dainty and Southern. "When did all of this happen?"

She stared into space. I knew it was hard to tell around here what day it was, but I could see her trying to think. She turned toward me. "I'd say a month."

I choked on my roll.

Novitiate Lalli came running over and Heimliched me. I think she bruised a few ribs—and enjoyed it. When I spit the piece of roll out into the air, it sailed across the table and landed on Jackie Dee's head. I turned away before I had to watch her snatch it up and eat it. Then again, it wasn't blonde.

"You all right?" Sister Liz called, running over. "My, my."

I coughed a few times and waved my hand in the air. "I'm fine . . . fine." I looked to see the staff starting to pick up the sharps. Margaret had retreated into her catatonic state of safety.

Since Novitiate Lalli had saved me, although I don't think I was knocking on the door of the pearly gates, I wondered if she was innocent of the fraud scam. She seemed really concerned. Then again, I had learned in this business that there are all kinds of people in this world and maybe she saved me so it wouldn't seem obvious in front of the entire room that she didn't like me.

I knew I had to see Jagger soon, but Novitiate Lalli's lecture from the last time I'd asked for him stuck in my head. I'd have to think of some other way to get in touch with him even though he'd left specific orders that I could call for him anytime. I just didn't want to listen to her again.

Damn.

Sister Liz and Novitiate Lalli left my side to help with counting the sharps. We had to remain seated until the all clear was given. I turned to Margaret and smiled despite my rib pain.

"They told my husband it'd be better not to contact me for four weeks when he thought I was coming to the special resort. Except for emergencies, of course. They said guests needed their R & R without the stress of home life. Four weeks." Tears ran down her cheek. "I didn't want to be here that long."

I didn't want to be there at all. I touched her hand.

"All clear," Novitiate Lalli yelled out. "Everything's accounted for."

The room exploded into patients shoving chairs and scurrying out, and my hand tightened on Margaret's arm.

I'd lost Margaret in the shuffle, but decided we needed to cool it so she wouldn't get into trouble. A few patients (surprisingly though, not Jackie Dee) grabbed at my arms, johnny coat and even my hair as I walked along the hall to the dayroom.

The day in the life of a patient in a mental hospital is very long and boring. I found this out right off the bat. I reread my magazines until the pages curled. I listened to every tape until Miss Myra told me not to sing along. If I had to watch TV any longer, especially Jerry S., I'd die.

Looking around the windowless room, I decided that dying was not a good analogy to make. Some of these folks could, in fact, be murderers here on an insanity plea.

On two of the red couches, several folks sat talking— but not to each other. From the cracked yellow chair, Ruby stared at the television as if interested. Lord only knows what was on her mind. And a few argued about nothing. Spike sat on his "throne," a tall brown stool near the doorway, and Novitiate Lalli glared at me through the glass wall of the nurses' station.

What the hell did she have against me?

And there was something about Spike that didn't set right with me. I moved him up above Novitiate Lalli on my mental list of suspects.

I decided I'd go to my room. Not that there was anything to do there. I couldn't even read a book, since I didn't have any, but at least it was a change of scenery. When I got up, Spike looked at me.

"What the hell are you up to?"

"I'm going to my room." I started to turn.

"What the hell for?" I'm pretty sure he growled.

"I . . . I want to lie down. I have a headache."

I heard him stand and stiffened. Before I could turn, I heard Sister Liz, darling Sister Liz, say, "Let her go."

Without turning, I hurried down the hallway and shoved open the door to my room and stepped inside.

Ouch! What the hell? A pain started at the base of my neck. Confused, I started to turn around while I automatically reached my hand up to my head to feel for blood. A second pain seared through my left ear.

Someone had smacked me!

I tried to turn, but my arm was grabbed, shoved behind my back and tightened while my head was forced forward so I couldn't see my attacker. All I could see was a flash of my bed then the floor of my room. "Ouch! Let go!"

Nothing.

Only more pain.

A kick to my right calf. A yank on my arm until I thought my shoulder was dislocated. And a bite on my neck.

A bite? Who bites when attacking except kids?

Only this was no kid.

This time I shook with all my strength and started to scream. Sure I was scared, but I was also determined to get free and fight back.

Outside in the hallway, footsteps clattered along. I actually wanted Spike to show up, so I yelled his name a few times.

My attacker eased up his hold. Before my room door could swing open, my arm was freed. The pain shot through my shoulder. I rubbed it and slowly turned, but not before vomiting on the floor. Damn it! Same thing had happened when I'd gotten my arm broken . . . by a killer.

I looked toward the door to see it swinging on its hinges, then Spike, Sister Barbie, Sister Liz and Sister Lalli ran in.

My attacker was gone.

Thank God. I was still alive.

A pungent taste filled my lips. I wiped them with my good arm, only to see red. I was bleeding. Nausea welled inside me like a shaken soda, but I swallowed it down, refusing to get sick again—especially in front of this gang.

I looked at them and weakly managed, "I need my doctor."

"That's a hell of a way to get in touch with me."

I didn't have to open my eyes to know Jagger was near. Suddenly the pain in my entire body subsided for a second, and then came back full force. "Shit. Ouch."

My eyelids fluttered. I forced them to open and hoped that seeing Jagger would take my mind off my attack.

He looked delicious, wonderful, hot—and pissed.

Pissed? Oh, great. Here I was assaulted in my room, nearly murdered, and he was going to be pissed at me. "I couldn't help it," I mumbled, realizing we were in my room and alone. I grabbed my pillow and hugged it to my chest. Small comfort. I really wanted Spanky.

"Help what, Sherlock?"

My eyes searched his. I'd never heard such a soft tone come from between his lips. And, having never been able to read Jagger's body language—this time I could see real concern in the depths of brown. Deep, chocolate brown. Reminded me of eating chocolate—warm, sweet chocolate.

"Hmm? Oh, I couldn't help getting attacked. No lecture please." I rubbed my ribs, then my cheek, which must have been the cause of the blood. "Ouch again."

Jagger remained still. He looked, well, insulted. "I'm not going to lecture you. Only get you out of here."

"This is my room."

"That's not what I mean."

I glared at him while still rubbing all my sore spots as if that would help. It didn't, but I ignored the pain and said, "What? What the hell are you talking about?"

"Look, Sherlock. The nuns think you did this to yourself."

"What? Are they crazy?"

"No, they think you are. Lots of patients self-mutilate—"

"Are you crazy too? Is everyone but me crazy?"

"I don't think you did this to yourself, Pauline. I know it has to do with the case. My case. I never meant . . ."

Jagger's lips kept moving, but my mind didn't comprehend that he was talking. Maybe because it had started out as an apology. A rarity with Jagger. Or maybe it was because somewhere deep inside, my gut instinct told me I didn't want to hear what he was going to say.

"Case is over for you. You're going home—for good."

I reached up, took his silver-and-black art deco tie into my grasp and eased him closer. "Over my dead body."

"That's what I'm trying to prevent."

I couldn't believe I was saying this, but somewhere,

obviously in my subconscious, I knew I had to stay. Margaret, and perhaps others, needed me. Needed *my* help.

And I needed Saint Theresa's help and a bodyguard.

"No arguing, Sherlock. I'll have them bring your clothes."

I yanked.

He gagged.

"I'm *not* going."

And when I released him—I saw pride in his eyes.

Pride! Pride for me!

At least I vowed to go to my grave thinking that.

And, hopefully, that wouldn't be too soon.

"Nice try, but you are done here," he said.

Ten

If I felt horrible physically, then mentally I was shattered after arguing with Jagger.

What was I thinking?

Sigh. I was thinking people needed me and if I was going to succeed at this career—and I damn well planned to—I had to stick out the tough ones. Besides, I needed to help Jagger—so he'd help me with my case. One hand washed the other and all that.

Jagger touched my arm. "You'll at least go out on a pass, so I can teach you some basic self-defense."

Let's see. Now I had another offer of help. Goldie had offered to teach me a while ago. Hmm. Jagger. Goldie. Jagger. Goldie. Although I loved Goldie as a dear friend, having Jagger help me with physical contact seemed like more . . . fun . . . er . . . in a business sort of way. "Fine. Then you'll let me come back?"

He looked at me.

Jagger didn't like being questioned. He'd said he was going to and that should be good enough for anyone.

"I'll have to make up a good reason why I'm letting you out on a pass again so soon." He ran his hand through his hair. "I suppose it's a good thing that I'm not part of the regular staff. Maybe I can get away with more, find a legit reason to convince the sisters that you need to get out of here."

Well, the nuns *were* women. "How about, say . . . my mother needs me. How's that?"

He looked at me. "For what?"

"Geez. You're the doctor. Why do you have to explain anything?"

"Because, Sherlock, I don't want anyone suspicious. If we don't fit in here, our case is screwed."

Our case? If he'd said we were screwed, I'm afraid I would have pictured us . . . never mind. I sucked in some stale air and blew it out. "Okay, make something up. I'll be ready to go." I touched my cheek and winced.

"A plastic surgeon needs to attend to that."

My eyes widened and my hand flew to my injury so fast, I yelled, "Ouch!" Then I hurried to the metal cabinet in the bathroom since we weren't allowed mirrors. "Where? What? Is it going to scar?" I leaned near. "Oh . . . my . . . God. I'm hideous!"

There was a bit of blood on my face, but in reality, it wasn't very bad, and I knew the cut was small. Still, when seeing yourself bleeding, one's perception sometimes got a bit skewed.

Jagger grabbed my arm. "Calm down or you'll be yanked off to solitary before I can say . . . that's the freaking excuse I'm going to use to get you out of here, Sherlock. I'm going to say I'm taking you to the emergency room for a plastic surgeon to stitch you up. You look . . . fine."

I looked fine.

That became my mantra since I, again putting my own spin on Jagger's words, decided it meant I looked damn good and close to "hot." Also, if I didn't keep repeating it, I would concentrate on Jagger's hand still holding my arm.

When I came back to reality, I said, "Oh. Gotcha. Good one. Good excuse." I chuckled. "Yeah, good excuse. No one should question—"

His finger touched my lips. Wow.

"Calm down or they'll never let you out of here." With that he was gone.

I remained motionless for a few seconds, collecting my confused thoughts and trying to return to my normal Pauline-Sokol-prior-to-meeting-Jagger reality.

I shut my eyes and then opened them.

There. I was back.

I sat in a special (locked) room off the main lobby crossing and uncrossing my legs far too many times, and then looking through the glass door at the receptionist and smiling. The last three times she seemed to ignore me. I couldn't help the leg thing though. Excitement did that to me. As much as I needed to stay and help, I was really glad to be getting out of here, even if only temporarily. I couldn't wait to see Goldie, Miles—hell, everyone. Okay, everyone except Fabio. Good thing he was still away.

A lay nurse, her nametag said Ms. Melissa Lawson, sat near the door, watching me. What the heck did she think I'd do? Well, I guess that was her job. Until I was safely out of here with my "mother," the nurse was responsible for me.

There was a knock at the door. The receptionist opened it and Nurse Lawson stood.

"Oh, my God! Suga! What happened to my baby girl?"

I looked up to see Goldie rushing toward me like a fullback in drag. Only this fullback looked very chic in a platinum wig and perfect makeup. He had on a periwinkle blue skirt suit with matching leggings that sparkled.

Goldie and his sparkles. They covered his face, too, shimmering in the gentle light.

He looked glamorous—except for the horrified look on his face.

He gently touched my cheek. "What the hell happened, Suga? Who did this to you?" I've never heard anyone's voice go from sympathetic to deadly in seconds.

Still, it touched me that he was so concerned.

I stood on my tiptoes, kissed him on the cheek, and said, "Get me the hell out of here. I'll tell you in the car." When I looked at the pain on his face, I was pissed at Jagger for not warning Goldie.

Nurse Lawson assured Goldie that I'd live and not be permanently disfigured while she walked us out, through the tunnel to the foyer, where Vito's body had been found. I shuddered when she said goodbye and reminded Goldie the time he needed to bring me back.

I had to smile to myself. The cut really wasn't anywhere near as bad as Goldie made it out to be. It was just not easy for him to see anyone he cared about be hurt in any way.

We walked to the parking lot, and once in the car, he turned to me. "Jagger had said you'd been . . . injured, but I wasn't ready for that."

I touched Goldie's arm before he started the car. "It's not even an inch long. Really not that bad."

He screeched. "Inch sminch. Any cut is too long."

I leaned over and kissed his cheek, the poor darling. "I need to learn how to defend myself, Gold. Jagger said he'd teach me."

"What for?" He cranked the engine and the Camaro purred out of the parking lot.

"What for? So I can prevent this from happening to me again."

Goldie stopped at the light before turning onto the ramp of Interstate 91. "It ain't going to happen again, since you ain't going back there."

I chuckled. "Don't you start that too."

"Suga, I ain't starting anything other than what Jagger said. Jagger said you ain't going back . . . ever."

I froze in the heated car. There was no sense in arguing with Goldie. The anger zooming throughout me was for Jagger.

How dare he!

Through clenched teeth I said, "Take me back. Take me back *now*."

Goldie looked at me and shook his head.

"Yes."

"Uh-uh. I'm no fool, Pauline. *Jagger* said."

I remained still with those words. Goldie had enough sense not to disobey an order from Jagger.

Me, I had other plans . . . only no idea how I'd implement them.

"Pauline," my mother said, leaning closely and squinting, "weren't you wearing those same scrubs on Sunday?"

She was observant. I'd give her that. That was also why I had Goldie do my makeup, much like a professional makeup artist, so that Mother wouldn't notice my injuries. It'd hurt, but the pain was worth not having to lie to her.

Lying to Mother never turned out well.

When we were kids she always seemed to find out, even if it was years later. Talk about "mother radar!" I supposed one day, eons from now, she'd ask me where I'd gotten that scratch on my face, but right now I wasn't volunteering anything.

Mentally exhausted, I collapsed onto the nearest

kitchen chair. I had the uncontrollable urge to eat kiel-basa. Mother's kielbasa and sauerkraut, which I *never* ate. As if that weren't scary enough, I'd insisted Goldie bring me there instead of to our condo. If I weren't so beat, I'd be in the bathroom inhaling pine. That mental stuff was getting to me.

And yet, I *was* going back.

Anger threatened to take over, but I put a stop to those feelings. I knew, just knew, if Mother noticed I was upset, she would interrogate me and find out way too much. I'd deal with Jagger and his "order" later.

"Mother, do you have any leftover kielbasa and kraut?"

She swung around and glared at me. "Tell me every-thing, Pauline. Everything that is going on in your life!"

What had I been thinking? Monday was meatloaf day and asking for Saturday's traditional kielbasa was a red flag big enough to send my mother into the truth-police mode. She was the captain of the squad too.

Even though Goldie hadn't been in my life for more than a few months, I looked to see horror and confusion and the question "what the hell were you thinking, Suga!" on his face.

In my exhaustion, I heard my mother calling my name again. Before I knew it, I was in Goldie's Camaro with him flooring it and mumbling about me.

I looked toward him. "Did we at least say goodbye?" There had been many times that I'd left my parents' house in the same kind of "hurry." But this time, I admit-ted, it was my fault for letting nostalgia make me tem-porarily insane.

"Yeah, you were polite as you scurried out, grabbing my arm. You need a manicure, Suga."

I looked down to see my half painted coral nails, which were way too long for me. As a nurse I'd learned to keep them short and couldn't stand when they grew a sixteenth of an inch or more. "You're right. Sorry about that. It's just . . . I didn't want to have to tell her about—"

We turned into the condo parking lot. "I know. I know. No sense worrying her. We're worried enough."

I knew he meant him and Miles. I leaned over, kissed his cheek, then turned and got out. When the fresh air hit me, I sucked in a deep breath and thought maybe I shouldn't go back. Maybe Jagger was right.

I could get hurt . . . killed. Maybe . . . maybe no one would ever help Margaret or others like her then. Even with Jagger on the case, it could take longer, and they'd all seen him. And he needed my nursing knowledge.

"I'll need a ride back tonight."

He turned toward me.

I touched his hand. "Cab. I'll take a cab." I had to remember to call for one early. In Hope Valley, the cabs drove into their cozy garages for the night at 7 P.M. sharp.

Goldie nodded rather solemnly.

"Don't worry. I'll be fine. As a matter of fact, I need to do some work on my case."

"Damn, Suga. I don't know how you do it. I'm so proud of you, ya know? You've gone from not knowing shit to working on two cases at a time. Proud as a mother peacock."

I smiled. "Hen. Mother hen."

He danced around with his arms waving.

I laughed. "Okay, with all your sparkles, peacock it is."

Goldie headed out, and I went to change. I was damn well not going to wear these scrubs to make a visit to Dr. De Jong. It felt good to slip into my jeans and a black-and-white sweater. I almost felt normal again until the pain in my face reminded me that I had to go back to the Cortona Institute of Life—sans Jagger.

Yikes.

I told myself that I could do it and he'd surely show up once he found out I'd gone back. With that comforting yet frightening thought in my noggin, I called the cab company and set up a pickup for five. I didn't want to take any chances of being late and facing the wrath of Spike.

I held Spanky extra long and then set him down. When he scampered off to his favorite spot on Miles's leather beanbag chair, I headed out. Thank goodness Goldie had gotten my Volvo back from the shop for me.

It felt good to be driving by myself, but I couldn't help looking in my rearview mirror over and over. Jagger was out there somewhere, and I didn't want him on the tail of my Volvo.

When I turned onto Oak Street, I slowed at the yellow light then stopped. A white van pulled up behind me. Rather close. I knew Jagger wouldn't be driving it, so I turned on my radio and ignored it.

"Let the sunshine. Let the sunshine in—" I sang along with an oldie-but-goodie station and decided I'd better keep my eyes on the road as I neared the doc's office.

The van turned in too.

I swallowed and told myself to ignore the fact that the van had followed me here from Oak Street, a grand total of three miles away. Big deal. No problem. Coincidence city.

I pulled into a space in the front of the house, then paused. My mind had been trained from day one in nursing school to think about the worst-case scenario. I had to notice if a patient's blood pressure bottomed out or there was a post-op bleed. Any complications and a nurse had to call the doctor. So, I had a lot of experience in looking for problems. Keeping the engine running, I glanced behind me.

The van had pulled over near the entrance, as if waiting for me to get out.

If I had to make a getaway, I would have to back out of the space. So I shoved the gearshift into reverse and backed out. Then I drove around the parking lot and into a pull-through space. I loved pull-through spaces. Those were the kinds of spaces that you didn't have to crane your neck around to see while you backed out. You just got in and drove off.

Which I might have to do soon.

I slowed. The van moved forward.

This was not looking good. My gut, which had served me so well in my nursing, told me this was not a coincidence.

I was being followed.

My first thought was that I carried a hammer in my glove compartment, since one of my biggest fears was to drive into a body of water and not be able to open my electric windows. That fear ran a close second to being arrested when I was innocent. I couldn't imagine that. And, some of the things I did in this new job had me thinking about that more and more.

The van was still behind me.

Now this was a worst-case scenario. Someone knew I was out of the hospital, unless it was some crackpot from a past case. That thought occurred to me as I drove out of the pull-through space and slowly around the lot. Then, I noticed Dr. De Jong come walking out of the front door and get into a red Jaguar. Damn! I could have gotten into her office and done some investigating.

Instead, I drove toward the exit of the lot—the van still

on my tail. Was it the same van that had picked up Margaret at the airport?

Where was Jagger when I needed him?

Wait, did I really need him? I'd gotten along so far by myself.

Maybe I wasn't really being followed.

Okay, Pauline, the world is chock full of coincidences.

But a van making every turn that you make isn't one of them.

Eleven

Before I could head out of the lot, Dr. De Jong pulled in front of me. I jammed on my brakes, amid the screech of her tires and smell of burnt rubber.

Wow. The doc must be in a real hurry. Hmm.

The van nearly plowed into my rear end. I didn't want the doc to recognize "Alice" so I quickly made a move and pulled in front of the doc. From the left, a tractor trailer barreled down on me.

I lifted my foot from the gas and held the brake. For a fleeting moment, I wondered what it would be like to charge out in front of the truck. Yikes. I must have been in the Institute too long. Way too long.

Clearing my weird thoughts, I slowly looked in my rearview mirror at the Jag. The doctor leaned forward, glaring.

I noticed the van behind her. I couldn't see the driver. Damn. Adjusting my rearview mirror, I tried to make out if it was a man or woman, but could only see a black hat, the wool kind that I myself have worn on stakeouts. Big help that was.

Honk!

Yikes again. I looked up to see the doc pointing to the

street and turned around. No traffic. Tempted to stay put so the van couldn't get me, I decided that was not a smart move so I looked both ways and started to turn left, then did a quick right out of the lot and headed down toward Maple Avenue.

Dr. De Jong could give Mario Andretti a run for his money, I thought as she peeled out in the other direction. Good. At least I wouldn't have to deal with her. I adjusted my rearview mirror and noticed no one was behind me.

I slowed, looked again.

Ha! I'd lost him. *Good job*, Pauline.

I'd looked forward to see the white van pulling out of Oak Street, right in front of me. Obviously he had been following me and had taken a side street to catch up. "No!" I shoved my foot so hard onto the brake pedal, a pain seared up my leg.

The van skimmed my right bumper. I couldn't afford to have my insurance rates go up, so I swerved to the left. Like a rabid dog, it followed.

We weaved in and out of traffic until I decided to head toward the police station on Main Street. I'd heard that was what you did when being followed. Relentlessly though, the van kept tapping my bumper.

I cursed and prayed. Prayed and cursed. Then just prayed.

Two more blocks to go and hopefully no one would be hurt or killed while this maniac kept attacking me. I neared the turn. The van's engine grew louder. He was probably going for broke and was about to smash me good.

Then a black Suburban zoomed out of Vine Street— and wedged itself between the van and an SUV just enough so that the van couldn't make the turn.

Jagger!

Had to be.

But it was my chance to get away, so I finished turning,

looked back to see I was alone and made a quick left onto Main toward my condo since I no longer needed to head to the police station.

I realized I was driving with legs of Jell-O and shaking hands.

Maybe I wasn't cut out for this job after all.

I couldn't help looking at the bathroom door over and over, as if I expected the white van to drive in while I soaked in the tub, lathered in Miles's honeysuckle bubbles. Sure, it was ridiculous, but I'd never been followed like that before. People, but not vehicles, had followed me. In the hot water I shivered. I could have been killed!

Jagger must be furious, but probably not as angry as he would be when he found out later that I'd gone back to the Institute. I looked at the clock on the counter, two cupids leaping in the air—one with a clock in its tummy, the other with a barometer—and realized I'd have to hurry.

Fifteen minutes.

I would have to rush to catch my cab. I looked over my bubbly shoulder one more time and asked myself what the hell I thought I was doing going back there.

Margaret popped into my thoughts.

I snuck out of the house so that Goldie and Miles wouldn't be involved in my "Jagger deception." When I turned toward the front of the parking lot, I froze.

"Seems as if you'd be recovering from your drive today, Sherlock."

I gulped exaggeratedly. Damn him. "I'm . . . I'm going to my parents' for dinner."

"Hmm. Monday. Meatloaf." He licked his lips.

I swooned.

"I could eat—"

I looked past Jagger as he again started to invite himself to my parents' for supper. This was becoming a bad habit. Not that there wouldn't be enough food. No problem there. All of Hope Valley could come eat. But if I did go there with Jagger to cover my lie, I'd be late for my check-in at the Institute. Over his right shoulder I noticed the cab pull into the lot.

Damn it.

How to fool Jagger?

"I . . . shit." I pushed at his chest, and relying on the element of surprise, succeeded in knocking him into the bushes.

"Aye!"

Without the spring leaves in full bloom, the sharp sticks had to hurt. I only hoped he hadn't cut himself, I thought, as I ran, flailing my arms, toward the cab.

I jumped in and yelled, "Get out of here! He has a gun!"

If I thought Dr. De Jong was a speedster, this cabby could make it from one end of Hope Valley to the other in a nanosecond. We were well onto Main Street when he looked over his shoulder, "Where to, babe?"

I gave him the address of the Cortona Institute of Life. He stared. "Don't look like no nutcase to me, babe."

I curled my lips. "Looks are deceiving." Then I gave him one that hopefully said to mind his own business and muttered, "Hm. Maybe *I'm* the one with the gun. Ha. Ha. Ha." The ride continued in silence. As he turned into the gate of the hospital, I thanked Saint Theresa for having the cabbie leave me alone to my thoughts and prayers—because those I really needed yet again.

I never saw a cabbie drive off so fast. I had barely

slammed the door shut. He didn't even claim his fare. I silently laughed to myself and then quickly stopped on the sidewalk to the main entrance.

Coming down the long, stone stairs that were bordered by white cement walls was my buddy, Spike, wearing a solemn—no, make that a mean—look. "Who the hell left you out here?"

Oops. "My mother had to run off. She was in a—"

He spit over the handrail. "Who cares? Get inside before you're late."

I could have argued that I got there in plenty of time, but thought I'd keep my body intact for as long as I could. Besides, Jagger wasn't around to protect me.

As I stepped up the cement front steps with Spike at my heels, that thought scared the stuffing out of me. The one about Jagger not being there, that is. Spike at my heels was another matter, but I refused to waste any emotion on it.

It wasn't long before I was back in my room, dressed in my damn fashionless johnny coat and sitting on the edge of my bed with Sister Liz babbling on about my cut and how did it feel.

Thank goodness I'd kept a bandage on it or else she would notice there really weren't any stitches. I watched Sister Liz for a few seconds as she tidied up my bed. It hadn't been slept in—by me, that is—but she still found a few wrinkles to yank at.

Gave me a warm motherly feeling just watching her.

At least I knew she wasn't a suspect. No way could she, particularly as a nun, be involved in anything shady . . . especially murder.

I shivered.

It warmed my insides thinking that Sister Liz had become a friend, in a way. There was that patient/nurse relationship, but I figured if we were on the "outside" she'd be my friend.

"You cold, Pauline?" She went to reach for the blanket that she'd just refolded and laid at the foot of the bed.

How sweet.

"I'm fine." I wanted to ask if anything happened while I was gone—like any more murders, but that would send up a gigantic red flag, even to Sister Liz. "You know, I kinda missed this place." I chuckled.

She gave me an odd look and a weak chuckle. "I would think you'd be happy to spend time with your family. Unless—" She looked at me a few minutes. "Oh, my, Pauline. Do you have problems with your family?"

I knew she was talking abuse or abandonment, but I thought of the same meal each day of the week, the house that the Cleavers built, and my mother's frequent offers to have me move back into that house. "Yeah, I have some problems with them. But . . . I'll make sure and tell my doc about them."

Then, it dawned on me.

I was utterly alone. I didn't have my "doc" around to save me from . . . whatever. I swallowed.

I could do this, I told myself. I was a professional and a strong, intelligent woman. I really could do it. After my little pep talk, I felt much better.

Sister gave me a pious smile and headed out the door.

I told myself to relax and work one step at a time. I would come up with some excuse so that whichever doctor treated me, he wouldn't medicate me into oblivion, fry my normal brain, or have me wrapped like a birthday present, only in wet sheets instead of fancy colored paper.

Without allowing myself to shiver again at any number of those thoughts, I went into the bathroom to wash off my face and perk up. When I shoved the door open, a clattering filled the room. I looked down in what had to be an expression of horror.

Spread across the black-and-white tile floor was . . . a broom handle.

A brown metal broom handle.

Like the one we'd seen harpooned into Vito's body.

Twelve

I knew screaming in a mental hospital was frowned upon. Yet, when I saw the brown metal broom handle in my bathroom, I couldn't keep the noise from blaring out. Thinking quickly, I shoved my hand over my mouth.

I reminded myself that I was a professional. So I shut my lips beneath my grip. Then I took ten slow, deep breaths. I looked out the bathroom door to see if anyone was coming into my room. The hallway was empty. Good. They must have figured my half-scream had been on television.

The damn broom handle glared at me.

Attached was a yellow Post-it note. *Wanna bee next?*

I didn't think they meant the flying insect. I also don't think the note writer meant anything good was about to happen.

I stared at the broom handle a few seconds, then stood silently. There. I could remove my hand now. As I did, I heard a shuffling of footsteps in the hallway. Quickly I shoved the metal culprit toward the wall and dropped two towels on it. The note stuck to my shoe. Great. I wiggled and danced a bit until I could reach my foot and grab it.

Then I shoved it into my pocket and hurried out of the bathroom.

"Everything all right in here?" Sister Barbie asked from behind me. I turned to see she held a tray of medication and was doing that squinting thing like my mother.

I wondered if that really helped someone see better like holding a book miles away from your face does once you hit forty.

Now, in my flustered state, I'd have to remember Jagger's instructions on how not to swallow a pill. "Yes . . . Sister. Everything is fine. I was about to go to sleep. Tired after my pass. You know, my cut and all." I prayed she wouldn't ask to see it.

Thankfully her hands held a tray filled with psychedelic colored pills. Seemed like hundreds of them. As usual, she was in a hurry to shove them at patients. When she gave me the little green one, Novitiate Lalli appeared at the door, flashlight in hand.

Damn.

With my mouth shut, I wiggled my tongue to get it exercised enough to do the trick. Sister started to turn.

"Take it *now*, Pauline."

Novitiate Lalli moved closer like some private dick investigating a case and not some novitiate nurse about ready to scrutinize my mouth. The woman gave me the willies. I mentally moved her up higher on my list of suspects. Tied with Spike now.

Hmm. A *new* nun. How convenient. Maybe she had pretended she really wanted to be a nun just to get this job to . . . commit fraud. My gut and my experience said she was a nursing student, but the nun part was still in doubt.

"Take the pill," Lalli reiterated. "We have plenty of patients to medicate."

I'll just bet you do. I opened my mouth, said a silent prayer and popped the pill in. Then I did the Jagger trick while swallowing.

"Stick out your tongue," she ordered.

The moment of truth. Suddenly fear gripped my insides when I realized there'd be consequences if I got caught. What they'd be, I had no idea. I only assumed I wouldn't like them, and, they could blow my cover. I looked to see Novitiate Lalli glaring at me, lit flashlight aimed high.

I wiggled my tongue, did as Jagger had said and opened.

As if digging for gold, she leaned so near I could smell the scent of cologne. Hmm. Nuns wear cologne? It was some kind of musk oil, light but sweet.

"Lift up your tongue."

Yikes.

After a sneeze, I did as I was told, praying at record speed that the pill was safely out of sight.

"Clean," she pronounced, shut off her light and turned toward the door.

Unfortunately, Sister Barbie Doll hesitated.

Soon the pill would start to melt. Melt mind-altering drugs right into my system, and I'd be a basket case. So, again with the nonexistent acting skills, I smiled at her and yawned. "My head is starting to hurt from my cut."

She looked at me a few seconds. "Then, my child, you should get some rest." Following Novitiate Lalli, she turned and went out the door.

Poof!

I spit the damn pill out across the room before it could leak anymore into my system. Quickly I grabbed it, hurried into the bathroom and flushed the pill into oblivion.

Had to keep a clear head around here now that I was alone.

Oh, my God! I was *alone*.

After what not only seemed like hours but must have been, I tossed and turned for the last time. In between tosses I had dozed but kept waking up. Deciding to get up and get a drink of water, I shoved off the covers and sat on the edge of the bed. An eerie silence filled my room.

Nighttime in a mental hospital is what scary movies are made of. I sat for a few minutes then shoved on my slippers and grabbed my robe. I started to head to my private bathroom and then realized—the broom handle was still in there.

Great.

A feeling of doom grabbed me inside, as if the metal object were some snake or other venomous reptile. I told myself to get over it. It was an inanimate object. Sure, one that was put there to scare the stuffing out of me. I decided to toughen up or I'd never be able to do a good job.

I stood, let my blood pressure stabilize and walked into the bathroom.

Empty.

No towels.

No broom handle.

Hmm. I didn't recall there being a maid service in this place. So who took it all?

I grabbed at the sink as if the absence of the damn thing was more horrifying than the presence of it earlier. The idea that someone had snuck in and took it while I dozed was a frightening thought. I took a deep breath and decided I'd go out into the ward.

I turned, walked to the door, opened it and looked

down the hallway. Empty and quiet. In the distance, faint snoring filled the air. Had to be from the patients who actually swallowed their meds. While I made my way toward the nurses' station to inform them I'd be sitting out in the dayroom for a while, I thought of Margaret. I really needed to be there to help her, and Jagger would soon realize that I was gone.

He'd come. I knew he would. Jagger was always there in a pinch—and sometimes I wanted to pinch his . . . never mind those kinds of thoughts. Preservation and growing old had to be my first priority.

A lay nurse sat at the desk. I hadn't been out here during the night before but figured with the shortage of nuns, there had to be plenty of laypeople working in this place. She looked pleasant enough in her floral scrubs while she bent over a computer keyboard.

I cleared my throat when I stood near the window of the glass-enclosed (shatterproof, I assumed) nurses' station. "Excuse me, ma'am."

She looked up and smiled. "Nurse Lindeman. Sharon Lindeman. Can I help you, Mary Louise?"

Not that again. Okay, I'd cut her some slack since she wasn't around during the days and probably had only seen my chart and me asleep most nights. "Yes and no. First, please call me Pauline. My doctor said to. Second, I can't sleep—"

She got up. "I'll check your orders for a sleeping pill."

"No!" I smiled. "No, thank you, Nurse Lindeman. I only want permission to sit in the dayroom for a bit. Then I'm sure I'll go back to my room and fall asleep like a baby." I'd been at my sister's during naptime and always wondered why the comparisons were made to sleeping like a baby. None of my nieces or nephews ever *wanted* to go to sleep. They cried until wiped out. Maybe there was too much on my mind to sleep tonight, but that couldn't possibly be the problem babies had. I figured crying around here would only get me heavily medicated or wrapped in the wet sheets like a tamale.

She stared at me a few seconds. "Fine. Just don't put on the television."

I chuckled. "What the heck would be on right now anyway?"

"Movies," a deep voice said from behind.

At first I thought it was Jagger in disguise, but I turned to see a damn fine-looking guy about my age, standing there in a white lab coat. Hmm. Maybe he'd replaced Dr. Dick.

"Movies? Well, that would be nice," I said smiling, "but I don't want to wake anyone. I'll just sit and meditate."

"I'll join you." He stepped closer. "Terry. Terry Myers. Dr. Terry Myers."

I looked to see Nurse Lindeman's reaction, but she had turned back to her computer. That was good enough for me. She didn't see any problem with me talking to this doctor. Maybe, without breaking any confidences, I could get some information that might help the case.

He followed me to the dayroom, sat opposite my chair and proceeded to tell me about his education, from Yale Medical School to his stint here. After I'd told him that I had gone to Yale for my master's degree, we reminisced about our alma mater.

"Small world," he said, staring at my legs. "Same school."

I had to believe that my Maciejko legs—inherited from my mother, grandmother and well, all the rest of the female clan—were of interest to him. I shifted and recrossed.

He continued to look down and told me how attractive I was.

Hey, wait a minute. Wouldn't that be considered unprofessional—even if true? "Yes, I guess it is a small world." I tried to gain some eye contact, but he kept staring at my legs—and it started to get creepy.

I had to keep my eye on this doctor and hope he wasn't assigned to my case.

Then he stood, still looking at my legs. My investigator instinct told me this was no ordinary doctor. Sure, some psychiatrists seemed whacky themselves and could use a dose of their own medicine. Yet, something bothered me here.

"Dr. Terry" leaned forward to whisper, "I've seen you around here a lot. Lovely blonde hair."

I pulled back and looked over his shoulder for Nurse Lindeman. With her back toward us, she looked as if she were typing at her computer.

Ruby suddenly appeared and grinned. "Hey, Terry. How's it hanging?"

"Don't ask me things like that, Ruby." He looked at her, and then back at me. "Gray eyes. Interesting. You must be of European descent."

I sucked in a breath and sat straighter, ready to bolt. "Polish." Good, I thought, if Ruby stays, I'll feel better.

I could see her watching us, but then she turned and walked away. Wonderful.

His staring moved from my legs to my face. "I know."

Gulp.

I got up.

"Well—" I yawned. "I think I could sleep now. Nice meeting you—"

"It wasn't our first time. And I love you, Pauline."

Whoa, boy. I pulled back. "Good night, Terry."

He went to reach out to me—I assumed for a hug—but when he reached out, his clothing shifted.

I gasped.

Beneath his lab coat was . . . *nothing*.

Thirteen

Well, it wasn't exactly nothing beneath Terry's lab coat. It was without a doubt—*something*. Something any man would be proud of.

Great.

Just what I needed.

A naked patient, pretending to be a doctor, shrouded in a lab coat and in love with me. Why the hell hadn't Nurse Lindeman said something? Did all the staff here get so jaded that they thought nothing of the patients masquerading as staff?

Okay. To cut them some slack I realized some patients' idiosyncrasies had to be tolerated to treat them. Now what?

Jagger! I really needed his help. I had to get in touch with him. I had to be able to make a phone call. Not only was Terry a nutcase, but also he was a bit suspicious. He knew my name! I didn't remember telling him my name. Actually, he had introduced himself and then we'd gone off on a tangent about our schooling. I was certain now that I hadn't introduced myself.

He also said he'd noticed me before. I didn't think he'd heard Nurse Lindeman and I talking to get my name.

Damn. Guess this was another one of the pitfalls of working in a mental hospital. I really had to get back to work and wrap up this case or I might *want* to stay here longer after my mind snapped.

Hm. Seemed "Dr." Terry's room might be worth checking out—when he wasn't there. I edged toward the nurses' station. Terry moved forward. "Okay, Ter, time for you to hit the sack. I'm sure I'll see you in the morning."

He grinned, rather an evil sight. "Why not join me?"

"That does it. Nurse! Nurse Lindeman?" I pushed past Terry and ran toward the desk. Two other staff members came from behind the desk. "He's bothering me," I said.

One staff member was a young male who looked like an assistant and the other Nurse Lawson.

She spoke first. "Terry, leave the other patients alone. Get back to your room now, or no television tomorrow."

I leaned forward. "You might want to remind him to dress properly or he'll catch a cold." Sure I knew you had to come in contact with someone who had the virus to catch a cold, but it was my subtle way of saying Terry needed some boxers.

She clucked her tongue. "And put on your pajamas."

Terry turned and skulked down the hallway as the male assistant followed a few feet behind.

I looked at Nurse Lawson. She'd taken me out to meet my "mother" the other day at the last minute when Sister Liz was called to an emergency.

Nurse Lawson had several body piercings with lovely diamonds, about six of them, in her right earlobe. They went well with her blonde, spiked hairdo. All in all she looked friendly. I liked her from the first time we met.

Momentarily forgetting I was supposed to be a patient

here, I held out my hand to the nurse. "Thanks. Please call me Pauline Sokol. I was a nurse too."

She gave me a "yeah, right" look, and I figured she'd worked psych for sometime and was rather attuned to patient behavior. But she smiled pretty nicely and said, "I'm Nurse Lawson. Melissa Lawson. We met the other day, but I didn't get to tell you my name." She had the courtesy to shake my hand. "You'd better head off to bed now, Pauline. It's after two."

Two A.M.!

I didn't even stay awake on New Year's Eve until two.

I started to turn, and then remembered I needed to talk to my partner. "Could I make one phone call, Nurse Lawson? Please."

She hesitated as if she was going to let me. "Since we are a private institution, some patients—very few, that is, and under the staff's supervision—do get to make calls. But it's very late."

Right. Hmm. Think fast, Pauline. "I know. My brother works the night shift over at—" I had started to say Hartford Hospital but then remembered Mary Louise wasn't from around here. Since I was to pick her up at the airport, she'd flown in, so she must come from another state. I cleared my throat and finished with, "—his job. I feel so lonely and we are very close. My doctor at home encourages me to talk to my brother whenever I need to." I took a step closer to engage her confidence yet not invade her personal space. "Please, Nurse Lawson. Please." After a few silent prayers, my best begging face, and several more lies, I stood and stared at her.

She let out a breath. "Follow me."

I thanked Saint Theresa that this was a private institution and the employees obviously had some leeway.

Nurse Lawson led me to the doctor's office and pressed one of the many buttons on the phone. "I have to stay with you."

I nodded and for a second couldn't remember one digit of Jagger's cell phone number. Then I told myself to be professional and the numbers flooded back. I smiled at Melissa Lawson while the phone rang three times.

"Yeah?" His voice now sleepy and sexier than usual had me hesitate.

"I need you. I *really* need you. To see you."

Silence.

"I said, I need to—"

"Damn it, Pauline. You went back."

Footsteps clattered along the hallway outside the office, and Nurse Lawson's eyes grew big. "I . . . you have to get off the phone. Now." She reached for the receiver, took it and shoved it down.

Startled, I knew she was worried we'd get caught, but I couldn't blame her. I wouldn't risk my job for a patient like me either. I smiled at her. "Thanks."

Jagger would come.

He would come.

On the way out, we ran into Nurse Lindeman in the hallway. She looked at us oddly and said, "Pauline, you have to go to your room now. Get some sleep or just rest."

I feared she might try to medicate me, and my tongue was too tired for any acrobatics so I nodded and turned toward the wing where my room was. Once there, I looked into the bathroom, behind the furniture and in every corner for someone hiding there—or for Terry.

Finding it safe, I flopped onto the bed and snuggled under the covers. Terry. Suddenly Terry became a real concern. A real possibility. A real threat.

Could it have been Terry in my room that night I was

sent off to Rain Tree Forest La-La Land? That would mean no one was after me—at least in this place. But wait. The white van. My tired brain became too confused, so I shut my eyes and heard Jagger's voice in my ear.

He'd called me Pauline. His serious name for me.

Yikes.

The next morning came way too soon. While I yanked my blanket higher, I heard Spike's voice. "Up and at 'em, Pauline. You miss breakfast and you don't eat until lunch. This ain't a hotel."

I peeked at him through one lifted eyelid. He looked enormous. I had to force myself to get up, which I did, all the while mumbling that I was sorry—even though I had no idea what for—so he wouldn't manhandle me.

Thank goodness he left while I washed up and brushed my teeth. Gigantic circles, dark as eclipses, had formed under my eyes. I needed some miracle facial cream but in this place would more than likely have to settle for Vaseline. I hurried out of my room and toward the dining room, hopeful that Terry had slept in today.

Why the heck didn't they keep the men and women separate in this place?

Guessing it would be too expensive to build two of everything, I found an empty seat next to Ruby and took my napkin off the table.

She stared at me. "You look like shit."

"Thanks." I managed a chuckle. "Couldn't sleep."

Ignoring my explanation, she took a sip of her black coffee and looked at me over the mug.

"Oh, hey, Ruby. I'm thinking of changing doctors. How's yours?"

"Fine."

Typical teenage response. "Who is she?"

"How'd you know it was a she?"

Oops. "I heard the nurses talking. You like her?"

"I've had better. But she's square."

I'm guessing she didn't mean Dr. De Jong was a geek. "Square" seemed to be a term kids used nowadays to mean something was okay. "Good. Been seeing her long?"

"Too long." She proceeded to tell me about her doctor. All sounded legit. Interesting.

"So you heard?" she asked, obviously changing the subject.

I looked up to see the breakfast line getting shorter. "Heard what?"

She sipped again. Actually she sipped several times as if taking her time. It began to seem as if Ruby was stalling until she said, "Margaret. Margaret is missing."

"What!"

Before I knew it, Spike was at my back, grabbing my shoulder. "What's going on here, Sokol? You want to start a riot or something. Maybe you don't want to eat today. All day."

"Take your hands off of her."

I spun my head around as much as possible, since Spike still had my collar in a death grip, only to see Dr. Dick standing there. I shoved free of Spike, jumped up and very unprofessionally, yet with every ounce of fear that Ruby had instilled in me, grabbed Jagger and hugged him.

Over my shoulder he said, "I need to talk to Ms. Sokol now. Fix her a tray, Spike, and bring it to the office."

On the way, and only after I'd pried my arms off of Jagger, I realized that Spike would probably spit in my food.

The pitfalls of investigation—there were many.

* * *

I poked at my food, looking for Spike's saliva, and decided to only eat the items that I felt certain he hadn't left his mark on. I munched on an individually wrapped bran muffin while Jagger sat on the edge of the desk, looking gorgeous, sexy and furious.

I waved my hand at him. "No need for a lecture. I had to come back, and you know it."

"What I know is that—"

"Let's just drop the whys and concentrate on the fact that Margaret is missing." That felt so good! I had actually taken control. I sat up straighter.

I thought I noticed a hint of surprise on his face and wondered if I had indeed found out some info that Jagger actually didn't know yet. *He probably won't admit it*, I thought as I opened my milk carton. Had to be safe and saliva free, since it was still factory sealed.

"How do you know about Margaret?" he asked, sitting up straighter himself.

Hmm. There could be some kind of power struggle happening. Imagine, me in a power struggle with Jagger. The winner would be him. Done deal, if that was the case.

But he, obviously being a stand-up kinda guy, said, "I didn't know she was missing. How did you?"

My shoulders sank. Maybe it wasn't true! Maybe I had heard wrong! Or maybe Ruby had made it up or was lying!

No, I had heard correctly and didn't see Margaret in the dining room before I'd been "handled" by Spike. Margaret was always there early since she hated cold food. Had to be part of her Southern upbringing.

"You didn't know . . . she is missing. She *is*," I reiterated. "We have to find out what happened to her. She's a nice person and doesn't deserve this." I sipped my milk but didn't even taste it. "She has a little boy." As if that would be the only reason we needed to find her.

Jagger nodded. "Finish up."

I bit the last bite of my muffin. "Then?" I managed as I tucked the piece into the side of my cheek very squirrel-like so as not to have it come flying out like the pill had yesterday.

"Then, Sherlock, we look for her."

Walking all the way down the hallway to the dayroom with Jagger, I couldn't help but think, he'd called me Sherlock.

All was right with the world now.

Except for a dead Vito, a missing Margaret, a stalking Terry, who knew how many patients held here fraudulently, my disarrayed undies in my drawer and, oh yeah, the white van, things were fine.

Maybe my world was still a bit askew.

Sister Liz strolled down the hallway toward us. "Good morning, Dr. Plummer. Pauline." She nodded toward me and smiled at him.

Typical female reaction. Unavoidable around him.

Maybe Sister Liz wasn't really a nun either!

Naw. She was too pious not to be one.

Jagger said, "I'm taking Pauline into the dayroom. She's had a bad night and we need to talk quite a bit. Don't want to tie up the exam room for too long. She's going to need a lot of therapy today."

Sister wrung her hands. "Oh, dear."

"What is it, Sister?" he asked.

"Pauline is scheduled for the ECT again. You know how—"

He nodded. "Yes. No need to explain. Let's get that done with and then she and I can talk."

Unless that head-exploding thing happens, I thought.

*　*　*

Jagger and I performed like Oscar winners. Even the technician, this time a timid, little male didn't question the machine or any of us. He merely marked the chart as treatment done after I had arched my back like an upside down cat and, of course, Jagger had managed to stand in the way so no one could see the equipment lights weren't on.

After Sister Liz came to take me back, Jagger once again had explained that we had to talk. She followed us to the dayroom where she left us alone and he assured me he'd write an order for no more ECT.

"Okay, Ruby said Margaret is missing?"

"Yep. I don't know how she knows but I didn't see Margaret in the dining hall and she's always there early. I picked a tiny glob of gel from my scalp where the timid technician had stuck a lead. I never could get used to nearly having my brain fried, even for a job.

"Okay. Let's take a look for ourselves."

I stared at him. "How do you propose we do that?"

I soon found out as I removed my johnny coat and told myself that I should have known Jagger would have had something up his sleeve.

In a few minutes, Jagger walked out from behind the changing screen looking very much like a stranger. He was dressed as a janitor, just like he'd been in the past, but this time younger and better-looking.

Me, I had stuck the brown cap on that he'd given me from his bag of disguise tricks and tucked my hair up as much as possible. I wasn't trying to look male, only trying to look like a janitor too. Hoorah for feminism, where we could both do the same job.

I knew my mother would say to tuck that hair up so it doesn't get in your face and you'll do a better job cleaning. Cleaning was not my major concern, however.

We slowly walked out of the room after he'd hidden his

clothing and my hospital pjs, and then we headed toward the wing where Margaret's room was. On the way Jagger stopped near a closet door, took out a key hanging from a chain on his belt and soon had us fitted for work, complete with dust rags, mop and bucket.

He had to have worked this place before.

Jagger looked at me and gestured to come with him. I followed him down the hallway as we peeked into each room, pretending to dust, mop and wipe.

When we got to the east wing, he opened a door and through the tiny crack I noticed Terry sitting there on the bed . . . naked. Geez. This guy was a pip.

Thank goodness Jagger had gone in first and said, "Lady in the hallway. Cover up, buddy."

Terry groaned as if he couldn't understand why he was not allowed to "dress" as if this were the Cortona Institute of Nudists of America. He did, however, cover up the important part with his pillow.

Not wanting to blow my cover, I shielded my face with my hat and mop handle. My hands shook a little at the cold metal reminder even though it wasn't a broom. I dusted the far side of the room while Jagger did around the bed, making small talk with Terry and very nonchalantly asking if he'd seen Margaret today.

Terry denied seeing her.

I swept faster until a pile of dust and dirt was outside the doorway. Jagger was right behind, bending down with a dustpan for me to sweep the stuff into. I was marveling that he did menial work like this for a case, and then my breath caught mid-throat.

Kneeling there below me, Jagger had fished something out of the dustpan pile and held it up toward me.

A piece of straw—from a *broom*.

Fourteen

I had to tell Jagger about my "incident" with Terry, knowing full well that Jagger would probably not only insist I get out of here, but maybe even physically drag me out.

For as much as being thrown over his shoulder sounded romantic and sexy, I really wanted to stay.

Too much was at stake for me to quit now.

I looked down at the straw Jagger held. He took a plastic bag from his pocket and put the "evidence" in it. Behind Jagger's shoulder, I noticed Terry staring. Oh, great. Now I really wasn't going to be safe around here.

We finished up and walked down the hallway.

At the end, Jagger opened another janitor's closet and we stepped in. Amongst the mops, brooms and buckets, we stood shoulder to shoulder, and I told him about Terry.

Silent for several seconds, Jagger finally looked at me and said, "You're out of here, Sherlock."

"Look, Jagger, I can take care of myself."

"Phoof!" Air flew out of my mouth when he grabbed me fast and swung my arm around my back. I in turn, did some kind of self-defense move where the next thing I knew, Jagger was up against the wall, and I had my face in his.

Damn! Where'd that come from?

He chuckled. "Good reflexes, Sherlock."

"Then let me stay."

He looked into my eyes—and I nearly forgot where I was. Before he could answer, he leaned forward . . . and his lips brushed against mine. Slowly. Very slowly. My heart started to pound so loudly I felt it vibrate against his chest. His kiss had me on my tiptoes, eyes shut, and hands pressed against his shoulders.

His hands ran along my back.

Oh, God.

His hands reached my neck and rubbed ever so gently, lifting my hair and letting it cascade down in a soft breeze.

Wow.

His hands slid around to cup beneath my cheeks while the kiss, the Jagger kiss, ended.

I had to take such a deep breath that my lungs actually hurt. I had good reflexes, but not good enough to react in an intelligent manner for several seconds.

"I'll always be one step behind you, Sherlock."

It seemed to take several hours before my legs could walk me out of the janitor's closet while I muttered my thanks on and on to Jagger for supporting my decision to stay at the Institute. I know it was only a few minutes in reality, but I wanted to let time slow to a crawl so that I could savor every blessed minute.

Jagger had kissed me.

Wa hoo!

But, once out in the hallway, it seemed as if nothing had happened. We were back to being partners in this job, and I could only console myself with the thought that I'd sleep like a baby tonight, dreaming about the kiss.

Jagger motioned for me to follow him. Back to work as usual. Okay. I had to scream inside my head that I was a professional and just because Jagger had kissed me, I had to clear the cobwebs out of my mind and pay attention.

Not paying attention could get us hurt, or worse.

From the end of the hallway, I noticed movement. Jagger kept going as if nothing had stirred. Right. *Act as if you are a janitor, Pauline.* Sister Liz and Sister Barbie came around the corner with several patients in tow. I wondered if they missed me, but then thought of how Jagger had told Sister Liz that we'd be talking a long time. Always thinking, that guy.

"You there," Sister Barbie said in her professional head-nurse tone.

We spun around. I covered my face as much as possible by turning my head toward my shoulder so my hair would fall forward while Jagger, in a disguised voice asked, "Yes, Sister. What is it?"

My heart couldn't take these frequent shifts in rhythm. On the outside when working a case, at least I got to go home and feel safe and off duty. Around there, it was 24/7 laced with fear.

Sister Barbie walked past us and over her shoulder said, "Make sure Room 84 is cleaned for a new patient."

I gasped.

Jagger nudged me so hard, I automatically pushed him back.

"What?" he whispered to me while smiling to the nuns. "My coworker has asthma. Dust sometimes causes it to act up." He took my arm and turned us the other way. "She's fine. Just fine."

"Thank the good Lord," Sister Liz said as they headed off.

I pushed at Jagger's arm. "That's Margaret's room. Or at least it was her room. Oh, my. Where do you think . . . you don't think she's . . . No. She can't be. They know she's not coming back. Not coming back! There's that little boy and all—"

He shoved a mop against my chest. "Stop that. Maybe she was released to go home."

He said that just to calm me down. Neither of us believed it though.

"Let's go," Jagger said.

I grabbed the mop, followed him, and mumbled all the way to Room 84.

I realized I'd never been in Margaret's room before. Of course, a patient visiting another patient's room was forbidden for various good reasons. But when I walked in, I froze. A hint of magnolia filled the air. Southern magnolia. Margaret's scent. The bed was tousled, as if she were yanked out of it. The door to the bathroom was partially shut, and I half expected her to come out any second.

Jagger reached down and picked something up from under the mattress. Something white had been sticking out. I'd noticed it too, but hadn't been able to move.

He held a photograph toward me. "That the boy?"

I swallowed and looked closely as if I could identify Margaret's son. "I've never seen him," I said, looking at the tiny snapshot, the size you get in one of those department store booths for a few bucks. "But . . ." My voice softened and my eyes burned. "He does look like Margaret."

"Maybe they moved her to another unit?" He tucked the photo into his shirt pocket and went about cleaning.

I stood there, floored. One because he thoughtfully didn't throw the picture away, and two because—he was still acting the janitor part. "You're actually cleaning." This guy was a real piece.

He looked at me. "Sherlock, when you work a case, you have to play the part or risk blowing your cover." With that he shoved the mop toward me and yanked the sheets off the bed.

"Right. I knew that. Like an undercover cop has to play the part of a drug buyer."

When the mop hit my arm, I grabbed it and started to clean. "I'll have to get back soon or they might get suspicious."

Jagger grinned.

"What? They might." I ran the mop in a circle, rather weakly, I admit.

He took it from my hands. "I know you're no house-keeper, Sherlock, but at least make an effort. Here." He proceeded to show me how to mop while I proceeded to wonder if there was anything Jagger *couldn't* do.

But all my darn brain would wrap around was the thought: He sure can kiss!

Once Margaret's room was done, Jagger and I had made our way out of the unit. Thank goodness he had the keys, which any patient would kill for. Well, I'd hoped not all the patients would do that but knew some would. It reminded me of my days of training in psych as a student nurse. The rule was to guard your keys with your life, because if they were lost (meaning stolen), the student would have to pay one hundred dollars. That was a lot of money back then, and a fortune to a poverty-stricken student nurse. It sure kept us on our toes.

Jagger's keys dangled off his belt, and I figured no patient, even mentally sick ones, would attempt to steal them from him.

We walked down the steps at the end of the hallway to the long tunnel that ran from building to building. I hadn't been this way before but couldn't help but think of Vito's dead body in the foyer at the other end of it.

"Have the police found out anything about Vito?"

"Nope." Jagger motioned for me to go ahead as he opened the door to another set of stairs. "Just that he was a con man and came from a family of crooks."

No need to ask where we were going, because it didn't matter. Jagger must have had a hunch to go to this part of the campus to search for Margaret. I only prayed that we wouldn't find her like Vito.

We climbed to the top of the stairs to another unit, and Jagger once again unlocked the door. When I stepped inside the dayroom, my heart jumped.

Sitting in a statuelike, catatonic state was Margaret.

The rest of the patients bustled about, talked to themselves or others, did crafts and even let out wild sounds on occasions, but Margaret didn't even look up.

I motioned for Jagger to look toward Margaret.

He nodded at me and worked his way over to her. I followed all the while, mopping as he'd shown me. Several nuns sat around the unit, and I figured they were on "constant" watch. Good. Now they couldn't pay us much attention.

Behind the nurses' station were two more nuns, a lay nurse and a male orderly. Much smaller than Spike, the guy still didn't look all that friendly. He looked downright sleazy. I knew sleazy from seeing Fabio. This orderly could probably manhandle someone with the best of them.

Jagger looked at me. Suddenly, through some telepathic form of communication, I knew he wanted me to talk to Margaret. I knelt down next to her, took out a cloth from my pants pocket and started to wipe an imaginary spot from the couch near her. With all the animation of the mental ward in full swing, no one paid attention to me.

"Margaret," I whispered.

Nothing.

Not even a blink.

"Margaret, it's me. Pauline. From the other unit. I came to find you. I know you don't belong—" I might as well have been talking to myself.

Margaret's eyes stared off into the distance, not really looking at anything. Damn. She was in her catatonic state, more than likely heavily medicated. Her pink lips were set as if she had never talked or laughed. The whites of her eyes were now pink. She had probably cried enough tears to flood the place when they'd moved her here.

And why did they?

Why had Margaret been moved?

I kept up my attempts of getting her to look at me, but to no avail. I rubbed the couch a bit harder until a hand covered mine. I turned to see Jagger with his cloth in hand.

"Need some help?"

"No" sat on my tongue because, after all, what dummy couldn't clean an imaginary spot off a couch? But before I could say anything, Jagger passed his rag over mine.

I felt something touch my fingers and lifted the cloth enough to see what it was.

My throat tightened and I lifted the object, then turned to look around the unit. Jagger had moved away and kept cleaning. A young man shouted to no one about Lincoln being assassinated. An older woman talked like a toddler as I bent to tuck the "gift" from Jagger into Margaret's hand.

At first I held my breath while she sat still. I worried she'd just let it fall to the floor, and we'd get caught.

But then . . . her finger moved.

It ran over the picture of her son a few times, then she lifted her eyes toward me. "Thank you," she whispered in a voice much hoarser than usual. I figured that was the result of crying.

Suddenly I felt a tug at my arm. Ready to gently ease free of some patient's death grip, I turned to see Jagger motion toward the door. He leaned toward Margaret and said, "We'll be back to help you."

When I turned to follow Jagger, I noticed the reason he had us leaving before I could talk more to Margaret. Two burly guys dressed exactly like us headed down the hallway with mops and buckets. Yikes! Our cover was nearly blown, I thought, as we hurried out the door and down the stairs. In our haste, Jagger hadn't even fumbled with the lock.

Things like that amazed me about him.

At the bottom of the stairs, I turned to go back toward my unit. Before I could take another step, I found myself upside down and slung over his shoulder like a sack of potatoes—although the sacks I bought were much smaller.

"What the hell? What are you doing?"

"Shh!"

Damn, he was right. I couldn't make a scene, since several staff members were coming down the stairs. Our cover really would be blown. Margaret would be left in limbo, and so would who knew how many other patients. And what of Vito's killer? Was all of this really related?

When the footsteps got closer, Jagger, still holding onto me dangling upside down, ducked into an alcove. Being an old building, the place was filled with them.

He set me down and held his hand over my lips. When he'd done that before I had been tempted to lick him.

Right now, I wanted to bite him.

Nurse Lawson walked by with what looked like a doctor. She must have been on the evening shift, since it was starting to get dark. In our investigating, we somehow missed lunch. I was actually hungry.

My stomach growled.

Nurse Lawson stopped at the alcove and turned.

I lowered my head to hide my face.

She said, "You two cut it out and get back to work."

Thank goodness she assumed we were fooling around instead of hiding.

Fooling around!

Jagger said, "Sure," took my arm, unlocked the door and yanked me out of the alcove. A late winter breeze slapped at my face, sending strands of hair dancing loose.

I pushed at his arm.

He took my hand. "Stop it!"

Before I knew it, we were inside his Suburban with the Cortona Institute fading away in the distance.

"I'll never forgive you for this," I swore. "Never."

Fifteen

Jagger kept driving silently while I ranted on about his being a liar. His being a jerk. His being a traitor and not letting us finish our job.

Before I knew it, we had turned into the Dunkin Donuts drive-thru, and he was ordering me a Hazelnut decaf— my favorite. He also included my French cruller.

When he turned to hand it to me, he said, "Figured you'd be hungry by now."

Not wanting to act childish, not to mention the fact that I was starving, I took them and bit half the donut off at once. "You lied," I reiterated with my mouth still full.

Jagger pulled the SUV into a space in the back where only the employees parked. After he shut off the engine, he sipped his coffee a few minutes and said, "You're going back, Sherlock. After I've taught you a few self-defense moves and gotten you some equipment to keep you safe."

I choked on the donut, took a sip of coffee and then said, "You ... I ... why didn't you?" I stopped, composed myself and finished with, "It would have made it much easier if you had explained that to me back there."

He remained silent, staring.

"And, Jagger, I'm not even going to give you the satisfaction of my feeling embarrassed that I got angry at you." I turned toward the window, pretending to fix my cap so that he wouldn't see my face—which was hotter than his black coffee.

I heard him sip his coffee and say, "Easier, sure, but not as much fun."

When we'd left the donut shop, I realized we were headed for my parents' house.

Jagger must have known I'd need a whiff of Renuzit.

He'd explained that he'd called Sister Barbie and lied about taking me out on another pass. Something about that fictitious plastic surgeon needing to see me again.

He was always a million steps ahead of me.

When we pulled into the driveway, Uncle Walt was getting out of his friend Henry's Oldsmobile. Walt's face lit up when he noticed us. I figured that was because he was so excited to see the SUV and not me. My uncle was a car nut and spent most of his time reading auto magazines, now that macular degeneration, causing some loss of vision, kept him from driving. I hoped he'd never lose his sight and not be able to read his magazines.

He hurried over and gave me a big hug after I stepped out of the Suburban. I wondered if he knew where I'd been. Then again, Uncle Walt and I had always been close so it made sense he'd be happy to see me. Henry waved and drove off.

"Where've you been, Uncle Walt?" I asked.

Uncle Walt gave me the once-over, and I remembered I was still wearing the janitor's outfit.

"Looks as if I should be asking you the same thing, Pauline."

I gave a nervous laugh.

Jagger came around from the driver's side, and I wondered what we'd tell my parents. "Pauline's been helping me with—"

He was going to tell him! Tell Uncle Walt about our case?

"—a cleaning job. I do it in my spare time to help out a friend."

Uncle Walt nodded and hugged me again. I'll never know if he bought that story or not, but he didn't seem to care. I myself had the feeling Walt knew more than he let on—all the time. After all, he did know about my last case since someone he knew had been killed. Murdered. He winked and I knew he enjoyed sharing the "espionage moment."

We walked inside and darling Uncle Walt said, "Stella? Michael? You have to see these getups. Pauline is helping out Jagger in a cleaning service." He winked at me and headed toward his room.

The house smelled of baking apple pie amid the scent of my mother's cabbage soup. Mother called it by its Polish name, *kapusta* soup. I loved the beef ribs that she cooked in it. When we were kids, my siblings and I used to fight over who'd get to whittle away at the meat on the last bone.

Daddy would always say, "The closer the bone, the sweeter the meat," and we'd then have to draw straws to see who'd get the last piece.

I inhaled and was glad she was cooking something so aromatic, so nostalgic. I could use nostalgic.

When she came around the corner followed by my father, she stopped so fast he bumped into her back. "Sorry, Michael, but I thought Walt was kidding. Pauline Sokol helping out to *clean*?"

I ignored Jagger's chuckle and kissed both parents on the cheek. "Just temporarily."

"What? No criminals to follow around today?" She didn't even smile at that one.

I only wish. "Sure there are, Mother. There are always bad people out there." Hopefully none who would hurt Margaret—or me.

She clucked her tongue and said, "Come. Eat. You two are just in time."

We all followed her into the kitchen. "Pauline, set two extra places." She turned toward Jagger. "What can I get you to drink, Mr. Jagger?"

I shook my head and mumbled that he could help out too, but then realized she considered him company. Yeah, right. I went about my chore and soon we were sipping the savory soup and, not wanting to look bad in front of Jagger, I cut the meat off the bone instead of chewing it, as I had wanted to do.

I looked up to see him, bone in hand, gnawing away like my father and Uncle Walt.

"Michael," Mother said, "we are not dogs." She picked up the largest bone with a fork and set it on his plate with a nod.

He kept gnawing away.

Uncle Walt did too, and occasionally took his piece of fresh rye bread, smothered with real butter—Mother abhorred margarine—and dunked it in his soup. Thank goodness Mother didn't notice.

My mother cut her meat off the bone with a knife and fork, so I kept doing the same with mine. Occasionally she'd give me a look that said she didn't believe I was really cleaning anything.

"So, Mr. Jagger, did Pauline do a good job?" Mother asked, taking a sip of her coffee.

I nearly choked on my *kapusta* soup.

He smiled and then said, "Well, to be honest, Mrs. Sokol, I had to show her a few things."

Mother grunted and continued sipping.

Daddy looked at me in sympathy.

Uncle Walt kept eating and not really paying attention. I think he was waiting for Jagger to give him another ride in his SUV.

As I helped to clean up after being given the order by Mother, I wondered why Jagger had brought me here. Why now? We could have stopped to get something to eat at a diner. I looked to see my mother watching me. Her eyes held concern, but she didn't say anything except, "Be careful not to chip my good dishes, Pauline," while I stacked the soup bowls.

Jagger had taken Uncle Walt and Daddy outside and, in fact, I saw them drive out of the driveway. How sweet. Surely that wasn't the reason we had come here.

Maybe, since he'd said I was going back to the Institute, he had wanted me to see my parents—in case it was the last time.

I gasped.

A bowl fell to the floor but only bounced softly on the indoor/outdoor carpeting Mother had insisted on installing in the kitchen. I could remember being a toddler and never getting hurt when I fell on this floor.

"Pauline, just what are you up to?" Mother stood above me as I bent to get the bowl.

"Oh. It slipped."

She bent down and touched my hand. "That's not what I mean. What are you doing dressed like that, and don't give me some baloney about helping Jagger *clean*. I mean, *really*."

I couldn't lie to her. Not from this distance. Over the phone would even be a long shot. "It's . . . I'm all right, Mother. It's part of the job."

"The criminal one?"

I stood and helped her straighten. "Yes, Mother. The criminal one. But I'm fine. Jagger—" How could I tell her that he would keep me safe? I felt it in my heart, but hearing the words come out might sound foolish. Unbelievable. Before I had to say any more, the front door opened and the three men came back inside.

The grin on Uncle Walt's face made my concerns fade.

"He let me drive," he said and turned toward his room where I knew he'd take his daily nap.

Mother looked more horrified than I felt. I turned to Jagger. "He has macular—"

He waved his hand. "It was only in an empty parking lot. I'd do it again."

Mother and I looked at each other and for a minute I felt some kind of connection. Something I'd really never felt with her, although I loved her to pieces. I hugged her and realized how tough all of this was on her.

Maybe she was ready to admit that I was an adult.

After we left my folks' house, Jagger drove me to my condo. As we pulled into the lot, I could barely remember my mother trying to get me to move back in with them, although I know those had been her parting words. Something about not having to clean.

In fact, she wasn't ready to admit that I was an adult.

Suddenly I couldn't wait to see Miles, Goldie and Spanky, as if I'd been away for months instead of days. Neither of their cars were in the lot, but I figured a tussle with Spanky would make up for it.

Once we headed toward my door, I realized I didn't have a purse or any key. "Damn, Jagger. We can't get in—"

He stood with the door open. A key dangling off his finger.

"How . . . ? Where did you . . . ? Oh, never mind." It wasn't worth asking about, so I chalked it up to a Jagger moment.

When we got inside, Spanky flew out of the kitchen into Jagger's arms. I hesitated, then Jagger turned and handed him off like a football. "Hey, my little guy, how have you been?" He nuzzled my neck, licked my face about seven times and then squirmed until I set him down. He followed Jagger, who was heading into the kitchen.

"I'll get some beers. You start moving the furniture to the side."

For a second I only stared. Beer? Me move the heavy stuff? Okay, maybe Jagger was too into equal rights here. But then again, he treated me as a partner so I shoved my knee against the ottoman and pushed it to the side. At first I wondered what the heck we were going to do, and that *kiss* nagged at my brain.

Naw.

From the kitchen he called, "You might want to go change into something more comfortable and that fits better."

More comfortable!

My heart started to speed up, and then Jagger came in the door and I realized we had some self-defense moves to learn. He handed me a Coors Light with a glass. I set it down on the coffee table and took a sip from the bottle.

"That's right. Not from cans, but you drink from bottles." He pushed the heavy couch farther toward the wall.

Amazed and, yes, a bit pleased that he remembered

something about me, I went upstairs and put on my navy jogging outfit with a Steelers tee shirt.

I hurried downstairs, realizing we really didn't have much time. Logically, I'd have to be back at the hospital soon, or our cover would be in jeopardy.

"Okay, first lesson. Forget what your mother taught you to do when a guy grabs you from behind."

I stopped at the bottom of the stairs. Obviously he didn't know Stella Sokol very well. My mother had never—nor would she ever—teach us girls to kick a guy—there. Instead she always taught us to avoid situations that might warrant the old knee to the groin. In fact, I think she truly believed nothing bad would ever happen to us and backed it up with prayers and lots of novenas.

I knew what Jagger meant and decided not to mention Mother. "Why?"

"Let's just say, every guy has a mother, sister, friend, cousin or some female who knows to go for where it hurts."

"And what is wrong with that?" I walked to the coffee table, lifted my beer and took a sip.

"Nothing. I'm not saying don't ever try it. Hell, the only wrong move in a dangerous situation is no move at all. What I'm saying is, the guy is going to *expect* it. So, you have to surprise him. The element of surprise might save your . . . butt."

I knew he meant "life" but was kind enough not to remind me.

"Makes sense."

"Come here." He held out his hands. "Lesson One. Make a claw of your hand and scrape it along the guy or gal's face and don't be shy or grossed out about digging into the eyes."

"Gal?"

"Yes, Sherlock, sometimes women are attackers."

I really hadn't considered that. I thought we were trying to protect me from Terry and whoever killed Vito, which very likely could have been Terry.

"Don't get hung up on the small stuff." He held his hand up toward me. "If the knee to the groin works, run like hell. If not, here's your second choice." He sprang forward and pretended to "claw" my face.

I screamed.

He pulled back. "Good. You could be hired for a B movie. Make sure you can exercise your lungs like that while acting though. Try it."

He grabbed my arm and I tried to do the move, but at first hesitated.

"Don't be afraid to hurt me. You'll never learn if you don't practice."

"Okay," I said while Jagger "attacked" me again.

"Go for the face, eyes, throat, and nose." He showed me how to hit with my solid fist against someone's lower throat—which could crush his or her trachea and be my saving grace.

After a gazillion moves and practices, I wanted to collapse on the carpet, but, being the stubborn Polack that I was, I refused to give into my exhaustion, even when he had me "raking" my clawlike hand down his face or learning a very disturbing yet probably effective move that involved fingers inside the attacker's nose.

Anything for self-preservation, he had said.

Then, to my amazement, he pulled this little thing from his pocket. He held it out toward me. It was smaller than a gun, black and looked a bit like a weird bracelet. "Fifty thousand volts of electricity shoot out of these probes in five-second cycles. Incapacitates the attacker."

"A stun gun?"

"A camouflaged taser gun, Sherlock. Cops use the ones that don't need to be camouflaged instead of having to shoot some suspects. This is only to be used as a last resort though. Fleeing the scene is your first. *Remember* that."

He proceeded to give me instructions on it. I insisted I understood and knew the effects it would have as I constantly mentioned how amazing it was that a taser gun could be made to look like a bracelet. Jagger only shook his head—once.

Okay, some things in this business still impressed me.

"You really want me to wear that thing?" I knew it sounded like a good idea but I also knew both Jagger and I worried I might taser myself.

He put it on my wrist. "I'll make sure the staff knows you are allowed to wear your mother's heirloom to help with your recovery.

I looked at the ugly bracelet. "Stella Sokol wearing a taser bracelet. I don't think so."

He chuckled.

Jagger finally stepped back and picked up his beer. "That'll do for now. Run the routines through your head over and over and practice them in your room when no one is around." He came closer and took me by the shoulders. "And, Sherlock, do not let your need to help people get in the way of your safety. If you ever, God forbid, have to use any of these techniques, *do not* stick around to help the assailant out and make sure he or she lives. In other words, no nursing the criminal, 'cause if it happens, you're a victim."

Jagger obviously had my number.

The old one though.

I told him and myself that I would do my best and not

feel sorry for anyone who had attacked me or hurt some-one else.

He leaned forward, touched my cheek and said, "I'm glad you finally believe that advice, Sherlock."

After I'd changed back into the janitor's outfit, Jagger pushed all the furniture back in order so that Miles and Goldie would not see it and have a collective fit. Just as we were about to leave, the door opened and my two best friends walked in, screeching, hugging and kissing me.

Jagger stood to the side and watched.

I could tell there were no derogatory thoughts in his mind. He actually looked a bit jealous of our friendship.

"What the hell?" Goldie said as he held me out to take a better look. "I didn't know Halloween was in March!"

Miles looked concerned. "That's part of the job, isn't it? I really think you should let me call my friend Hammy and set you up with a job in his furniture store."

I smiled at both of them. "I'm fine. Really. Jagger just taught me some self-defense moves—"

"Whoosh!" flew out of my mouth.

Before I knew it, Goldie had me in some kind of body lock. I didn't even think, but reacted with what I'd been taught by stepping on Goldie's little toe, causing him to let go, then I grabbed his arm and flipped him onto the floor. I knew then that if it had been for real, I would have done my moves with a hell of a lot more force.

Goldie got up and kissed my cheek while Miles hugged me. "Okay, get the hell on out of here," Goldie said like a proud mamma, taking a zebra handkerchief out of his black furry purse. He dabbed his eyes and waved me off with the hanky.

I walked on air past a smiling Jagger.

Sixteen

I barely had the energy or appetite to go to the dining room to eat that night. Jagger had gotten my hospital gown and pants back, walked me to my ward and left me in my room after reporting to Sister Liz that I was back.

I sat on the bed contemplating poor Margaret in the other ward. Why on earth did they move her? I figured that someone knew this place was being "looked at." But how? Jagger and I had been so secretive. Still, maybe I was wrong. Maybe my imagination had me thinking someone had found out about our investigation, but they really hadn't. But there was the broom handle . . . maybe I was a target for another reason.

Maybe I should just chalk it all up to bad vibes from being in here. After all, the aura of these patients had to be in shades of gray to black. Sad but true.

"Hello, Pauline."

I swung around to see Terry in my doorway!

"Oh. Hey, Ter." I shifted on my bed ready to get up and react if need be. "You know you can't come in here. No visiting in other patients' rooms. Sister Barbie . . . Barbara Immaculatta's rule."

Terry poked his big toe through the doorway.

Despite my exhaustion, I pushed myself up to stand. "Where are your shoes, Ter?"

He wiggled his toe. "Why do I need shoes for what I need to do?"

Yikes! My throat went dry. "Er . . . what is it that you need to do, Terry?"

He stepped forward.

Instead of my life flashing before my eyes, Jagger's self-defense instructions played like a video before me. I ran my finger across my bracelet. "I'm going to have to call Spike or whoever's working this shift if you come any closer."

Terry laughed. What a God-awful sound. Talk about chills running down your spine. Mine were on speedboats. He wiggled his naked foot. Even that looked sinister.

I backed toward the wall, wishing I could get past him and out the door. But Terry was a decent size in height and a generous portion in weight.

I couldn't take him.

What I could do was protect myself with Jagger's techniques and taser Terry's butt if necessary, along with screaming for help.

"Well, it's time to go to the dining hall, Ter. You hungry?"

He stood still. "Don't call me 'Ter.' *He* called me that and look what happened to him."

Whoa boy.

"Who called you that?"

He clucked his tongue. "You know. *Him.* He called me 'Ter,' so that happened to him."

"Um. What is that, Terry?"

"You know."

"No. I don't . . . remember."

He walked toward the bed. "Stop fooling me, Pauline. You know. You are smart. That's why you're here."

Oh . . . my . . . God. Terry knew! "Hooow?" my words kinda croaked out.

This time Terry came within taser distance.

Good. I actually felt rather brave with the knowledge that Jagger had given me, not to mention the weapon on my wrist. I could do this, I told myself. Of course, I could scream too, but knew full well what happened to screaming patients around here. Terry would be out the door in a flash and no one would believe me as I rambled on while tucked in the wet sheets. The nuns already thought I'd hurt myself.

He clucked his tongue. "You know you are smart and they have you here for that. You know that I only wanted him to see the light. You know all that, Pauline. I don't see why you are pretending."

Suddenly I knew what it meant when someone's eyes grew cold. I eased back and swallowed.

"Pauline. Pauline. Pauline." He started that laugh again.

Oh, boy. Terry's elevator didn't go to the top floor. It was actually plummeting to the basement before my eyes, like the Tower of Terror at Disney. "Okay, I'm just hungry. So, let's go see what there is to eat." I called his bluff and started to walk past him. Not knowing where the courage came from, I let adrenaline power my legs as I looked him in the eye and walked toward the door. Then I stopped and realized maybe I could get more info out of Terry.

He must have killed Vito. He'd just about confessed.

"You're not afraid to die, Pauline?" He closed the door.

Got my attention with that one. I turned around. "Die? Why would I die, Terry?" I stood firm and decided I had to do my job and part of that job might just involve Vito's death.

Terry started to hum and wiggle his toes. If I wasn't facing a probable murderer, his actions would be comical. Instead, they came across as disturbing. Evil.

"I guess we all have to die someday, Ter." I'd purposely used the nickname to rile him. I figured he might spill more beans while losing what little control he actually had.

I preferred him spilling his beans instead of spilling me. I held my bracelet with the other hand.

"And you want to see the light on Tuesday?"

Today was Tuesday. "No, Ter. I want to see my grandchildren's children grow up. No light for me yet."

He came closer and looked much larger.

Gone was the pleasant doctor look that I'd originally seen when we first met. Mentally ill folks do have some chameleonlike qualities. That's what makes psych so hard to work in. One never could tell if someone was sane . . . or not.

I was going with "not" for Ter.

For a second, I wished Jagger would come running in the door and zap Terry. But then I decided I could do this. I was an investigator and needed to face the risks of the job on my own.

So, going for the sixty-four-thousand-dollar risk, I asked, "Hey, Ter . . . did Vito see the light?"

"Vito!" he shouted then lunged at me with all his crazy force. I fell against the wall and started to call for Spike or anyone. Someone! Terry had wrapped his gigantic hands around my neck and wasn't about to let go. He started to squeeze as he asked, "Is the light getting brighter yet? Is it?" he raised his voice.

The damn light is about to wink out, I thought. I tried to move, but ended up flailing about under his weight. Taking a hint from Spike, I spit at Terry. He shifted and cursed while I lifted my knee to his groin enough to get him to jerk up and yelp.

Then he grabbed my wrist against his shoulder . . . and tasered himself.

His eyes bugged out. His body had some kind of convulsion. And Terry landed like a limp, gigantic rag doll on my chest, with a *whoosh* of air into my face.

Geez. I would have thought his reaction to being stunned would have been different. More stiff. I pushed at him until he tumbled to the side.

In the meantime, I jumped up so fast my head spun, while a gang crowded into the doorway. The first row of spectators consisted of patients. Staring. Mumbling. Hollering. Some woman with a Barbie doll stood in front shaking it at us.

From behind, I could hear Spike and the staff yelling at the spectators to move. Spike shoved past everyone.

I straightened up and said, "Terry's not feeling well."

Kneeling next to Terry, Spike said, "He's *dead*."

Seventeen

"I killed him. I killed a man," I wailed, as Jagger held me. Thank goodness he had appeared only seconds after Terry's demise and whisked me off to the treatment room after I had experienced "the trauma of seeing Terry die directly on top of me."

I'd seen patients pass away before my eyes, but I had never been the *cause*.

"You didn't kill him. He killed himself. And besides, you didn't know that the taser gun could affect him like that because of the medication Terry was taking. There's only been a few cases where cops tasered perps who happened to be on medication for some form of mental illness . . . and they died. It's controversial and it's rare. Very rare, Sherlock."

"But it happened." He held me tighter. I wondered how Jagger had known that there had been some very rare cases where cops had tasered suspects and they had died.

I figured he didn't tell me because then I'd hesitate to use the taser around here—even to save my own life.

"True, it did happen, Sherlock, but you said he was going to kill you. You said he had killed Vito. And he killed himself instead. Ironic, but justice nevertheless."

"No. I . . . well . . . he—" I sniffled again and Jagger handed me a tissue from the box on the counter. "He actually didn't say he had killed Vito. He kept talking about 'seeing the light' so when I asked him if Vito had seen it, he attacked me." I blew my nose and continued, "Kinda odd. Isn't it? I mean I only had to ask about Vito and Terry went off like crazy."

"He *was* crazy." Jagger touched his finger to my forehead, this time so gently I had to struggle to *feel* it. I did feel my hair being moved back again. Real nice touch.

As I basked in Jagger's hold, he continued, "Terry was in here for hurting his younger brother. Terry denied it though."

"That's not uncommon."

"No, but Terry tried to throw a hairdryer on full blast into a Jacuzzi with his brother in it."

I shuddered. "Oh, my."

"But good old Terry had said that he only wanted his brother to experience 'seeing the light.' Never meant to hurt him. He said he planned to pull the plug right after his brother had the opportunity to see the light."

"He wanted me to see the light," I whispered.

"I'm taking you home tonight, Sherlock."

"I guess that would be a good idea. Then I can come back tomorrow and find out more. I mean, Jagger, Terry killed Vito. Now it's safer for me to be here. We only have to find out about the fraud ring and get Margaret safely out of here."

"We don't know for sure that he killed Vito," he said.

"But he must have. I feel better knowing he is the one who did it."

"Yeah, whatever." Then he pushed the hair back from my face and kissed me on the forehead.

I held my breath. I could have taken the gesture as one of friend to friend, adult to child, or Jagger to woman.

I was going with the last.

Yeah, whatever? That was not something one would expect to hear from confident Jagger.

When I got home, I found that Goldie and Miles had gone out for the night. I wondered, only for a few minutes, what story Jagger had concocted to get me another pass, then found out he'd wowed Sister Barbie enough so that she had me temporarily moved to another unit—or so she thought—after Terry died on me. But in reality, Jagger had sneaked me out.

The guy could be crafty.

Besides, who would they report missing, Mary Louise?

I actually thought that maybe Sister Barbie or someone higher up there knew all about Jagger and me. Well, at least Jagger. He knew his way around the Institute too damn easily. Maybe that's how he got away with so much—thank goodness. Before he'd sent me upstairs to bed and said he'd be bunking on the couch, he'd mentioned that now I'd have time to finish my case.

I'd thanked him for getting me out of there for a few days to do that.

But once tucked in bed, I realized that Jagger had no intention of my ever going back to the Cortona Institute of Life.

Three strikes and Pauline was out.

Percolating coffee. Frying bacon. Citrus.

I opened one eye and inhaled. Breakfast. I was starving

since I never did make it to dinner last night in all the hubbub of Terry killing himself.

Throughout the night I'd tossed and turned, feeling horrible about his dying, and did come to the conclusion that it wasn't my fault. I did, however, still say some prayers for his confused soul.

When I looked at the clock to see it was after nine, I jumped up. No Spanky on my duvet. Jagger was downstairs and Spanky, the little rascal, knew it. He also must have known that Jagger was making breakfast. Miles and Goldie only did the big breakfast on the weekends. Today was Wednesday. Jagger had turned into a chef again.

He'd done it before for me.

I heard laughing—male laughing with a few giggles interspersed—and knew my roomies were downstairs with Jagger. Feeling as protective as a mother lioness, I jumped out of bed, not sure how Jagger and my roomies would get along. I didn't want them to feel uncomfortable with someone they didn't usually hang out with. I loved them both too much.

Since I couldn't appear in my nightie and robe, I shoved on undies and a jogging suit, headed to the bathroom, brushed what needed to be brushed, combed what needed to be combed and tried to cover up any facial wrinkles with makeup. My cut had scabbed and looked well on its way to healing. I needed Goldie's expertise right about now but had to settle for something more along the lines of what a mortician's makeup artist would come up with.

On the way down the stairs I stopped and listened. More laughter. I could tell Miles's since I'd known him for so long, and Goldie—well, there was that giggle again. But the new laughter, the deep, sexy laughter had to be coming from Jagger.

I nearly ran into the kitchen to be sure.

There, seated on the counter, holding traitor Spanky, was Jagger, smiling, sipping coffee and, yes, laughing.

"You're sitting on the counter," was all I could manage, knowing Miles must be having a fit.

But Miles laughed again and said, "Ease up on him, Pauline, we like him."

They like him? They like him? They *like* him!

Something had transformed around the condo during the night, and it wasn't me. I did, however, accept the cup of green tea Goldie handed me. He was wearing a peach cashmere sweater, peach suede slacks and a white ostrich feather pin to the left side of his chest.

"Thanks," was all I could get out. Goldie must have known how flustered I was as he led me to the table and practically had to sit me down.

I whispered, "He's sitting on the counter. Miles can see him!"

Goldie patted my shoulder. "Suga, you all right?" He sniffled.

I looked up to see Miles wipe his eyes too.

"You shouldn't have told them," I said to Jagger. "They have a tendency to worry." I smiled at Goldie and Miles. "Guys, I'm fine. I wasn't hurt."

"Well, I for one am glad that whacko offed himself," Goldie said.

"He was sick, Gold."

Goldie waved a hand at me and held his fingers out. "Don't you go feeling sorry for some nutty nut who could have hurt you, Suga." He snapped his fingers with a *crack*.

Miles gasped.

I jumped.

And Jagger shook his head—twice.

Goldie and Miles both stood and started to clean up.

"I'll get that, guys. You go ahead," I said.

Goldie leaned over and kissed my cheek. Miles gave me a bear hug that had me nearly out of breath. "You two stop acting as if I was nearly killed. I can handle . . . I handled myself. I'll be fine when I go back."

Goldie screeched but not as loudly as Miles. They both spun around toward Jagger as if he could help them.

"Guys, don't look at *him*. I *am* going back." I actually *couldn't* look at Jagger. If I did, I was afraid he would put some kind of Jagger-influenced curse on me, and I'd be following an order not to go back to the Cortona Institute of Life.

"I am," I reiterated.

Silence.

Spanky jumped down from Jagger's lap as a squirrel had the nerve to tap his paw at the glass of the French door that led out to the patio. Miles opened the door. "Get the varmint, Spanks!"

While the dog barked, the squirrel jumped to the brick wall and turned around as if to laugh at darling Spanky. Miles and Goldie excused themselves to head off to work. "Chickens," I mumbled as they both went out the door. Goldie said that neither would be home until late tonight, so we were on our own for dinner.

I looked up. "I am going back, Jagger. I *am*."

Jagger and I never began a "discussion" about my going back or not going back to work on the case. Instead, we headed off to Dr. De Jong's practice, and before I knew it, we were in the backdoor, down the hallway and into the reception area sooner than anyone could see us.

"Isn't this breaking and entering?"

Jagger merely looked at me. I knew it was, but I also

knew he had friends in the police department, and we were not going to do any harm or take anything or break anything. Jagger had jimmied the lock without leaving a smudge.

Still, in the distant memory of my mind I thought about going to prison and still being innocent. I would not make a good prisoner. I hated change.

"What if the doctor comes in?" I asked.

"Her first case isn't until noon. We have two hours."

I marveled that he knew about her first case and said, "How'd you know that?"

"Because it's ten and the first case is noon."

I curled my lip at him. "I know ten from twelve is two, but how did you know—"

He pointed to her schedule book, which was clearly opened on the desk. Damn.

"How'd you know she wasn't already in here?"

"You see her car in the parking lot?"

Shoot. Fraud Investigation 101 had just progressed to 102. Way before our two hours were up, Jagger had taken all the teens' charts from the file cabinet and had them in a pile. I read through them, noting that several had authenticated diagnoses from other physicians. I had worked with three of the doctors at the Hospital of Saint Greg's so could vouch for their skills, and what they all said made sense.

Some kids even had blood work done, test results and family input all leading to a correct diagnosis. From all that Ruby had told me, her chart corroborated her information.

I looked at Jagger. "De Jong's not committing fraud."

He shrugged, obviously believing me.

"Still, it is too bad there are so many messed-up, depressed kids."

"Things are different nowadays, Sherlock. Teens have so much peer pressure, more stress and sometimes way too much rotten luck." He stared off into space.

And here I thought Jagger knew little to nothing about teens. There had to be something in Jagger's past that led him to that statement.

I could only wonder though, since I knew he wouldn't tell me. We finished up documenting the cases, and I also wondered if damn, cheap Fabio would pay me.

Hey, it wasn't my fault that Dr. De Jong was an honest psychiatrist!

A door shut in the back of the office.

I blinked and then looked at Jagger with my eyelids in the full open position.

He touched his finger to his lips, as if I weren't smart enough to keep my mouth shut. Okay, truthfully I wanted to scream. Jagger touched my shoulder and soon I was standing by the door.

He'd closed up the charts and shoved them back into the file cabinet as if in a film on fast speed. I had to blink again to see that the files looked as if we'd never touched them before he shut the drawer.

Jagger took my arm and soon we were out of the office doorway, facing . . . Dr. De Jong.

"Alice? What are you doing in here?" Dr. De Jong asked, as if I were alone.

She smiled at Jagger.

I shook my head and thought the woman needed a man. Her own man. "I—"

"Alice is horrible at directions, Doc. Sorry. She wandered in here while I was parking the car. You know," Jagger leaned near her, and I knew pheromones were wielding their powers on her thoughts. "I couldn't remember when our next appointment was. Alice insisted it was today."

I stuck my tongue out at him while the doctor couldn't see me. No sense in her thinking I was a spoiled, childish woman.

"It's *next* Wednesday," Dr. De Jong purred.

I wanted to rip her diplomas off the wall. A doctor acting so unprofessional, despite pheromone intoxication, should not be allowed to practice.

Within seconds, Jagger and I were off scot-free and out the door. Safely inside his SUV, I turned to him. "You didn't have to make me sound like such a bimbo airhead, you know. Save that for buxom blondes."

When I'm holding my great grandbabies, I think I'll still remember that devious yet delicious expression on Jagger's face when he looked me up and down—even if I have a full-blown case of dementia.

"What do you mean you won't pay me for my case?" I screeched at Fabio. Then I slammed my fist down on his desk. Papers went flying.

"Look, doll—"

I leaned forward, "*Don't* call me 'doll.' Ever. It's 'Ms. Sokol' or 'Pauline,' to you." My feet were numb, my hands were tingling, but I managed to keep my voice from shaking.

Yes!

"Look, doll . . . Ms. Sokol, I lost a bundle at the crap tables the last few days—"

"Which has nothing to do with me, Fabio, and you know it. I investigated Dr. De Jong's practice and found out her claims are legitimate. She's on the level. You have to pay her clients' claims, *my* fees and that's that."

He reached over and took a dead cigar from the ashtray. When he picked up the lighter, I leaned over farther, but was careful not to give him any thrill if my breasts got too close. "Don't even think about it. I hate smoke."

He flicked the lighter.

I gave him one of those looks that my mother always used on us kids when we were doing something wrong—or even *thinking* about doing something wrong.

While I triumphed over the fact that Fabio had shoved his lighter and unlit dead cigar down on the desk, I thought—Oh . . . my . . . God.

I'd just acted like Mother.

My *mother*.

Eighteen

Fabio finally paid me—not in full(he promised the rest later), but enough to make my payment on the Lexus I not only never drove, but also never even had seen. Sometimes I'd wake up at night and wonder what color it was. Money. The root of all evil, yet necessary.

Rent was still due, so I had to get back to work. Maybe because I wouldn't let Fabio smoke his cigar, he'd said my next case could take a few weeks to have ready for me. He wasn't firing me, more like punishing me in a way I had no control over. Stalling my earnings. That's what he was doing.

Slimy creep.

I couldn't get out of him the reason why my cases had to coincide with Jagger's and whose idea that was, but figured Jagger had some kind of gag order on Fabio—even if he owned the business. Jagger didn't work for Scarpello and Tonelli Insurance Company, but being Jagger, he seemed to have influence wherever he went.

I decided that I had to go help Margaret, despite what Jagger, Goldie, Miles or Spanky said. Yeah, the little doggie had given me a mean look when I told him where I was going, so I bribed him with an extra doggie treat and headed back to the Institute in my own car. Couldn't waste money on a cab.

I parked in the most distant section of the parking lot and made sure no one was around when I got out. This way, no one would question whose car it was. They'd figure it belonged to some visitor.

When I got out, I pressed the button on the key chain Nick had given me and felt a bit down. Too bad it couldn't have been different between Nick and myself. He was a nice guy. Why hadn't there been an attraction there for me?

I started to put the key chain into my pocket, telling myself not to dwell on Nick because then my mind would find some reason to think of Jagger, and then I realized that I couldn't take the keys inside with me.

Surely Spike or someone in charge would confiscate them.

Shoot. I looked around the grounds. Empty.

I started to walk around the parking lot, trying to think of what I could do with my keys. Hide them. The thought struck me, and while I walked back to my car, I worked the ignition key off the key chain, pocketed it and stuck the chain into the glove compartment. A single key would be much easier to hide and if someone found it, they wouldn't know what it went to.

After locking the car, I headed for a sitting area beneath the leafless trees. No patients would be out in the cool March weather, so I tried to lift the leg of the wrought-iron bench to stick the key under it. No such luck. The bench weighed more than me and there was still ice on the ground.

In the center of the sitting area was a lily pond complete with a naked statue of a little Cupid that peed water into the pond when turned on in the summer. He held a bow and arrow, and I leaned over the water to tuck the key safely in the crook of Cupid's arm. I had to shove a bit so that a strong wind wouldn't shake it free.

It had to be a good omen that Miles's clock had two Cupids too.

The evening was starting to darken, so I hurried toward the front entrance. I'd have to think up some excuse why I had been outside, so I told the receptionist that I was lost. She looked at me horrified, as if I was going to harm her. Because I scared her, she didn't interrogate me as to how I got to the lobby. I'm sure she just wanted to get me locked up again.

Within a few minutes I was taken back to the old unit after telling the nuns that I felt it would aid my recovery to get back to the familiarity of my old room. It didn't hurt that I also said if they sent me back to the other ward, I'd find another way to "get lost" again. Soon I was in my old room, dressed in the stylish hospital garb.

Novitiate Lalli came to my door. "Glad to see you back here, Mary Louise."

I'll just bet you are. "Pauline. Call me Pauline." I plopped down on my bed, feeling the taser bracelet press into my skin. For a second I felt a bit tempted to taser the insincere novice's butt.

Sure, not a Christian attitude, but she bugged me.

Feeling very bold, I asked, "Why did Margaret move?"

Novitiate Lalli's eyebrows wrinkled. "How did you know she moved?"

Eek. Good question. "Well, she's not here, is she? She's here, then not here. Then she's moved. Then she's here. Then she's . . . who knows where?" I decided to use some psych-patient jargon and maybe confuse her. I was certainly getting confused myself.

Novitiate Lalli blinked. "That doesn't mean that we moved her. She could have gone home, you know."

I got stuck on the "we" part. Lalli had made it sound as if she was involved in something.

"Where did *we* move her to?"

"I didn't say that she moved, *Pauline*."

What an un–nunlike tone she had used on my name. I don't think Novitiate Lalli liked me. Damn. I hoped *she* didn't suspect me of knowing something. And here I prided myself on making a good first impression, yet she'd used this attitude with me from day one.

Okay, Pauline, time to shift to Plan B.

I gave her a smile, trying to look as sane as I was. "Please tell me where Margaret is. I really liked her. She has a son, you know."

She touched two fingers to her chin.

Wow. A nun with a French manicure. That had to be telling in some cosmetic/religious fashion.

Before I could contemplate the nail thing, she said, "I can't discuss other patients with you." She started to turn.

I chuckled. "Come on, Sister Lalli, you know there's a grapevine around here that could make enough jelly to slather on peanut butter sandwiches to feed every kid in the Hartford elementary schools. Might as well just tell me where my friend is and why she's not here anymore, since I'll find out soon anyway." If any of these whackos gets a moment of sanity, maybe that statement could actually be true. The grapevine part was indeed true, but most of the rumors were figments of the other patients' imaginations.

And what rumors they came up with.

If you don't eat your meal, the staff will tie your tongue with special tape and feed you next time. If you talk to yourself, you will not get dessert. (This one was not enforced as far as I could tell, probably due to the overwhelming number of self-talkers.) And if you didn't turn your lights out at the correct time, the sleep fairy wouldn't come. Her, I didn't want in my room. I knew she'd scare me to death.

Novitiate Lalli looked at me.

Paging Meryl Streep, I thought, then went into dramatic action. I sniffled, wiped at my eyes and started to talk more about Margaret's little boy. Not knowing that much about him, I drew on past remembrances of my nephew Wally. My face contorted in concern mixed with a tad of pain until Novitiate Lalli glared at me and . . . her face softened.

"Margaret is on Ward 171. She was moved because . . . well, she was causing trouble here." Lalli turned and started to leave.

"Wait!" I reached out then, realizing grabbing a nun, even a novitiate was frowned upon, I calmed my voice and said, "Trouble? Margaret? You know she was very cooperative and even a bit shy." I forced a huge smile. "Come on, Sister Lalli. Margaret wasn't trouble."

She stared at me a few minutes then said, "I'll be back with Sister Barbara Immaculatta to give you your medication."

Novitiate Lalli had pulled a chameleon transformation—much like ol' Ter had.

I dressed and got ready for breakfast after a very peaceful night's sleep. Being back and not having to worry about death and Terry calmed me enough to really get some rest. Despite the fact that Jagger wasn't around, I felt very good today. Positive. Had that "I can do it" attitude.

So I made my way to the dining hall and looked around

the room. Whom should I target today? Ruby sat eating by herself, as usual. She glared at me through squinty eyes. Wow. Someone woke up on the wrong side of the manacles.

Miss Myra sat talking to herself. I hadn't seen her around much lately, but patients came and went and were moved to other wards depending on the types of care they needed.

Behind her sat Jackie Dee, and I knew my appetite couldn't take her coiffure snacks this early in the day. I really missed seeing Margaret . . . Oh . . . my . . . gosh!

Margaret was *back*.

She sat at a table near the window, eating and not talking. Bingo. I made my way over there, despite a few patients mumbling something about my having had some fun with Terry before he croaked. I kept silent and shook my head, hoping they really didn't believe that Terry and I had been having sex when he died. I wanted to shout, "We were fully clothed when you all saw us, you morons!" but there was that frowning-on-outbursts thing around here.

Having sex with Terry. Yuck.

That I could not handle.

I got into the line near where Margaret sat and took my oatmeal, skim milk, tea and wheat toast with a packet of butter. When I neared her, I asked, "Margaret, may I join you?"

She kept eating.

"Margaret. Everything all right?"

In robotic motions, she lifted her coffee cup, took a sip and didn't even look at me over the rim.

Damn. Maybe they'd zapped Margaret's brain to cause her to forget. Forget where she belonged. Forget that she sure didn't belong here. And forget her family, her son.

I sat down without an invitation, jiggled my green tea bag in the lukewarm water—that was so patients wouldn't harm each other by throwing hot water—and leaned near her. "Margaret. It's me, Pauline. I'm back to help you."

I noticed a twitch in her lip as if she were trying to speak. I eased my hand over and felt for Margaret's pulse. Bradycardia. Her heartbeat was slower than my Uncle Walt trying to walk around the block.

Margaret must have been highly medicated.

Thank goodness, I thought. That had to be better than the long-term effects of brain shocking. At least the meds would wear off and I'd be able to talk to her eventually.

After breakfast, I shadowed Margaret for the rest of the day. When I'd see Sister Barbie, with her little Novitiate Lalli shadow in tow, I gently took Margaret's arm and walked her in the other direction. We managed to avoid the medication cart for now.

And Margaret's glassy stare was subsiding.

I walked to the western section of the unit where there was a dayroom without a television. Subsequently, it wasn't the most popular place on the unit. A few older gentlemen sat staring at each other, in some form of nonverbal communication, I guessed. All three wore red pajamas.

A young woman sat talking to her doll—Career Barbie. I recognized her from the "Terry incident." She had shaken Barbie at us.

A teenage boy slept on the couch while sitting upright, and I wondered if he wasn't a drug patient. His hair was spiked out in blue threads and rings of silver hung from most features of his face. He snored softly, and I felt saddened that someone with so much to live for would be hidden away here in sleep—while his life passed him by.

"Let's sit by the window, Margaret. The sun is nice and

bright today. You can even see new buds on the trees. Soon spring will green up the depressing sight."

She turned to me. "I'm the depressing sight around here."

My eyes burned with tears, and I told myself I had to suck it up and avoid emotions if I was to try and help Margaret. "No, you're not. Did they give you a lot of medication?" I eased her down by the arm.

Margaret sat in silence, looking out the window. Maybe a layperson had no idea how much medication they received around here. For me I knew one green pill was way too much.

She turned toward me. "I think . . . so."

I'd almost forgotten the question, but I took in a breath and said, "Well, I think it's wearing off. You are looking perkier."

A faint smile crossed her lips, and she touched my hand. "Thank you."

I figured that was for the picture of her son or maybe for trying to help. Either way I winked at her. "Do you know why they moved you?"

Our voices, although in a whisper, filled the nearly empty dayroom. It was difficult to keep them down enough and yet still hear each other, since the woman with the doll kept talking louder and hollering to her doll, "Just wait until you have dollies of your own! You just wait, young lady. I hope I'm around to see the day and see them treat you like you treat me."

Margaret and I smiled at each other and she said, "No, Pauline—" She yawned.

I hoped she could remember something.

"—I don't know why."

Shoot. "Then just tell me what happened."

She nodded. "I was sleeping. It was in the middle of

the night as far as I could tell. The next thing I knew, the night orderly—Vinny, I think his name was—came into my room and started gathering up my things. Oh, he was nice about it . . ."

She drifted off, as if in thought, as she once again looked out the window.

"Margaret?" I said softly.

She remained still and yawned a few more times.

Damn. I was losing her, and to make matters worse, the woman with the doll was getting rowdier. She had its head in one hand and was about to yank. I knew the staff would be descending on the dayroom any second. One of the red-pajama men told her to cut it out, which helped for a few minutes.

Although not a touchy-feely kinda gal, I reached out and rested my hand on Margaret's arm. "Please, Margaret. Come back for a minute. What did Vinny do?"

Slowly as if half asleep, she said, "He . . . took it all and my hand. The picture fell . . ." She pulled free and touched against her heart.

I imagined she'd hidden her son's picture there securely in the pocket.

"Yes, go on."

She let out a loud sigh. "I cried that I wanted to get the picture, but a nun was standing in the doorway and ordered him to get moving."

Great! A nun!

"Which one?"

"There's only one doorway to the room, Pauline."

Damn. Confusion was not what I wanted to hear. "No, Margaret. I mean what nun? What nun stood in the doorway the night they moved you and ordered Vinny to hurry?"

Suddenly the ward erupted into chaos. Several staff

members hurried down the hallway. While trying to pull the info out of Margaret, I hadn't noticed that Doll Lady and one of the men in the red pj's had started a ruckus. They hollered at each other. Spike shouted for them to quiet down, and then the doll's head flew through the air, smacking one of the men in red pj's in the cheek and causing a huge welt. If it were December, the color would have been perfect with his outfit.

I quickly turned to Margaret. "Which nun? Which nun was there when you were moved?"

Sister Barbie came walking toward us, followed by Novitiate Lalli, Sister Liz, two other nuns whose names I didn't know and Nurse Lawson. Damn. Busted.

"Margaret, time for your meds," the nurse said.

I grabbed Margaret's shoulder. "Which nun?" I whispered.

She looked from them to me and mumbled, "The tall one."

I swung around. Except for Sister Liz, everyone else in black was about the same height.

Nineteen

Margaret had said the "tall" nun had been there the night Margaret was removed from her room, and up until now, I never realized how many tall nuns there were around here. Damn.

Not much to go on. But I did figure that whoever the nun was must have known something. Something like why Margaret had to be moved from this ward. Talking too much about not belonging here? Then again, if that were the case, she'd probably do the same on the new ward. What was the difference? And why was she moved back to the old ward?

I scurried back to my room before they somehow caught and medicated me. Had to keep a clear head since I was Jagger-less. My heart fluttered. More from safety concern than from the usual Jagger lust. I wondered if I'd made a mistake in not convincing him to join me.

I touched the taser bracelet. Okay, I had that security weapon and, as evidenced by Terry, it worked. Then a frightening thought struck. If it had killed Terry because of his being on a certain medication, wouldn't it do the same to just about *every* patient in here? Suddenly the taser bracelet wasn't such a good idea. I sure didn't want to kill anyone else. As a matter of fact, I'd have to be really careful when I got close to them.

Jagger would say stop thinking like a nurse—but it was in my blood. Once you are a nurse, you are a nurse all your life.

The bracelet could be dangerous to some sick patient who might threaten me. But if the suspects were members of the staff, as I thought, I wouldn't hesitate to incapacitate any one of them.

For several hours I practiced Jagger's moves, thinking they would be my best and safest defense. Luckily no one had come into my room. I hoped Sister Barbie had gotten too busy and had forgotten my medication. But as a nurse, I knew that wasn't possible. She'd be at my door soon, and I'd have to exercise my tongue in addition to the rest of my body, which, by the way, had been getting a super workout from the defense moves.

I flopped on the bed and wondered more about why they had moved Margaret back there—so soon after I'd mentioned it to Novitiate Lalli. Had Lalli said something to whomever was in on the fraud? Had she talked to whomever was in charge, and gotten them to let Margaret come back because I missed her and she thought it might help Margaret and I get better? Be well enough to leave?

Or had Novitiate Lalli gotten Margaret moved back to avoid any more of my snooping, my suspicions? Or to send me a message—that someone was in control?

Maybe she figured if Margaret came back, I wouldn't have to try and find out anything else. Margaret and I could commiserate together, and no one would believe us.

I shut my eyes and tried to think of what was the best, most logical answer.

"Medication time, Pauline," Sister Barbie said, startling me.

My eyes flew open. I sprang into a sitting position. Yikes. My head spun inside. "Oh. Hey. Thanks." Get ready for action, Ms. Tongue.

Directly behind Sister Barbie was, you guessed it, Novitiate Lalli with her flashlight in hand.

Okay, I told myself, you can do this. Jagger taught you well and you've done it before. So, I took the Green Demon, gave an insincere smile to both women and shoved it in my mouth. With the little maneuver going, I opened for the flashlight beam.

Sister Barbie sneezed, blowing a gust of warm air into my face.

My reflex was to instantly inhale on a gasp—and the pill shot down my throat.

I tried to cough it up and even hurried to the bathroom, saying I had to go, when I, in fact, planned to stick my finger down my throat until the pill came back.

Novitiate Lalli was fast on my heels. "Don't even think about spitting the medication back up, Pauline."

I felt her staring at me and realized it was futile. She was either a real bitch or a damn good psych nursing student—or a criminal.

As I started to feel weak and sleepy, I went with the criminal part—merely out of principle.

The rain forest appeared in my hospital room once more. I tried to ignore it and think clearly, but the damn frogs or toads hopped about, making a racket with the other creatures.

My inclination was to lie there and watch the entertainment, but in the deepest recesses of my mind, I knew I had to keep my wits about me, no matter how drugged I was.

Lives were at stake, and some were already snuffed out.

It wasn't easy to fight the sleep that had my eyelids weighing a gazillion tons and threatening to shut at any second. I told myself to get up, do some exercises, fight the Green Demon, but my body felt as if I'd just gotten a spinal gone bad. Felt as if it had paralyzed my entire body. No extremity would cooperate and move.

The nuns, as far as my foggy brain could remember, had partially shut the door when they'd left. I figured they thought I'd fall asleep and not cause any trouble. Suddenly, it started to open.

I could only lie there and watch.

Amid the greenery of the rain forest, the frogs jumping and butterflies the size of fighter jets flying about, a figure walked in once again.

I lay in my bed, watching the figure, which was carrying something, move about my room. Talk about déjà vu. Geez. There really was no privacy in this place.

But this time I refused to give in to the confusion that the drug tried to shroud my mind with. No easy feat, but I knew that when I took a Sine-off for my hay fever and lay down, I'd fall asleep, and if I kept active, I wouldn't feel the drowsiness. At least I was able to remember stuff like that. I thought that my battle with the Green Demon was working. I was winning. I sucked in some air and struggled with my brain, screaming to stay focused and also screaming to my limbs to move.

My left leg lifted into the air. I wasn't sure if that's what I had planned it to do, but at least it was a start.

The figure opened the top drawer and started to poke around.

Not again! How many times was I going to have to rearrange my undies?

Good. I was thinking. Getting perturbed. My arms

moved to the side, and I grabbed onto the railing that was down but close enough to the mattress so that I could reach it and sit up . . . very quietly. I swatted away a butterfly and stood up on shaky legs. Kicking away three frogs, I slid my feet along the floor, all the while holding on so I wouldn't collapse into the greenery of ferns.

Getting close enough, I reached out to grab the figure but had misjudged the distance. Damn the Green Demon.

The figure spun around. I couldn't see who it was—only that it was dressed all in black. Before I could reach it, a long object swung out, smacking me right in the forehead.

Then I realized the supposedly lush green of the rain forest ground was as hard as the linoleum of my room.

"Pauline? Pauline?"

Pain shot up my spine while I listened to the voice. Sounded familiar. Female. Hmm. Not sure who it was, but I was sure that I didn't care. My body ached too damn much!

After the voice called my name a few more times and kept asking if I was all right, I opened my eyes to find myself lying on my back. The figure that stood above me was rather cloudy-looking but did, in fact, look familiar.

My vision started to clear. "Oh, hey. How are you, Margaret?"

She looked concerned. I ran my hand along the back of my head, half expecting some sticky, bloody mess, since now I remembered landing on my back on the floor.

Guess the good old lessons I was taught in high-school basketball had paid off. Ms. Franklin, the gym teacher, had always said to hold our head up when we fell.

Margaret touched my arm, and I recognized that I was

in my bed. No rain forest scenery. My mind, despite the pain, was much clearer.

"They drugged me again, Margaret," I moaned. "How . . . what are you doing here?"

She sat on the edge of the bed and ran a damp facecloth over my forehead. Actually felt nice, comforting. "I found you on the floor. You must have slipped when trying to go to the bathroom. I started to call for help, but you grabbed my arm and insisted I didn't so I helped you into bed instead."

Hmm. I didn't remember that part, but felt damn good that my drug-induced self had the foresight not to report this to the staff. "Oh, right. Yeah. You shouldn't be in here though. But thanks for helping me."

She looked me straight in the eye. "You didn't fall, Pauline. Did you?"

I gently patted her arm and sat up despite a tornado of pain slamming into my back. "What did you see? Anyone? In black?"

She shook her head. "You were only on the floor. No one was around. No nuns."

"In the hallway. Did you see—" I winced and decided to ease myself down. "Ouch. Did you see anyone in the hallway? Think."

"There were lots of people. The staff, patients. It's lunchtime, so everyone was walking toward the dining room."

"Oh, great. No one with a . . . broom?"

The scary thought hit me.

The attacker had smacked me with a broom. The metal handle part. Just like the one that had been stabbed into Vito and like the one found in my bathroom.

Margaret shook her head. "No, Pauline. No one—"

She paused. "Wait a minute. I saw someone sweeping the hallway when I came to get you."

I sat upright and grabbed her by the shoulders despite my muscles shouting at me. "You did? You saw someone with a broom?"

"Or a mop. Not sure. Why is that so important?"

"I . . . that's what they hit me with." I reached up to my forehead and pushed the hair to the side. Ouch! An egg-sized bump sat on my forehead above my left eyebrow. Thank goodness my Polish skin must be thick, since the force didn't split it open—only knocked me over. And good thing my bangs hid the bump so the staff wouldn't notice.

If there weren't so many people and commotion out in the hallway, maybe the broom handle would have been stuck into . . .

I couldn't go there. Not productive to my working this case. I asked Margaret a few more questions, but unfortunately her medication still had her a bit up in the clouds. She was now certain the person sweeping was a janitor named Bob, and she really hadn't seen anything else. Damn. Janitors wore brown. A chocolate shade that couldn't be confused with black like the nuns wore. Besides, the nuns wore habits, not pants. If Margaret was remembering correctly, that wasn't of any use to me.

But I might be dead right now if it weren't lunchtime.

After I washed up a bit and splashed enough cool water onto my face to at least reverse some of the effects of the Green Demon, Margaret and I headed to lunch.

The dining room was in its usual chaotic, chatty state. No one looked suspicious and no one had on all black like the intruder had worn. Besides, many of the patients looked as if they belonged here.

Margaret and I got our sandwiches on white bread—no health-conscious nutritionists in the bunch—and headed to find seats.

"Over here," Jackie Dee called out.

Margaret and I looked at each other. I felt sorry for Jackie but really didn't enjoy my meals when I sat with her. Actually, that's why I never sat with her. Still, she seemed like a nice girl, even though she must have had some whopper of a problem to eat her own hair. Jackie called out a few more times since very few patients ever wanted to sit near her at meals. "It's fine with me," I said to Margaret.

We headed to sit near Jackie Dee.

Margaret settled on the opposite side of the table, with me next to Jackie. I figured if she snatched a strand of blonde, I could stare at Margaret while I finished my lunch. Actually, my body hurt from the fall, so I really didn't have much of an appetite. I took my cold drink of water and held the plastic cup to my forehead.

Jackie stared at me.

Oh, boy. She probably figured that my gesture had something to do with eating silken locks. I turned to her. "Sinus headache today. Say, Jackie Dee, your room is across from mine. Did you see anyone come out of it, oh, a little while before lunch?"

She shook her head.

"Then did you see anyone come out of my room all day? Even just in the morning? Maybe one of the staff? In black. One of the nuns, I mean."

Seemed my questions were a bit much for Jackie Dee. She set down her fork and reached for her bangs. Before I knew it, she had a handful of hair in her fist and had yanked. Then she stuck some into her mouth.

I turned away but heard her soothing herself and felt

horrible that I'd caused her to relapse. By the looks of her hairdo, it'd been days since she'd pulled out a snack.

"Pauline."

I ignored Jackie and looked at Margaret. She gestured with her head toward the door. I swung around to see the nuns standing there with Nurse Lawson and Nurse Lindeman. It wasn't unusual for all the staff to come and watch the patients while they ate. For a few seconds, I thought they were all staring at *me*. Then Sister Barbie came toward my table.

Yikes!

Twenty

I tried to nonchalantly munch on my tuna sandwich as Sister Barbara Immaculatta came forward. She didn't look all that pleased. I quickly made sure my bangs covered my bump.

When she got near my seat, she gave me a cold stare and said, "Stop that. Stop that!"

I dropped my sandwich onto my plate, causing a spoon to knock my glass of cold water over in a splash—which landed on the dish of the gentleman who sat next to me, soaking his sandwich.

Between his curses and several patients' laughing, Sister Barbie continued hollering until I shouted, "Stop *what*?"

The room grew silent.

Everyone looked at me.

Margaret mouthed, "She was talking to Jackie Dee."

And my face burned so that I thought my white bread would soon be toast.

"Pauline, please do not cause a ruckus around here," Sister Barbara ordered. "Unless you want the wet packs." Then she stood over Jackie Dee. "You were doing so well, my child. Don't give into the temptation. Do not give into the evil that causes such destructive behavior."

I could only sit and listen. The nun sounded like some television evangelical minister preaching to the masses. At first I wasn't sure if it was good nursing or bad. But when I turned to look at Jackie Dee, she had taken her handful of hair from her mouth and set it on the dish.

Yep. My appetite was done for it now.

Sister Liz came forward in her usual perky manner and waved her hand about like a Disney fairy godmother. "Everyone go back to eating their meal. Go ahead." One more wave and the room settled down to its usual roar.

But at least everyone else was eating.

I figured this was a waste of my time so I gathered up my tray and said to Margaret, "I'll meet you in the dayroom."

She had resumed finishing her egg-salad sandwich, and I figured she really *had* been here too long. When I stood, Jackie Dee tugged on my johnny coat. I turned to look at her.

"I'm done here, Jackie. Please let go."

She looked so very sad while she released her hold. "Ruby," she said and eyed the tuft of hair on her dish.

I wanted to bolt out of there before she seized it and munched, but suddenly it dawned on me what she'd said. "Ruby? Ruby was . . . you saw Ruby come out of my room before lunch?"

"Big deal, bitch."

I turned around to see Ruby standing there glaring at Jackie Dee. "Eat it. Go ahead, you whacko."

"Leave her alone, Ruby."

She cursed at me.

"Why were you in my room?" I asked.

She curled her lips in a typical teen fashion and said, "I . . . had come to get you for lunch."

I wanted to call her bluff, then looked down at her. She had on black slacks. Ruby had always worn jeans. *Blue* jeans. Beneath her johnny coat was—a black turtleneck.

Oh . . . my . . . gosh.

I stuck my tray on the conveyor belt and hurried after Ruby. I decided to stay a few feet behind so as not to let her know that I was following her.

Ruby?

Could Ruby have whacked me? Did she have anything to do with Terry killing Vito? Or did Terry really kill Vito? Of course he did. He'd just about admitted so. And how well did Ruby know Terry? When you ask someone "How's it hanging?" I'm guessing you know them pretty well. Then again, Ruby could have been teasing him. She aggravated and teased plenty of the sick patients around here.

Ruby had headed down the hallway toward the dayroom without the television. But before she got there she turned into her room. Damn. I huddled in the alcove near the nurses' station to wait and see if she came out.

Several minutes passed and no Ruby. I noticed Margaret walk from the dining room and head down the hallway. I waved for her to come over. "Did you see that Ruby had on black slacks? She never wears black slacks."

Margaret seemed to contemplate Ruby's wardrobe. "No, I've always seen her in jeans. Did you ask her about them?"

I grimaced and figured I might be loading too much info on a layperson like Margaret. After all, she was a Southern housewife and mother, not some PI. "No, let's not say any—"

Nurse Lawson came down the hallway, gave us a look and went into Ruby's room. Before I knew it, Ruby was coming out—with her suitcase!

The nurse turned to her, "Say goodbye to the other patients, Ruby."

I wanted to melt into the alcove, but Ruby turned around with the most devious look in her eyes and said, "*Goodbye*, Pauline."

That speedboat of chills maneuvered up my spine again.

When Ruby and Nurse Lawson disappeared from the unit, I leaned against the wall and sighed.

"How nice that Ruby is getting out. I guess she is all cured," Margaret said.

I could only sigh again and think that was good news for me too. With Ruby gone, I was safer—until I realized we didn't know who had put her up to attacking me. Of course she could have done it on her own, but I doubted that. In my gut I knew someone must have influenced Ruby. She had no reason to attack me otherwise.

I sat in the quiet dayroom after Margaret decided to go take a nap. Her medication must have made her sleepy. My Green Demon's effects had been overridden by my astonishment. Ruby had to have been the one to attack me. But why?

I needed some outside help.

When I saw the Doll Lady come by with a brown ripped teddy bear, I hurried out of the dayroom to the nurses' station. Sister Liz was on the phone. Nurse Lawson was charting and Novitiate Lalli was writing on what looked like the medication records.

Sister Liz it was.

I made my way over to her side of the desk and waited by the glass window until she looked up. Finally she did and said, "Hello, Pauline. What can I do for you?"

"I need to talk to my doctor. I'm feeling very—" I had

to choose my words carefully in this place. One mention or hint of suicide could have me on constant watch. "Well, you know, Sister, I just need to talk to him."

She looked as if she was trying to find his number, and I said a silent prayer to Saint Theresa that Jagger/Dr. Dick was still listed as my doc. Please. Praying to a saint with a nun as an interceptor had to garner extra points. In a few minutes, Sister Liz was sliding the glass window to the side. "Please be brief, Pauline. We can't tie up this line before . . . Sister Barbara returns."

I smiled at her, knowing that Sister Barbara would more than likely not let me talk on the phone. I pulled the receiver close to my ear and said, "Dr. Plummer, I need some help."

Silence.

I half expected to hear the dial tone at any minute.

Instead, I shut my eyes a second when Jagger's voice said, "What do you need?"

No argument. No lecture.

Of course, he knew I was probably standing in front of some staff here and didn't want to risk my getting caught. I was also quite sure, however, that the next time I saw him in person, he'd let me have it.

I whispered to him to find out about Ruby and how she had gotten released. I was certain she would have been here much longer by the sounds of things when I first met her.

I knew Jagger had nodded and then hung up.

What I didn't know was that within a few minutes, Dr. Plummer would summon me to the examination room. My escort, Spike, seemed to take pleasure in bringing me down there as if he thought I was going to get zapped again.

When Spike walked out, Jagger turned around. "Ruby was released early. Two months early." He leaned against the wall and for a few seconds I thought, *Great, this is going to be business as usual.*

Then Jagger came closer. "What the hell were you thinking, Pauline?"

I could barely think when he used my real name. "Well, I had to . . . Margaret is back on this unit. They moved her back right after I questioned Novitiate Lalli as to where Margaret was and why she was moved." Damn, I sounded as if I really did know what I was talking about.

I didn't let him say anything but waved my hand like Sister Liz and told him all about my theories, what I'd found out and my attack earlier that day.

Before I could go on, he moved closer, gently eased my bangs to the side and cursed—but not at me. He let go and looked as if about to ask a question.

"I'm fine. Just fine. So, by moving Margaret back, and taking Ruby away, I think someone is trying to tell me something. Something like *they* are in charge."

Jagger remained silent.

I assumed he was upset and needed to compose himself. In a few minutes, he grabbed the rolling doctor's stool with his foot, sat and said, "I'm going to assume you and your skills were the reason you didn't get killed this morning, and not some dumb twist of fate. That you used your skills, what I taught you, and your brain."

I nodded since I knew anything I said would be a lie. I found I could lie with body movements better than with words.

Jagger then proceeded to review the case with me—no more mention of my coming back—or leaving anytime soon.

"So this means I get to stay?" I asked, smiling.

He looked at me.

"Come on, Jagger. You know we . . . I need to be here. To do this for Margaret and anyone else involved."

Jagger rolled his stool toward the wall and leaned back. "You're on probation, Sherlock."

I straightened up in a flash as if that would give more credence to my words. "Fabio let me off probation—"

Jagger leaned near. His nose barely touched mine. I felt his warm breath on my right cheek. "*My* probation, Pauline. *My* probation."

I looked at him. "Fine. Your stinking probation." I didn't want him to think he'd gotten one over on me. "But, Jag, this is the last time I take a nursing job. If you want my help, you'll have to ask for it as an *investigator*."

I know I'll always wonder what that look on Jagger's face meant—because I sure didn't think it was agreement.

Jagger had left me with the "order" to find out if there were any other patients here that didn't belong—who could have been kidnapped, admitted and had their insurance cards stolen.

Ha. No easy feat.

Half the chameleons around here looked sane one minute but in the next instant were tearing off dolls' heads or carrying on conversations with Napoleon. Still, it was a good idea, and I had agreed to get to work on it.

So I headed out to the dayroom with the television set, the hub of Psych Ward 200.

While Oprah talked to actor Johnny Depp about a newly released movie, I sighed a few times in honor of Johnny and sat myself down on the couch, ready to study this gang.

Sometimes my job was really easy.

Talking to Johnny from her seat on the dayroom's re-

cliner was Suzanne, a wannabe actress. She'd corrected
me several times that her name was pronounced, "Su-
zonne" with a French accent. Then she argued with
Johnny about why he got movie contracts and she didn't.
Ha. Ruby had told me once that Suzanne had played in
local high school productions and a few bit parts at the
off-Broadway theater, the Shubert, in New Haven. Now
she worked at a fast-food restaurant to pay her bills and
had started to smoke pot to fight depression, not to mention that she argued with stars on television.

Conclusion: Suzanne belonged here.

Next to me on the couch was the Doll Lady, who was
snoozing with a stuffed rag doll tucked beneath her arm.
No one would believe that only yesterday she was a doll
decapitator.

Belonged here.

My gaze spun past three men in their red pj's who were
all sitting in a catatonic state and were well into their sev-
enties. I figured they belonged in a nursing home rather
than here, but must come from money, and maybe kids
who put them here. What they most likely needed was
loving family members—and had greedy heirs instead.

Didn't belong here, but weren't hijacked either.

"Is anyone sitting here?" a deep, male voice with a
slight French accent asked.

My female instincts perked up and I turned to see a
damn good looking, dark, swarthy guy—in navy silk pj's
with a navy silken robe and Italian leather loafers on.

Wow. I sure hoped *he* didn't belong here.

Suddenly I was beginning to like the policy of patients
wearing their pj's. I knew it was so they couldn't escape,
but damn, some looked real good in them.

"No. Have a seat." I inhaled some very expensive

cologne. It had to be expensive because everything about this guy dripped money, and it didn't smell like anything any of my male relatives wore. Then again, this guy could be a poverty-stricken chameleon.

He held out his hand before sitting. "Mason Dubois."

I scanned the room to see none of the staff was watching, shook his hand and said, "Dubois. Sounds French. I have a dear friend who is French Canadian." For a second I missed Adele and the gang terribly, but told myself I'd be out of here real soon.

"Cajun French." He sat down with the grace of a dancer.

My eyes widened. "Cajun French, as in from the South?"

"New Orleans."

My mouth went dry. *New Orleans.* If this guy was "recruited" here by the same sleaze that kidnapped Margaret, we could have something soon. "Oh. New Orleans. Small world."

"Have you been there, *mademoiselle*?"

The accent and the looks sidetracked my mind. *Mademoiselle*? How cute. How European. How *sexy*.

Suddenly I hoped this guy wasn't a nutcase. He appeared to be too suave to be a real patient.

"The name's Pauline. You know, Mason, I haven't seen you around here before." *And you stick out like a swarthy sore thumb.*

His eyes darkened. More like anger than sadness. "I only just arrived."

Hmm. We needed to talk. I looked around and saw Nurse Lawson approaching. Didn't the woman ever have a day off? She walked to the Doll Lady and checked her pulse. Geez. Had she gone to that big dollhouse in the sky while I sat here?

Evidently not, since Lawson smiled at Mason and went

back to the nurses' station, where several nuns worked. Spike was on his perch at the end of the dayroom, glaring at me. I nodded and smiled. No reaction. Good. At least he didn't come slap me upside the head.

"Pauline? I asked you if you'd been to New Orleans."

"Hmm? Oh, no. But a friend . . . another patient from here has. Well, she lives there. Margaret Seabright. Do you know the New Orleans Seabrights?"

"I've heard the name, but no, not personally." He looked around the room and shook his head. "How sad."

I nodded and my gut said Mason Dubois did not belong here.

Spike was coming toward us.

I motioned for Mason to watch the television.

"Everything all right here, Pauline?"

"Why wouldn't it be? We are watching Johnny Depp, for crying out loud."

Mason chuckled.

Spike glared at me.

I grabbed the arm of the couch in case he got the idea to lift me up and shake me like the Raggedy Ann doll that Doll Lady held and was now twisting its head around and around. Must have had a bad daydream.

"Everything is fine," Mason reiterated.

Spike turned and over his shoulder said, "Better be. Don't annoy the new patient, Pauline."

Well! I could have given him a good piece of my mind, but knew my place here and wasn't in a "wet sheet" sort of mood. I turned to Mason. "Don't pay any attention to him. He's a bully."

Mason looked at me as if I were the Doll Lady. Oh, no! He wouldn't confide in me if he thought I'd flown over the cuckoo's nest.

I had to gain his confidence to investigate more. So I

decided to tell him the daily schedule of Ward 200 in case he hadn't heard it. Then he seemed to be paying attention, so I looked around to see Spike embroiled in a conversation with Nurse Lindeman. I made my move.

"Mason, what brings you here?"

He hesitated, but I could tell he was dying to say something. Did it have to do with fraud? For a few seconds he remained silent. Smart man not to trust another psych patient. I gave him extra points.

"Look, I don't belong here," I said, then followed his gaze up and down my outfit. "Oh. Don't let appearances fool you. The policy is that they take all your stuff around here to keep you safe." I waved my hand. "Not that I'm not safe with my stuff."

Now he looked confused. How to convince him?

"Mason, I am . . . not who you think I am."

His eyebrows rose and I could tell I was losing him, and no wonder. I was beginning to sound as if I not only belonged here, but should put up a shingle naming it my permanent residence.

I took in a breath and let it out slowly.

Then I told him a little about Margaret, her family, where her house was and how she got here.

Mason's interest peaked.

"Did you come here in a white van?"

"I flew from New Orleans, and, yes, a white van picked me up at Bradley International Airport."

I nodded. "So did Margaret."

Finally he said, "My ex-wife caused me a great deal of pain. Left me. I was totally unaware, and she did it with a note on the refrigerator. We were going to start a family soon."

Wow. How cold. "I'm sorry."

He nodded. "When Francine left, I was very down.

You know, Pauline, it really wasn't from her leaving, but more the prospect of not being able to have a child. I love children."

My biological clock alarm sounded.

What a guy. Good-looking. Money. Nice. And *wants* kids. I was ready to sign us both out and put a down payment on a house with a white picket fence.

"I have several nieces and nephews."

He smiled at me, gently. "No children of your own?"

"No husband of my own." Then I stuck up my hand. "No one else's husband either!"

Mason laughed. "So, I called my travel agent, a new one, mind you. Arnold, my regular agent, had recently retired and moved to his cottage on the Gulf. So, this new agent, whose name I will not mention, suggested I come to a resort in New England. I needed a change of scenery and climate. I could rest, relax, forget my problems and play tennis . . . indoors."

Mesmerized by Mason, I muttered, "We have Ping Pong on the unit."

His laughter yanked me out of my cloud.

"So, you didn't know you were coming to a psychiatric hospital?"

He looked insulted. "No, *mademoiselle*."

"Did they . . . do you have very good coverage for mental health? Insurance coverage that is."

"Excellent."

"Mason, you don't belong here, and *I* can help you."

He leaned over and took my hand, bent and kissed it.

When I looked up in a tizzy, behind Mason stood . . . Dr. Dick.

Twenty-one

Great. There I was, making . . . er . . . making progress in my case with Mason, and Dr. Dick had to show up.

And he didn't look all that friendly.

"Doctor, this is Mason. He's from New Orleans—"

"It's time for your treatment, Pauline." Jagger glared at me and ignored Mason.

I started to stand. Jagger took my arm. Behind him I could see Spike starting to get up. Geez. I stood and smiled. "Fine. Fine. I'm all set." I turned back to see Mason, looking at me as if I would make a perfect nutty snack for any squirrel.

Once inside the examining room, I yanked free of Jagger. "What the hell are you doing?"

"Saving you, Pauline."

I rubbed my arm where he'd held me, although it didn't hurt a bit. He winced. Good. "Don't call me that."

"Okay, Mary Louise."

He didn't even grin.

I pushed past him and sat on the edge of the exam table. "You shouldn't have pulled me away from talking to Mason. I was making progress with him!" I did not need saving.

"More like time," he muttered.

I had to smile to myself.

"I wasn't flirting with Mason."

"No, he was flirting with you. French accent, my foot." He sat on the doctor's rolling stool. It rolled into the wall with a thud.

I think he smacked his head, but ignored it.

"Jagger, Mason Dubois is from New Orleans. Like Margaret—"

"Small world."

"No it isn't. He's been brought here under false pretenses too. He thought he was coming to a resort, but they took his insurance card, airline ticket, and all his stuff. And he has damn good mental-health coverage."

Jagger looked at me. "I'll take you back now."

I smiled. That was enough of an apology from Jagger.

I have to get Margaret and Mason together soon, I thought as I headed toward the dining room. When Jagger had dragged me away from Mason, he looked as if he thought I was a real patient. We had to convince him otherwise. Hopefully there would be something Margaret could say that would get him to open up to us.

Jackie Dee sat at the table near Mason. Damn. I did not want to cause her to relapse again, and she was just nosy enough to listen to everything we said. Margaret was a few seats down. It would look too suspicious if I asked her to move near Mason and we all started whispering. Darn it all, it'd have to wait.

Since I was late and had spent some time surveying the room as usual, the only seat left was next to the Doll

Lady. She was feeding Raggedy Ann a slice of white bread. I only hoped she hadn't buttered it.

So I got my tray of chicken Parmesan and watery Jell-O and sat next to the Doll Lady. That was rude, I told myself. I needed to find out her name. "Hi. I'm Pauline," I said as I sat and opened my napkin.

She kept feeding the doll then she shoved the chunk of bread into her own mouth.

"She's very cute. What's her name?" I took a bite of my white bread.

The Doll Lady watched in horror. "You stole that! Give it back to my baby!" With that she yanked the bread out of my hand, scratching my wrist in the process and causing me to scream, "Ouch!"

I tried to calm myself, but my wrist hurt, the Doll Lady was now swatting me with Raggedy Ann and the room was focused on us. I grabbed my napkin to use it as a shield. A little stuffed, buttery doll leg ripped through it followed by a splash of milk.

By now Spike was upon us, yanking *me* up. "Now it's off to the funny-farm relaxer for you, Pauline." He had me by the scruff of my johnny coat as if I were a kitten. Okay, in some circumstances I wouldn't mind being called "kitten" in a sexy connotation, but this was more derogatory.

While the nurses and nuns shouted for everyone to settle down, Spike yanked me toward the door, and Mason looked at me with a "yeah, right, you don't belong here" look.

Great. The Doll Lady may have just blown my case.

Thank goodness the wet packs were used for calming so as not to have to medicate the person. Okay. I was tickled that I wouldn't have to fight the Green Demon, but being wrapped in wet sheets was not my idea of relaxation.

Give me Cancun with ninety degrees.

"Please," I begged Nurse Lawson and Spike. "Don't do this. I'll behave. Though, I really wasn't misbehaving. The Doll Lady started it!"

"She has a name, Pauline," Spike spat.

"I realize that, but I don't know it. And why don't you like me?"

Nurse Lawson chimed in. "Pauline, Spike does not dislike you, but patients and staff cannot have any interaction . . . you know. Like that."

As if I were romantically interested in King Kong! Damn. This place was getting to me, and where was Jagger? Surely he wouldn't let me get . . .

As was customary, Sister Liz pressed her finger against the side of my face to take my temporal pulse while I lay wrapped mummy-style in a closet of a room. At first my heart rate had sped up and the feeling of claustrophobia couldn't be ignored. I hated elevators. But pretty soon riding one didn't seem so confining. Finally, I started to relax.

Wet packs are surprisingly calming.

I hated to admit it, but they were. Not that I'd want to be swaddled in them again. Maybe it was just the momentary reprieve from Ward 200 and my case. I shut my eyes and felt her fingers pressing lightly.

"Sister?"

"Yes, my child?"

"I . . . I'm feeling much better." I could have bitten my tongue over that one. Made it sound as if I really *needed* this treatment—and I didn't! I'm quite sure I could have calmed myself if—

"What is the woman's name? The one with all the dolls?" I asked.

"Joanna. Joanna Hamilton."

"Oh. Joanna. That's—" I yawned. "—that's nice. I didn't want to hurt her, you know."

Sister remained silent.

Great. I must have fallen down a few notches in her book, not to mention that I'd probably never be able to get any more info out of Mason.

After drying off and being allowed to put my johnny coat and bottoms back on, I decided I needed something from home. The "comforting" experience had me missing everyone. I asked Sister Liz to call my doctor and ask if my "mother" could bring me my own pajamas.

Because now I felt too vulnerable and too patientlike in the hospital garb.

For several hours, I sat in the dayroom looking for Margaret or Mason, until Sister Liz came up to me and said my mother was there.

Goldie!

I followed Sister Liz down the hallway and passed Margaret walking toward the nurses' station. I smiled at her and gave her a wink.

Seemed Margaret had been medicated too heavily to wink back. Damn. But she did, however, seem to recognize me. I'd have to get to her before the next medication time. Somehow I'd have to find out if she got her meds BID, TID or QID (twice a day, three times a day or four times a day). I needed to plan my days around here to get clear heads from whomever I spoke to—within reason.

Sister Liz unlocked the last door to the lobby. Patients were able to meet visitors there and then were ushered into a private room, which was locked—from the outside.

When I saw Goldie sitting there, dressed all in black, it touched my heart. How fitting. He shrieked and jumped up to grab me. On his chest was a plume of peacock feathers, which tickled my cheek.

It felt wonderful.

Next to him sat Miles, dressed in business-casual navy pinstripe and holding our darling Spanky, who jumped from Miles's grasp and ran toward me.

I started to cry as if I really were a patient, and while wiping my eyes reminded myself I could get out of here any second if I wanted to.

But in reality, I had to stay.

"Well, it is nice to meet Pauline's parents," Sister Liz said in a very Christian way. I knew she had to be wondering how they could be my folks and look so young.

Or maybe look so . . . different.

"I'm thrilled to see them," I said and with Spanky tucked under my arm, grabbed Goldie's hand while he held onto Miles with the other.

"Your daughter is a very nice woman," Sister said.

Miles and Goldie looked confused until Goldie's eyes widened. "Our Suga is a doll. She really is. Smart and beautiful." He touched my arm.

"Yes. I pray she returns to you soon."

Sister Liz led us into the visiting room and looked very apologetic when she shut the door and had to lock it.

"Oh . . . my . . . God. Oh, my God!" Goldie screeched again. "You look awful, Suga. Just awful."

I laughed. "Thanks. And here I just had a relaxing treatment of wet packs."

Both of my "parents" shrieked in unison.

Miles took my shoulders, hugged me again, and then held me out to look at me like some long-lost relative. "You don't have to do this, Pauline. You know it's only a case.

You don't get paid enough to get locked up and wrapped up and whatever else up"—he sniffled—"whatever else they do to you around here."

"Oooooooh!" Goldie shouted.

"Guys, I'm fine, and pipe down, or Sister Liz will throw you out and who knows what she'll do to me."

Both glared at me.

"Kidding!" I poked at Miles's chest and winked at Goldie, then hugged Spanky. "Just kidding. Lighten up." I gave them each a few minutes to compose themselves. "How are my folks? Uncle Walt?"

Miles smiled. "All fine. We stop by to see them every day. Jagger had told them you were working a case and they seemed . . . okay with that."

"Thanks for the lie. I know my mother."

"Okay, but your dad and uncle seemed okay."

"Just keep seeing them and make sure they are all right."

Both nodded.

"Did you bring my nightie and robe?"

Goldie held out a shopping bag with a Saks Fifth Avenue label. How Goldie. I knew he didn't have time to shop there today, but it was his favorite store.

"You didn't have to buy anything. I have plenty of nightwear."

Goldie waved a hand. "We couldn't rifle through your intimate apparel, Suga."

I laughed. "Why? It wouldn't be the first time. I've seen you do it!"

"I know, but it's not the same with you not there," Miles said. "With you there it doesn't seem as . . . invasive."

Goldie shook his head. "No, Suga, it wasn't the same . . . We couldn't."

I realized what priceless friends I had.

I touched his arm. "Let's see what you brought, guys."

As if animated, Goldie sprang to life. He lifted out a silken animal-print nightshirt with V-neck plunge and lace trim. "By Natori," Goldie exclaimed.

Yikes. Who the heck was Natori? Beyond my budget, I'm sure. How not to hurt my friend's feelings? But if I wore *that* around here, I'd be attacked by more than a Raggedy Ann doll. "Hm. Gold, that's beautiful, but—"

He looked at Miles and they laughed. Miles said, "That's not for you."

I laughed too. Felt so good. "It'll look gorgeous on you Gold." I rubbed Spanky's ears and wished Sister Liz would forget the time and let us visit indefinitely.

Goldie reached into the bag. "I bought all this on Miles's and my last shopping trip into New York City. This was going to be for your birthday, Pauline, but I found that necklace instead." He grinned.

I had visions of the night the original necklace broke when Nick and I . . . never mind.

"So, do you have anything in that bag that I can wear around here? Some of these folks are . . . different."

Miles looked at Goldie. "Maybe we should take her out of here?"

I shook my head. "No. I'm not going. Here, give me the damn bag." Goldie released it, and I reached in and pulled out a pair of pink-and-beige-checked pajamas. The tag, still on, said Burberry Nova Check, and was labeled $265.00! That was more than my share of the rent. "You guys, these are way too expensive."

"Nothing is too good for our Suga. There's a robe too," Goldie said. He reached over and yanked out a Burberry terry robe and held it toward me. "Our little girl is worth it."

The tag said $220.00.

Between the two, I could have made the Lexus payment and had some cash to spare. Still, I hugged and kissed both of my friends and then whispered, "Thanks. You guys are dreams."

Sister Liz gave us a five-minute warning, so Goldie reviewed a few self-defense moves with me and assured Miles that Jagger would keep an eye on me.

I hugged them both, and the nun ushered out the two.

I stood next to her and waved, muttered to Spanky, then said, "I love you all," and they were gone.

My mother was wrong. Expensive clothes really do make you feel better. Back in my room, I looked down to see myself clad in Burberry and hoped it would make me look saner to Mason.

My visit with my "parents" was fun, touching. I truly needed to get out of there soon.

Determined to finish this case up, I went out of my room and down the hallway. Margaret was in the dayroom, watching reruns of *JAG*. Suddenly I realized I'd called Jagger "Jag" and he didn't blink an eye. I felt a bit closer to him since I'd inadvertently made up a nickname for him.

Jag. I liked it.

"Hey, Margaret." I looked at the clock in the nurses' station. After eight. Her medication had to have peaked by now, and she'd be more coherent.

She looked at me. "Oh, Pauline. I didn't recognize you in that outfit." She yawned. "You look nice. Burberry is one of my favorites."

I remembered that Margaret could probably afford this outfit, which would have taken me weeks to pay for. She held the little picture of her son in her hand. I leaned over and touched her wrist. "Close up your hand so no one sees the picture."

I didn't think they would take a family photo away from the real patients, but whoever knew Margaret didn't belong here more than likely would.

Soon the room emptied except for Joanna, with a Raggedy Andy doll. She didn't even pay any attention to me, and I figured she was very sick and didn't think twice of how she'd accused me of taking Raggedy Ann's bread. Sad. I smiled at her.

She ignored me and crooned something to Andy. Probably about me, the Carb Thief.

Margaret closed her hand tighter around her son's picture. "I'm sorry about what happened to you earlier."

My body stiffened. "It really wasn't as bad as I thought it would be."

She looked at me sadly. "I know."

I patted her hand and wondered how many times they'd wrapped Margaret in the wet sheets—just for speaking the truth. Spike must have been off tonight, because Vinny was sitting at the other end of the room. Much mellower than Spike, Vinny let us talk in a low whisper and didn't seem to mind. He was reading *Sports Illustrated*— the swimsuit edition.

We had plenty of time to talk.

"Margaret, did you meet the new patient, Mason, yet?" I hoped she had and my case could take a giant leap.

She shook her head and held tighter onto her picture. This wasn't a good night for Margaret.

I let out a sigh as I tried to think of what to say next. Getting to the point to get her out of here was first and foremost so I told her about Mason. "From New Orleans. Came in a white van, too, and used a travel agent who was new since his boss retired—"

She turned toward me, a tear in her eye. "Arnold, my husband's friend and our travel agent—retired to his cottage on the Gulf."

Bingo.

Twenty-two

"Tomorrow is Kyle's birthday," Margaret said while I was celebrating the fact that now I knew both she and Mason clearly had been hijacked here against their will for the insurance money.

"I worry that he thinks I'm not coming back to him. My poor baby."

My heart sank.

"I'm so sorry. But you know what, Margaret? I think . . . no, I *know* you will be seeing him very soon. Very soon."

She gave me a look that said she was close to hopeless yet willing to give me one last vote of confidence.

I couldn't let this mother down.

I walked her to her room, where she flopped on the bed. I pulled the covers over her and took her son's picture from her hand. "If it falls when you are asleep, it could go missing." I tucked it under her mattress at her request and patted her on the shoulder. "Good night. I'll see you tomorrow."

When I walked out of the door, making sure that no one saw me coming out, I leaned against the wall and silently cursed whoever was so evil, so money-hungry that they'd separate a mother and child—and commit *murder*.

Thoughts like that made me realize that I was way out of my league sometimes and it was right of Fabio to give me easier cases like Workers' Comp and Dr. De Jong's treatment of teens. I could see that he assigned me cases that coincided with Jagger's so I could learn from him—although I felt certain that Jagger didn't work for Fabio. I was kinda glad the doctor wasn't committing fraud, because right now I needed some belief that humans were inherently good.

Some, however, got sidetracked.

I walked away from Margaret's room and toward the quiet dayroom. I needed to sit and vegetate like a real patient. Today had been a long, difficult day. Too much action for my taste and investigative skills. When I came around the corner, I stopped.

Sitting on the couch a few feet away from the window was Jagger, talking to Mason.

Yikes.

They looked up simultaneously and both smiled.

My female instinct said their smiles came from the same place—noticing me.

Oh . . . my . . . gosh.

I walked toward them and wondered if Jagger had told Mason exactly who he was. Then again, *I* didn't know who Jagger exactly was. And he damn well better not have told someone else—some stranger—first.

Mason jumped up. "You look nice in your outfit, Pauline." His French accent did something to my name that made my heart flutter. Then I looked at Jagger and felt my cheeks burning.

I must be as red as the pj's of the elderly gentleman

who was fast asleep on the loveseat. At least he wouldn't be eavesdropping.

"Please sit down, *mademoiselle*."

If the Cheshire Cat wore Burberry, I'm quite sure I could have passed for him at that moment, with the grin on my face.

Jagger grunted.

I sat next to Mason. "Hey, Jag—"

His eyes flashed what had to be a warning.

"*JAG*. Did either of you watch that television show about the military tonight? *JAG*?"

Jagger shook his head.

I thought I did a damn good job of sidestepping my faux pas, and thought that Jagger just didn't want to give me the satisfaction of doing something correct.

He really did seem as if he were a bit perturbed at Mason.

But, ever the professional, Jagger sat there, just looking at me—and more than likely transferring his dismay to me.

I leaned toward Mason. "Margaret's husband booked her trip with your new agent. Arnold, the old agent, was her husband's friend!"

Mason gave me a look of trust but flashed his eyes at Jagger.

I quickly said, "He's all right. He's my doctor. We can talk in front of him."

Jagger looked at me as if I should just shut up, so I leaned toward him. "Mason knows that I can help him. Margaret does too."

"How are *you* going to help them, Sherlock?"

Mason looked confused. "Sherlock?"

Now I looked at Jagger, accusing him of a faux pas, and then turned to Mason as if I could wave away his confusion with my hand gesture. "Don't pay attention to that. What we need to do is get more info to corroborate. It certainly sounds as if both of you, and we don't know how many more, were brought here just to get the insurance money. Maybe not only from the New Orleans area, but from all over the country."

I asked a few more questions about the van, the driver and anything else Mason could think of. "Tomorrow I'll see if these match what Margaret says. Then we'll be home free."

Jagger leaned near. "And whom are you going to accuse, Pauline?"

I pulled back. In my excitement, I didn't realize that we still were no closer to finding out about Vito's death or who was the ringleader in all of this fraud. Oh, I knew that we'd have to complete that, but with the horrible day I'd had, I'd let my excitement get away from me.

Mason excused himself and told me he'd meet me for breakfast tomorrow. I smiled and agreed, then turned to see Jagger standing there shaking his head.

"What? He's a nice guy."

"Darling. Just darling." He took my arm and led me toward the examining room, stopping at the desk long enough to inform Nurse Lindeman that he'd be "seeing" me right now.

I grinned all the way down the hallway.

When we got to the exam room, the door was closed. Before Jagger could open the door, Vinny came bounding out.

"Oh, hey, Doc. This room is in use. You can use the one on Ward 200B. It's down the hallway and to the right. No locked doors in between. It's part of the same unit, but the more . . . sicker patients are kept there."

"Thanks," Jagger said, taking my arm.

I heard a female's snicker. Apparently *Vinny* was using the exam room.

I smiled at Vinny and followed along like the ever consummate, cooperative psych patient that I'd become.

When we got to the end of the hallway, I realized I'd never ventured this far, thinking all the doors were locked. Then it hit me: the *sicker* patients?

"Maybe we should wait until tomorrow and stay on Ward 200. Plain old 200?"

Jagger shook his head—twice.

"Hey, you're the one who can come and go around here. They get me on Ward 200B, and they might make me a permanent resident."

He chuckled. "What? Are you afraid they'll think you are a bit . . . different, Sherlock?"

I looked around to make sure no staff was watching and slapped Jagger's arm. "No, Jag, I'm not. Oh, hell. I . . . yes, I am. Do you know what it's like to be wrapped in wet sheets like a mummy?"

Suddenly, he had me in his arms. The feel of his heart next to mine nearly had me drop to the floor. Instead I struggled on wobbly legs. Jagger gently stroked my hair and whispered, "I'm really sorry about that, Sherlock. Really sorry."

I knew he meant that he wasn't around to stop it, and I sure as hell wasn't going to tell him that the sheets were a bit comforting and at least not as bad as I'd thought it would be.

Instead, I leaned closer to him and said, "It was *horrible*. The *worst* thing that's ever happened to me."

His kiss came softly, gently, as if stealing into the night. Before we could continue, a door clicked shut in the distance—and Jagger released me.

It was well worth my little white lie.

* * *

Jagger guided me down the hallway, following Vinny's suggestion and instructing Nurse Lawson to make sure we had time to talk uninterrupted. She agreed and as we headed down the corridor, a woman's scream filled the air.

I froze.

Jagger yanked at me and said, "Ignore it. The staff will take care of her."

But before we could get past Room 201, the door swung open and a pillow flew out, hitting Jagger in the back of the head. If it were a much heavier object, I wouldn't have laughed.

Suddenly I sobered when the culprit came out the door shouting.

Mary Louise Huntington!

Jagger's grasp on my arm tightened.

I grew faint at the comparison of her standing there in the johnny coat, which I no longer wore since getting my Burberry outfit, her hair as messy as mine, and her face, a bit younger (which I attributed to a more expensive facial cream than I could afford), but very similar to mine.

Way too similar.

She started to curse at me—mostly incoherently. I figured the Green Demon had visited Mary Louise too.

Jagger ignored her and pulled me toward the exam room.

Once inside the room, he grabbed the stool with his foot, yanked it over and sat. "Sit down." It came out very much like an order and I wondered if Jagger was just as shocked as I was.

Then I looked at him.

"She was here all the time." I sank onto the exam table as the accusatory words came out. "And you *knew* it."

Jagger stared, but there was no look of apology in his eyes. "She fell into my lap for this case, Sherlock."

"Call me Pauline."

"I needed to get into this place to crack this fraud ring and when I saw her picture in a file on Dr. Pinkerton's desk, I knew you would be perfect for this job.

"Not because of my skills?"

He ignored that and continued, "Mary Louise was brought here from Minneapolis. She's a convicted felon who got off with an insanity plea. Her family had her transferred here because her brother worked here and they thought he could keep an eye out for her." He rolled closer. "Vito was her brother."

I gasped.

"But you should have told me she was here—"

"She wasn't."

"Mary Louise might know who killed Vito," I mumbled more to myself than to Jagger, as if I wanted his approval.

I felt him touch my hand. "I'm proud of you, Sherlock."

Do not let that be your undoing! I shouted in my head. I was still angry with Jagger for all of this.

"Does she know you? Did she recognize you?"

He shook his head.

"But, unfortunately, Pauline, I'm sure she recognized *you*."

Twenty-three

Jagger continued to explain how Mary Louise was to come to the Institute with me. It had been a perfect plan to get me on the inside and once there, disguised as a patient, I'd be free to investigate with no one the wiser. Jagger would have given me a fake patient ID, and Mary Louise would be safely admitted nowhere near me. But Vito, dressed up like a nun, had interfered.

Why?

Did he know something about the fraud ring and that's why he was trying to stop his sister from coming here? Or, was he just trying to free her? Help her escape? Had he planned to drug me or was it all on the spur of the moment to save his sister? Blood is thicker than water and all.

Jagger swore that he'd followed Vito to make sure I got here safely.

I wasn't sure if I was angry at that or glad. Go figure.

Jagger thought the fact that Mary Louise and I looked so much alike would be a benefit. Now, we weren't sure.

Vito was dead.

We had no idea how much Mary Louise knew—and I still resembled her.

Someone could confuse us. Easily.

I could see the cogs working in Jagger's brain. He'd taken out his usual toothpick and started to chew on it. I wondered if he wished it were a cigarette.

"Did you used to smoke? Cigarettes?"

He looked at me as if I really did belong here. "Long time ago."

"During the Gulf War?" That had been a sore subject with Jagger and Nick. They'd known each other, flown together, and separated from the service as adversaries. After hearing about their story, I'd assumed it had all been too much for them to handle, and since they both went into the investigative field, they were way too similar to get along.

"What does this have to do with the case, Pauline?" He threw the toothpick into the wastebasket.

"Nothing. I was only curious."

"Then be curious about what we are going to do. Mary Louise could have a coherent moment . . ."

Not if the Green Demon has its way.

I knew Jagger was talking, but fear had my ears shut. I really didn't want to hear that my life was in more danger—again. I'd gotten over that with Vito dying and Ruby gone. I felt safer with Jagger around and now he was tearing away that wall of safety.

Then again, Jagger didn't talk idly. He really must have been concerned about my knowing Mary Louise was here—although he hadn't given me any details of how that happened—and what she'd do now that she knew *I* was here.

Jagger had walked me safely back to Ward 200 and turned me over to the evening nurse, Ms. Lindeman. She made sure I got to my room and to bed as "Dr. Dick" had ordered.

"Good night, Pauline," she said and left the door ajar.

I wished it could be closed all the way and locked. But that was against policy around here. I focused on the light coming from the hallway, and my body felt as if I'd drunk ten cups of coffee. But I knew I was worried about the case, Mary Louise and my future with my grandkids.

I must have fallen asleep at some point, since I woke before the sun was up. Not a very restful night. After tossing about until the muscles of my legs ached, I decided to get up. I put on my new robe and smiled.

I really missed my family and friends.

Funny how it had only been a few days, but being locked in this place made it seem like forever. I said a silent prayer for all the patients, brushed my teeth and hair and went out to walk the hallways.

A new nun was at the desk. Actually, she was probably here before, but since I didn't make a habit of leaving my room during the middle of the night, I'd never met her. I walked closer to the desk.

She shuffled some papers about. "Yes?"

I smiled, but she didn't look at me. "I'm Pauline Sokol. Just wanted to say hello."

The nun looked up. "It's four fifteen in the morning, Pauline. You should be asleep." She stuck the papers inside a large file.

"I . . . I did sleep, and now—" I laughed. "That's it for me for tonight. Maybe I had too much caffeine," I said, and then laughed.

She smiled. "I'm Sister Janet. Just don't turn on the TV and wake anyone else up. I have too much work to do and need to finish it by morning. You can walk around outside your room if you are quiet."

I nodded and pretended to lock my lips and throw away the key as Uncle Walt used to do. When we were kids, he'd say his "noise box" was full and we all needed to lock up. I smiled to myself and turned to walk down the hallway.

I really missed my jogging, so I walked back and forth and around and around. Not a soul was up besides me and the small staff from the night shift. Sister Janet had seemed very nice, I thought, as I rounded the corner and landed directly in front of Ward 200B.

For a second I hesitated. There was no good reason for me to go through the doors. Mary Louise had to be asleep right now and more than likely highly medicated after her pillow incident.

"Move along," a voice said from behind.

I turned to see a night orderly, carrying a stack of sheets. Looked heavy.

"Oh, here, let me get the door," I said and held it open. Before I could step back, he had me grabbing at sheets as the pile started to shift and the door closed.

"Damn it!" he said. "I got it. Go back to your room."

I started to turn and heard a faint noise, actually music like from a radio, coming from the direction of Room 201. Mary Louise must be awake and listening to it.

I smiled at the orderly, who couldn't care less as he went down the hallway with his lopsided bundle. In the distance someone shouted and two other patients screamed out. I said another prayer for all of them and added I was thankful that I wasn't on this ward.

Then I walked closer to Mary Louise's room.

Maybe, that is if she didn't freak out when she saw me, I could get some info out of her. Maybe learn more about her brother. I paused at the doorway and listened to the radio commentator's soft voice announcing the next song. He'd put me to sleep if I listened to him. Gingerly, I pushed the half-closed door open.

I touched my taser bracelet, which I would use if absolutely necessary, but sure didn't want to. "Mary Louise?" I whispered ready to bolt if she aimed a pillow or something harder at me.

Silence.

The room was dark except for the dim lights from the hallway. As the radio played a soft instrumental with lots of strings, I tried to get closer. "I came to talk to you, Mary Louise." I waited, not wanting to wake her and startle her.

No reply.

I sighed and turned. No way would I wake up a sleeping psychiatric patient who was a convicted felon. Jagger never did tell me what Mary Louise had done—and I figured he really didn't want me to know. Because then I might bolt out of this job.

When I got to the door, I took the handle to open it further.

"Then talk," Mary Louise said in the darkness.

Not expecting her to be awake, I jumped. I realized psych patients "played 'possum" very well. Slowly I stepped back and closed the door more. If I shut it all the way, any staff member walking by would surely be suspicious.

She lay in bed, restrained like a madwoman. My heart slowed and I felt like yanking her free until I realized she probably could hurt herself or someone else—like me.

"Oh. Hi. My name is Pauline."

She curled her lips as if to say, "I already knew that."

I stepped back and told myself not to try and second-guess a mentally ill patient. Also, not to get too close.

"What the hell do you want?"

Her voice sounded quite coherent but then again, I really had never had a real conversation with her. Still, the tone sounded much like it had in the airport. So, I had to conclude that her medication might be just about wearing off by now. I summoned my long ago repressed psych training.

"Look, Mary Louise, I'm sorry about your brother."

She remained silent. Then a low laugh started in her chest. Both hands were shackled to the bed rails on each side. I noticed her fingers twitch.

"Vito's dead."

"Yes. I know, and I'm sorry."

"Why?" She looked at me now with a glassy stare. "Did you kill him?"

I stepped back more. "No. Absolutely not. I was hoping you could tell me who did." I moved closer. "Do you have any idea why someone would want to hurt your brother? Or who would?"

"Hurt? He's dead, you bitch."

Maybe the Green Demon still swam in Mary Louise's system. "Sorry."

Her fingers moved more swiftly. "He saved me . . . and I couldn't help him."

"He saved you from prison?"

Her head spun sideways. *The Exorcist* came to mind, but it stopped short of a three-sixty turn.

"Of course from prison." She laughed.

I quickly looked at the door. Thank goodness no one came in. I softened my voice, hoping she'd get the hint, and moved near the bed.

"You look familiar," she said.

Not wanting to go into details of our similarities or remind her that she'd met me before and jog her memory to an unhealthy place, I ignored her statement and said, "So your brother took you from the airport so you wouldn't have to go to prison?"

"Or here."

Damn. Not a veritable font of information. Reddish

rays of sunlight peeked above the trees outside and I knew I had to hurry and get out of there. I'd be in more than wet sheets if I was found breaking the rule about no patients in others' rooms. "Mary Louise, tell me if you know anything about who killed your brother. Did you know he was in on a fraud ring?"

She started to laugh.

I started to tell her to be quiet.

And the door started to open.

Damn.

I looked at her and figured if I was going to get punished, I might as well make it worth it. "Did he tell you about people being brought here that were not really sick?" I spoke so fast she probably thought I was using a foreign language.

The door swung all the way open.

Mary Louise stopped laughing and said, "Sure. He made a bundle on that scam," while a stuffed elephant peeked at us from the doorway.

Joanna.

Darling Joanna, I thought as I hurried out, careful not to knock her and Dumbo over. She stood there shaking him at me like some voodoo doll.

I only hoped she wasn't allowed to have pins in this joint.

Thankfully Ward 200 had come to life with the rays of the sun. As I walked down the hallway, several patients milled about and I figured they were heading to eat breakfast. Maybe I could make it there on time today.

With the little sleep I'd gotten though, I had to keep my wits about me. The info from Mary Louise could pole-vault this case forward.

Despite my hunger, I had to talk to Jagger.

I hurried to the nurses' station to see the usual staff on duty. Sister Liz was heading out the backdoor, most likely

on dining-room watch. Sister Barbie stood with a tray of
pills in her hand, Novitiate Lalli right beside her.

Not wanting them to see me and give me the Green Demon, I pulled back. I'd lost faith in my ability to not swallow after the sneeze incident.

They, too, walked out the backdoor. Nurse Melissa
Lawson sat there, reading someone's chart. Hopefully not
mine, although it was probably a doozie of a read.

"Excuse me, Nurse Lawson," I whispered.

She looked up. "What's wrong with your voice,
Pauline?"

"Oh. Nothing. Just, I don't want to wake anyone up."

She looked at me as if I were either crazy or deaf, since
the unit buzzed with noisy, hungry patients.

"I need my doctor. Now."

"Why?"

Damn it. Couldn't these nurses just do as the patients
requested? I couldn't come up with a quick enough lie.

She waved at me. "Go. Eat your breakfast. Dr. Plummer will be on his rounds soon. I'm sure it can wait." She
waved me off again.

Having avoided some ancient psychiatric punishment
once already this morning, I told myself she was right and
headed to the dining hall. I'd see Jagger soon enough.

Margaret was sitting next to Mason. Great. There
wasn't a seat next to them, since Margaret was on the end
and one of the "Jo's" sat next to her. Callie Jo was from
New Orleans, I'd learned from her once.

I quickly got my tray of watery eggs, white toast and
OJ, and then sat next to her. I wondered if she really was
Callie Jo right now. Once Ruby had told me that Callie Jo
had come here with the problem of thinking she was
Patty Jo, Bobby Jo and Mavis Jo, whom I actually liked
talking to, since she was an elderly Southern woman

who'd been through the war—the Civil War. Patty Jo was only three years old and difficult to understand with her Southern drawl, and Bobby Jo was a teenage boy who didn't talk to adults. I wondered what the heck Callie Jo had been through in her life to cause her illness.

I sat next to her and looked at Margaret and Mason. "Hey. Good morning."

They both nodded and Mason said, "We had the same van driver. Tall, very built and not too bright. First a nun led us to the van, but she didn't drive. He did."

"Spike?" I asked in horror.

Margaret took a bite of toast. "We're not sure. He had on a white shirt and white pants. And a Red Sox baseball cap. I couldn't see his face and neither could Mason. But we agreed he acted very rudely."

Spike for sure.

I took a giant bite of my toast, nearly choking. I had to talk to Jagger real soon. "Try to listen to Spike today. See if the voice, the tone of the voice sounds familiar."

"If you can get him to talk," Callie Jo said. Her voice was very rough, deep.

I looked at her. "Hey, Bobby Jo, is it?"

He or she nodded. I really didn't want to encourage Callie Jo's illness, but she'd interrupted—and might know something. The folks around here had heaps of time to observe what was going on.

I leaned near. "You know Spike?"

"I can take him, the shit."

I had to smile. Callie had the teen attitude down pat. How sad when someone's mind split them into so many other personalities. "I'll bet you can. Did you ever see Spike in a Red Sox baseball cap?"

Callie started to shake. Her toast fell onto her dish.

I leaned over and patted her hand. "Never mind. You're

all right." I looked around to see if any of the staff noticed.

Spike stood guard by the doorway, watching.

God I hoped he couldn't read lips. Callie started to calm down when Margaret talked softly in her ear. A mother of a son. An expert.

Soon Callie Jo was eating peacefully. I'd lost my appetite. And Margaret and Mason stared at Callie Jo as if she held some deep secret.

Once the sharps were counted and everyone was released from the dining room, Callie Jo tugged at my arm. Before she said anything, she wiped her arm against her nose like a kid would do.

"That you, Bobby Jo?" I asked.

Spike came toward us.

Callie Jo said, "I saw him bring that man in the other day."

"Did he have on his white uniform? And a Red Sox cap?" I asked before King Kong descended upon us. If he ushered me off to the wet packs, it'd be worth it to get some info that he was involved.

"I'm a Yankee fan," Bobby Jo said proudly.

Shoot.

"But what was Spike wearing—"

"Stop annoying her," Spike ordered and grabbed my arm. "Come with me."

I gulped.

Margaret and Mason looked on in horror.

And Bobby Jo spat at Spike, missing him and hitting Joanna's elephant with a gob of saliva. She screamed, and Sister Liz hurried over.

Amid the ruckus, Spike cursed at me for always making trouble and Bobby Jo said, "Yeah, he had them on."

Twenty-four

I yanked free of Spike's hold when Bobby Jo, the little sick darling, had confirmed my suspicions about Spike. Even though Bobby Jo was ill, I believed that she was correct. She wasn't as zonked out as some patients.

Spike must have picked up Margaret at the airport too.

"Where are you taking me?" I asked, about ready to accuse him of fraud, but biting my lip instead.

He glared at me and this time it scared me. I stepped back. At least this place was crowded and he wouldn't pull anything now.

I touched my taser bracelet and figured old Spike didn't take psychiatric medication—so he damn well better watch out!

"Your doc is here," he said and grabbed me again.

"I'm coming. You don't have to manhandle me. Besides, my doctor—"

Jagger stepped out of the alcove. "If I have to tell you again not to treat her like that, you'll be fired."

Spike let go, mumbled something I think was a curse and stomped off.

Jagger gently took my arm and didn't let go until we were safely in the exam room with the door shut.

"You can't fire him."

He shook his head. "*He* doesn't know that."

"No, I mean. We don't want him fired. He's the one who brought Margaret *and* Mason here. He's in on the fraud, Jagger."

I don't think I'll ever forget the look of pride in Jagger's eyes—or how my heart felt at that moment.

I, of course, had to explain it all in detail, as Jagger was not one, smartly I might add, to take my opinion without proof.

"Good job, Sherlock." He sat on the stool, took out a toothpick and chewed.

I debated whether to tell him about Mary Louise. He might let me have it for sneaking into her room. It was a risky thing to do, and I wasn't sure if I wanted Jagger to holler at me right now.

"You what?" he shouted after I told him about my visit to Mary Louise. "They *should* lock you up on Ward 200B."

I sat on the edge of the exam table and fumed. "I can handle myself, Jag, as evidenced by my still being here. And alive and kicking I might add."

I liked that he didn't tell me not to call him "Jag."

"Well, do you want me to finish telling you what I found out from Mary Louise before we were interrupted by Dumbo?"

Jagger shook his head—once.

"Okay. I'll skip the Dumbo part. Anyway, she knew. Mary Louise said she knew her brother was involved in the fraud around here."

Jagger took his toothpick out of his mouth, snapped it in

half between two fingers and said, "In your medical opinion, Pauline, do you think she'd make a credible witness?"

I started to say that she had probably been medicated very heavily and then realized his tone. Jagger was being sarcastic. "What's so wrong about me finding that out?"

He sighed. "Oh, I don't know. Maybe because she's a psych patient, a criminal and under the influence of drugs? She's barely useful to us, Sherlock, unless she knows whom Vito worked with. We need to find out who else is involved. Vito's death already had him implicated, and since Mason arrived after Vito was killed, the fraud is continuing."

I chuckled. "Of course I already *knew* that." My face burned yet again.

I also knew Jagger didn't believe me—but I was getting used to embarrassing myself in front of him.

Jagger walked me to the dayroom and said goodbye. After stifling a few sighs, I said I'd see him in the morning and wondered where the heck he went at night. My guess was some doctors' quarters around here. He never would go far, that much I knew.

Joanna came into the dayroom, this time with a Barbie Doll dressed as a nurse. How appropriate for this place. I laughed to myself but ignored her so she wouldn't have some kind of attack. There was no bread around to feed her doll, but I came to realize that anything could set off anyone around here.

I turned to watch the television and wondered where Margaret and Mason were. Since Ruby left, there weren't many patients that I talked with anymore. Too risky.

One of the men in red pajamas had the remote control and kept clicking through the channels. Joanna ignored it and told Barbie that she'd take her outside for a walk soon. Callie Jo sat talking to herself, and I wondered if she was able to communicate with her other "selves." Interesting yet very sad. And a new woman remained silent on the couch.

Did she belong here?

I ignored the television and watched her. Several patients milled about, and she didn't seem to pay them much attention. By the expression on her face, she could be depressed or plain furious that she was here. I couldn't tell yet. I would have to talk to her.

I got up and headed toward her. When I got near, a shriek filled the unit. I realized it was from the new woman.

Novitiate Lalli was on my heels in seconds. "What did you say to her?"

I shook my head. "Nothing. I merely walked near her."

She ignored me and stroked the woman's arm. "It's all right, Kathy. She won't hurt you. You are safe here."

"What happened to her?" I asked, figuring the novitiate would say it was confidential, but I had to say something to show my concern. I was like some kind of "freak-out magnet." Seemed I got a lot of these patients riled up without doing anything.

"Kathy was robbed in her own apartment, and he was still there, dressed in her clothes when she came home."

I wondered why she associated me with the robber. I tried to give her a smile and softly said, "I won't hurt you, Kathy," then walked back to my seat and flopped down. I should just go to my room. I was tired after the night I'd had but thought if I went to sleep too early, I'd start a bad habit and keep waking during the middle of the night.

One of the drugs kids took the remote away from Pajama Man and put on *CSI*. Great. Maybe I could learn something and figure out the case before the actors did. That'd keep my mind busy. I yawned, curled up and watched.

My eyelids fluttered at the sound of talking. I slowly opened them to see I was still in the dayroom, *The Tonight Show* was on, and most of the patients were gone. I reached my arms up to stretch through a yawn and decided to go to bed.

I stood, and something fluttered to the floor from my lap. With my blurry vision, I bent and looked closer.

A straw from a broom.

My hands flew to my mouth so I wouldn't scream out. But who . . . how did it get there, on my lap?

And what did it mean?

There goes my night's sleep. With shaky fingers, I picked it up and stared at the damn thing as if it could tell me. Vinny sat on his perch near the doorway, reading a book. Good for him, but that didn't help me. I thought about asking him if he noticed anyone around me, but then wondered what I'd say if he asked why.

I waited a few minutes then walked toward the nurses' station. Sister Liz had the evening shift. Thank you, Saint Theresa. A cooperative staff member. "Hi," I said through the window.

She rolled her chair over and slid the window aside. "Not sleepy tonight, child?"

Suddenly I missed my mother—and Goldie.

"Oh, well—" I chuckled. "I just took a long nap on the couch."

She smiled. "So I noticed. I told Spike not to wake you before he left."

Spike?

"Why . . . thank you." I started to turn. "Why would he? Wake me, that is?"

She looked pensive. "I really don't know. It's just that I noticed him near you when I went to pass out the medication." She shrugged. "No telling why Spike does things around here."

She didn't much care for him. I could tell by her tone. Good. That tidbit might come in handy in the future. "Sister? Could I? . . . Have a nice night."

She smiled again.

I needed to talk to Jagger but couldn't have the nurses keep calling him. So, I decided I'd look for him. Jagger was never too far. Where would he be that I could get to?

Ward 200B. Maybe he was talking to Mary Louise without me! I looked around to see that Vinny was engrossed in his book. The only word in the title that I could see from here was "Sex" so I guessed old Vin wouldn't pay any mind to me.

Operating under the theory that if you looked as if you belonged, you'd blend in, I walked down the corridor to Ward 200B, still holding the piece of straw. As I put my hand up to push the door, it swung at me, hitting me in the face.

"Ouch!" My hands flew up and the straw became airborne.

"Great. It's you."

"Don't get so excited, Jag." I touched my nose.

"Are you hurt?"

I looked at my hand as if it would be covered with blood. "No, I'm fine." Even though my nose felt as if a train had rammed into me, I didn't want to make a big deal about it in front of him. "I need to talk to you." I looked around for the straw. Nothing. Damn.

"I . . . what are you doing?" Jagger followed my gaze

as it bounced off the floor, walls and door. "Did you drop something?"

"No, I didn't drop something. You knocked the *evidence* out of my hand!"

"Evidence?"

There it sat on Jagger's shoe. "Don't move." I bent down and grabbed the straw and then held it out toward him. "This evidence."

"Where'd you find it?"

"I didn't find it. It found me." I waved the straw a bit as if that would give my words more punch. More credibility.

"Sherlock, where did you get it?"

"I fell asleep in the dayroom—"

He grabbed my arm, pulled me through the doors near the window. "You fell asleep in the dayroom? Do you know how dangerous that can be for you?"

I do now.

"Someone dropped it near you?" Jagger asked.

I was annoyed that he figured that out, but nodded. "It was on my lap. When I got up it fell. Sister Liz said Spike was near me earlier."

"While you slept. He could have stuck a syringe into you."

I shuddered, remembering Vito in the airport. "Let's forget that and go on."

Jagger took my arm. "I'll go on, but I won't forget. You have to be more careful, Pauline. Start thinking like an investigator all the time and not like a nurse . . . or a patient."

"I resent that."

"You are a nurse," he said, and then grinned.

"Did you talk to Mary Louise?"

He shook his head. "She was asleep."

"I thought you said she wasn't of use to us."

He merely looked at me. Oh, well, it didn't matter. "Let's go see if she woke up since you left her. Maybe she knows more about Spike. If she'd seen her brother with him or someone else. We might luck out." Still holding my arm, he turned me toward Room 201.

I smiled to myself.

I'd done well again. I knew it, since Jagger hadn't shaken his head. At the door, we stopped, looked around and eased it farther open.

A night-light burned in the bathroom, and I figured that was so the nurses could check on Mary Louise without waking her. The room lay silent. No radio on tonight. Jagger led us closer, but his body blocked what little light there was.

I could barely see Mary Louise, but she looked as if she was still on her back with her hands shackled to the side rails and the chest restraint on. Mary Louise lay very still.

Damn, I thought, *no info from her tonight.*

When Jagger shifted, I could see the restraint was too high on her chest. I reached out to pull it down.

Jagger grabbed my hand.

"Don't. Don't touch her." Then he pulled me closer. "Damn it," he whispered.

Figuring he was thinking the same thing I had been, I started to nod. "We shouldn't wake her even if we won't get any more info tonight." Then I looked down.

Her eyelids never fluttered. She had to be heavily sedated. I tried that squinting thing to better see if her chest was moving up and down without being constricted. I looked closer. Then, I grabbed Jagger's arm.

Mary Louise Huntington was dead.

Twenty-five

Mary Louise had been strangled by the restraints . . .
or at least made to look as if she was.

After Jagger had gotten me back to my room and noti-
fied the staff about Mary Louise, he came to see me.

I jumped when he walked in the door.

"Maybe it was an accident?" I said quickly.

He looked at me.

"No. Really, I remember reading an article in *The Hartford Courant*. Yes, now I remember. It was years ago.
About the number of patients who died while restrained.
Accidentally. Over one hundred fifty. She . . . Mary Louise
looked as if she might have tried to get up and the . . . the
restraint tightened on her neck."

"Then why didn't she pull back? Give herself some
breathing room? Call for help?"

Damn. Good question.

"Maybe she was too medicated. Did she look as if she
had tried to move? To pull back?" I hadn't studied her
since Jagger'd whisked me out of the room so fast. I guess
he figured it was too late to try and save her so no sense in
us getting caught in there.

Jagger sat on the foot of my bed. "No."

I desperately wanted a "yes." I wanted to know that it was a horrible accident, and not *someone*, that had killed Mary Louise.

Someone who also killed Vito and left his calling card on my lap tonight.

"Do you think Spike did it?"

Jagger shrugged. "He could have."

I held my covers tightly as if that would protect and comfort me. It didn't work. "Well, then we need to—"

"But even if he did, why did he? Spike is not the ringleader, working this scam alone."

I wanted to ask how he knew, but Jagger just knew those kinds of things. Agreeing with him, I nodded. "He's not smart enough to orchestrate something so huge and on such a large scale that it reaches out as far as New Orleans."

Jagger smiled.

I eased up on my sheets.

Jagger got up. "We could have a big day ahead of us tomorrow. Get some sleep." He touched my face and pushed back a strand of hair.

The little gesture was almost as good as a kiss . . . almost.

Ever the mysterious Jagger, he pulled an object out of his pocket. The dim light caught it—something small in the palm of his hand. He held it out toward me. "For emergencies only. Patients can't get it."

A key. I took it. A key to get me out of here if I needed it. How very Jagger-like.

Thank goodness.

He left without a word. There was no point in thanking him. To Jagger this was all business as usual.

After he left I lay in my bed thinking about Terry, Spike and Mary Louise. Yeah, Jagger was right. They were all just pieces of the puzzle—with the end pieces that bordered it still missing.

There had to be someone in the hospital running the scam. Someone who had started it and was keeping it a secret. Surely all the staff didn't know that these patients were really not patients.

But who did?

At breakfast the next morning, I avoided Joanna, who was feeding cereal to Barbie the doll. Good thing it didn't have milk on it. Maybe Joanna wasn't as bad off as she appeared. Then she started talking to Barbie. I took that thought back.

Mason came up next to me with his tray. "May I?"

I nodded. "How are you doing?"

A sadness covered his face and I touched his hand.

"Horrible."

"I hear you." If anyone knew what it was like to be locked up here when they didn't belong, that would be me. I nonchalantly touched the key Jagger had given me inside my outfit. I'd finagled a piece of tape from Sister Liz. "Hopefully it won't be much longer."

His eyes brightened. "You know something? Did you find out something?"

Sister Barbie Doll appeared in the doorway. This time her flashlight-wielding shadow was Nurse Lawson. Novitiate Lalli must be off today. Good. They approached the table and gave Joanna a handful of pills. Red ones. A green one. The Green Demon. She swallowed them as if starving. No need for the flashlight with her.

"Good morning, Pauline," Sister Barbie said.

I smiled. "Hi."

She went past me and gave Callie Jo her medication. Then the nun and nurse made their way down the table. I leaned next to Mason. "If you can, hide the pill under your tongue, but make a gulping sound so they think you swallowed it."

He looked at me as if I were brilliant.

"We need clear heads around here." I looked over to see Margaret swallowing. Damn. Still, I couldn't blame her. I actually think she took the medication to escape this place even if only while she slept. Margaret would be out of commission for hours. I wished I'd gotten to talk to her about Spike first.

"Good morning, Mason," Sister Barbie said. She smiled at him.

I thought that was a good sign. Maybe the nun would be less likely to suspect he wouldn't take the medication. After all, she and Nurse Lawson thought he was a real patient.

A page came over the intercom. "Sister Barbara Immaculatta to the nurse's station STAT."

STAT. Wonderful. Thank goodness I knew the familiar medical term for "immediately."

"Here, Pauline," she shoved the pill at me, and she and Nurse Lawson hurried out.

It must have been about Mary Louise.

I stuck the pill in the pocket of my robe and turned toward Mason. "Did you—"

He was wiping the napkin across his lips and the pill landed in the crease.

"Perfect," I said and winked at him.

We ate in silence so that no one near us would hear anything that we said. I knew I could no longer trust anyone around here. It pained me to think that way about Sister Liz, but I had to be very careful.

Mason and I put our trays on the conveyor belt and waited to hear Sister Janet say that all the sharps were accounted for.

We stood by the wall and watched the staff in the kitchen counting. Margaret sat very still. I motioned for Mason to follow and we walked over to her and sat for a few minutes.

"Hey, Margaret."

She gave a faint smile and nod.

"We are getting closer. Hang in there. You go rest and think of Kyle—"

"There's a knife missing," Sister Janet called out.

Damn it!

Now what? This was the first time we couldn't leave, and I had so much to do. Hopefully Jagger was out there finding *something* out.

"Everyone line up by the door," Sister Janet called.

Then, I looked up in horror as the staff proceeded to frisk all the patients. I ran my hand to my robe and felt my pill in the pocket. Shoot! I sure didn't want to take it, and if I tried to throw it out before they got to me, some patient might find it and be harmed if they ate it.

My head started to pound. This place was getting worse and worse. I should have shoved the pill in a napkin and threw it away like Mason. "You go in front of me," I said to him.

He gave me an odd look but appeared to trust me enough not to say anything. I stood there trying to think, when suddenly, Barbie—the plastic doll, that is—smacked me in the head!

"Ouch!"

Everyone turned around again.

"Sorry. She bumped into me. Joanna that is," I lied in my defense.

Joanna gave me a wicked smile, then shook the doll at me. I pretended to be scared so she'd leave me alone while I thought.

"Next," Nurse Lindeman said.

Mason moved up, was checked and released to go.

I only had Joanna the nutty Doll Lady between cold wet sheets and me. For a few seconds I thought of pretending that I was sick, but that would ruin the rest of my day and maybe I wouldn't get to investigate. They might send me to my bed and put me on constant watch. I moved forward as if going to the gallows.

Joanna fussed when Nurse Lindeman took her doll. Just as she did, a clatter sounded. We all looked down to see the knife, which had fallen out of Barbie's nurse's whites.

"All clear," Nurse Lindeman shouted.

I sighed so loudly, Joanna swung around. "You touch my baby and I'll cut you!"

Yikes!

They whisked Joanna off—maybe for a few ECT jolts of sanity.

As if I didn't have enough on my plate to worry about, now I had to hope that Doll Lady Joanna didn't whack me one with stolen cutlery.

Thank goodness the staff had taken her away. I assumed she'd be heavily medicated or get shock treatment. I was glad that Jagger had changed the routine order on my chart for having shock treatment, too. One less thing to worry about.

I motioned for Mason to follow me, and soon we were seated near the window of the dayroom without the TV. Two of the men in red pajamas were sleeping on the couch. The new lady, Kathy, was also sleeping in the chair by the entrance. Good. No one to snoop. No interruptions.

I turned to Mason. "I wish Margaret could be here."

He nodded. "But it seems as if we are onto something, with what she and I have already talked about."

I nodded.

Mason shifted, moving himself closer.

Our hips touched—and I *noticed*. This was not a good sign. After all, there was Jagger and his kiss. I thought for a moment and told myself I was being crazy. Jagger's kiss certainly meant more to me than it did to him. I was out of my league with him. Actually, all women were out of their league with Jagger.

But sometimes it felt good to end up in left field, even if only for a few seconds.

"Pauline, I'm still not clear as to why you are here," Mason said, moving just a wee bit closer.

I didn't budge, but for some stupid reason, did look up to see if Dr. Dick was in sight. The only person walking in the hallway was one of the red pajama men. That was good, I thought. He was getting some exercise. I couldn't tell Mason about my job, so I took a page out of Jagger's book. "I work for someone. We need to find out more about this fraud ring. That's all I can say." I gave him a gigantic smile as if that would prevent him from asking any more questions.

He smiled back and leaned near. With one finger, he brushed the hair away from my eye. "I could not resist. Sorry."

Making my heart do a jig was nothing to be sorry for. "I'm . . . no problem." I took a deep breath to clear my head and forget, for a few minutes, that I was a woman and he was a man . . . all man. "Mason, do you . . . Can you think of anything else that might help us? We seem to have lots on Spike, but that's it. Do you remember if he spoke to anyone, maybe on his cell phone while he was driving?"

Mason leaned back, yawned and had his arm around me in a heartbeat. Smooth. Very smooth and not even sophomoric like two kids in a movie theater. Maybe his French accent helped to make any move that he made seem charming.

"My mind is so cloudy since being here."

I chuckled. "I hear you. It's as if the air in this place is filled with some mind-altering drugs. We're all a bit foggy. But think. Start with when Spike picked you up at the airport. Was he friendly?" I'd have a hard time believing he was, but then again, he seems to have some personal grudge against me.

"Yes, as a matter of fact, he was very friendly. Not at all as he appears around here. We talked of golf and how the course would already be open yet the air cool. I looked forward to playing . . . Wait."

I turned so fast, our shoulders banged together. Mason smiled and touched my face. This time, just touched it. No moving any hair. What the heck were we talking about again?

"What?" I asked after a moment of clarity returned. "What do you mean, 'wait'? Did you think of something?"

"When we drove across this bridge over a river—"

"The Connecticut River," I said.

"Yes, I read a sign that said it was that river. Well, I was trying to take in the scenery, but I do remember Spike answering his cell phone."

"And?" This could be a break for us. For the case.

"Mind you, Pauline, I did not pay too much attention to his private conversation."

I curled my lip. "I know. You thought he was a chauffer taking you to a resort. But did he at least sound friendly? Angry? Sad? What?"

Mason looked out the window for a few seconds. I felt him grow tense as he said, "Yes, now I remember."

"Here you are, Pauline," a voice said.

I swung around to see Jagger. "Oh, hey, Ja . . . Dr. Dick. We were just—" If I said too much in front of Mason, I could blow our teamwork. So I just laughed and said, "Did you need me for my session now?"

Mason's hold tightened.

I didn't know whether to push his arm off my shoulder and jump up like a kid caught in a naughty act, or just sit still and let Jagger "observe" us.

I sat still.

"I . . . we do need to talk right now, Pauline. I have other patients to see today."

"You do?" I coughed. "Oh, of course you do." I turned to Mason. "We'll finish this later. I'm very curious to find out what you were going to say."

He eased free, stood, took my arm and lifted me from the seat. Then, he touched my face and said, "I enjoyed talking to you. Spending this time with you."

My legs wobbled.

I vowed that when I got done with this case that I'd go out with lots of guys. I had to get back in the dating scene. For a fleeting second I even thought I'd take a date that my mother fixed me up with. Then, I told myself I was in a mental hospital, and any thoughts that I had in this place could not be taken to heart.

"I'll see you before lunch. Let's meet out here. I'll try to get Margaret to come too."

"Agreed." He smiled and nodded. "Doctor." He smiled at Jagger too.

Jagger growled, a low, soft sound. I was probably the only one who could hear it.

I laughed to myself.

*   *   *

Once we were down the hallway and into the exam room, Jagger let my arm go.

I chuckled.

"What's so funny?"

"Oh, nothing."

"You aren't going to finish this case by sitting and chatting with that guy all day, Pauline."

I stifled the next chuckle. Wasn't easy, but I managed so I wouldn't rile up Jagger too much. This was actually fun. "Jag, we were making headway." I told him what Mason and I were talking about, finishing with, "And then you interrupted. Right when he was going to tell me something about the phone call."

Jagger didn't offer any apology. No great surprise. But what he did do was take out his toothpick, break it in half and throw it away—never touching it to his lips.

The poor guy.

"I'm taking you out of here *now*."

I felt my eyes widen and my temper ignite. "What? No you are not! You're not taking me out just because of Mason putting the moves on me."

He merely looked at me. "Let's go." He took me by the arm.

"But . . . I . . . look, Jag—"

"Jagger." He eased me to the door. I knew I couldn't make a scene, or our cover could get blown. "Don't call me Jag."

I stopped for a second and could only stare. So that's the way it was. If he'd allowed me to call him that when he was in power, that was fine. But when I got him riled up, it wasn't.

Talk about a control freak.

We walked to the nurses' station, where Jagger explained that I needed some detailed therapy so we'd be off the unit for a while. The nurse on duty was a lay nurse I didn't recognize and she didn't seem to care much anyway. She merely nodded and I couldn't help wonder if Jagger's looks had anything to do with her "hypnotic" state or if she was just a burned-out employee.

Jagger let go and I followed him through the locked doors into the tunnel. Before I knew it, he was opening the door to the outside, easing me through and walking us toward his SUV.

"What the hell?" I yelled.

This time he opened my door. "Get in."

"Not again! I . . . what are you doing?"

"Working our case, Pauline."

We drove out of the grounds of the Cortona Institute of Life. Not sure when I'd be back or even *if* I'd be back, I looked out the window.

Margaret stood in the bay windows of Ward 200. My heart sank.

"I have to go back. You can't take me out of here for good."

Jagger didn't even look my way. "If you weren't so preoccupied with Mr. New Orleans, you would know that we were only going out for a short time."

"Why didn't you tell me that?"

He kept his eyes on the road and said, "You didn't give me a chance."

I turned to him to argue, but when I studied his profile, his concentration on the road, I decided to shut my mouth.

I think Jagger just lied to me because *he* was more preoccupied with my being with Mr. New Orleans than even I was.

We rode in silence until we reached the interstate. When he got on the ramp of 91 South, I asked, "What's going on?"

"We're paying a little visit to Ruby."

"Ruby? Why? She's out of the picture."

He took his eyes off the road and looked at me quickly. "Is she?"

Got me there. Jagger must have found out something more about the rich drug addict.

He took the exit for my condo. We parked and hurried inside, and I went to change. No one was home, and I wished I could have seen them, so I settled for a few Spanky hugs.

Soon Jagger and I were back in the car with my Burberry outfit in a bag. Jagger drove us to the side of town that bordered West Hartford—the ritzy side of town.

Then he turned into the driveway of what looked like a giant mansion. Its driveway was longer than the street that I lived on. Surely we were not going to see Ruby at her house.

When he pulled onto the circular area in front, I noticed a very discreet sign on the door: ST. CLAIR HEALTH SPA.

I looked at him. "What? Are we going for a mud wrap or something?"

Jagger was out of the SUV and waiting while I got out too.

"Something," he said, leading me inside the gigantic mahogany doors, which were bigger than my parents' garage doors.

At the entrance, the foyer bigger than my parents' house, a woman sat at a reception desk of fine, carved wood. She looked back and forth between us and then settled on Jagger.

What a surprise.

"We only see clients with appointments."

"Dr. Plummer," he said.

She flew up from her seat. This broad, in her Chanel suit of black and white, had nothing on Adele in her Frederick's of Hollywood. And Adele was much more courteous and pleasant than this society woman.

Soon we were led to changing rooms (Separate ones. Damn!) and were told to meet out near the pool. We'd be assigned our personal trainer, masseuse and a third person who would do who knows what else to our bodies.

I'd been so swept up in the hoopla of this place that I'd forgotten to ask Jagger about Ruby. Surely she didn't work here. Naw. Ruby didn't work anyplace. She'd never mentioned a job, and with her parents footing her bills, I figured she didn't need a job.

After taking off my clothes, I slipped into the silken robe that was handed to me by a woman dressed in a black uniform. She looked like the upstairs maid you see in old movies. Sexy and pretty.

Cautiously stepping out of my dressing room, which had more supplies sitting on the counter than Goldie and I had put together, I looked around.

"Right this way, Mrs. Plummer. Dr. Plummer is waiting for you," the upstairs maid said.

I followed her along until it dawned on me. "Mrs. Plummer?" Not that again. This wouldn't be the first time I'd masqueraded as Jagger's wife.

Only it was the first time I'd done it *naked* in a silken robe.

Twenty-six

I hoped the spa had resuscitation equipment was my first thought when I saw my "husband" waiting by the entrance to the pool. He looked so delicious in a black silk robe, which I guessed was killing him to wear, that I started to have SOB (in laymen's terms, shortness of breath).

"Hi," I said, walking up to him.

The upstairs maid kinda drooled at Jagger and then mumbled something about waiting for our masseuse. We could get a health drink or yogurt while we waited, she'd said.

"No thank—" I started to say.

Jagger grabbed my arm. "We'd be delighted to. Thank you."

I wrinkled my forehead at him and whispered, "I'm sure they don't have black coffee."

In silence we followed the upstairs maid into a gigantic room decorated like something out of the Gilded Age. I never saw so much gold in any of the Catholic churches I'd been in. When we got close to a long bar, which was marble with carved wood for legs, I stopped.

Ruby sat on a lounge chair sipping a drink from a goblet bigger than Miles's largest floral vase.

I looked at Jagger and motioned with my head in her direction.

He looked back at me as if to say, "Do you think we came here for the carrot juice?"

The waitress, dressed in all white, asked, "What may I get you, Dr. and Mrs. Plummer?"

I looked behind me. Oh, right. *I* was Mrs. Plummer. I wondered how Jagger was going to explain all of this to Ruby.

I didn't have to wonder for long.

The girl set my coconut banana smoothie with extra Vitamin D and Jagger's plain yogurt (no imagination) on the table near Ruby. We sat on the lounge chairs opposite her.

At first, she didn't pay us any attention. Ruby kept reading her *Cosmo* and drinking something that smelled like onions and strawberries.

Jagger took a spoonful of his yogurt and winced. I could barely keep a straight face. I sucked on my drink and thought it very sweet and pleasant. This beat the heck out of the Cortona Institute of Life's skim milk in the plastic cups.

Jagger set his yogurt down. "Ruby, we need to talk."

She took her time in finishing what she was reading, took another sip and then looked up. "Shit. What the hell are you two doing here?"

Good question. I looked at Jagger for the answer. How was he going to tell her and keep our investigation a secret?

In order to avoid an explanation, he began interrogating Ruby.

"Who had you sneak into Pauline's room?"

Ruby looked at me as if I could help her. She must have felt as if she sat in a locked room with a bright light shining directly on her while Jagger, smoking away, stood over her.

I shut my eyes a second and said, "Just answer. You'll be better off. Believe me."

She started to get up.

"Lieutenant Johnston is very interested in the drug use that goes on around here," Jagger said.

His voice held more threat in it than if he'd pointed a 357 Magnum at her. I also figured that Ruby was well aware of who Johnston was—and that he knew about her drug habits. Maybe he was the reason she'd ended up at the Institute.

Jagger recognized when to hit below the belt—and he did his homework.

"Look, I never did anything like breaking into anyone's room before. I was told that if I did that one time and only to scare you, Pauline . . ." She looked at me with a pleading glance and her fingers started to dance on her glass.

I wanted to reach out and comfort her, but held back. Of course Jagger's steely glare had something to do with it. "Go on," I said as firmly as I could.

"If I scared you, then I could get out early."

I looked around the room. Smart girl. Guess I would have done the same, and she actually hadn't hurt me that badly. But could we trust her? If she'd gotten the chance, would she have smacked me more?

"You could have really hurt me with that broom handle."

She looked like a little child. Reminded me of my niece.

"Pauline, I never had a broom handle with me. I punched only with my fists and only that one time. I swear."

For some reason I believed her, although now I had more to worry about.

"Really," she pleaded. "They said I'd get out early so I only did it that one time. Then I was out."

"Who told you that?" Jagger asked in a no-nonsense tone.

I almost felt like that light was shining on me. Soon Ruby was telling us everything she knew, which, unfortunately, wasn't much. Spike had been the messenger yet again.

"I don't know who they are. They only communicated by leaving me notes. What the hell did I have to lose?"

"Great," Jagger mumbled.

"Who *are* you people, anyway?" she whined.

Jagger said it didn't matter, cursed, stood and reached for my hand. *Damn. No massage*, I thought, until a husky woman of Scandinavian descent walked up to us. "I'm Greta and will be doing your hot stone treatments."

"We're all set. Thanks anyway," Jagger said.

Greta looked him in the eye. "You. You *need* it. You look angry about something. Come." She yanked on Jagger's sleeve. His robe opened to reveal his chest.

I swallowed and mumbled, "Please. You *owe* me some R & R."

In this classy spa, couples were treated together in special "partner" rooms if they arrived together. Probably half of them were wealthy businessmen and their "secretaries." So Jagger and I were treated as Dr. and Mrs. Plummer so our hot stone treatments were on twin tables.

I silently prayed that we wouldn't have to remove our robes.

"Take off that robe, Mrs. Plummer," Greta ordered like a Marine sergeant.

I turned to see Jagger already prone on his table with a sheet up to his waist—his head turned toward me. Even his naked back looked luscious.

I stared him in the eye while saying, "It's a bit cool in here."

"The stones will warm you. I have other clients coming soon. I need to start."

Put in my place, I kept staring at Jagger until he had the decency to turn his head the other way. My robe dropped. I was prone on the table in seconds. Greta must have used some kind of Swedish karate move to get me there. She did have the decency to cover me to my waist too, and soon something hot touched my back.

"Ouch!" I almost sprung up but glued myself to the table instead.

"Relax," Jagger muttered in an almost dreamlike state. Guess he was enjoying the sweltering rocks on his back. Well, they weren't really sweltering, more warm and very smooth. This just wasn't a situation in which I could relax.

Jagger moaned.

Not like a moan of pain, but one of sensual feeling. Me, I could barely stay still while Greta went back and forth sticking hot stones on my back and then on Jagger's. That's when he'd moan again. The next thing I knew, she was pressing the damn rocks into my spine. It might have felt good if I was alone in there, but having to listen to Jagger moan, groan and all out ah, I couldn't relax worth a damn.

With my senses heightened, I heard everything, felt every pressure point of the warm stones and inhaled pheromones that filled the air so thickly, I think Greta herself moaned.

I wondered how much Jagger was paying for this torture.

Soon, she had us slathered in some herbal cream that smelled to me like tuna with basil, but Jagger remained silent, breathing so softly, I wasn't sure if he was asleep or awake.

When I refused to turn over, I found out Jagger was still awake. He said, "Enjoy it, Sherlock, before you have to go back. You deserve it."

Greta agreed, although she had no idea where I was going back to and why I deserved it.

But I felt wonderful having Jagger admit that.

"Fine. Do your massage, but I'm not turning over. My back hurts if I lie on it flat like that," I lied, feeling like some senior citizen instead of a healthy thirtysomething without any back problems.

Greta started at my lower spine, circling her thumbs in a motion that had me nearly asleep. She continued on, and my body soon felt like Jell-O. Wonderfully relaxed Jell-O without a care in the world. Without a tense muscle in my body.

Greta whipped my sheet off, revealing my naked bottom!

I tried to reach out to grab it back, but didn't want to lift up too much to reveal more. I couldn't think of an excuse to make her cover me back up—and Jagger lay there watching.

I sucked in a breath and, holding my head up as high as I could while plastering myself to the table, let Greta continue. Jagger would see just as much if we were at a beach where women wore those thong bathing suits.

Only not this woman. No thongs for Pauline Sokol.

I'm not sure which came first, Jagger's chuckle, Greta's yanking of *his* sheet off—or my gasp.

I swallowed back the next one, deciding when all else fails to resort to humor. "This job keeps getting better and better."

Silence.

On the way back to the hospital, Jagger and I remained quiet. I shifted in my seat, thinking about being naked in front of him, and then him being naked too.

At the age of thirty-five, I had my first hot flash.

"Hey, you missed the turn onto 91 North," I said.

Jagger kept silent and then took a left. Without a word, the white, metal-sided house with the familiar black shutters came into view.

The St. Clair Spa was a mansion, but my parents' house looked a gazillion times better to me right then.

Jagger pulled into the driveway and got out. When I followed him to the front walkway, I said, "Thanks."

He rang the doorbell and a Brahms lullaby rang out.

Mother never had changed the tune since we children were born, and each time I heard it, I got sleepy. She always sang it to us at naptime.

The door swung open a few seconds later. I knew Mother had first peeked through the peephole in the door. "Oh, my! What a surprise!" She reached out to hug Jagger. "It's so good to see you, Mr. Jagger."

"What am I, Mother, chopped liver?"

"Don't be so dramatic, Pauline. *You* I can see anytime." She stepped aside to let me in. "Anytime that is, when you are not on some horrendous, dangerous case."

Ah, so that was it.

I hugged her and decided not to argue. "Actually, Mother, I just had a wonderful day at a health spa."

"Health spa shmealth spa." She still held on to Jagger. "Michael, we have company, and Pauline is here too."

I had to laugh to myself, then hugged her again. "It's good to see you, Mother."

She let go of Jagger. "See?"

"See what?" Daddy said as I hugged him and kissed him on the cheek when he came into the foyer.

"See how she behaves now since she left nursing? Since she took this foolish, dangerous job? Away on some secret mission. She can't even tell her parents where she goes! Telling me it's good to see me. Ha! Where would that come from unless she was in danger? She's never said anything like that to me before. Come, eat."

Jagger chuckled.

Once again my magician mother put out a spread the likes of an army platoon's buffet. And she did it in seconds, before I could help or even see what the heck she was doing. Oh, she'd order me to do things like set the table, get Mr. Jagger a drink or go wake Uncle Walt—to which she added, "So he gets to see you before it's too late."

I don't think she was talking present time here.

Poor Mother. It pained me to see her worry. I'd have to allay her worries. Somehow.

Uncle Walt came into the room and gave both Jagger and me a big hug. I hoped that he wasn't concerned about me too.

Earlier Mother had served her usual Thursday meal of roast pork, so Jagger and I got to have the leftovers. Only when Mother fixed any leftovers, they tasted as if freshly made. She did have a way with cooking.

Made me love her even more.

"Yeah, Mother, we spent the day at the St. Clair Health Spa. We got massages and the woman even used warm stones on our backs."

She looked at me as if I were nuts. "The yard is filled with rocks, Pauline. You want them heated, there's the microwave."

Jagger chuckled. "Actually, Mrs. Sokol, it is a wonderful experience. Someday I'll treat you all to a day at the spa. It's good for the soul."

"Church is good for the soul," she said, ladling more gravy onto his pork and oven-baked potatoes without even asking. "But, if *you* treated, Mr. Jagger, I'm sure . . ."— she laughed, then patted him on the shoulder—"that I'd enjoy it."

Oh . . . my . . . God.

Was Mother flirting with Jagger?

Had her hand lingered for a second?

I excused myself and headed for the bathroom.

After a few whiffs of Renuzit, I sat on the edge of the tub and told myself I was crazy. Too much influence by folks like Joanna, the red-pajama men, Kathy and everyone else had me thinking Jagger had any bearing on Stella Sokol's thoughts. Yes, I was certifiably mad. After a few more whiffs, I heard a commotion in the living room. Then a shriek.

I scurried out and ran down the hallway into the arms of Goldie. "Hey, even though it's been a short time, I missed you guys!"

He hugged me back and moved to the side so Miles could get in a squeeze. "We missed you too. When you coming back?"

I looked at Jagger sitting on the love seat by the bay window. Daddy was reading the newspaper in his recliner and Uncle Walt was catching some z's on the couch. Made me smile.

Jagger looked at me. "Soon."

"It should be soon, guys. We've made some great headway. I think we are about to crack—"

"As long as you don't crack your head open," Mother said, coming in the living room with a tray of tea. She set the pot down and slapped Miles's hand when he tried to help her pour.

He helped anyway.

And she let him.

Goldie, dressed casually in a chartreuse velour-jogging suit, wearing his bright golden-colored wig with a barrette of chartreuse roses, chuckled. On his wrists he must have had ten colorful bracelets. Instead of common white tennis shoes, Goldie wore Nikes with springs in the heels. They were bright pink to match the camisole top he wore beneath his jacket.

Gotta love him.

Jagger excused himself and went outside to make a phone call. Through Mother's sheer curtains, I could see him sitting on the edge of the porch banister talking on his cell. I wondered to whom, but knew I'd only find out if Jagger wanted me to.

"Pauline, go get some extra coasters in Mary's old room. You know where I keep my stuff," Mother said.

I turned to see she had poured all the tea, and Miles must have gone into the kitchen to make more. Goldie sat sipping away and occasionally looking at me as if I'd disappear at any minute. I was in no hurry to get back to the hospital. That was for sure. Until I thought of Margaret standing in the window as Jagger and I drove off.

"Pauline," Mother said, shaking her finger at me. "Ever since you left your nursing job you've not been yourself."

"That was the point, Mother."

"Don't interrupt me. You seem to be here yet not be here. Then you are saying something, and then you go running off to the bathroom. I've had to re-stock my pine-scented Renuzit three times since your new job."

Goldie tried to hold back a laugh, but his shoulders shook, sending his pink dangling globe earrings a-swinging.

"Mother, I'm still the same me. Only with a more . . . interesting job."

She made the sign of the cross.

I walked over, took the teacup from her hand and hugged her. When I kissed her cheek, I whispered, "Please don't worry about me. I'm fine. Jagger makes sure."

She looked at me. "Oh. Well. Then if Mr. Jagger is always around to watch over you, I guess I'm fine with that." Then she walked out of the room.

I looked at Goldie. He smiled. Daddy shrugged and Uncle Walt snored.

"I'll get the coasters," I said and walked out.

Jagger was still on the phone when I passed by the window.

Mary, being the oldest girl had a room of her own until Janet, ten years younger and the last kid, had come along. But Janet married right out of high school so Mary got her room back after she left the convent.

I walked into the room and paused. Talk about nostalgia. Mother had kept everyone's room pretty much the same, as if we would all move back in one day. Oh, my. I had to sit on Mary's twin bed with the patchwork-quilted bedspread after that thought. After a few seconds I got up.

In the bottom of Mary's closet, Mother kept a hope chest of things she had no place else for after five kids had filled the house up with their treasures. I went over and opened the closet to see if the coasters were in there. At the bottom of the left side was a set of new ones with lighthouses on them. I took the package, stood up, looked around.

I guess Mary's education, thanks to the nuns, was part of the reason my sister was such a neat freak. She was even more organized than Miles. Being a nurse, I was way up there in the skill, but no one beat Mary. The top of her shelf was filled with books from her past. I noticed her yearbook from when she graduated high school and then went into the convent. On top was the booklet of novitiates that were in the convent at the same time. There had been a ceremony where they handed them out. I picked up the booklet.

I needed a laugh, and seeing a picture of Mary in her old habit would do the trick. When I opened the booklet and started to flip through the pages to find her though, my hands froze.

Sister Barbara Immaculatta.

There she was in all her glory, and beauty, I might add. She'd been in the same class as Mary! Talk about a small world. I'd have to ask my sister if she remembered Sister Barbie.

I sat on the edge of the bed, gently so as not to wrinkle it, and thumbed through the booklet. There was Sister Liz too! How neat. I recognized a few more of the nuns from the Institute, including Sister Janet.

When I set the booklet back on top, I paused. At least I knew these gals were the real thing.

I was still betting on Novitiate Lalli as my number-one suspect.

"Pauline, are you *making* those coasters?" Mother yelled.

"Oops." I hurried out and into the living room. I couldn't remember if I'd shut Mary's closet door, but I'd hear about it on my next trip here if I hadn't.

My next trip here. I hoped it was real soon.

Miles and my mother passed out homemade chocolate-chip cookies. Mother kept saying how lucky it was that she happened to have them in the refrigerator by chance, but I knew she *always* had something ready for company.

Jagger took a sip of tea, winced, and finished his cookie.

I smiled to myself. How nice and polite not to refuse my mother's tea and ask for coffee instead.

"Well, I think it's time Pauline and I get back to . . . work." He walked over to my mother and gave her a hug. "Thanks. Everything was wonderful."

Mother turned and I felt a hitch in my throat and noticed the concern in her eyes. "You take care of her."

Jagger nodded and kissed her on the cheek. When he went to shake hands with all the men, Mother stood there rubbing the spot.

Damn. What a guy.

I gave her a hug and kiss, and then whispered, "I'll be fine, Mother."

Goldie held me for several minutes while Miles stood silently by.

I slapped both of them on the arm. "Stop it, you guys. I'm only going to work. Not the gallows!" I laughed.

They did too, but theirs seemed forced.

Then again, they knew where I was working.

Jagger had stopped at a filling station so I could change into my Burberry outfit. I'd missed lunch and dinner by the time he'd sneaked me back into the Cortona Institute of Life. I wondered if Mason thought I'd stood him and Margaret up. Maybe he'd lost faith in me. Once in my room, I slumped on my bed just in time before Sister Janet made rounds to check on me.

I almost mentioned seeing her picture in Mary's book, but caught myself. Then I touched my shoulder to make sure the key Jagger had given me was still taped on the inside of my top. Hopefully, no one would ever know about it—and more important: hopefully, I'd never need it.

I hurried out to find Margaret and Mason, but when I passed the "wet pack" room, I heard sobbing. Through the glass window I could see Margaret, wrapped in the sheets with Sister Liz at her side. Fighting the urge to yank open the door and free Margaret, I clenched my fists and turned toward the dayroom.

When I walked around the corner, I noticed Spike sitting on his chair by the door. He grinned at me. What the hell?

I think he liked intimidating me. So, I smiled back, nodded and flopped down on the couch. Joanna and her Barbie doll had the TV controls. Well, Barbie had the controls. Shoot. Guess I'd have to watch whatever the inanimate object chose, because no way was I going to argue with her.

Suddenly the door from the tunnel between the buildings opened. Sister Dolores, looking very serious, walked in followed by two men in suits.

Lieutenant Shatley!

Jagger's friend and a local detective.

Before I knew it, they were talking to Spike and walking him out the door! I jumped up and went to the door. Through the tiny window, I could see them putting handcuffs on Spike.

Yes!

They'd arrested him for his part. Now I felt safer. I slumped into a chair near the doorway and started to laugh. Novitiate Lalli came hurrying out of the nurses' station as if I were having some kind of fit.

"Keep it down, Pauline," she ordered.

"Um, where'd those men take Spike?"

She looked at me for several seconds. "Where *they all* belong."

Yikes!

Twenty-seven

I needed to share Novitiate Lalli's comments with Jagger. Not wanting her to get suspicious if I suddenly asked to see my doctor, I merely smiled and tried to think of what I could do to find him.

She wrinkled her forehead at me and I think she growled. The woman had no love lost for me and vice versa. *She and Spike are two of a kind*, I thought.

Without a word, she walked away and headed toward the nurses' station. I walked down the hallway, turned into my room and entered the bathroom. I looked around to make sure no one had come by, and then stuck my hand under my robe and pajama top to pull out the key.

My heart raced at the thought of using it—and getting caught. I stuck the key in the pocket of my robe, walked to the door, and looked both ways down the hallway.

Cautiously, I walked out. At the dayroom door I stopped. Joanna and Barbie Doll (the plastic one) were arguing over the choice of television shows. I watched from the sidelines and could only stand at the ready in case the doll came flying. Before Joanna noticed me, I eased past a few patients and went by the nurses' station.

At the alcove, I decided to turn toward the stairs leading to the tunnel. After I looked over my shoulder, I touched the key. The cold metal sent a chill up my arm, but I grasped it and took it out. Checking once more to see that no one was around, I stuck it into the lock, turned, heard the click and opened the door. On the other side now, I shut the door, leaned against it and let out my breath.

I listened for any footsteps or voices. After sticking the key back into my pocket, I gingerly walked down the stairs. At the bottom was an alcove with a set of windows and a door to the outside, which looked like the one Jagger had taken me out of.

To the right was the tunnel leading under the buildings. Surrounded by beige walls and, above my head, pipes that occasionally gurgled, I didn't relish the idea of traveling through the tunnel and getting lost. So I decided to look out the window first.

With the outside security lights on, I could see the Cupid fountain through the branches of the trees. A taxicab pulled around the curved drive and stopped. I eased back from the window. A man dressed in a suit got out. Maybe a doctor. Maybe a visitor. Didn't matter to me right then. I looked past him to see the black Suburban in the physician's parking space.

Bingo.

At least I knew Jagger was on the grounds. After sucking in a breath, I stuck the key into the door's lock.

"Ha! He's a shit anyway."

My hand froze at the sound of a female voice. Within seconds, I yanked the key out of the lock, stuck it back into my pocket and ducked into the alcove. I pressed myself as far back behind the wall that bordered the door as I could. Then I looked down to make sure my feet didn't stick out and pulled both back a bit more.

"Yeah, he sure is," said another female voice, much closer now.

I held my breath as if getting an X-ray and waited and prayed.

The voices grew distant.

I let out all the air from my lungs and leaned a bit forward. One of the women was Nurse Lawson. The other didn't look familiar, but at least they were passing through the door and up the stairs. With a sigh, I ran out, unlocked the door, and was outside, relocking it before I could sigh again.

Looking around to make sure no one was about, I hid behind tree after tree until I was closer to the SUV. I also used up a few novenas hoping Jagger was inside. A long shot, but I figured, where else would he go?

When I got near the suburban, I could see a shadow in the driver's seat and smiled. Once at the door, I whispered, "Jagger," and tapped on the window.

He quickly turned. "Damn it, Pauline. What the hell are you doing out here?"

Before I knew it, I was sitting on the passenger's side, saying, "They, Lieutenant Shatley that is, just arrested Spike." I was so proud of myself.

Jagger took out a toothpick, unwrapped it, placed it between his teeth and remained silent for a few minutes.

Geez! "Did you hear me?"

He looked over. "Questioning. They took him in for questioning."

"I . . . you . . . damn it! How did you? Why didn't you *tell* me?"

He broke the toothpick in two and threw it on the dashboard. "After I finished my coffee, I was going to do just that."

I looked to see his half-empty cup in the holder between us.

"I'll bet you don't know what Novitiate Lalli just said about Spike."

He remained quiet.

"Ha! See, you don't." I sat there and started to twirl my thumbs.

"Of course I don't. So you are going to tell me."

As if he had lassoed my tongue and pulled my words out, I babbled on what she'd said about Spike ending with, "Where *they all* belong! That's got to be a clue. Spike should go where they all belong."

"Where *who* belong?"

"Um. I don't know that part, Jagger. But she knows something. I just feel it."

"I trust your instincts, Sherlock."

"You do?"

"That's why you're here." He took his cup and polished off the rest of the coffee, opened his door and got out. "Let's get you back inside before you get caught."

Getting back in was much easier with my "doctor." A few nurses walked past us in the tunnel and didn't even pay attention to me. They did, of course, look at Jagger.

At the top of the stairs leading to my unit, he turned toward me. "Keep an eye on Novitiate Lalli. Try to find out who she's talking about—but don't be obvious. Find out where she thinks they all belong, too."

I stood there still marveling at the words, "I trust your instincts, Sherlock." I'm not too sure what he said after that, but it had to do with the case. Oh, yeah, me finding out more about what the novitiate had said.

How the hell was I going to do that?

* * *

I ended up safely in the dayroom, observing. Jagger had left and no one was the wiser. The unit bustled with its usual after-dinner activity. One red-pajama man slept on the chair by the door to the tunnel. Another sat arguing with Joanna and her Barbie doll about what he wanted to watch on television. And Kathy, the new patient, sat on a couch sniffling.

I sat down next to her. "Hi. I'm Pauline," I said very softly, refraining from touching her in any way.

She turned to look at me.

"Hi," I repeated. "Did you eat your dinner tonight?"

"I didn't see you there." She kept looking at me.

I felt like a specimen under a microscope. "Oh, well, no. You are correct. I was with my doctor."

"Even my doctor can't help me. *He* ruined everything." A tear escaped her eye.

I wanted to give her a friendly hug, but knew better than to make contact. "Things will get better. You'll get better and go back home soon. Don't give him—don't give *anyone*—that much power over you. It'll take time."

"You think so? Sometimes I feel so . . . like I really do *belong* here." Suddenly her eyes widened as if she thought she'd just insulted me. "Sorry."

"No need to be." I smiled to lighten the mood. Kathy wasn't brought here like Mason or Margaret, but Kathy did need to be here. Only temporarily.

"Where'd they take that orderly?" she asked.

I looked toward the door to the tunnel and realized Kathy must have seen them take Spike in for questioning. Maybe she heard something.

"Gee, I don't know. Maybe they arrested him!" I laughed again.

"They arrested *him*. The one that did that to . . . me."

I felt like a creep. "I'm so sorry, Kathy. I didn't mean to bring up—" I sighed. "He deserved to be arrested."

She waved her hand. "There's no need to be sorry. I have to toughen up. That's what my psychiatrist says. I have to let go and be thankful that I am here. Alive, that is."

"True. That sounds like good advice."

She let out a sigh and touched my hand. I didn't pull back.

"I think you might be right about that orderly though," Kathy said.

"Spike?"

She nodded.

Great. Now we were getting somewhere. "How do you know? Did you hear something?"

She looked around. Vinny had replaced Spike on the chair and was watching a DVD on a handheld screen. Good old Vinny. Couldn't trust him to watch the lot of us, but he was good as far as keeping his nose out of our business. I'd bet my next paycheck that his movie was X-rated.

She tightened her hold on my arm. "I heard what the men who took him said."

I wanted to jump up and shake her but thought better. Seemed Kathy had to be handled very delicately. She'd been through quite an ordeal, and I didn't want to cause any more stress.

"He said he didn't do it and the man in the dark suit said they only wanted to talk to him."

That much I knew.

She continued and finally released my arm. "Spike. That was his name?"

I nodded. "That'd be him."

"Spike said he was not taking all the blame. He said he'd spill his guts to get back at . . ."

I felt myself leaning closer and closer to Kathy, wishing that I had that imaginary lasso that Jagger always used on me. She couldn't have forgotten what she was going to say! What she heard!

"Go on," I nudged.

She looked behind me. I turned to see Novitiate Lalli sweeping down the hallway like a tornado. As she got closer, I knew she didn't want me talking to Kathy.

But was it because Kathy had been traumatized? Or because Kathy had heard something?

It didn't matter what Kathy had been about to tell me, since Novitiate Lalli whisked her away, but not before she scolded me with, "Do not upset the patients, Pauline."

As if I weren't a patient!

Well, I wasn't, but she didn't know that. Hopefully.

I got up and walked around the unit until I found Mason in the dayroom without the TV. Two men in red pajamas were sitting on the couch talking; the third was asleep. I had to laugh to myself. They were like a club, like the ladies of the Red Hat Society, with those outfits on. The fellow sleeping seemed to be the oldest and had been sleeping nearly every time I'd seen him.

"Hey, Mason." I sat down opposite him at the table.

He was playing solitaire. "Hi, Pauline. Did you have a good day? I missed seeing you at the meals."

"I did have a good day. Went out on a pass." No need to fill him in on nakedness in a health spa, Mother's special hidden cookies, or Jagger's butt or chest or . . . no need.

He looked up sharply. "And you came back?"

Oops. I merely nodded. "The cops came and took Spike in for questioning."

His eyes widened. "I'll be damned. Good. So, will I be out of here soon?"

"One can only hope. We need to know more about whom Spike worked with." Or more likely for. "Did anything go on while I was gone?" I pictured Margaret in the wet sheets.

Mason set the cards down. "I had a nice lunch with Margaret. Her son sounds like a wonderful child. I have no children of my own, but I have a niece and nephew. Twins. About Kyle's age. That's Margaret's son."

I nodded.

"Oh, she told you. Well, the woman with that fool doll—"

"Joanna."

"Yes. Well, Joanna made a scene in the dining room yet again."

"Did it involve bread?" I chuckled.

"No, actually it involved the younger nun."

Younger nun? I'd guess since Sister Liz, Sister Janet and Sister Barbie went to the convent with Mary, they were younger than Sister Dolores, but that didn't help. "The tall one?" I asked with no one special in mind. I hoped it would jar Mason's memory to give a better description.

"The one who wears a different outfit."

A novice. Novitiate Lalli. I gave him a brief description of her and he nodded.

What the heck went on between her and Joanna? I figured it was a mental-health issue, since Lord knows, Joanna appeared to have a slew of them.

"Joanna kept talking to her doll, saying things about Spike."

My ears perked up like Mr. Spock's.

"Mason, you have to tell me everything. Everything, even if you don't think it's pertinent." I leaned over the table as if to pull more information out of him. A few cards flew onto the floor. "Geez. Sorry."

"It's only a game."

We bent to pick them up at the same time. Our hands

touched, his on top—and I didn't pull back. Actually I didn't want to pull back. Mason was a good-looking guy and nice to boot. He held my hand a few minutes, then leaned near, placing a kiss on my lips.

Wow!

Before this case, I'd recently been forced into celibacy by my ex-boyfriend's arrest, and now two kisses in one week. From two different men!

Could life get any better?

We pulled apart, and Mason picked up the cards. When we sat up, we just looked at each other.

And behind Mason, was my shadow, Dr. Dick.

He walked past us, down the hallway to Ward 200B. Maybe I should follow him and explain. But explain what? There was nothing between Jagger and I other than a physical attraction—on my part.

I knew not to go sniffing around where I didn't belong.

Mason, on the other hand, was right for me despite the fact that he lived over a thousand miles away. I ignored what just happened and said, "What else do you remember?" I croaked out, and then cleared my throat.

He smiled. "Joanna must have heard Sister Lalli talking to Spike at one point."

"Novitiate Lalli."

He lifted the cards and restacked them into a pile. "Oh, sorry. I'm not Catholic."

Oh, boy. He was now off Stella Sokol's Characteristics of Pauline Sokol's Future Husband list.

"That's all right. What did she hear?"

Mason continued on, with lots of information that Jagger and I already knew. It had been established that Spike was the "brawn" in the fraud scam, but we had yet to identify the "brains."

Maybe it had been Vito? I looked at Mason. "Did she mention Vito at all?"

He thought for a minute. "Vito. Vito. I'm not sure. Joanna was not too coherent at times. Mostly she'd talk to her doll. Then Novitiate Lalli would tell her to be quiet. Almost as if she was trying to silence Joanna. Soon after that, Nurse Lindeman came and medicated Joanna. She fell asleep very quickly."

Roadblock. Another dead end. Courtesy of the Green Demon.

I wasn't going to give up though. We'd gotten Spike out of there, and maybe the police, much more skilled in interrogation than I was, could get something out of Spike. Then Jagger would tell me.

In the meantime, I had to do something. I had to tail Novitiate Lalli.

Because I was damn sure she knew *something*.

After we had left the dayroom to do some spying, I nodded to Mason to sit in the dayroom near the door to the tunnel. Certain that I could trust him, I had explained the next step of keeping the novice nun within earshot.

Meanwhile I dropped down on the couch near a sleeping Joanna. A stuffed Mickey Mouse sat on her chest, almost falling to the floor, but no way was I going to fix Mickey. He'd have to take the fall before I got that close to Joanna.

One thing I'd learned in nursing school was not to let a patient in pain grab onto your hand (give them the metal side rail to squeeze) and never wake a sleeping psychiatric patient unless absolutely necessary.

I looked around the room. Most patients were either talking to themselves, arguing with each other or watching the television. Jackie Dee was nibbling on something, this time a cracker. So I stayed next to Joanna and waited.

Every once in awhile I'd look over at Mason and wink. Callie Jo came over to him and stood there, talking up a storm. I had no idea who she was at the moment, but her distraction seemed to work. No one paid attention to Mason or me. Sister Lalli came out of the nurses' station with Nurse Lindeman and the medication tray.

Mason stood and pretended to be watching television. I guessed he was listening to whatever went on while still talking to Callie Jo. Most patients ran toward the nurse as if she were passing out gold. I guessed to some of them, the Green Demon was gold. Sadly, many of them needed it.

One of the red-pajama men got his pills, swallowed them down, opened for Novitiate Lalli, and then walked over toward me. He smiled as he sat next to me. It did look as if he'd had a handful, so I figured soon he'd be fast asleep. How sad. Life, nearly the end of his life, was passing him by.

Once the pills were gone and everyone was getting happier as the medication melted into their systems, the nurse and nun left and Joanna started to stir. Oh, boy. I had to be on my toes now or I'd be wearing Mickey on my head.

I smiled at her. "Did you have a good nap?" It must not have been her time for medication, since no one had waked her up.

She held Mickey tighter to her chest. "What nap?"

I'd better change the subject, I thought. But what the heck was a safe subject to talk about with her?

She started telling Mickey to watch out for me. Me! I was the one. The one who *knew*.

Now *I* was freaking out. Joanna was scary, to say the least, and now she was downright creepy.

How much did she really know?

"What are you talking about, Joanna?" I asked as softly and nonthreatening as I knew how.

She hugged Mickey tighter.

"I'm not going to touch your doll."

She clucked her tongue at me and cackled. Yes, cackled. It sure wasn't a real laugh. "Mickey Mouse, you fool, is not a doll."

Nor is he real, you fruitcake. "Oh, sorry. Anyway. What were you telling Mickey about me?"

She leaned near. "I know. I heard you talking to him."

"To Mickey?"

Another cackle. "You're dumber than you look. No, you fool, to the doctor."

Jagger? She'd heard me talking to Jagger? "The doctor. What did I say that was so wrong?"

Joanna's eyes darkened. She was actually a very attractive woman if her eyes didn't show her mental illness so readily. A little makeup and combing of her brunette locks would do wonders for her. One thing about this place, very few patients cared about personal grooming.

She'd better not start with that "you know" business when I asked her a question, I thought. I was losing my patience with Joanna although I knew the woman was sick. So I bit my tongue and waited.

"Ha! You said you'd sleep with him. He told me so!"

Jagger said that?

Now I was getting more confused than Joanna. "I never said I'd sleep with anyone."

She looked at Mickey and ignored me.

Fine. Let her talk to a stuffed mouse.

"He told me so. You remember hearing it. Don't you?"

I looked at the mouse, waiting for a response. Then I came to my senses and got up. "This is crazy," I mumbled. "Good night, Joanna. Mickey." I nodded to the damn mouse.

Joanna cackled again and then said, "He really did tell me. Then when he went to her room, she killed him. He was lying right on top of her when we all came to the door."

I shut my eyes.

Great. She was talking about the late Terry and his *accidental* death.

But, damn! Had Terry really told her I'd sleep with him?

After ordering myself to ignore the fact that Joanna had started some rumor about Terry and me, I motioned for Mason to come next to me.

The man in the red pajamas woke up, glared at Joanna and Mickey and said, "Shut the hell up, you two. Can't Santa get some sleep around here?"

Mason and I chuckled. I wanted to ask him if he'd heard the lies that Joanna had told, but decided it wouldn't benefit the case. Terry was gone and no matter his part in the fraud, we couldn't prosecute him or stop the scam from continuing with her information.

I actually believed Terry was not involved and was merely a sick man.

"Did you get anything out of her?" Mason asked.

I sighed and shook my head. "Poor woman is worse off than I thought. She almost had me talking to Mickey Mouse."

Mason laughed and put his arm around me. We walked down to the other dayroom to talk privately, and I surprised myself with the fact that I didn't shrug off his arm.

I heard shuffling behind us, and turned to see Santa following us. Guess he was fed up with Joanna.

The two other red-pajama men were there fast asleep. I watched "Santa" take a seat next to them and smiled. What a threesome. I only hoped that they'd all be out of here by next Christmas.

We sat in the love seat by the window. It was so dark out tonight that I could barely make out the Cupid fountain in the distance.

Mason looked around. "Lalli—Novitiate Lalli—and Spike used to date."

I felt my jaw drop. "What?"

"I heard her talking to Nurse Lindeman. You know when they pass out the medication, they chat. It's as if they are robots doing the job. I guess they give out so much medicine around here that they barely pay attention."

"What?" I repeated, still floored.

"You heard me right, Pauline. She told Nurse Lindeman that she was glad Spike got hauled off."

"And you knew she was talking about the cops taking him."

He nodded. "Yes. So, I moved closer when I heard Spike's name. The bastard."

Now I nodded. "Go on."

"Okay. The nun said she used to date him. Said when she was in nursing school, he was her first patient that she had to give an injection to."

I smiled, remembering my first time.

Mason grabbed my hand and held it. "Pauline, Spike had just gotten out of jail. He had an infection, and she had to give him an antibiotic shot. Then, she started to get to know him better each day, she said. Nurse Lindeman didn't seem too interested, but she was polite and let Novitiate Lalli talk."

"Her conscience must be eating away at her. Guess she thought Nurse Lindeman was a good sounding board. She seems very passive and nice."

"I guess. But, imagine, Novitiate Lalli and Spike were . . . lovers."

"And a scorned lover makes a wonderful snitch," I said.

Twenty-eight

"So, Novitiate Lalli and good ol' Spike were lovers," I whispered to Jagger as if anyone could hear us in the exam room. The staff must have thought I was getting intensive therapy, since Jagger and I met so often. He'd come to get me before lights out, which worked out perfectly. For once I didn't have to call him to give him the information that I'd found.

Mason had politely excused himself, and Jagger's glare followed Mason all the way down the hallway.

How cute.

"Good job, Sherlock."

I smiled. "Thanks. Now we need to find out more from her. From Lalli. Don't you think?"

"Do you?"

"Why, yes—" I curled my lips at him. "Don't give me that psychobabble, Jag. I catch onto medical stuff too easily."

We both laughed. It was nice, for a change. All in all, today wasn't such a bad day. Especially since I got to get out of the Institute, even if only temporarily.

I thought of the spa and felt my face burn.

Jagger took out a toothpick, unwrapped it and held it near his lips.

I couldn't take my eyes off the little stick of wood.

Before he touched it to his mouth, he said, "Look, Sherlock, forget about this morning or we're not going to get past it enough to work together." He popped the end of the toothpick into his mouth and stared.

If my face had been burning, it had just exploded from the heat. But he was right. I had to forget that he'd seen my butt and I his. That was going to be hard to do, but I would force myself. So again with humor, I said, "Oh." I laughed. "Sure, it's already forgotten. A butt's a butt."

He grinned. "I was talking about you missing your parents, because if you get too emotional, you could mess up. It could get dangerous."

I wondered if my face was redder than "Santa's" pj's. "Yeah. I knew that, but a butt is still a butt," I mumbled, and had to cover my mouth with my hand to shut myself up.

Maybe I really couldn't work with a guy like Jagger.

I let out a breath, removed my hand and said, "So, I'll see if I can get anything else from Lalli. I'm not even going to call her Novitiate Lalli. She doesn't deserve it, and maybe she isn't even going to be a nun. And with the info from Mason and Margaret, I'm guessing Spike was driving the white van that followed me from Dr. De Jong's."

He nodded. "Lieutenant Shatley said there were no fingerprints on the broom handle that was used to kill Vito. They have no leads."

"Not even Terry? He did seem like a real sick man. I mean, didn't Terry kill him?"

"Or Spike."

I disliked the guy, but murder? "Do you think he did?"

"Sherlock, I don't think in this business. It's all common sense. We find evidence and tie two and two together, then deliver it to the cops." With that he stood, leaned over and kissed me on the forehead. "Get some sleep."

I stood and walked to the door. "Okay. You too." When I walked toward my room, I touched my forehead. Couldn't I have come up with something better, maybe more romantic? Then again, he had kissed my *forehead*, like one of my brothers.

The next day passed along as usual. A few patients had "incidents" that ended them up in wet packs or solitary confinement. I successfully avoided swallowing the Green Demon all day and met up with Mason and Margaret for meals. Novitiate Lalli was nowhere to be found. We concluded that she either had the day off or was working another shift since she'd worked last night. It seemed the staff changed shifts around here quite often. That was odd to me, but then again, this was a mental institution. I couldn't compare working here to working on an obstetrical ward at a regular hospital.

After dinner, I sat in the television dayroom while Margaret and Mason went to the other one to see if they could find out anything. *Good luck*, I thought. I hoped they would do better than I could around here. My only hope was talking to Joanna, who was once again arguing about the television remote with the older man in the red pajamas.

Oh, well. It wasn't as if I had anything better to do. I got up and went over to the glass window of the nurses' station, which was part of the dayroom. Sister Barbie was working the evening shift. "Hi, Sister."

Ignoring me, she kept working on the computer. Damn. I leaned a little closer to the opening in the glass window where patients had to talk into. "Good evening, Sister Barbara."

She slowly finished typing and looked up. "Oh, Pauline. I didn't hear you. Sorry. Have you been there long?"

Good. I didn't want to be on all the staff's black list. "No. I just wanted to tell you that Joanna and . . . I don't know the gentleman's name but he is wearing the red pajamas—are arguing about the remote—"

The plastic Barbie doll came flying at me, hitting my shoulder. I felt the key Jagger had given me pinch into my skin. "Ouch!"

Sister and Vinny were up and hurrying over to Joanna. They talked to both patients while I picked up Missile Barbie. The staff had Joanna fairly calm now though she insisted she had nothing to do with the doll flying at me. The man in red was watching whatever was on the television.

I started to walk toward Joanna and had a thought. I learned "Santa's" name was Stanley when I heard Sister Barbara call him. He moved to a chair that was closer to the television. I smiled to myself wondering why he even cared what was on TV, as he'd probably be fast asleep soon. They didn't whisk Joanna off. She sat there silently. I held the Barbie doll close and sat next to her.

Joanna didn't look at me.

I looked around the dayroom. No one was paying attention. Vinny, now back on his perch, was reading a magazine. So I held the Barbie doll up on my lap and in my best high-pitched tone said, "Joanna, I'm glad you are all right."

She looked at Barbie. "Yeah, right. Big help you were."

I bent Barbie forward in an apologetic stance. "I am sorry. Will you still be my friend?"

Joanna paused. Thank goodness she didn't look at me. I think the poor thing really thought the doll was talking to her. Then again, judging by her past behavior, I guessed a doll talking to her wasn't anything new to Joanna.

I leaned Barbie closer to her. I pushed her left hand out with my finger. Good thing I had nieces that I'd played with in the past. "Hey, Joanna, let's talk about that nun. The young one who dresses differently from the others."

Joanna stared at Barbie and then patted her plastic hand. I couldn't believe she didn't yank the doll from my hold. I wondered if Joanna was enjoying the Barbie doll being animated on its own.

"Lalli. I told you her name was Lalli."

"Yeah, she's the one. Let's talk about her. It'll be fun!"

Santa snored.

Joanna's attention was broken.

Damn. Thinking quickly, I raised both of Barbie's hands and "hugged" Joanna. "I love you," I sang out.

She pulled her glance back to the doll. "Then eat your bread at breakfast."

Barbie doll nodded. "Tell me more about Lalli. I think she's mean."

"We know she is mean. She always makes me put you to bed when you are done with breakfast. I hope that man gets her in trouble."

My eyebrows rose—and I think Barbie's did too.

"Trouble?" Barbie asked.

"Yeah," Joanna whispered. "You know they are dating. They actually live together. Ha. Ha. Ha." She looked as if she'd just told a hilarious joke.

Me, I was stuck on the "are" part. Spike and Lalli were *still* living together?

"Tell me more! Tell me more!" Barbie insisted. I almost felt that if I let her go, she'd still keep talking—as if she was taking control.

I shook my head and persisted.

"Shh!" Joanna ordered. "Don't be so loud."

I thought my "ventriloquist" voice was barely audible. But I softened it further. "Yes, Joanna. And I will eat my bread."

She smiled. "Okay. Well, they live in such a poor neighborhood, with her father too, that Lalli's relative came up with a wonderful idea to make money. They are all so smart!"

"What relative?"

"I . . . Joanna doesn't know. Lalli never said a name, but she did say she was pissed at them and hoped Spike would go back to jail with them all." She leaned close to the doll and stroked her hair. "Lalli doesn't think she's getting enough of the money. Wants a bigger cut."

Bingo!

Suddenly I caught the Barbie doll looking at me and wanted to say, "What?" Then I realized what she was trying to tell me. How reliable was Joanna? Damn it all. This sounded too good to be true.

Motive.

I may have stumbled upon the motive for the fraud scam.

Joanna was yanking at Barbie. "I asked you a question!"

Darn. I hadn't heard it. "Sorry, Joanna. I didn't—"

Before I knew it, Barbie was flying across the room yet again. Joanna had grabbed her and scratched my hand in the process. Vinny was up and out of his chair in seconds, subduing a freaked-out Joanna, who kept screaming about the insolent Barbie.

I rubbed my hand and sat back.

Santa, obviously awakened by the noise, looked at me. "If she thinks she's getting another one of those for Christmas, she's whacky."

I could only wonder at the thought of Santa speaking like that.

In all the hubbub, Dr. Dick came walking into the unit. He whisked me off to the exam room, and before I knew it, I was filling Jagger in on the entire scoop.

He nodded. "Good job, Sherlock."

That was better than getting out on a pass.

"So, can you check on all of that to see if it's real?" I asked.

"Done."

"You already did?" My voice sounded shocked and disappointed all at once.

Jagger chuckled. "No, Sherlock, I didn't already do it. I meant 'done' as in, 'You got it.' I'll do it."

"Oh." I leaned back on the exam table. "Now we need to find out who Lalli's relatives are."

Jagger looked at me as if to say, "No kidding," but he didn't. He didn't say the words and embarrass me further. What he did say was, "I'll see if I can find out. Shatley may have more info now or at least maybe get more with all that you have given us."

I puffed up like a stupid peacock. Made me think of Goldie.

"Shatley did say Spike is out after being questioned."

Damn. But I wasn't going to let that get me down. I needed my moment of glory.

Jagger must have noticed my peacock stance and said, "Well, Sherlock, guess it was worth it to get you into this place."

My bubble broke when I remembered him standing in the doorway at Bradley International Airport and watching me get taken away. But, damn it all, he was right.

We were getting very close to ending this fraud ring and sending innocent victims like Mason and Margaret home.

Deciding to be big about it, I said, "You know, Jag, it was worth it. I can just picture Margaret getting back with her family and hugging Kyle."

"Kids should be with their folks," he said.

Taken aback, I looked at him and noticed a sadness in his eyes. Where had Jagger come from, and was he talking about something to do with him? His childhood?

Before I knew it, he gently lifted me to stand and took me into his arms! He held me for a few seconds and then looked at me. "You have the key?"

I nodded.

"I'm going to talk to Lieutenant Shatley. When I find out where Lalli and Spike live, I'll take a look. In the meantime, stay out of your room and in the dayroom with the TV. The busier room. I'll be back as soon as I can."

He brushed some hair from my forehead and after I nodded (since I couldn't speak), he leaned forward and kissed me again.

Not at all like a brother.

I watched a rerun of *Gilligan's Island* with Santa and a few other patients. Jackie Dee, now terribly bald on the back of her head, had been moved to Ward 200B. I said a prayer to Saint Theresa for her.

Callie Jo slept near Vinny, who apparently was doing a double shift since Spike was gone.

I know Jagger had told me to stay out here, but I had to go to the little girls' room. So, I walked down toward my room with an eagle eye out. No one seemed suspicious. But when I got to the end of the hallway, I noticed the night staff coming in the door from the tunnel.

Novitiate Lalli was there.

Damn.

I scooted into my room and went into the john. There on the sink sat a can of pine-scented Renuzit. For a second I feared someone had connected me to my mother. My family. But that was ridiculous. Even if there were spies on this unit, no one could have ever known about my "always soothing, nostalgic fetish."

My fears were relieved when I noticed a toothpick, the flat kind, still in its wrapper next to the can.

I lifted the Renuzit. There was no red dot on the can either. *Jagger must have paid full price*, I thought, and smiled.

'Cause he sure didn't get it from Stella Sokol.

After I hid my Renuzit, I was back in the safety of the dayroom. Not much had changed since I'd left, but now Margaret was sitting next to Santa, telling him about her son. My heart ached. We had to get her out of there soon. Mason seemed to be holding out better, but then again, Margaret had been there longer, and as a mother, missing her child had to be devastating.

She started to weep. I couldn't take it, so I got up and went to her. "Let's take a walk." Sitting next to Santa, even a nutty one, had to be too much of a reminder for Margaret.

Remembering Jagger's warning, I figured walking around with someone was safe. Margaret and I headed down the hallway away from the nurses' station. When we passed by Jackie Dee's old room, I noticed a janitor cleaning.

"Hold on, Margaret. Wait right here for me." I went into the room.

At first the guy jumped. Guess he didn't like being in a room alone with a "patient." "Hi. I'm just curious."

"And I'm a janitor, lady. Go on now." He started to sweep. I noticed a few broom straws on the floor.

"Looks as if your broom is coming apart."

He cursed. "Cheap place. Won't even buy us good brooms."

"Has that been happening long?"

He looked at me as if I were certifiable but said, "Last few months these old ones have all given out."

So that could be why I found so many straws around. Maybe they really weren't some kind of warning to me. Maybe no one had any idea who I was. Maybe my mind had been playing tricks on me after being in here too long.

Way too long.

I hurried out to share my news with Margaret.

"Hey—" The hallway was empty. Suddenly something didn't feel right. My old "gut" instinct from my nursing days kicked in. Margaret wouldn't just take off without a word. She seemed pleased to be talking to me. Damn it.

"No!" I heard a shout coming from the hallway near the tunnel entrance. Sounded like Margaret.

I ran in that direction and stopped short when I saw Spike dragging Margaret out the door!

"Stop it!" I shouted.

He turned and glared at me. "Get the hell out of here."

I could *not* let him take her. So, I summoned up the lessons Jagger had given me and slammed Spike one with a fist to his throat. He let go of Margaret.

"Run!" I shouted to her.

"I've been waiting a long time for this, bitch!" He tried to punch me in the face, but I turned with the motion of his fist and only got a slight blow to my cheek.

"Damn!" I did a few more moves and told Margaret to leave. "What do you have against me anyway, you jerk?"

He laughed. "Maybe the fact that you could ruin everything has something to do with it."

Spike knew about me. But how?

"Ruin what, jerk?"

He pushed me up against the wall. "The money. The perfect money scam we got going. You ain't going to take it all away from us."

I couldn't resist. "How the hell did you know?" No sense in denying who I was. It was all coming to a head real soon anyway.

"Let's just say, Santa don't need any little elves. He does fine by himself."

Santa was in on it too! Pretending to be asleep, he must have heard lots of conversations. If you couldn't trust Santa, whom could you trust?

Margaret reached out. Spike grabbed her arm. With all my weight, I stomped my foot onto his little toe, remembering that Jagger had said it was a more sensitive area.

Spike yelped.

Margaret pulled free.

And I yelled, "Get out of here now!" I waved my hand toward Margaret and my bracelet went flying. The clasp must have broken!

She hesitated while I let Spike have another taste of my Jagger lessons. This time I used the finger to Spike's nose. He moved his head back before I could scratch him, but still cursed in pain.

"I can't leave you, Pauline." She tried to grab at Spike's hair.

"Yes you can. Do it for Kyle!" I couldn't even tell her to go get help. We were way too close to solving this crime and I didn't want to blow it. And now I had much more to blow it all wide open with. *I can handle Spike*, I thought, smacking him in the eyes with my clawed hands. "Get out . . . of . . . here, Margaret! Go get my doctor!"

With fear in her eyes, she turned and ran.

Good. Now all I had to do was deal with King Kong—all by myself.

Spike is a force to be reckoned with, I thought, as we battled it out. Sure, his strength was no match for mine, but my brains beat the heck out of his.

I was holding my own, since I managed to duck and twist to avoid several of his punches, but I still couldn't get my taser bracelet from the floor to stun him one.

I had to fight dirty with this creep, so I said, "Lalli sure punked you." I could hardly believe that I'd used the word "punked."

"What you talking about, bitch?"

He didn't let go, but I could feel him relax. Good. My words found his Achilles' heel. His macho self wouldn't let a female insult him. "Lalli, your girl. She's spreading it around that you belong in jail. With all the others. The whole lot of you. Ouch!" He'd tightened his hold. I could only imagine his anger, this time, was against Lalli.

"What'd she say?"

I made a few moves that maneuvered us closer to the doorway. Then, I sneezed in his face and grabbed the key from under my top.

Spike cursed at me and wiped at his face. "You're gonna pay for that." He reached out to me.

I tried to flip him as Jagger had shown me, but his foot caught on my robe, sending us both down on the hard tile floor.

The *smack* sounded in the emptiness.

The grossness of landing on top of Spike was more than I could bear, even in my dizziness from the fall. I pushed up, noticed my bracelet near the radiator and grabbed for it. Before he could get up, I aimed it at him.

He didn't move.

Oh, shoot. Had I been responsible for another death?

Gingerly I touched his neck. A full pulsing from his carotid artery said he was still alive—but I wouldn't be for long if he woke up.

I had to get the hell out of there, but first I bent—and tasered the sucker—just in case he woke too soon.

Taking the key, I fumbled in haste to get out of the unit and into the tunnel—not sure where the hell I'd go.

Twenty-nine

"Don't fail me now, Saint T," I whispered as I hurried through the tunnel, stopping only to unlock each door that got in my way. After several turns, I think I made a giant circle. Thank goodness it was the night shift and the tunnel was empty. Lights out must have arrived by now, and everyone would be back in their rooms. Soon they'd notice I was gone—and probably find Spike's body if he hadn't already gotten up.

I looked behind me to see the tunnel empty.

Phew. At least he wasn't following me.

Ahead was a section that proved to be a veritable maze. There were twists and turns and pipes on the ceiling spewing steam, along with cameras on the walls. I envisioned some loser of a security guard watching me—and having hysterics. Nothing looked familiar or like an exit. I had to have taken a wrong turn. Surely I should be outside by now.

I slowed and stopped to get my bearings. There were no windows in the tunnel since it was a system of walkways built under the wards. There had been a similar tunnel structure in the psychiatric hospital that I had trained in, and as students, we used to take little "detours" on the way to the wards to see what was down there.

I was trying to think of a way to escape when I heard a noise.

Footsteps. Running footsteps.

My feet were soon running too, as I tried to think of a way out of there. Then it hit me.

An emergency exit. That was it. There had to be one of those red signs posting an exit in case of fire or some other catastrophe.

I ran down a long tunnel and at the end noticed a glimmer of red. Heading in that direction, I ran as fast as I could.

Something whizzed past my head. I didn't stop to see what it was.

Okay, this was a catastrophe now—an attempted murder! Mine!

Up ahead I saw the sign. The red exit sign. Thank goodness I was a jogger.

Over my shoulder I could see a figure in a black hat, black shirt and dark pants, and I could hear the person gasping for breath.

Good, maybe he'd pass out. Obviously he wasn't a jogger.

Thank you Saint Theresa!

With shaking fingers, I hit the push bar on the door. When I ran through, I wasn't outside, but in a hallway, headed toward the main entrance. The giant public lobby.

Of course, it was empty at this time of the night.

Thank goodness I knew my way around. I also knew that the front doors were locked, since it was way after visiting hours.

I said a quick prayer that the same key unlocked all the doors in this place. Surely Jagger would have known if it didn't. He wouldn't have wanted me trapped in the maze of tunnels like some hunted animal.

The receptionist was long gone I noticed as I ran past the desk. "Damn." I could grab her phone and dial 911 and be killed, or just get the hell out of there.

I went with get the hell out of there.

There wasn't even a guard around that I could call to. I had no idea where the guards worked. I knew from experience that the buildings were pretty darn soundproof. No one walking by outside needed to hear the ranting of a whacked-out patient.

Or the screaming of a normal person being hunted by a killer! I slowed for a second and turned.

Nothing.

Maybe I'd lost him. I sucked in a breath and blew it out slowly. I couldn't keep running like that, and the searing pain in my lungs told me that I had missed way too many days of jogging. So I figured I'd rest a second or two.

I heard a door slam and decided I'd had a long-enough rest. I rushed to the front door and stuck the key in the lock and jiggled. Then jiggled some more.

The door swung open.

Thank you very much, Jagger *and* Saint Theresa.

In the darkness it was a long shot to find the Cupid statue and get my car key. But, I was damn determined. Loving life and wanting to keep living it had my adrenaline gushing. The fountain could be seen from my ward, so I headed in that direction, hoping for the best.

If I got the key and made it to my car, I could lock myself in and drive off to safety. Surely the police would come as soon as Jagger found I'd gone missing. Or, hopefully, Margaret had told him. How I wished I had my damn cell phone.

Whoosh! Whoosh!

I screamed as I saw something swing by my arm. My legs had no choice but to carry me as fast as they could.

Damn it! The killer grazed my arm and ripped my Burberry robe. Now I was furious. I didn't see the guy, but I did get a glimpse of the weapon.

A brown metal broom handle with the tip fashioned into a point. Just like the one that had killed Vito.

The tip must have caught onto the fabric of my sleeve. My arm hurt and I reached over to feel something warm. Blood. Shoot. I'd been cut. Growing even more furious, I yanked a small branch from a nearby tree. I swished it frantically in the direction of the figure, made contact and heard a yelp—but didn't stay around to see the effects.

Too bad I hadn't seen the guy's face while he was swinging the broom handle at me. I could then tell Jagger who the fraud-committing killer was. The ringleader. Because I knew in my heart that this guy chasing me meant business and was the "brains" behind the fraud.

In the darkness I wasn't sure if it was Spike or not. The guy was tall, but maybe not as wide. Hell, I really hadn't gotten a good-enough look to be sure. Running did that to me and the darkness didn't help.

I ran until my lungs were about to explode and then hid behind a giant oak tree to listen. Nothing. Silence. Good. I slowly walked toward where I thought the fountain would be, making myself as light as I could so as not to crunch the fallen leaves beneath my feet.

Being early spring, the old leaves of fall were still scattered on the ground. Some trees still had brown leaves on them, which only fell off as the new growth approached.

I hoped I got to see the new leaves.

The grounds were, naturally, empty. To be expected in a psych hospital. No one was allowed out, visiting hours were over and no one, not even the local teens, hung around this place. Besides, it was so far off the beaten track that you couldn't expect anyone to come by.

Footsteps tapped along the ground, the sound getting louder. I let out a few "Help me" shouts, a waste of time, but I thought I'd go for it, in order to stay alive. Nothing. No reply. No cars coming in the drive.

From here I could see a light glowing on the second floor. Ward 200. It had to be. I ran my gaze from the window to the grounds and followed the line. Soon, in the distance and barely visible, was good old Cupid, standing in the water.

I ran so fast, I felt certain the guy following would pass out from lack of oxygen. Either that or I would. When I got to the fountain, I reached for the key. I patted Cupid's arm and grabbed at the cold stone.

Nothing.

No key.

I poked further into his elbow, and then I felt it! The key must have been blown down his arm by a strong wind. I touched the metal and nearly cried. Footsteps crunched in the distance. I snatched at the key and felt a sharp pain in the cut of my arm.

And heard a *plop*.

"No!" I whispered. It couldn't be. The damn key had fallen out of my grasp. There was neither time nor any way that I could find it in the murky water of the fountain.

Fighting the urge to collapse into tears, I sucked in some much-needed air and turned around. Determined to get out of there alive, I took off toward the parking lot on the western side. My car was there. If I could get to it . . .

It'd still be locked.

Mother had always drummed locking our cars into us kids. Who else locked their cars when they were parked in their own garages? She would be so upset if she knew the cause of my death was her raising us to always lock our cars.

Maybe I hadn't locked it. I told myself there was a slight possibility that I'd forgotten to lock the car when I'd driven back here.

Even I didn't believe it though.

How I wished I'd been able to wear my own clothes. Then there might have been a chance I'd have my car keys on me.

My keys.

My parents.

Nick, Goldie, Miles, Spanky, all my siblings, their kids, and spouses.

Jagger.

I slowed to rest. Tears welled up in my eyes. Hurriedly I brushed them away, looked around, and took off again.

Landscapers had worked magic on this place, but the trees seemed to pop in front of me at every turn. The grounds of the Cortona Institute of Life were picturesque, to say the least. That is, unless you were being hunted on them.

Still, the plentiful maple trees, oaks and pines gave me some place to run through, like a tree-filled maze. Had to make it harder on my pursuer.

The idea of dropping down and crying filtered through my brain again, but only temporarily.

Pauline Sokol was no quitter.

I sobbed and ran around a large oak's trunk. My ankle twisted when my foot caught on the roots sticking out of the ground. "Ouch!" I grabbed onto the trunk, sliding my hands down and scraping the skin in the process. Damn, it hurt, but I wasn't about to stop. I'd long forgotten my first injury and told myself nothing hurt. I was fine. Just fine.

So, I plowed on with a slight limp. Every once in a while I'd hear the footsteps crunching on the grass. But, determined, I decided I'd only think of my family. I'd pretend I was one of the Steelers running backs going for a touchdown with fifty seconds to go and fifty yards in the Super Bowl. Uncle Walt would be proud.

Uncle Walt!

Uncle Walt had learned caution from my mother too. As a matter of fact, I just remembered, he'd made me put a magnetic metal container under the rear bumper of my car. And inside was a spare key!

If I could make it to my car alive, I could get it. I *would* get it.

The campus was not well lit since no one usually came or went during the night except the staff. It wouldn't be time to change shifts for hours. But "someone upstairs" was looking out for me, since the moon cast a pallid glimmering between the trees. I turned to look behind me.

A black figure stood amidst the naked trees, the moon's glow catching the metal handle . . . and sparkling.

"Oh damn!" I sucked in a breath and sucked up the fact that my arm hurt, my Burberry was ruined and my ankle killed me, and decided that would be the only part of my body killed tonight.

For a second I silently watched the figure. No movement. I guessed he was scanning the area, looking for me. Slowly I turned and eased toward the parking lot. If he didn't see me, I could sneak quietly over there and give my legs and lungs and every part of my body a much-needed rest.

When I got to the edge of the tree-lined walk, I moved behind a giant oak—and stopped. Damn it all. I had to cross the drive. The wide-open drive without any protection to hide behind. I looked around.

No one.

If I ran across, the moon that had helped me earlier would surely highlight me like a spotlight. Then I'd be a perfect target for the hit. So, I shut my eyes a second to think of what Jagger would do.

Jagger.

Then I decided he'd shake his head twice at me if he saw me hesitating, so I swallowed back any tears and bent down. Jagger would use his experience. He'd use what he knew to survive.

A branch crackled in the distance.

I sunk to the ground. I had no idea what Jagger did in the military, but it gave me a survival idea.

Like a giant snake, okay maybe a big worm, I eased onto my belly and started to slither commando-style across the road. If a car did come by, I'd be road-kill.

Broken gravel dug into my skin through the expensive fabric, which was surely not designed for action like this. A long time ago, I'd ordered myself not to think of the cold. All the other pain from my ankle to my abdomen to my arm was plenty to make me want to scream. But I bit my lip, the lower one. Really bit it. And before I knew it, I was across the road, flying up from the ground and high-tailing it behind the safety of the cars.

I looked back. No one. Thank you again, Saint T. My car was parked on the far side. After nearly slipping from the pain in my legs, I looked down to see a red streak along my robe. Obviously I'd torn some more skin when being a commando. But that was little worry compared to staying alive.

I'm sure Goldie and Miles wouldn't mind the ruined outfit.

I nearly wept when I saw my Volvo. It sat there in front of me screaming "safety." Before the killer caught on, I leaned down behind the bumper and ran my hands across the freezing metal.

Nothing!

I had to bite back another scream. What the hell? Uncle Walt had said he'd stuck the spare key there for me. What if he'd forgotten? A few tears did escape, but hell, I was in danger and allowed them. My favorite uncle wouldn't let me down. I knew it. I'd feel awful if this was the cause of my death. That is, looking down from heaven, I'd feel awful.

"Come on, Uncle Walt." I reached around some more. Where would I hide the key if I were an elderly man? *That had to be it*, I thought, as I reached around. He probably thought some thief would find the key there, so he made it harder to find.

Thank you very much, dear Uncle.

I hurried to the side and fiddled around above the wheel. There was lots of metal there, but no key box. Damn it. I kept feeling around the car until I looked up and saw the dark figure in the distance. I gulped. He'd made it to the caretaker's house. Good. Maybe he thought I was hiding in there. It would have been a good idea, but, wait, no it wouldn't have been, since he had figured it out first.

I pulled back, my hands frozen, dirty and stinging from the cold metal. "Please, Uncle Walt. Give me a sign."

My Steelers' bumper sticker glared at me.

I reached underneath the bumper, felt what I'd hoped for and shut my eyes. "Yes," I whispered then grabbed the metal box, pulled it open and took out the key.

With the key in my bloody fist, I stuck it in the lock, praying it wouldn't be frozen. How I wished I lived in sunny Florida.

The key turned. I let out a breath, yanked open the door and jumped inside. When I went to stick it in the ignition, the key fell to the floor. "Shoot!" I fumbled around under my cold feet but couldn't bend down far enough and there was no way I was going to get out to look. Quickly I sat up and shoved the manual locks on all the doors.

Then I swung down again, hitting my head on the steering wheel. Stars danced in front of my eyes, and they weren't celestial ones. A warm liquid trickled down the bridge of my nose. I was about to ask myself what Jagger would do when a figure leaped in front of my car.

I screamed.

A metal handle thrust at my windshield.

I screamed again and was pretty sure that I'd keep it up as long as he kept prodding the glass with the handle. I hoped the promise of "shatterproof windshield glass" was not false advertising.

A heard a crack, and a spiderweb pattern spread across the glass.

"No! Get out! Leave me alone! I won't tell anyone!"

"Too late, Pauline."

I froze.

The female voice had stunned me into temporary silence. Despite the fact that *she*—not a he as I'd assumed, kept stabbing my windshield—I had to look past the web to see. . . .

Barbie Doll.

"What the hell are you doing, Sister Immaculatta?"

Sister? My injuries had me so mixed up that it just dawned on me that Barbie was as much a nun as the late Vito Doran had been.

I looked around the car. There had to be some weapon in here that I could use. I could take her. She was too beautiful and built to beat me. Then I watched her arms as the glass shattered more.

I couldn't take her.

I fumbled around in my glove compartment, pulling out a map, a bottle of water (Mother always made us carry water, as if we lived in the Sahara instead of Connecticut) and then the hammer I'd use if my car ever plunged into a river or something. I knew I could never get close enough to whack her, but I pulled it out anyway. Then I touched the key chain Nick had given me for my birthday.

I grabbed it.

I stuck my sore fingers on the center button, appropriately named the "panic" button.

I held it up and pushed the button, then the car started to honk and lights flashed. Barbie pulled her weapon back and cursed worse than I would.

She really was no nun.

"I'm gonna kill you, Sokol!" Barbie yelled.

I aimed the panic button toward her as if that would make a difference. All it did was make her curse more and start swinging the broom handle like a baseball bat.

Ex-sister Immaculatta had a darn good swing.

My car kept up its racket as I kept poking the button. Now Barbie ran from door to door yanking at the handles and swinging her weapon. She kept this up as I cried louder and louder for her to stop and let me live. I'd sunk to begging, but hey, who would worry about being embarrassed at a time like this? I paused only to see if my life was going to flash in front of me.

Nothing.

Yet.

Then I looked at my side window. The driver's side was only a few inches from my head.

The tip of the broom handle, the sharp metal tip, was poised directly on the other side of the glass. I wondered, only for a second, if that glass was as strong and shatterproof as the windshield.

I refused to be harpooned in my Volvo like Moby Dick.

I hit the panic button again.

The lights flashed, the horn honked and Barbie screeched.

Very unbecoming of a nun. Oh wait, exactly like a psycho-crazed killer though. "Get away!" I screamed over and over until the next thing I knew . . .

The tip of the broom handle punctured the window. A piece of glass flew off, and embedded itself in my left cheek. I screamed. "Now you did it! Now I'm pissed!"

She screamed louder, pushing the broom handle forward.

I think I screamed too, but it was getting confusing as to who was making all the noise.

Bam!

The window blew out and she reached in and opened the door. Before I could move to the other side, she had me by the robe and had yanked me out of the car. I tried to get to my bracelet, but noticed it was hanging off my arm. In my commando maneuvering, I must have damaged the clasp on it. I tried to reach for it to taser her ass, but couldn't get a grip.

She was standing above me, holding my neck—and squeezing.

I kicked at her, and she released her hold a bit.

"You stupid fool. You ruined everything!" she shouted at me.

With enough air to speak, I said, "Ruined what?"

"You know, you bitch. I had my family almost set to move into someplace . . . nice. Lalli and Spike and my father."

I pushed at her face, stabbing a finger into her eye. She let go. I tried to run, but she grabbed my robe and ripped the belt off. "Your father?" While she wrestled me to the ground, it dawned on me. "*Santa* is your father?"

"His name is Stanley and he's not crazy like the rest of

them." She yanked the belt and held me for a few seconds.

"*You're* crazy if you think you are going to get away with this. Doctor Dick is at the police station right now. He knows about Lalli, Spike and . . . you."

She cackled more eerily than poor Joanna. "Yeah, right. You had no idea about me. You never figured out that I wasn't really a nun anymore. I gave up on the convent when I went home to see how my family lived. I couldn't let them stay in that squalor. I was responsible for them.

"Daddy couldn't take care of Lalli and Mother had split years ago. And you. I recognized you from the time you came to see Mary." She pushed me to the ground and straddled my back.

Damn it! Mary and that convent. I tried to grab the bracelet, but Barbie held my hands above my head, leaning all her weight on top of them and pushing my face into the ground.

Barbie was no doll.

"So why kill Vito?" I figured if I lived this could come in handy at her arraignment. That is, *when* I lived.

"Vito, the jerk." She pushed down at his name.

"Ouch!"

"Sorry."

I'll bet she was. The word must have snuck out from her old upbringing.

"Stupid Spike came to work one night drunk. Spilled part of our scam to Vito. That's why he had to go. Couldn't let anyone spoil it. Daddy and Lalli didn't deserve to live in a place like that. They should be happy."

"Are you really a nurse?" Grass stuck into my mouth.

"Of course. I wouldn't harm patients."

Only kill those who get in your way. Very logical.

"So Vito was only trying to save his sister when he attacked me at the airport?"

"The damn fool. When she got to Ward 200B, I got all kinds of information from her. That, and my daddy listening to you, is how I found out what you were doing—you are a fake, Pauline Sokol."

"No, I'm the real Pauline Sokol. I was a fake patient." I'd gotten her talking and for a second had a tiny window of opportunity. So, I took a shot and lifted my hands enough to get my bracelet lined up with her arm and press.

"Aye!" she shouted. "What the hell did you do?" She sat up and rubbed at her arm.

Apparently the shock wasn't enough to stun her or else the taser had been damaged. Either way, I forced her off of me with a shove and kicked her in her pretty face.

She shrieked and cursed at me. Wow. Who knew an ex-nun knew such language. "I should have run you off the road when I had the chance!"

It had been *her* driving the white van and not Spike.

I fiddled with the bracelet and tried to get close enough to zap her, but still stay far enough away so she couldn't grab me. She didn't even try. Nope. Instead, she reached into the car and pulled out the broom handle.

Great! Her weapon of choice yet again.

Barbie swung and hit me upside the head. My world started to wink out, but I refused to let it. Instead I aimed my arm at her, bobbed up and down, and kept pressing in case I touched her skin.

It worked and sent her flying back toward the car a few times, but she was still coherent.

Damn, but lunatics are strong and persistent.

We kept going at each other with our weapons and alternately screaming and cursing.

Boom!

Suddenly one of us stopped screaming. The broom

handle dropped away. Barbie fell forward, her eyes glaring at me.

I pushed her back. What the hell?

She grabbed onto my side-view mirror and just hung there.

I kept screaming.

What the hell was she doing? Trying to play 'possum, like the nutty patients? Like her father?

Red lights flashed, and headlights lit up the darkness.

She merely glared.

Then, my voice froze as I saw her get up. Actually, she was lifted up, blood staining her black turtleneck and slacks. All I could think of was, someone so model-beautiful could have been more creative than to wear that clichéd black outfit for hunting me down.

Then again, she'd been wearing black since I'd known her.

After he'd shot Barbie, I nestled my head in the crook of Jagger's arm. It wasn't in any sexual way, since the red flashing lights of the cop cars, the staff from the hospital bustling around and a group of nuns, standing next to us reciting a litany of prayers, kinda put a damper on anything romantic—not to mention my looks. I had to look scary covered in grass, dirt, blood and ripped Burberry. I looked over to see Sister Liz. She made the sign of the cross and nodded at me.

I smiled.

After Jagger went through how he'd, in fact, figured out that one of the nuns really wasn't a nun, he'd rushed back to the hospital to make sure I was safe, and Margaret had told him about Spike and me.

"Timing is everything," I'd mumbled to him.

He chuckled, a deep sound that vibrated beneath my ear. Then he'd explained how "Sister" Barbara had left the convent a while back, so was able to impersonate a nun to run a fraud ring here. She, Spike, Lalli and their father had lured people to this place with the promise of R & R in a luxurious New England resort, just as we'd been told. Apparently Barbie had been here as a novitiate, so she knew about the place and her way around.

What we hadn't known was that Dr. Pinkerton, the head of the staff—and Barbie's lover—was also in on it. That's how she got in here. They hijacked people from the airport, took their personal belongings, medicated them and then filed for the insurance reimbursement and pocketed it. Spike got four thousand dollars for each person he brought in. They had a contact at the insurance-company end who found the likely "patients."

"I'll bet Pinkerton was pissed to find out he hired *you* to fill in for him," I said.

Jagger chuckled.

He told me a woman in billing was in on it too. Poor Terry was innocent of all criminal activity. Spike had used Terry to scare me a few times with the straw, Margaret had been moved as a warning to me, and Ruby was not lying about only trying to scare me once. Barbie had been the attacker with the broom handle. I didn't have the strength to ask Jagger how he'd learned all of this, or more important, how he knew to come save me—I figured his cop connections had paid off again.

After all, this was Jagger I was leaning against.

Suddenly I felt something on my left cheek.

His touch.

"There's a piece of glass in your cheek," he said.

"I'd forgotten about it. I'll get it out when I get home."
Home. I couldn't wait to hold Spanky, kiss Miles and
Goldie, and call my folks.

"Look, Sherlock, I'm sorry it has led to this."

I should have said that it was all part of the risky job
we were in, but instead I said, "You damn well should
be."

"Next time I'll clue you in a bit more about the case."

I sat forward, ignoring all the new pain the movement
had caused. "Next time? Next time? Next time!"

He reached up to my cheek and whispered, "Take a
deep breath, Sherlock." He eased out the glass so swiftly,
I didn't feel a thing. Besides, it wouldn't have mattered if
it hurt like hell when he said, "*Of course* there'll be a
next time." Gently he kissed my good cheek. "Oh, I forgot to give you your birthday present."

Now we'd come full circle. My thinking the envelope
from Fabio was a present from Jagger had gotten me here
on the ground in damaged Burberry. But a Jagger-present!
My heart danced at the thought. "Well, where is it?" I
sounded like a kid, so I added nonchalantly, "I could use
something to cheer me up now."

He reached into his pocket and pulled out a little box.
Jewelry box. Geez. Didn't Jagger know that I wasn't the
jewelry type? Even Nick had figured that out.

"Sorry I didn't get to wrap it."

I took the box. "My birthday was days ago." This time
I shook my head and opened it to see a beautiful pink
locket. Actually it was rather nice and was rather me. Not
too fancy. Not gaudy. And not shiny. "Thank you. It is
beautiful. It's . . . me."

"No, Sherlock, it's to keep you being *you*."

"Huh?"

Jagger laughed. "It's a special kind of locket."

Wow. I felt wonderful. No pain right now, thinking Jagger thought I was special. "I'll wear it all the time."

"Good, since it's a container of . . . pepper spray."

How very Jagger-like.

I smiled.

And don't miss Lori Avocato's next
thrilling Pauline Sokol mystery,
DEEP SEA DEAD,
coming in 2006

"What? A boat? I mean a *ship*? I could fall over-board and drown! It could sink! Look at what hap-pened to the *Titanic*!"

My skuzzy boss, Fabio Scarpello, glared at me with, well, one could never really know what Fabio thought, so I decided not to even try. It was more than likely X-rated anyway. He puffed on a re-lit cigar. "The ship sails from New York to Bermuda."

I wanted to argue that there might be pockets of cold water out in the Atlantic that could form into an iceberg, but I knew my imagination was going wild in order for me to come up with some excuse not to go.

After a few more puffs, he said, "Look, doll—"

"Don't call me *doll*. Ever." I sat straighter in my seat across from his mold-covered desk. Okay, maybe mold-covered was a bit strong, but I was guessing there had to be something growing beneath the used paper plates, cof-fee cups, piles of ashes and files. He had my folder in his hand.

"Okay, newbie—"

"Pauline, Ms. Sokol or Investigator Sokol will do fine," I started to sip on my decaf café latté that my co-worker, friend and roommate Goldie had made me earlier, then decided it had been contaminated when I'd walked into Fabio's office.

Fabio cursed under his breath. "*Investigator* Sokol is a stretch, but if you want to keep your freaking job, you better take this freaking case. High seas or not."

A nurse on a cruise ship.

I should be excited about the assignment, I mean, come on. Salty sea air, wind in my hair, sun, bronze males, coral sand of Bermuda and...waves. My stomach lurched.

And back into the old nursing career!

He shoved the file toward me. "Want it or not?"

Not would have been my first choice. Pauline Sokol was not one for change. Pauline Sokol was not one for water transportation. And Pauline Sokol was not one to be stuck out in some nautical God knew where investigating medical insurance fraud...alone.

Admittedly I've never been out of New England for a vacation or any other reason, and that thought probably had something to do with my reluctance to try new things. Ethnic Hope Valley had been my home for thirty-five years—and I kinda liked my feet on mother earth.

But there were those nasty things called bills that had invaded my life. And they required being paid.

I looked up to see Fabio tapping his cigar into the dirty ashtray. "Well?"

I snatched the folder. "When do I leave?"

"Friday."

"Friday? It's already Wednesday."

"One of the staff nurses on board got sick. It's perfect. Just perfect. Bon voyage, doll."

* * *

I decided to ignore Fabio calling me doll again since my mind got stuck on Friday. April 13. Perfect. My new assignment would start on an unlucky day. I hurried out of his office and paused in the hallway for a breath of fresh air.

"Suga!"

I spun around to see my tied-for-best friend in the world rushing down the hall. My other roommate and other tied-for-best friend in the world and Goldie's "honey" was Miles Scarpello. Fabio's nephew.

Goldie dressed in Gucci, Prada and Armani. Sometimes from the ladies' dept. Sometimes the men's. But I still loved him, and he always looked like a movie star. Today he ushered in spring with a pink, black, white and orange spiral patterned sweater over black slacks and a pink camisole top. He wore a Sandra Dee blonde ponytail wig that didn't look a bit fake. Looked very sixties. And very beachy. How fitting.

Maybe I could borrow them for my cruise.

"So, Suga—" he yanked me into his office, which looked like a cross between New Orleans, Goldie's hometown, and the jungle. Gotta love him. "—what's your new assignment?"

I held the folder out toward him as if it were a snake. "Here, you look. I don't have the stomach for it so early in the morning."

Goldie patted my head in a very Goldie-like sort of way. "Let's take a looksee." He ran a pink colored nail across the envelope and amid the tearing sound mumbled, "Shit."

"Shit? What does *shit* mean?" I slumped down on the zebra couch, feeling a bit faint.

Goldie looked at me for a few seconds. I had the sudden thought that he was making up some kind of lie. That hurt, but if Goldie lied to me, it would have been for my own good.

"I . . . well, what I meant was . . . shit, you get to go on a cruise to some warm, sunny island, and I'll be stuck in stupid Hope Valley, Connecticut, with temperatures in the 50s all month."

I could only stare. Was Goldie really concerned with the temperature? Or had he seen something in the folder that I should be worried about? After several minutes of silence and him offering me another latté over and over, I finally asked, "Gold, are you lying to me?"

"Yes!" flew out of his mouth on a breeze. He flopped onto his leopard chair and looked at me with a pitiable glare. "I'm sorry, Suga. But, Bermuda. *Bermuda!*"

"I guess I'll give you credit for your honesty even though I don't know what the hell you're talking about. As a matter of fact, I *will* take a regular latté since I think I may need a dose of caffeine."

Before he stood he said, "You don't drink caffeine, Suga."

"I do now. Seems as if I'm going to need it on this case. What is so wrong about cruising to Bermu . . . the triangle. You are worried I may get sucked into some paranormal triangle of ocean?"

Goldie screeched.

I jumped up and hurried over to him. "I'm sorry, Gold. I didn't mean to . . . wait a minute. Why am I consoling you? I should be the one being comforted. I'm the one going on this fool assignment."

He eased free and looked at me. "I'm so sorry. I never should have said anything. I mean, folks sail to Bermuda every day. Planes fly overhead. And, well, bon voyage, Suga!"

* * *

"Bon voyage!" my mother shouted as she served me a piece of the ocean blue cake she'd designed for my going away party. Inside was chocolate with a mousse filling.

All I could think when I heard that third "bon voyage" was, three strikes and you're out.

"Thanks, Mother," I mumbled as she set the dish in front of me. I loved cake. I loved sweets. I drank very little alcohol, not counting beer and wine to avoid calorie overdose so I could have the sweets. Nothing could top chocolate. But right now I had this inner feeling telling me I should eat sweets like there was no tomorrow and drink plenty of liquor—because I was going on a cruise to *Bermuda*.

My sister Mary, ex-nun, leaned forward. "You're getting to be such a professional, Pauline. Imagine. A cruise." She leaned back and shut her eyes. I figured Mary was saying a novena for my safety. She never did quite lose that "religious" persona.

Several nieces and nephews stabbed at the white waves, fashioned out of cream cheese and frosting. Everyone ate and laughed and chatted.

I turned to see Uncle Walt, my favorite uncle who had lived with us forever, smiling. He leaned near and tucked a white envelope into my hand. "Meet some nice young man and have a ball."

"I'm going to be working, Uncle Walt." I fingered the envelope. Had to be money. God bless Uncle Walt.

"Work. Ha!" He forked a piece of cake, ate it and said, "How sick can passengers get? Meet someone. Dance. Eat. Old Widow Kolinsky tells me that cruises are the best. She said she danced so much heading to St. Martin, that she wore out her shoes." He chuckled.

I smiled, leaned over and kissed his cheek. "I'll be sure to bring a spare pair. Thanks for the gift." I winked at him just in time to catch Jagger in my view.

My face burned hotter than the candles on the cake my mother insisted on lighting even though I'd argued it wasn't my birthday. I hoped Jagger didn't think I was winking at him! I felt my cake rising in my throat at the thought.

He sat down opposite me and graciously smiled when my mother set a plate in front of him with half of the cake and a tidal wave of frosting on it.

"Here you go, Mr. Jagger," she said.

Actually she gushed like a teenybopper, but no way was I going to admit to myself that my mother was flirting with "Mister" Jagger! Yuck! Even though he only had the one name—that we all knew about—she insisted on the title for him each time. I couldn't help but cut her some slack because, well, Jagger had a way with women and obviously Stella Sokol was not immune. Guess I should be glad my mother was "normal."

"So, Sherlock, any questions before you set sail?" He took a sip of his beer. Gotta admire a guy who drinks beer with his cake—and, damn, but I admired lots of things about Jagger.

I looked at him and realized—I was finally working on a case by myself. Jagger usually ended up involved. But not this time.

My heart skipped a few needed beats.

I was really going on my own.

Back in my condo, I flopped on my bed and looked into the dark little eyes of my joint-custody dog. Weighed in at seven pounds now after a doggie diet. "When's the last time a cruise ship sank, Spanky?"

He looked at me, curled into a ball, and shut his eyes.

"Right. The *Titanic*. Ages ago. I know there have been fires onboard and epidemics of gastrointestinal problems, but in this day of modern—"

Spanky snored.

I had to smile while I petted his squirrel-sized head. "Modern technology. No problem. Where's my grocery list?" I leaned over, grabbed my paper and pencil and added, bracelet thingie for motion sickness. God, I hoped the ship's movement didn't affect me, since admittedly I couldn't sit in the backseat of a car without needing Dramamine. Damn.

Spanky snored on so I continued packing, making sure to grab my stethoscope, bandage scissors and several pens. Back to nursing. I knew it made sense that my skills would be best served for the medical fraud cases, but, hell, Jagger wasn't a nurse and he did fabulously. At least I didn't think he was a nurse. No one really knew who he worked for. I'd learned not to care.

After several hours, I stood back and looked at my luggage. Full to the brim. I used the extra strap that my mother had insisted on after seeing it advertised on television, which wrapped around the bag in case the zipper popped. I assured her it wasn't going to get thrown around like on an airplane, but, being Mother, she had convinced me I didn't want the world to see my panties if, God forbid, the zipper gave way. Not that I expected that tragedy, but I'd learned from infancy that if Stella Sokol said something was going to happen—look out—because it always did.

As kids we used to cringe and fuss when she'd say, "Don't go out in the rain because you'll catch your death of a cold."

Even at our young ages we knew you had to come in

contact with someone with the cold virus, but inevitably we'd go out, and the next day (always a Saturday) we'd get sick and spend our day off in bed.

So, I yanked at the strap to make sure no passengers were exposed to my "essentials" and shoved the biggest suitcase with my foot until it was at the doorway.

Tomorrow Goldie and Miles were driving me to the dock in New York City to start my next case. That alone was reason to lose sleep tonight.

My night was not as sleepless and fitful as I had expected. It was *worse*. But once my roomies had the car packed— and they wouldn't let me lift a finger to help—we were well on our way.

The traffic on Interstate 95 was at its usual standstill near Bridgeport so I snuggled up to Goldie's shoulder while Miles drove. I shut my eyes.

"Suga. Suga?"

"Hmmm?"

Something nudged at my arm. I peeked out to see Goldie and realized the car had stopped. I yawned, stretched and screamed.

Goldie grabbed my arms and hugged me. "It just looks so big because we're so close up."

I looked out the window to see the "ship" I was going to be living on for the next few weeks or so—and strained my neck without being able to see the end of it. There had to be a million decks. "Don't heavy objects sink like rocks in the water?" I mumbled.

They laughed, and Miles gave me a quick physics lesson and assured me that the *Golden Dolphin*, the mother ship of the Dolphin line out of the U.S. was quite safe. He'd done some Internet research about the private line and told us much more than I wanted to know.

I think even Goldie had dozed off.

We shook him back to reality and after Miles found a parking space, we all three got out—and stared at the ship.

The gigantic mass of white sat proudly at the dock, dwarfing the surrounding buildings. At least that's how I saw it from this angle. Hundreds of passengers were waiting in lines for what I guessed was some kind of processing before embarkation. We asked one of the staff what was going on and found out they were checking passports and getting credit card info.

I looked at my friends. "Well, this is it." After tearful goodbyes (mine) to Miles and Goldie, I turned to walk away then looked back. "I'm going to miss you guys." I sniffled.

Both had dry eyes.

Now that hurt. And it really wasn't like them. Nope. Inside they were both blubbering fools. "Well, I'll keep in touch although I have no idea how—"

Goldie waved a hand. "I can't stand it any longer!"

"About time. I thought you two weren't going to even shed one tear to see me go."

They glared at me with a collective grin.

"What the hell is wrong with you two? You're acting . . . weird. Weirder than usual." I chuckled.

Goldie grabbed my arm, spun me around and despite my shouts to stop, Miles joined in.

"What the hell? You're going to make me seasick before I even get on the ship." I yanked free.

Miles laughed. "You have your anti-nausea bracelet on. And," he leaned near, "where'd you get that pink locket?"

"You like it?" I fingered it and smiled.

"It's you. Not too pretentious. Not too much like real jewelry."

"Jagger gave it to me. Inside is pepper spray. For self-defense."

They looked at each other then back to me. "You won't need it!" they shouted together.

Once again they wrapped the three of us together like a pretzel.

"You guys are driving me crazy. What is going on? How do you know I won't need my locket?"

"Because we are coming along!" shouted Goldie.

After shouts and cheers, I left my friends to go get processed with the promise that I'd find them later.

After I was checked in within an inch of my life for security purposes, I headed up a slight incline of a gangplank. Once inside, I had to stop and take a breath. I wished I could experience this with Goldie and Miles.

The inside of the ship, like a lobby of sorts, was gold, purple, glass, chrome and decorated like a Las Vegas hotel. Glass elevators glided gracefully up the walls. Chatter filled the air, but in the background soft music from a string quartet gave the *Golden Dolphin* the class of what it must have been like climbing aboard the *Titanic*.

For a second I couldn't believe I was actually still in New York City. No horns beeping. No sirens screaming. No "scents" of the city.

It smelled like a fresh ocean breeze in here.

After asking several of the crew for directions, I found my way to my quarters, which were located across from the infirmary. Very convenient. I opened the door to see twin beds along each wall, covered in white spreads, and sitting in a room no bigger than a closet. The walls, too, were white as the two stuffed chairs near each bed. I guessed ships had the market on white. Smelled freshly Lysol clean, but instead of windows, there were tiny portholes in the walls.

Oops. My elevator phobia came to mind.

I ignored it, telling myself this was a job. A job that I needed and *could* do.

I had to share the room with another nurse, Jacquelyn Arneau, who I'd learned was French. No kidding. Real French as in came from France for this job. Seems as if the entire crew was a mixture of nationalities.

Should be an interesting job.

PERENNIAL DARK ALLEY

More Than They Could Chew: **Rob Roberge** tells the story of Nick Ray, a man whose addictions (alcohol, kinky sex, questionable friends) might only be cured by weaning him from oxygen.
0-06-074280-1

Like a Charm: Karin Slaughter gathers some of the hottest crime fiction writers around in this suspense-filled novel in voices.
0-06-058331-2

Men from Boys: A short story collection featuring some of the true masters of crime fiction, including Dennis Lehane, Lawrence Block, and Michael Connelly.
0-06-076285-3

Fender Benders: From **Bill Fitzhugh** comes the story of three people planning on making a "killing" on Nashville's music row.
0-06-081523-X

Cross Dressing: It'll take nothing short of a miracle to get Dan Steele, counterfeit cleric, out of a sinfully funny jam in this wickedly good tale from **Bill Fitzhugh.**
0-06-081524-8

The Fix: Debut crime novelist **Anthony Lee** tells the story of a young gangster who finds himself caught between honor and necessity.
0-06-059534-5

The Pearl Diver: From **Sujata Massey**, antiques dealer and sometime sleuth Rei Shimura travels to Washington D.C. in search of her missing cousin.
0-06-059790-9

An Imprint of HarperCollinsPublishers
www.harpercollins.com

DKA 0705